MURDER IN MALMÖ

Torquil MacLeod

MᶜNIDDER
GRACE | &
CRIME

To Lyra and Ally. They make me smile so much.

Published by McNidder & Grace
21 Bridge Street
Carmarthen
SA31 3JS

www.mcnidderandgrace.com

Original paperback first published 2015
Reprinted in 2021

© Torquil MacLeod and Torquil MacLeod Books Ltd
www.torquilmacleodbooks.com

A catalogue record for this work is available from the British Library.

ISBN: 9780857161147

Designed by Obsidian Design
Printed and bound in the United Kingdom by
Short Run Press, Exeter, UK

ABOUT THE AUTHOR

Torquil MacLeod was born in Edinburgh. He now lives in Cumbria with his wife, Susan. He came up with the idea for the Malmö Mysteries after visiting his elder son in southern Sweden in 2000. He still goes to Malmö regularly to see his Swedish grandson.

Murder in Malmö is the second book in the series of bestselling crime mysteries featuring Inspector Anita Sundström. *Missing in Malmö* and *Midnight in Malmö* are the third and fourth stories.

ACKNOWLEDGEMENTS

I would thank my wife, Susan, for all the hard work she has put into this book. It has improved it immeasurably. I'd like to thank Fraser, Paula and Ally for putting up with me on trips to Malmö. Also thanks to Kriminalinspektör Karin Geistrand, yet again, for the red wine and help in answering questions on Swedish policing. Any mistakes or liberties taken are all down to me. And a big thank you to forensic scientist and Senior Lecturer in Policing at the University of Teesside, Helen Pepper, for researching a particular problem and coming up with jelly. I'm also very grateful to Göran Brante for going to the trouble of ironing out Swedish inaccuracies – and to Eva Wennås Brante for her enthusiastic support. I'd like to thank my novelist sister, Janet MacLeod Trotter, and husband Graeme, for their practical advice and encouragement. I'd also like to thank again Nick Pugh of The Roundhouse for his striking cover design. Finally, to say to Calum, Sarah and Lyra that these books prove there is life on the planet Torcal.

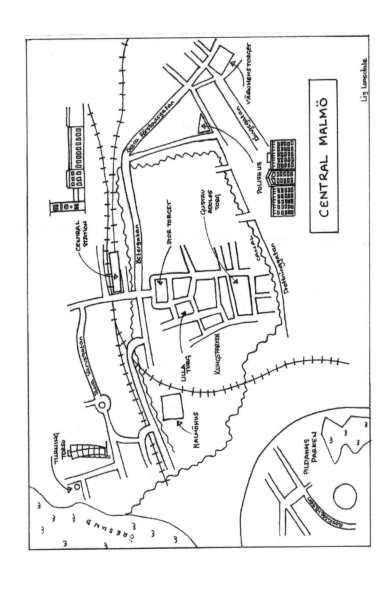

CENTRAL MALMÖ

Liz Lonsdale

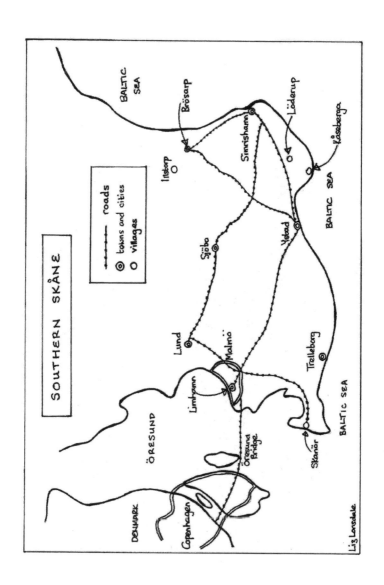

SOUTHERN SKÅNE

roads
⊚ towns and cities
○ villages

BALTIC SEA

Brösarp

Löderup

Kåseberga

Simrishamn

Ittserp

Ystad

BALTIC SEA

Sjöbo

Lund

Malmö

Limhamn

Trelleborg

ÖRESUND

Öresund Bridge

Skanör

BALTIC SEA

DENMARK

Copenhagen

Liz Lonsdale.

PROLOGUE

It was a fine, clear, tranquil evening and there was nothing to hamper his line of fire. He could see the two women chatting animatedly. They waved their arms extravagantly as they spoke, to add emphasis to whatever they were discussing. Their actions were caught in the lights of the entrance to the drab block of apartments. The whole area was a sea of faceless, formless concrete. Unimaginative buildings filled with unwanted people.

Rosengård wasn't a part of Malmö that he had been to before. It had taken him time to get his bearings. To get a feel for the urban terrain; his new war zone. And he was in enemy territory. These people weren't his people. They were invaders from foreign lands. Intruders, like these two women in front of the apartment block who were now the centre of his attention.

He moved further behind the bush. No one else was around. He could hear snatches of music and voices coming from televisions because windows were open due to the warmth. He smelt the faint whiff of cigarette smoke from somewhere nearby; probably someone on a balcony. But he wasn't worried about being spotted. He could deal with any situation. And he had his favoured large-calibre handgun, which gave him an automatic advantage.

Now the women seemed to have come to the end of their conversation. They looked as though they were about to part. He raised his gun and lined up his targets. Each of the women was wearing a brightly coloured hijab. Somehow it made it

1

easier that he couldn't see their faces clearly. He would need to shoot quickly as he wanted to hit them both. His finger hovered gently over the trigger. He steadied himself. There was now a gap between the women. He tensed.

Two shots. The women silently slumped to the ground. There was a shout from a nearby window, but he didn't hear it. He was gone.

CHAPTER 1

The mirror caught Tommy Ekman's self-satisfied smile. The brilliant white teeth between open lips were the most obvious sign, but it was the sparkle in the cool blue eyes that really reflected the inner delight. Despite it being seven in the morning, his eyes weren't fogged up with sleep. He had been lying awake for the last half hour. He had been thinking about *her*. Not his wife Kristina, who was staying over at her father's country place near Illstorp, but Elin.

He took out his toothbrush and squeezed on some toothpaste. Must keep those teeth looking dazzling. The smile again. Yes, he had made love to Elin at last. Over his office desk. He had been trying to engineer the opportunity ever since he had employed her as an account executive six months before. She had rebuffed his advances for a while. 'We're both married,' had been her defence strategy. He started to brush his teeth vigorously without ever losing sight of himself in the mirror. But last night he had breached her fortifications. His advertising agency had won that important pitch. Elin had led the successful team. They had broken out the champagne in his office. Others had slipped away over the next hour or so until they were the only ones left. Elin was a little high on her first big success with the agency. From then on, it hadn't been that difficult to get into her knickers. Even he had been surprised at how easily she had succumbed. He would give her the rise he had pantingly promised her shortly before he had manoeuvred her onto his desk – but only as long as she was happy to provide "extracurricular" services to the boss.

Tommy rinsed out his mouth. He would still have to be careful with Kristina. He wouldn't want her to find out. Her money was still useful – and her father's business contacts. He didn't want to rock the domestic boat, though he found it harder to make love to Kristina these days, despite the fact she was still an attractive woman. Maybe it was familiarity that had led to boredom on his part, or perhaps because she hadn't been as interested in the physical side of their relationship since the kids arrived. But the business was doing well, despite all the economic doom-mongers. Still, he didn't want her to take him to the cleaners.

Kristina's father had been useful with the "group", too. Given him a foot up. Now he had cemented his place with his strategy ideas. They had gone down very well. One of the suggestions had been acted upon within a week. And the film had been a real success. He was confident that he would be running the show very soon. Then the "group" would make people sit up. On this beautiful, sunny May morning, life couldn't get any better.

He slipped off his pyjama bottoms and admired his naked figure in the mirror. He was still finely toned, despite all the client business lunches. And he still had stamina. Just ask Elin. Once aroused, she had been very accommodating. He was still laughing to himself when he stepped into the spacious wet room cubicle, closed the door and flipped on the shower. It sprang into life, and he tilted his head upward and enjoyed the hard spray of hot, refreshing water hitting his face. It was invigorating. As he soaped his body, his mind began to wander again. Back to Elin. It had been so exciting. That triumphant moment of conquest. He could feel the first stiffening in his groin. It was only as he put the soap back in its cradle that he became aware of a strange tingling in his throat. He looked down at the silver circular outflow cover on the floor beneath his feet. The water was running out as usual, but something didn't seem quite right. His head began to swim and he started to feel giddy. His eyes were misting over.

Tommy flapped at the shower tap and the water stopped flowing almost immediately, except for a few final drops. He swayed in the cubicle, not sure whether he would be able to keep on his feet. What the hell was happening to him? With great difficulty, he managed to slide the cubicle doors apart. In front of him the bathroom was a blurred vision of dancing pale green and blue tiles. He stumbled out of the cubicle, still dripping wet. He tried to steady himself against the wash-hand basin, but his grasping fingers missed the edge and he sank to his knees as he retched up some dribbled green saliva and the remnants of last night's champagne. Why was his skin so itchy? Frantically, he ripped at his arms and chest with his nails. With a huge effort, he half-staggered to his feet and fell forward towards the door of the bedroom. He didn't make it and he sprawled on the bathroom floor. He tried to call out for help; not that there was anybody in the apartment to hear him at that time in the morning. But all that came out of his mouth was a fresh burst of vomit. The dizziness was sickening. He couldn't fight it any longer. Why was this happening? His throat, his skin, his eyes, his head were all on fire. He lay in a heap on the floor. He could feel himself slipping into a void of unconsciousness. His limbs, totally independent of his fast-evaporating will, gave a last defiant jerk.

Rays of early morning sunshine speared through the frosted glass of the bathroom window like a prism and bathed the dead body of Tommy Ekman in a brilliant light show. Below the bulging eyes, his mouth was wide open; frozen in the moment, in the cry for help that never came out. The sunlight made his teeth sparkle.

CHAPTER 2

Michaela Lindegren yawned. She didn't know why, because she had slept soundly all night. Normally, when Jörgen was away on business she would fret the night away, even though she knew he would be fine. Maybe it was insecurity. Now that the children had flown the nest, she had the house to herself, and that never felt quite right. During the day, she enjoyed the freedom. At night it was different. Jörgen was always considerate and phoned from wherever he was to make sure that she was all right. She always locked up carefully, but perhaps it was the size of the house that made her nervous. Lots of empty rooms. That's why when Jörgen wasn't there, she would have the radio on when she went to bed. Noise was reassuring. Often she went to sleep with it still playing and would wake up in a fright because she could hear voices. Come daylight, and all the fears would disappear, like the early-morning mist outside their seaside home. It was going to be another lovely day. And Jörgen would be back tonight. His flight into Kastrup Airport was due in the late afternoon.

Michaela wandered into the kitchen and fixed herself a coffee. Nice and strong. The perfect lift for the day. She missed having to make breakfast for the children. She had enjoyed the routine of fussing over them and making sure they had everything they needed for school that day. It gave her a role within the family. She was the organiser. Now there was very little to organise. Meals for Jörgen. Accompanying him to the theatre or one of his business functions. She had become a trophy wife without the requisite glamour. Home was her province. The other wives in their circle were far more sophisticated. They were up with the latest fashions, knew the names of the trendiest interior designers and chefs, and could drop into any conversation the expensively exotic locations where they had been on holiday, without the slightest hint of humility. Jörgen could afford to take her to anywhere she wanted, but she was a home bird and he travelled so widely in his work that she was content to stay in Sweden. So they usually went to the island of Öland, or even closer to home in Österlen, which wasn't much more than an hour's drive from Limhamn.

After another coffee and a light breakfast – she wanted to save herself for the special meal she was cooking to welcome Jörgen back – Michaela wandered down the corridor to the front door where she picked up the morning newspaper. She would have a quick read of it before heading off to the shops. She walked into the living room. The curtains were drawn. As she opened them, a weak sun was trying to penetrate the sea mist. Soon it would burn it off and it would be a lovely day. Then the wonderful, sleek lines of the Öresund Bridge, the link between Sweden and Denmark, would emerge.

It was as she turned from the window that she instantly knew something was wrong. For a moment she couldn't put her finger on it as she stared at the opposite wall. She suddenly found herself gasping for air. It couldn't be. She steadied herself against the table. She looked again. There was no denying it. What was Jörgen going to say? She was now feeling faint. However hard she stared, it wasn't going to bring it back. It had definitely been there when she went to bed last night.

This morning it was gone.

CHAPTER 3

'I shot the wrong man. That's why I'm here, isn't it?'

'I wouldn't put it as brutally as that,' he said quietly.

Inspector Anita Sundström absently patted down her short, blonde hair before adjusting her glasses slightly as she stared hard at the young psychologist with the goatee beard and long, wavy, black hair. Why did everyone look so young these days? After recent events, Anita was feeling every one of her forty-two years. Was she weighed down with self-reproach over her actions, or was she feeling guilty because she needed therapy? Certainly her employers, the Skåne County Police, thought she required help. Or was it just that it would make them look better after the fiasco over the case of murdered film star, Malin Lovgren? She had got their man, but only after she had shot the star's innocent husband, Mick Roslyn, on the top of Malmö's iconic Turning Torso tower.

'Take me through the events again, Anita.'

Anita sighed and glanced towards the window. It was sunny out there. Swedes should be outdoors when the weather was like this, not stuck in a featureless hospital office telling some child with a psychology degree the same story for the umpteenth time. Like most of her fellow countrymen, she accepted therapy as a necessary adjunct to modern-day life. She had had some sessions when trying to come to terms with her father's tragic death some years before. That had been her decision. This time it was different. It was beyond her control. She was being forced into it. She felt that, in her own way, she was coping well enough with the consequences of her recent actions. Maybe the problem was that she knew she would have to touch upon matters that were too sensitive to discuss, even in the cosy confessional of a psychologist's consulting room.

'I became convinced that Malin Lovgren's husband had killed her. I had established that he was having an affair and he seemed to be pinning the blame on someone else.' Anita realised that she was looking at her hands twisting on her lap. She knew she was avoiding eye contact.

'And this someone else?' Doctor Axelsson gently prodded.

'He was an old university friend of Roslyn's from England. Well, they had been friends until they fell out over a young female student. It was only this year that they'd met up again. The friend was a journalist, and he came over to Malmö to interview Roslyn because he'd become a famous film director over here. Roslyn tried to throw him off the top of the Turning Torso. The only way I could stop him...' Her thoughts flashed back to that moment on a bitterly cold February day when she had rushed to the top of Scandinavia's tallest building and found the two men fighting, Roslyn just about to heave his one-time friend over the edge to plunge to a certain death. She had been too far away to physically break them up. She had called out, but Roslyn had ignored her. She had had to make a split-second decision. Her pistol was the only way she could save... She had never shot anyone before. The thought still made her tremble.

'I only realised later that Roslyn had worked out that his friend had murdered his wife.'

'Why do you not refer to the journalist by name?'

Why? Because she didn't want to go there. This was the part that she still had difficulty getting her head around. She had accepted the problems her actions had caused when the truth came out. One minute lauded as the cop who had solved

Sweden's most recent high-profile murder, the next bringing in the real killer shortly after all the public plaudits had been dished out. The department had looked so stupid. "Incompetent" had been one of the lesser accusations tossed about in the press. "GUN-HAPPY COP SHOOTS STAR'S INNOCENT HUSBAND" had caused the Skåne County Police particular angst. As always, they had pretended to close ranks in public, but behind the scenes the blame game had kicked-off almost at once. She had been suspended immediately, and as part of her rehabilitation she was now sitting in Doctor Axelsson's office. All the details had been leaked to the press, although her name had been withheld. The papers had quickly put two and two together and had realised it must be her. It was important that the public knew that there was a scapegoat. The fact that she had brought in the real killer was now totally overlooked – as was her intervention at the top of the tower, which had stopped Roslyn committing murder himself.

'Ewan,' she said quietly. 'Ewan Strachan. That was his name.'

Axelsson tapped his pencil thoughtfully against his pursed lips. It was a habit that was beginning to irritate Anita.

'Was?'

'Is. That *is* his name.'

Axelsson smiled to himself.

'So how did you discover that Ewan was the real murderer?'

It sounded just as ridiculous as it did when she told her story to her immediate boss, Chief Inspector Moberg. He couldn't believe it any more than she could when Strachan had confessed.

'He just told me.'

'Just told you?' Axelsson asked quizzically.

'Yes.' Ewan had admitted it as he sat opposite her in a restaurant. He had let slip a piece of information that had made her suddenly realise that he was the guilty party. When she had challenged him, he had admitted, without a murmur of protest, carrying out the crime. And, furthermore, he had also put his hand up to the killing of the girl in Durham who had come between himself and Roslyn twenty-five years earlier. Anita wasn't sure why she hadn't mentioned that part of his confession to Moberg. The next few hours had been like a dream. Ewan had meekly allowed her to take him to the polishus, where she had officially charged him with the murder of Malin Lovgren. She was still wearing her one decent evening dress. That had become a running joke among many of her colleagues. As a result, she felt some relief that she had not been allowed to spend much time at police headquarters in the last few months.

'So why do you think he was so compliant?'

The question gave Anita a jolt. It was one that, fortunately, Moberg, or in fact anybody else connected to the case, hadn't bothered to ask. She didn't want to reply, but Axelsson's eyes were fixed steadily upon her. He wanted an answer and he would know if she was lying.

'He... he was in love with me.'

'And what about you?'

'What do you mean?' she said defensively.

'What did you feel about him?'

She glanced towards the window. The sun still shone, but there was no help in that direction. Since that night, she hadn't even admitted to herself her feelings for Ewan.

'I was falling in love with him. I suppose I...'

Axelsson made a note on his pad.

'Do you still love him?'

'He's in prison.'

'That's not an answer, Anita.'

No it wasn't. She didn't want to confront her feelings. Not in front of this young man. All she wanted to do was get out of his room, run back to Simrishamn and walk along her favourite beach by herself, and forget about the police, psychologists and the people who complicated her life.

'Do you still love him?' he repeated gently.

Very slowly, Anita nodded.

Axelsson snapped his notebook shut. 'Now we're getting somewhere.'

CHAPTER 4

The light from the bedroom was momentarily blotted out. Chief Inspector Erik Moberg's giant frame filled the doorway. He wasn't much shy of two metres tall, and carried an unhealthy amount of bulk around with him. It was many a year since he'd been able to slip into size 54 trousers. The most disconcerting aspect of his appearance was the strange colour of his dyed hair, which could best be described as nicotine yellow. Beneath it, all the features of his face were exaggerated by their mass, from the heavy jowls to the increasingly slitting eyes, caused by the collision of drooping eyebrows and puffed-up cheeks. He moved forward into the bathroom and towered above the body. With Moberg inside, the room seemed a lot smaller than it had before. Quite a crowd now, with senior forensic technician, Eva Thulin, bending over the corpse, Inspector Henrik Nordlund examining the shower cubicle, and Inspector Karl Westermark, with a wooden toothpick sticking out of the side of his mouth as a substitute cigarette, leaning casually against the basin. All three had on plastic suits.

'Well?' Moberg boomed. 'What the hell happened here?'

Westermark took the toothpick out of his mouth. 'He's called Tommy Ekman. Runs an advertising agency in town. Cleaning lady found him.'

'How did he die?' This time Moberg addressed Thulin.

Eva glanced up. 'Somehow he seems to have been gassed.

Or certainly the physical signs point in that direction.'

Moberg snorted. 'How do you gas someone in a shower?'

'I have no idea yet,' said Thulin rising from her haunches.

'OK. Is there a fru Ekman or is he a gay bachelor?'

'There is. And a couple of kids, too.' Westermark twirled the toothpick round his fingers. His cropped blond hair, piercing blue eyes and lantern-jawed ruggedness gave him the good looks that he assumed no woman could resist. Not many had. 'They're in the country at the moment.'

'And the cleaning lady?'

'She's in the kitchen with a constable,' explained Nordlund. 'In a state of shock. Swedish isn't that good. Bosnian, I think.'

'Bloody typical,' snarled Westermark.

Moberg ignored Westermark and shook his head. 'But gassing?'

'I might be able to tell you once I've examined the whole scene,' said Thulin with some exasperation. 'So, if you gentlemen would like to leave... Until then, your gas is as good as mine.'

Even Moberg managed to raise a faint smile.

Anita drove out of the hospital car park. Were the Axelsson sessions doing any good? Only time would tell. What was inescapable was the fact that she would be returning to work tomorrow. It made her feel nervous. How would she be received by her colleagues? Sympathetically? Resentfully? Mockingly?

Anita turned the car into the stream of traffic. Chief Inspector Erik Moberg would probably treat her with his usual suspicion. He was uncomfortable with a female detective on his team. He didn't like anyone standing up to him, particularly a woman. And just when she thought she had won him over with her discovery that Mick Roslyn had murdered his wife, it was all blown away by the revelation that Ewan Strachan had been the killer all along. Henrik Nordlund, the oldest member of the team and her unofficial mentor, would provide the sympathy and a shoulder to cry on if necessary. A widower nearing retirement, Nordlund had already taken the time to come round to her apartment in Roskildevägen and talk to her. But her real worry was Karl Westermark. In his late thirties, this coldly handsome man was a danger. She knew that he both loathed her and lusted after her. He had made both emotions perfectly plain. He was ruthless, and she knew he would have exploited her fall from grace whilst she was on leave of absence from the polishus. Westermark had believed Strachan to be guilty all along and felt that she had been protecting the British journalist because he could see – even when she hadn't initially – that she was falling for him. This had infuriated Westermark because she was one of the few women he had failed to add to his impressive list of conquests. Her pointed rejections of his obvious advances had only increased his hatred of her whilst heightening the sexual tension and desire. It was a volatile combination that would only strain the atmosphere within the team on her return.

Anita now found herself at a standstill. The traffic was going nowhere. It was unusual to have a jam at this time of day. This was annoying. She only lived across the park but had taken the car as she wanted to do some shopping at Mobilia after her hospital appointment. Now that she was stuck, she just wanted to get back home, put on her running clothes and jog away her worries in Pildammsparken. Living in Malmö meant she hadn't a quiet space to run or walk along. In the summer, too many people came out to enjoy the sun on the city beaches. She had managed to escape to Simrishamn during her suspension, staying with her old school friend Sandra. There, she had been able to wander by herself up towards Baskemölla and onto her favourite beach, Lilla Vik. It was her mental sanctuary. Out of season, there would be just her on her own, the clean, shining sand, and the Baltic stretching away to the horizon.

Anita looked around to see if there was another way out. The car was trapped. She smacked the steering wheel in frustration. The sun was now beating down, and her old Volkswagen was getting decidedly stuffy, despite the open window. Like some of the other drivers, she got out so see what was holding them up. Further along the street, she could see a large group of bystanders. She also spotted a couple of uniformed policemen. She slammed the car door shut and walked towards the crowd. On reaching the group, she recognised one of the officers, Carl Svanberg. Her attempts to attract his attention were drowned out by the blaring of an ambulance siren. The ambulance wove its way through the traffic until it stopped in the middle of the street.

'Carl.'

The officer turned and looked at Anita in some surprise. Once he recognised her, was that a smirk he was trying to hide? Or am I being paranoid? thought Anita. 'What's up?'

Svanberg pointed through the throng. 'Someone's been knocked over. Probably wasn't looking when crossing the street.'

'Can I help?'

For a moment she could see the confusion on his face. Like everyone based at the polishus, he would know her situation and be aware of its aftermath. 'I thought you–'

'I start tomorrow. Any development on the Rosengård shootings?' The press had lost interest when it became clear that both immigrant women would survive. She hoped the police attitude hadn't been the same.

'No.'

Fortunately, Svanberg was saved by his colleague calling to him. The paramedics were dealing with what Anita could now see was a man lying on the ground. He was soon lost to view, and as she walked back to her car, the ambulance siren started up again.

CHAPTER 5

Chief Inspector Moberg stared out of his office window over the canal that encircles the old centre of Malmö. The sun glinted on the calm water. It didn't reflect his disposition at that moment. He was irritated – and he was hungry. The two weren't mutually exclusive. It took a lot to satisfy his appetite. He knew he ate and drank too much, but it was more out of habit these days. He had long given up on the idea of diets and controlling his weight. He had always been big. Now he was gross. He realised that colleagues must make comments behind his back, though his temper ensured that no one would dare make derogatory remarks to his face.

He hadn't eaten properly because he had been called out to the Ekman case. It had been bedlam since, and he hadn't had time for even a sandwich. On returning to the polishus, he acquainted Dahlbeck, the Commissioner of Skåne County Police, with the facts. Then he had had a first briefing session with the team. They were as nonplussed as he had been. A respectable businessman possibly gassed in his own shower. The commissioner thought Moberg had been winding him up at first. By the time he appreciated the fact that the crime was for real, he had made it clear that they were only to state that Ekman had been found dead at his apartment and that the police were looking into the circumstances. He didn't want the press to have a field day with such a potentially gruesome story until the case was further down the line.

After making brief, initial enquiries, there was certainly no obvious motive for the murder. What was clear was that it was meticulously planned. The shower must have been tampered with somehow. Then there was the gas. He had come across accidental gassing before, usually in workplaces where toxic fumes had escaped. Suicides, too. But in all his years of policing, he had never come across a murder like this one. For it must be murder. Otherwise, it was a very strange suicide. It was beyond him. That was why he was waiting for an initial report from Eva Thulin when she got back from the forensic lab at nearby Lund. But before that happened, he hoped the food he had ordered from China Box on the corner of Värnhemstorget would arrive. Then he would be in a more receptive mood to take on board whatever bizarre information Thulin had for him.

Anita slumped down in front of the television. She knew she should be out in the park opposite her ground-floor Roskildevägen apartment, yet she was unsettled. She was wearing her running gear and she rested the TV remote on her bare thigh. It was unseasonably warm outside and the apartment was clammy. So why was she idly flicking through the channels on the TV? She knew that it was worry about tomorrow morning and her reception at the polishus. Her attention was brought back to the telly when she heard an English voice. It was not uncommon on Swedish television as many of the programmes were British or American imports that had Swedish subtitles. Many younger Swedes were virtually fluent in English through watching undubbed telly. Anita's was even better because she had spent two years in the North East of England as a child when her father was working as a designer at the Electrolux factory at Spennymoor in County Durham. Then, a few years ago, she had been on secondment to the Metropolitan Police in London. She pricked up her ears. The man was well-spoken but had a definite trace of a northeast accent. Educated Geordie.

He was obviously a cleric, judging by his dress. Maybe about sixty, he was tall with wispy grey hair. It was the thin lips that Anita found herself focusing on. Only when she started to listen to what he said did she become incensed.

"Just look at the historical evidence. It certainly suggests that six million Jews weren't deliberately gassed in the gas chambers. In fact, I think that Fred Leuchter has proved beyond doubt that there were no gas chambers at all in the concentration camps. Extermination was not a deliberate policy by Adolf Hitler, and I doubt whether more than about three hundred and fifty thousand Jews died during that time."

As he carried on in the same vein, Anita shouted at the screen and then violently turned off the television before throwing the remote angrily onto the sofa. She went for a run.

'All I can say is that it might have been some sort of crystals or pellets that had been placed in the drain. There are no traces of anything in the shower head. My guess is that the hot water started off the process, but what probably did for Ekman was when he turned the water off. The crystals probably reacted with the air to create a lethal gas. Certainly, a preliminary look at the body suggests hydrogen cyanide poisoning. The extractor fan would have helped the poisoning process because it speeded up the circulation of the gas. It would have been a quick but agonising death.'

Moberg turned away from Eva Thulin and glanced at Nordlund. 'If it was that simple, I could have got rid of my first two wives without being taken to the cleaners.'

'So the murderer just lifted the drain cover and placed these crystals or whatever inside?'

Thulin nodded in answer to Nordlund's question. 'The beauty of it all is that the evidence was flushed away by the shower water. I've got my people scrabbling around the drains to find traces, but they may be long gone.'

'The wife was away. No sign of a break-in, yet someone got in,' mused Moberg. 'That's very convenient. She's got an automatic alibi. She plants the crystals and buggers off to the country while her husband dies horribly. She's in the clear.'

'That's assuming that the wife wasn't the intended victim.'

Moberg looked at Nordlund. 'That's a point. The killer might not have known that she was going away. Do we know exactly when she left for the country?'

'According to the cleaner, it was the morning of the day before,' said Nordlund.

Moberg looked at Thulin. 'OK.' This was a dismissal. She left the room.

Moberg picked up the empty noodle box on his desk and dropped it unceremoniously into the plastic bin. He eased his massive frame out of his chair and heaved himself over to the window.

'So, where does this leave us, Henrik?'

Nordlund paused before speaking. Unlike Moberg and the equally bullish Westermark, Henrik Nordlund was a quiet man of few words. But when he spoke, he was usually worth listening to. That's why Moberg showed the older detective the respect he withheld from most of his colleagues. Nordlund was nearing retirement but still believed in what he did, despite the general sense of disillusionment that surrounded him at work. His grey pallor and permanently sad expression had more to do with becoming a premature widower than the rigours of the job.

'It was carefully planned. It could be fru Ekman, who was out of town at the time, and she could have set it up before she left. Or it was someone who knew that she was out of town. Or else fru Ekman was the intended victim. But whoever it was seems to have had access to the apartment and presumably knew they wouldn't be disturbed while setting the whole thing up.'

Moberg stared out of the window. There were a few pedalos on the canal. When the weather was good, people took to the water. He couldn't understand why they did as it looked too much like hard work.

'We need to check if there were any visitors to the apartment yesterday. Workmen, delivery people. And I want to speak to the grieving widow. When's she due back?'

'Late afternoon.' Nordlund paused. 'It'll be interesting to see what Westermark comes up with after his visit to the advertising agency. Some of his colleagues might have known his movements – or those of his wife.'

Moberg pursed his large lips. 'We need to build up a picture of Tommy Ekman. A cut-throat business like advertising must throw up some tensions, business rivalries; that sort of thing. And what did he get up to out of work? I'll bet he played around. They always do. If his wife knew, she'd have a motive. If she didn't, then someone else will have one. Jealous husband. These things usually boil down to sex.'

'What about the MO?'

Moberg turned around. 'It's a good way of murdering someone without having to be there. I think our killer is clever, but I don't think we need read anything more into it.' Nordlund shrugged thoughtfully. 'Come on, Henrik, let's brief the rest of the team and then we'll have a word with the widow.'

As they were about to leave the office, Nordlund said. 'Anita's back tomorrow.'

Moberg sighed heavily. 'I know.'

'She'll be useful on this case.'

The chief inspector shook his head. 'I've got something else in mind for Inspector Sundström.'

CHAPTER 6

This was the sort of place where Inspector Karl Westermark felt at home. The building in Stortorget might be old, but the interior was anything but. The room was almost entirely white, except for the light grey flecked carpet. It had a large, round, white table in the centre. The table had no legs but was supported by a circular tube in the middle. Round it were six ergonomically designed swivel office chairs. To one side, there was a tripod floor lamp with a big shade. The walls were artfully adorned with "creative" work; posters, advertisements and a flat screen TV, which was silently spooling the agency's commercials. Westermark noticed that not all the well-known ads came out of Stockholm. He was a man of modern tastes. And he liked to be around money. The Ekman & Jonsson Advertising Agency reeked of it. In an understated way, of course.

It was full of attractive women, too. Westermark already had it in his mind to ask the receptionist out on a date. He had chatted to her while waiting to interview Ekman's business partner. She was posh but thick – a great combination as far as he was concerned. They always liked a bit of rough. Then there had been the secretary who had brought him a cup of coffee. Long dark hair, short skirt and nice tits. She hadn't liked it when he had eyed her up and she had scuttled out of the conference room. Silly bitch. Didn't know what she was missing.

Now, sitting opposite him was the twitchy figure of Daniel

Jonsson, who was distractedly fiddling with his iPhone. In his late thirties, Jonsson was going prematurely bald. He wore red-rimmed spectacles, which looked as though they would slide off the end of his nose as he peered at his phone. His dress was extra casual. It cost money to dress down as easily as this. Westermark had already established from the chattily indiscreet receptionist that Jonsson was the creative director of the agency – the ideas person. Tommy Ekman was the business brains – the smooth front man, the persuasive presenter of Jonsson's creative work, and the amusing friend of clients at meetings and numerous out-of-office social occasions.

Jonsson explained that he had only just got back into the office from doing a recce for a TV commercial they were shooting next week. He wondered why Tommy hadn't been around to answer any questions.

'Tommy's usually in first thing, but maybe it's because last night was a fairly late one.'

'Working late?'

'No. We'd just heard that we had picked up a new account. Big one. Geistrand Petfoods. Had a bit of a celebration with the winning team.'

'Ekman... any enemies?'

That stopped Jonsson fiddling with his iPhone. Westermark concluded he was one of those annoying people who couldn't leave the damn thing alone. A social prop. Jonsson gave the policeman a startled look.

'That's an odd question.'

'Just answer it.'

Jonsson's attention strayed back to his toy. 'We have business rivals. But that's normal. Advertising is a very competitive industry. Anyway, shouldn't you ask Tommy that?'

'I'm asking you.'

'Right. Look, you haven't really explained what you're doing here. Has one of the staff got into trouble?'

'You could say that. Were you the last person to see Ekman in this building last night?'

Jonsson shook his head. 'He was still here when I left at about nine. There were at least a couple of other people in his office. Elin Marklund was certainly still here. Look, what's this all about?'

Westermark wrote down Marklund's name. 'I'll have to speak to everyone who was at your "celebration" last night.'

'Why?' Westermark was amused to see that he had actually put his phone down. 'Has something happened to Tommy?'

'Put it this way, you might think about taking his name off your company letterhead.'

Kristina Ekman fitted Chief Inspector Moberg's image of what he expected of the spouse of a high-flying businessman with the obvious trappings of wealth. She may have just become a widow, but she was still immaculately turned out. The long, blonde hair cascaded down to her shoulders and framed a very pretty face. Her creamy complexion was complemented by only a small amount of artfully applied make-up. She had the air of someone who knew she didn't have to exaggerate her beauty with cosmetics. Whether by design or accident, she wore black. Her clothes were from the sort of stores where it was considered vulgar to put prices in the window; the places that Moberg's previous wives had always wanted to frequent, though he had made sure that they never had quite enough to buy anything too budget-busting. She sat opposite Moberg and Nordlund in the opulent open-plan living room of the apartment in Drottningtorget that she had shared with her husband. Her perfectly formed lips held a cigarette momentarily in place. Was the cigarette being used to keep seething emotions in check or as a smokescreen? What Moberg couldn't decide, as he watched her, was whether he was talking to a woman who had lost her life's soul mate or a calculating husband-killer. Or, if she was the intended victim, would the murderer come back? He found her calmness unnerving.

'I know it's a difficult time, fru Ekman, but we needed to talk to you as soon as possible. The more we learn now, the quicker we can find your husband's murderer.'

Kristina Ekman held the cigarette elegantly at an angle, the wrist cocked so that the smoke wafted away from her. 'You are *sure* that he was murdered?'

'Yes. Our forensics people say that it couldn't have been an accident.'

'I can't believe...' Her voice trailed off. Were her feelings beginning to show? She concentrated on her cigarette again, which seemed to have the effect of snuffing out any signs of emotion.

'All I have been told was that he died in the shower. If it's murder, did someone attack him?'

'No.'

'So how was he killed?'

'I'm sorry, fru Ekman, but I can't reveal anything until we know more.'

She turned her head away and stared out of the window. The brightness outside mocked the gloom that immersed the room.

'What we need to know,' continued Moberg, 'is who knew that he would be alone in the apartment last night?'

She took another delicate puff on her cigarette as she contemplated the question. 'Myself. The kids. Monica, the cleaner. My father. We were staying the night with him. That's about it. Unless he mentioned something to people at the agency.'

'Why were you away last night?'

A mirthless smile played on her lips. 'He had a new business pitch on yesterday. I always keep out of the way at times like that. If he wins, he usually stays out late celebrating and comes back smelling of drink. If they lose, he gets really down and he's hell to live with for a day or two.' She realised that she had been talking in the present tense. 'He *did* get down,' she corrected herself before violently stubbing out her cigarette in an expensive cut-glass ashtray.

'Who else has a key to the apartment? There were no signs of forced entry.'

'Only the people I have already mentioned.'

Moberg shifted his bulk in the massive sofa, which he managed to make appear small. 'I'm afraid I have to ask the obvious question, but are there any people who would have a motive to harm your husband? Business rivals?'

'Tommy was successful, so I'm sure there would be a lot of professional jealousy. There was no one whom he ever mentioned being a bitter rival. He thought he was above that sort of thing. He thought he was better than everybody else in the ad world.'

'What about his personal life?' This was Nordlund's first contribution.

'What are you implying by that?' she snapped.

'Fru Ekman, all I'm saying is that there may be a more personal angle to this crime.'

'You mean a love rival,' she sneered. 'I can tell you that Tommy was a faithful husband.'

'I was thinking more about your husband's social circle. We need to build up a picture of his life, both at work and away from the office.'

She quickly regained her composure. 'He didn't have much spare time away from work. But he liked to relax with the family when he could. We have a weekend place in Österlen. He liked to sail. Bit of golf. We didn't socialise much; he spent so much time entertaining clients that he wanted a break from that when he was with us.'

Moberg nodded to Nordlund and they both stood. 'That's all for the moment. We'll have to speak again at some stage.

I'm afraid you can't stay here while your apartment remains a crime scene.'

Kristina Ekman remained seated. 'I'll go back to my father's home at Illstorp to take care of the children. I haven't told them yet.'

'Before you return there, you'll need to officially identify your husband's body.'

She gave him a startled glance. Moberg didn't know where to look when Kristina Ekman suddenly burst into tears.

CHAPTER 7

Anita was grateful to seek the sanctuary of her office and shut the door. It had been a nerve-racking walk from the polishus car park up to her room. She had deliberately got in early so that she wouldn't bump into too many people. Coming through the main door, she had passed Carl Svanberg. He had greeted her with a half-smile and told her that the pedestrian knocked over that day was going to be all right. He was just off to interview the driver of the car. Fortunately, the only other person she had come across was Klara Wallen, another inspector in the Criminal Investigation Squad, who had given her a reassuring smile and a hasty 'I'll catch you later' as she rushed off on some unknown errand. Wallen was the nearest thing Anita had to a female friend at headquarters, though their only real areas of common ground were red wine and a dislike of Inspector Karl Westermark. From the few others that she had scurried past, she had got some strange looks, which she hadn't been able to interpret. Scorn or disinterest?

After a sleepless night she was tired, and her nervousness only made her feel more lethargic. She leant with her back against the closed door and sighed. The office hadn't changed; just a hell of a lot neater than she had kept it. There were still two desks squeezed into the small room. Apart from the chairs, the only other piece of furniture there was space for was a wooden bookcase, which was more a general dumping ground for files, notebooks, unread memos and mugs than it was for holding anything more intellectually stimulating. What prevented the office from being totally claustrophobic was the window, which overlooked the green swathe of Rörsjöparken. Her desk was bare except for her computer and the small photo of her teenage son, Lasse, in a wooden frame. He had bought it for her as a birthday present some years before. The other desk meant that Mats Olander must still be here. She liked Mats, who was a police assistant; she was meant to be showing him the ropes. Fine example she had set. Yet she was a bit sad that he hadn't tried to contact her when she had been off "sick". Maybe he was embarrassed by the whole escapade and it wouldn't do his career any good to be associated with the detective who had killed one of Sweden's most famous film directors and become the authorities' official scapegoat.

As she put her bag down and sat at her desk, she idly pulled open the top drawer. She started. Her throat went dry. She felt a pang of panic. She hadn't expected Moberg to be so efficient. Next to her warrant card was her Sig Sauer in its holster. The P225. The pistol she had used at the top of the Turning Torso. She began to tremble as she slumped in her seat. Images of that awful day replayed themselves in her mind for the umpteenth time. The sight of Mick Roslyn about to tip a struggling Ewan Strachan over the edge of the skyscraper. Her shouting at Roslyn to stop and the split-second realisation that he wasn't going to. And then the explosion in her hand as the weapon went off, and then... Anita stared at the pistol and swore to herself that she would never use it again, whatever the circumstances.

She heard the door opening and guiltily shoved the drawer shut. The young man who entered was unfamiliar. He was tall and thin with short-cropped, jet-black hair, a swarthy complexion, and a face that was too youthful to be anywhere near a police station, unless on a school trip. At first glance he looked distinctly Middle Eastern. A broad smile spread across his features, and she noticed that he was holding a coffee mug in each hand. One was being offered to her.

'It's strong. Inspector Nordlund told me that Inspector Sundström likes her coffee strong.'

'And who are you?' asked Anita ungraciously.

The young man put the mug down in front of her. The pleasant smile was still in place. 'Khalid Hakim Mirza. I'm your new trainee assistant.'

'Where's Mats Olander?'

'He was sent back to Stockholm just after...'

Just after she had fucked up. She couldn't suppress her growing annoyance. She was being palmed off with another trainee. She had got used to Olander and didn't want to have to start with another one. Why couldn't someone else have this bloody kid? Why was it always her? Because she was a woman? She wasn't going to be a bloody nursemaid again!

'I'm sure there's been a mistake, em... Sorry, what was your name again?'

'Khalid Hakim Mirza. But people call me Hakim.'

'Well, Hakim, I wouldn't get too used to that desk.' Hakim was now sitting behind it, opposite her.

The smile had been replaced by a perplexed expression. 'I was put here on the express orders of Chief Inspector Moberg.'

The bastard! He had done this deliberately. It was Westermark's turn. They had probably laughed about it as they assigned Hakim to her. She took her coffee grudgingly. 'Thanks,' was all she could muster.

Hakim sipped at his coffee. He looked disappointed. Hurt. 'Oh, I was to tell you that Chief Inspector Moberg wants to see you in his office at nine.'

Moberg had been in since 6.30. He wanted time to reflect before catching up with Nordlund and Westermark. He was stumped. A neat murder carried out while the murderer could be on the other side of the world. As yet they had no suspects, unless you counted the possibility that it was Ekman's wife. But even if they found a motive, they would have a real problem proving it. The murderer would have a watertight alibi. Literally!

He opened the discussion by asking Norlund, 'What did you make of Kristina Ekman now that you've had time to think about what she said yesterday? I suppose I'm asking if she could have done it.'

Nordlund stroked his chin. 'It's possible, but we'd have to find a motive. Would she have more to lose than gain from her husband's death?'

'Yes, Tommy Ekman was obviously successful. She was too damn calm for my liking, until the waterworks at the end. Maybe they were for our benefit.'

'People react to tragedy in different ways.'

'We need to look thoroughly into her background. She might have skeletons which would point to her being the potential victim.' Turning to Westermark, 'What about the advertising company?'

'I spoke to Daniel Jonsson. He's the co-owner. Strange bugger. Creative type. From what I gathered, it was Ekman who was the silver-tongued front man, with Jonsson doing all the arty-farty stuff in the background. Obviously a combination that worked. They were growing fast and had been planning to open an office in Stockholm before Christmas. Jonsson couldn't think of anyone who would want to kill his partner. Really shaken up when I broke the news.' Westermark smirked at the memory. 'I think he could see his rising business career crashing to the ground. But Ekman seems to have been popular among the staff. Well, certainly among the women. They seemed devastated to hear the news. A whole lotta crying goin' on.'

'What about Tommy Ekman's movements the night before?'

'They'd just won an important piece of business and there were a few celebratory drinks in Ekman's office for those involved. We don't know what time he was there till because Jonsson says that Ekman was still there with an Elin Marklund when he left. I haven't been able to ask her as she called in sick yesterday. But I'll get to talk to her today whether she's sick or not.'

'Good. And keep digging at the agency end. There'll be something there that'll provide a motive.'

There was a knock at the door. 'Come!' bellowed Moberg.

Eva Thulin popped her head in. 'I don't know if this will be of any relevance, but our man had sex a few hours before he died.'

'How long before?'

'The night before. There was a pair of his pants on the floor of the bedroom. Traces of his sperm on them. So he probably had sex somewhere else and pulled his pants back on after. Left a telltale dribble.'

Moberg looked at the other two officers. 'Well, well. That can't have been the delectable Kristina. She was at her father's. We need to find out who the lucky lady was. And if Kristina knew he was carrying on, that would give *her* a bloody good motive.' He slapped an ample thigh. 'I'm feeling happier already.'

Anita's heart was racing. She hesitated outside Moberg's door. She had been dreading this moment. How would her boss react? He was difficult at the best of times. Would he start shouting at her or would there be outright resentment? Sarcasm was his weapon of choice. She had no idea how he had felt about the final outcome of the Malin Lovgren case, as it was Commissioner Dahlbeck who had sent her packing after the arrest of Ewan Strachan. She hadn't seen Moberg, as they were so keen to get her out of the building and on sick leave that her feet had hardly touched the ground. And then nothing. No call to offer her support, as Henrik Nordlund had done. The trouble was she didn't much like the chief inspector. He was a perfectly good policeman. Better than most. He was just a rather unpleasant person. She took a deep breath and knocked.

'Take a seat.' Then, as an afterthought, 'Anita.'

She sat down opposite his intimidating bulk.

'It's good to be able to call on a full team again.' He watched her closely. She tried not to squirm. 'For the record, I don't blame you for what you did up on the top of the Torso. You had no choice.'

She was grateful for that. But he wasn't going to let her off lightly. 'Of course, if you hadn't persuaded me that Roslyn was our killer, I wouldn't have let Strachan loose for Roslyn to chase after.'

She had to bite her tongue and take the flak. Moberg was dead right, though she could have pointed out that they would never have been able to actually prove that Strachan was Malin Lovgren's murderer. It was only his confession over their romantic dinner together that had clinched it.

'Anyhow, I've got something for you to do.'

'The death of the advertising man?' Anita was surprised at the level of enthusiasm in her voice. Hakim, after she had broken the awkward silence that she had created, had told her of all the activity in the polishus the day before.

'You're not going to be working on that case.'

'And why not?' she demanded.

'I can't let you near a murder at the moment. Not after...'

'In case I cause the department embarrassment.'

'Yes, if you fucking well want to know.' He was getting as annoyed as she was. 'It's a tricky case and the press will jump all over it if they think you're involved. I'm keeping it as low profile as possible, so you're not going to get in the fucking way.' He brought his rising temper under control. Why did this bloody woman bring out the worst in him? The trouble was he had never worked out how to handle her.

He pushed a thin file in her direction. 'You're going to find a missing painting.'

'You're joking! That doesn't come under serious crime!'

'It does if you're the guy who's had it nicked.'

'But Economic Crime handles that sort of thing.'

'Not this time. The art collector just happens to be a pal of our beloved commissioner. This is your chance to keep your job and make him love you again.'

'What about the shootings in Rosengård? Couldn't I work on that?'

'Inspector Larsson's on that one. Probably just a local dispute,' he added dismissively. 'Take Mirza with you. It'll give you chance to get to know him,' he added caustically.

'Why have I got stuck with another bloody trainee?'

'Because we're too busy trying to catch a murderer.'

Anita slammed Moberg's door shut behind her. She had nearly thrown the file in his big, fat face. But that would have really finished her career. Even through her red mist she was beginning to realise that she had to watch her step. Everything she did would be monitored, noted and reported back to the commissioner's office. And she knew that certain people would do their utmost to make her life as difficult as possible.

'I'd recognise that lovely arse anywhere.'

A shiver went up Anita's spine. She immediately regretted putting on a tight pair of black jeans that morning. Slowly she turned round and faced a leering Westermark. Still handsome. Still slimy. And still a problem she was going to have to learn to deal with.

'Hello, Karl.'

His eyes were undressing her as he spoke. Anita might be in her forties but she was still in excellent shape. Particularly that backside snuggling into those figure-hugging pants. And her face had aged well. Not many lines. The short, blonde hair helped to accentuate the bright, green-grey eyes, the high cheekbones and the shapely mouth – not too wide, the lips not too thin. He remembered how quick she was to smile and how her whole face lit up when amused. That didn't happen often these days when he was around. Then there were the glasses. They were a definite turn-on. What always amazed him was that she didn't seem aware of how sexy she was. Not naïve, more disinterested. 'Nice to see you again.' There was no warmth in his voice. 'I'm not sure if Moberg was too keen to have you back. But I'd have you any time!'

Anita wanted to tell Westermark to sod off but resisted the urge. He moved a little closer. Too close.

'Pity I was right and you were wrong about your British "boyfriend". He's not much use to you in prison, is he? If you're lonely...'

'I'll never be that lonely.'

He gave a grunt of derision. 'You will one day.'

'I've got a case to solve. So I won't keep you.'

Another snort of mirthless laughter. 'I've never been into paintings. I'm more cut out for serious crime. Anyhow, it'll give you a chance to show the immigrant the finer things in Swedish life.'

'What do you mean "immigrant"?' It came out almost as a screech.

'The Arab from some shithole in Rosengård you've got stashed in your office. I think it's the commissioner's way of showing the politicians what a multicultural force we are.'

'You should go on a course with our hate crime educator.'

'Hate crime educator!' Westermark repeated in a childlike voice. 'What is Skåne County Police coming to? Can you think of anything more pathetic?'

Anita glared at him. 'Yes.' As she stalked off down the corridor, the thought of taking Hakim under her wing didn't seem as bad as it had done half an hour before.

CHAPTER 8

They hadn't been able to find a spare police car, so she had to take her own vehicle. She had been compelled to apologise to Hakim for the state of the inside of the car, which was full of sweet wrappings, a couple of old newspapers and an empty soft drinks can rolling around somewhere under the seat. She would *definitely* clean it out at the weekend. The young police assistant was sitting in the passenger seat with the file that Moberg had given her on his lap. She navigated her way through the well-to-do suburbs of Limhamn. Though part of the city of Malmö, Limhamn was seen by its residents as a separate entity – and a far more desirable place to live. A Limhamn address was a prized thing indeed, even if the most famous resident had been, briefly, Hermann Göring. Ironically, the area's most high-profile modern home owner, when not plying his trade in Italy, was the international footballer, Zlatan Ibrahimović, of Bosnian and Croatian stock. Like Hakim, he had been brought up in Rosengård, a district mainly made up of immigrants. With Hakim by her side, she became conscious of how few ethnic faces there were on the streets of Limhamn. She suspected that behind the walled residences, the luxury apartments and the few remaining traditional cottages, sympathies were more for Göring than Ibrahimović.

'What have we got?'

Anita had only glanced at the file in which there was a photo of the stolen painting. To her jaundiced eye, it was a streaky splodge of muted yellows and blues with lines of glinting silver running through the composition. It probably looked far better in real life. And she had also established the address in Strandgatan where the painting's owners, Michaela and Jörgen Lindegren, lived. Her heart wasn't in the case. It was humiliating.

'The painting is called *Dawn Mood*. It was painted back in the 1980s. Pelle Munk.'

Anita squinted sideways at Hakim and then quickly turned her attention back to the road.

'I know him. Well, his daughter really. Karin. She was at school with me in Simrishamn. Same year. They lived just outside on the Vik road.'

'Did you meet him?'

'A few times. I went to stay overnight with Karin once or twice, but her dad only appeared for supper and then disappeared off to his studio again. Not very communicative as I remember.'

'Is he still alive? The price usually goes up when they're dead.'

'I think so. Haven't seen Karin for a few years.'

They had passed down the main shopping street in Limhamn and were nearing the sea. She halted at the junction at the bottom. On the grass opposite was a statue of the "Limhamn King", engineer and industrialist R.F. Berg. Away to the right loomed the large cement works, which was totally out of sync with its well-heeled surroundings. Immediately to the left towered the Strand Hotel. She turned the car to the left into Strandgatan.

'I've heard his name, though I don't know much about him,' Hakim said.

'He was really "in" during the Seventies and Eighties. Abstract concepts are probably the best way to describe them. But instead of canvas, he sometimes painted on sheets of metal. He was as likely to use a screwdriver as a conventional brush. It created startling, shiny effects. Not really my thing, but the art establishment loved him and his prices went through the roof.'

'Does he still live near Simrishamn?'

'Think so. He came down from Stockholm because of the quality of the light in Österlen. It makes the area a magnet for artists in the summer. One year he didn't go back to Stockholm. Been down here ever since.'

They drew up outside a large villa set back from the road beyond a tidily trimmed hedge. It was in a good spot. On the opposite side of the road was a line of plane trees between which could be seen the sea, and the Öresund Bridge stretching all the way across to Denmark. A tanker was ploughing its way towards the middle of the bridge, where its twin towers, like a tent, were pegged into place by massive wire guy ropes. To the right, a forest of masts idly swayed in the yachting sanctuary of Gästhamn. The house itself was a squat, cream-coloured building with a red-tiled roof. The large windows, each curved at the top, were neatly painted white. Judging by the outside of their home, Michaela and Jörgen Lindegren were fastidious folk. Anita and Hakim walked up the short drive at the side of the house and turned right to reach the stout wooden front door. Anita rang the bell.

Jörgen Lindegren let them in. He was a small, fussy man in an expensive business suit. There was a blur of quick hand movements. He used his arms to usher them swiftly into the living room, which was sumptuously decorated. However, Anita had little time to take in the eclectic mix of furnishings as Lindegren was already pointing animatedly at the space on the wall where Pelle Munk's *Dawn Mood* had been proudly displayed.

'It just went during the night. Michaela didn't hear a thing. How they got in, I have no idea. No obvious signs of a break-in. I just don't understand it. It could have been resold already. It cost me a fortune. That's why I got straight onto Commissioner

Dahlbeck. I wanted a top person on this; a proper detective. He promised me.'

'OK, herr Lindegren,' Anita managed to get in when Lindegren's flow began to slow. 'Let's just go through this methodically. I know that colleagues of mine have been and inspected the premises.'

'But they didn't send a detective.'

'I can assure you that they would have done a thorough job. That's obvious from their initial report,' she lied, as she hadn't actually read it. 'As there was no sign of a break-in, I have to ask if the house was left unlocked. Or a window open?'

'Of course not! Michaela always locks up.' Lindegren sounded horrified at the thought, probably because if the house hadn't been secured, he wouldn't see a krona in insurance money.

'So your wife was here alone that night?'

'I was away on business. It should be in the report.'

Anita caught Hakim's eye. His hint of a nod confirmed that Lindegren's absence had been noted. She realised that she was going to have to be more professional than this. Make an effort, even if her mind was straying to what Moberg and the rest of the team were up to. She glanced round the room and took in the other works of art adorning the walls. She wondered whether Lindegren had been drawn to them for their aesthetic qualities or financial worth.

'As the Munk painting was the only thing stolen, the thief or thieves must have targeted that particular picture. Is the Munk your most valuable piece?'

'Possibly.' Anita assumed that meant it was. 'I only bought *Dawn Mood* three months ago.' Lindegren was now talking to the blank wall. 'From a dealer in Stockholm. It was painted in 1985. One of Munk's best.'

'I believe he's not as popular now. Surely that will affect the value.'

Lindegren turned with a hint of a smile. 'Ah, but there's news that, after a few quiet years, Munk is going to hold an exhibition of some new paintings soon. The art world is waiting with bated breath. The value of his old works will rocket.' That answered one question.

'Is Munk's new work general knowledge in the art world?'

'Yes. Or so the art dealer told me. And Munk himself.'

Anita looked at Lindegren in surprise. 'Munk?'

'Yes. I invited him to a soirée I had when I first got the painting. Friends and business acquaintances. Munk came along and seemed delighted to see the picture again. Though he wasn't making anything from the sale,' he added as an afterthought. 'It was a resale.'

'In that case, it's not surprising it was targeted. And, if it was a professional job, then it probably won't reappear until after Munk's exhibition if what you say about its value is true. Yet how they got in remains a mystery. While I take a look around, will you give my colleague the names and addresses of all those who attended your "soirée"?' Anita had difficulty keeping the sarcasm out of her voice.

'You cannot be serious,' Lindegren almost shouted, throwing his arms in the air. 'Surely it's not necessary. Some very important people came that night.'

Anita stared hard at this annoyingly gesticulatory man. 'Herr Lindegren, if you want your painting back, we have to look at all the possibilities. It was targeted by someone who knew that you owned it – and knew where it was in the house. Now, everyone at your gathering did. They may have innocently passed on the information to a third party who got word back to our thieves. We have to start somewhere.'

Westermark couldn't take his eyes off Elin Marklund. She was taller than he had expected. Her short, spiky, black hair was immaculately unkempt. The prominent cheek bones gave her face a sculptured look. The nose was strong without being distracting. The mouth was wide and inviting without being out of proportion. The confident, dark eyes were defiant. The combination was striking. The short, black skirt and matching jacket were businesslike yet alluring. He put her at about thirty.

They were sitting in the same conference room that he had interviewed Jonsson in the day before. Moberg had wanted someone with him to interview the staff, which was why Klara Wallen was seated next to him. Westermark had little time for Wallen and had told her in no uncertain terms that he was conducting the interviews and she was to take notes. He had brushed aside her 'I'm not a bloody secretary' protest.

'Feeling better?'

'Yes.' Marklund didn't offer an explanation for her absence yesterday.

'I need you to tell me about two nights ago. I believe that there was a small party going on to celebrate some business success.'

'We'd won a new client.'

'And?'

'We had a few drinks in Tommy's office.'

Westermark leaned forward with his elbows on the table. 'You and Ekman were the last to leave, according to Jonsson.'

'I suppose we were,' she said offhandedly.

'What time?' He didn't know whether to be angry or to flirt.

She squinted up at the screen with the spooling commercials. 'About half nine. Might have been nearer ten. I wasn't keeping an eye on the time.'

'Didn't you have a husband waiting for you at home?'

'I have a husband, but he's away at the moment.'

'Did you leave at the same time?' This was Wallen. Westermark gave her a filthy look.

'I went first. I got a taxi home. I left my car. I don't believe in drinking and driving.'

'That's what we like to hear,' smirked Westermark. 'So, when the taxi came, where was Ekman?'

'Still in the building. I assume he was locking up.'

'You don't seem very upset that your boss is dead.'

Marklund fixed him firmly with a stare. 'Of course I'm upset. But I'm not going to burst into tears for your benefit. Grief is a private thing.'

'And did anything happen between you and Tommy when you were alone?'

'What do you mean by that?' Marklund appeared momentarily to be caught off guard.

'I only mention it because Tommy had sex with sometime that night. To put it bluntly, was it with you?'

'I'm married.'

'That's no answer.'

'It's the only one you're going to get to such a question.'

Anita parked the car behind the ICA supermarket on Linnégatan. She had promised to buy Hakim lunch in an effort to get to know her young assistant and make up for her less-than-welcoming attitude that morning. They walked past the supermarket and came to the end of the same block. In a window in the wall was a falafel shop. Next to the window were pictures of various celebrities who had patronised the eatery, including Zlatan Ibrahimović. Obviously, when the great man was home from Italy, he wasn't above slumming it. She ordered two falafels and a couple of cans of coke.

'And before you say I'm being condescending and buying these because you have a Middle Eastern background, it's because I like falafels and I'm starving. And they're cheap.'

Hakim just smiled. 'I like them, too.'

They stepped into the sunshine and starting biting into their pitta breads.

'So what do you think of the robbery?'

Hakim didn't answer straightaway as his mouth was full.

'If fru Lindegren didn't leave a door unlocked or window open, then someone must have talked their way in or had a key. According to fru Lindegren, only a cleaner, the next door neighbours and the Lindegren kids have keys.'

Anita nodded. 'You notice that he kept his wife well out of our way, which makes me think that she was inadvertently responsible. What did you make of him?'

'A man used to getting his own way.'

Anita laughed. 'We've quite a few like that at the polishus.'

'And he wasn't very happy about giving me the names of his guests.'

'Neither will his guests be when we have to question them – especially Commissioner Dahlbeck.'

That thought made her feel better as they munched quietly and enjoyed the warm rays of the midday sun. Anita loved days like this. Swedes loved days like this. It's what they spent all winter dreaming about.

'Obvious question, but what made you want to join us lot?'

'Sometimes I wonder.' He nodded towards the picture of Zlatan Ibrahimović. 'When I was growing up in Rosengård, I wanted to be a footballer like him. It's the only way out. It's that or crime. I was OK; attacking midfielder – but not good enough.' He took another bite of falafel. 'My parents left Iraq because the law was distorted by Sadam Hussain and used against them. Despite everything, they instilled in me that you must respect it. It wasn't an easy belief to stick to when many of my friends were being drawn into petty crime. There's not much else to do when you think the world's against you.'

'I'm afraid you're going to get a lot of shit from both sides as a cop. Some of our colleagues aren't going to welcome you with open arms. And your own people–'

'*My* people!' There was a flash of anger. 'I'm Swedish!'

'Sorry, I didn't mean...' Christ, she had fallen into the trap that she so often accused others of stepping into.

'I suppose you think the two women who were shot the other night were just *my* people.'

'Look, Hakim, what I meant was that the community you grew up in might not take kindly to you being on this side of the law.'

Hakim didn't answer but finished his falafel in moody silence. Anita was mentally kicking herself. Though it was Hakim who should be officially trying to make an impression on his senior officer, it was she who was feeling like an idiot, for the second time that day.

They put their empty falafel wrappings in the bin and wandered back to the car.

'One thing that struck me as being odd. At the house today.'

Anita glanced sideways at the young man. He was talking as though they hadn't had an altercation minutes before.

'What?'

'The Munk painting is worth a lot of money but, whatever Lindegren said, there were at least a couple of other paintings in there that were probably even more valuable.'

'Know much about painting?'

'A bit. My father ran a gallery in Baghdad before...'

'So, why just the Munk?'

'Exactly.'

Anita smiled to herself as she unlocked the car door. This boy might not be such a burden after all.

CHAPTER 9

It was well over an hour's drive, even at the speed that Chief Inspector Moberg liked to do. The car raced through typical Scanian countryside. Neat, long, low farmhouses dotted among wide, hedgeless fields. One farm seemed to run into the next. The landscape was broken up by clumps of mature trees and lazily twirling wind turbines. The countryside started to become more undulating as they got further away from the coast and headed over towards the eastern side of Skåne.

Moberg was glad that Nordlund was with him. He didn't feel comfortable with the likes of the region's powerful and wealthy, nor did he have much time for them, which might explain why he hadn't climbed higher up in the force. He didn't posses the social skills and contacts that Commissioner Dahlbeck had so carefully cultivated to reach the top of the tree. Moberg was more interested in being a policeman than pandering to politicians and the press. Nordlund was steady, reliable and tactful. He wouldn't upset the servants or startle the horses at the Wollstad estate near Illstorp. Everybody in southern Sweden knew about Wollstad Industries. The corporation was a big employer. What Moberg hadn't known much about was the company's figurehead, Dag Wollstad, until Nordlund had done a bit of background research before they set off. As well as being a man who kept out of the public eye, Wollstad was very successful, immensely rich, impeccably connected, and, more relevantly, the father of Kristina Ekman and father-in-law of their murder victim.

Moberg swung the car off the main road and onto a country lane. This would meander for kilometres before they reached Wollstad's home, which he assumed would be large and ostentatious. He also knew that the chat with Wollstad would not be an easy affair. The reason given over the phone – and the one that had persuaded Wollstad to meet them – was to find out more about Tommy Ekman. His father-in-law might know more about his business dealings in a way that Ekman's colleagues might not. If Moberg was a betting man – and he was – then the odds were pretty short on Ekman having exploited the Wollstad contacts to get on. What was trickier was the growing suspicion that Kristina was a possible suspect in the murder of her husband. She could quite easily have planted the poisonous crystals before she left. She would know his washing habits and be aware that Tommy would probably use the en suite shower instead of the apartment's main bathroom. It would certainly be safe to assume that no one else would use that shower. Where she had got the deadly crystals from was another matter, but her father was a player in the Scandinavian pharmaceutical market. Nordlund had spotted that on the list of business interests that came under the Wollstad Industries' umbrella. So, she had means and opportunity.

But what about motive? If Tommy had been playing away from home, Kristina would have reason to get rid of her husband. He might have been a serial philanderer. That had yet to be established. Kristina struck Moberg as a proud woman; a woman of privilege who probably wouldn't countenance the potential shame and embarrassment that a wayward husband would cause in her social circle. Not that he had the faintest idea what her social circle was like, but he could imagine.

They came to a curve in the road and to their left was a pair of gates. Spread out on both sides of the road was parkland.

They started to negotiate the drive and slowly moved round the edge of a large man-made lake. It was only after the lake did the house appear. "House" was probably the wrong word. "Château" would be a better description. It had two elegant wings flanking the main part of the building, which was set slightly back. Over three floors, rows of dark, perfectly aligned windows gazed out of the stippled ochre walls. Like watchful eyes, they stared straight down the neat driveway, inspecting visitors bold or foolhardy enough to approach. Dag Wollstad's home was too grand to be inviting.

Wollstad himself was an impressive figure. He was tall and in very good physical shape. A good head of fine, white hair made him look distinguished. The blue eyes were sharp and observant. Despite his seventy years, his face had few lines. This was a man who took care of himself. He was casually dressed in cream trousers and an open-necked checked shirt. Despite the relaxed clothing, this was a man who took his authority for granted. He didn't seem in the least intimidated, as many people were, by Moberg's aggressive demeanour. Moberg got the immediate impression that few would dare to cross Dag Wollstad. If they did, they wouldn't do it a second time.

Wollstad had kept Moberg and Nordlund waiting twenty minutes before appearing in what was one of many reception rooms. Moberg suspected that this was where he met his less important visitors. It was still tastefully decorated, though the elegantly curved Louis XV chairs were rather uncomfortable. Appearance was more important.

'This is a terrible time for our family, as you can imagine. My daughter is devastated. She is comforting my grandchildren. I assume you will not have to talk to her again.' This sounded more like an order than a request.

'Herr Wollstad, we need to find out as much as we can about your son-in-law. Your daughter has already told us about his personal life, but we need to dig a bit deeper into his business life. This maybe is where he's made an enemy or two?'

'Business can stir up emotions, though I hardly think that advertising is important enough to merit murder. That's why I find it hard to believe that a rival would go to such lengths as poisoning Tommy in his shower.'

Moberg and Nordlund exchanged surprised looks.

'How do you know that? Nothing official has been said, not even to your daughter.'

Wollstad waved away Moberg's angry objection. 'I know people.'

Probably the bloody commissioner, or someone in his office. God, he hated all this "friends in high places" bollocks. Wollstad probably had half the government on his payroll.

'Did you have much to do with your son-in-law's advertising business?' This was Nordlund coming to the rescue, as he could see that his boss was having a problem controlling his temper.

'I had contacts that were useful to Tommy when he started up his own agency. He handled the marketing accounts of some of my companies. But not exclusively. I like to keep my options open. Not that Tommy really needed much help. He was a natural salesman. Very charming. That's how he won over my daughter. And it's Kristina who needs protecting right now. I expect you're using every means available to catch his killer?'

'We are doing our best.' Moberg managed to inject some servility into his voice. 'If you think that a business angle can't provide a motive for murder, then it might be a personal vendetta. I know he was married to your daughter, but do you know if he was as faithful a husband as your daughter believes?'

'Chief Inspector, he would have had to answer to me if he wasn't.'

Moberg wasn't sure how to phrase the next question, but it had to be asked. 'Our problem with this case is that no one appears to have broken into the apartment. We know who has keys. The cleaner, the children, yourself and...'

'And Kristina? If you are trying to imply that my daughter had anything to do with this appalling crime then you won't be working on this case much longer.'

Moberg was having serious difficulty curbing his tongue. In other circumstances he would let rip. Again, Nordlund was on hand to help defuse the situation.

'There's one other thing we have to consider, herr Wollstad. Maybe your son-in-law wasn't the intended victim. Your daughter would be the only other person who would use that particular shower.'

For the first time, Wollstad appeared vulnerable. The thought had obviously never crossed his mind. He quickly regained his composure.

'I very much doubt it. But I'll make sure that she's safe. She will remain here.'

Moberg stood up. Despite having size on his side, it was still Wollstad who commanded the room. 'Thank you. If you can think of anything that would help us, please let me know.'

'My advice is to look beyond the business community. Nor should you be trying to find some lurid sexual motive.'

Moberg didn't even bother to acknowledge the suggestion. He turned towards the door.

'Is that Gustav the Second?' asked Nordlund as he glanced towards a portrait of a pale-faced man with a swish of reddish hair, a blond goatee beard and swirly moustache, which was hanging above the fireplace. Beneath the flamboyant, lace ruff collar was a gleaming armour breastplate. While they had been waiting, Moberg had assumed that it was some ancient ancestor of Wollstad's.

'Indeed. Gustav Adolf. Arguably, our greatest king. Are you a student of history, Inspector?'

'I take an interest.'

'Sweden was a great country then. Respected. Feared. Now we have to make our impact through more passive means, making our presence felt in the world through the likes of Ericsson, Tetra Pak, IKEA and Volvo.'

'And Wollstad Industries?'

Wollstad stared hard at Nordlund for a moment and then a smile played on his lips. 'I like to think so.'

Anita put down the phone. She stared towards the window. It was still pleasantly sunny outside. She was deep in thought. She knew she had to go through with it. But she knew she shouldn't. What was the point? What would it achieve? What would be the reaction? Would it enable her to move on? Or would it unleash further demons? She shelved the unanswered questions the moment the door opened and Hakim came in with a couple of plastic cups.

'Thanks,' Anita said as she took the proffered coffee. 'I've just had an interesting conversation with a gallery owner in Ystad.'

Hakim took his seat behind his desk and looked at her keenly. Had she been that enthusiastic when she began years ago? Probably.

'She says that she had a Pelle Munk painting stolen from the gallery a few months ago. It was on permanent show. Stolen during the day. Someone must have just marched in and walked out with it.'

'I'm surprised they noticed,' smirked Hakim. He was making reference to the theft the year before of three important paintings from Malmö Art Museum. The works by Gustav Rydberg, Pär Siegård and *Two Friends* by Edvard Munch hadn't been spotted missing for nearly a fortnight.

'She didn't admit that their security was lax, but she has insurance to think about.'

'So someone must definitely be targeting his paintings. Someone who knows that they will increase in price when his new exhibition takes place?'

'It seems that way. Which brings us back to the Lindegren party and their guests.'

Hakim pulled out of his jacket pocket the piece of paper on which he had written down the names that Jörgan Lindegren had given him. It was now heavily creased. He smoothed it out with the palm of his hand.

'I was looking at the list when I was at the coffee machine. Apart from the commissioner, there's one name that I recognised.'

'Who?'

'The man whose death Chief Inspector Moberg is investigating. Tommy Ekman.'

Moberg was still fuming twenty minutes later when they hit the main road and headed back to Malmö. He rammed his foot down on the accelerator. Nordlund knew his colleague well enough not to say anything when he was in one of these moods.

'I can't stand bastards like that!'

'Well, you did virtually accuse his daughter.'

Suddenly Moberg laughed. A deep roar. 'You certainly put the wind up him with the suggestion that she might have been the intended victim.'

'It's true.'

They travelled swiftly through the sun-drenched countryside. Nordlund would have enjoyed taking in the scenery if they hadn't been going so fast. He loved the landscapes around here. He had been brought up on a farm in Skåne. Sometimes he wished he had stayed put and taken over from his father, but there was little money in it. And he wouldn't have met his beloved wife, who had been a fellow police officer. He had missed her dreadfully since her premature death from cancer a few years ago. He steered his mind back to the case in hand.

'Something struck me about Wollstad.'

'And what was that, Henrik?' Moberg asked. He was now in better spirits. He reduced his speed.

'If he had found out that his son-in-law had been two-timing his daughter, as we suspect Tommy Ekman was, then he doesn't seem like a man who would stand by and let her be humiliated. And, by association, humiliate him.'

'That thought had occurred to me, too. Not that he would have done it himself, but I suspect he would be able to find someone who could do a neat job for him.'

'That could explain why there's no evidence of a break-in.'

'And he has at least a couple of pharmaceutical companies in the Wollstad Industries' portfolio.'

Moberg gave a heavy sigh. 'Imagine the shit we'll get into if we try and prove that old man Wollstad was responsible for the murder.'

Moberg put his foot down again.

CHAPTER 10

It was the last interview of the day. Westermark was fed up talking to advertising people. The women were fine, as most were attractive. There were a couple of stunners he would seriously consider contacting later. He thought the men were either too smooth or too arty or too arrogant, like the Danish senior copywriter, Jesper Poulsen. He couldn't get over the confidence of some of the younger members of the firm. And most of the employees were under thirty. So, he was surprised when Bo Nilsson entered the conference room. Nilsson was far from what he had expected to see in such a thrusting organisation. Westermark put him at nearly sixty. His bald head seemed to elongate an already thin face. He had deeply sunken eyes that gave little away. The rest of him was thin too, though he was only about one and a half metres tall. Despite the heat, he was neatly dressed in a smart suit, which was in sharp contrast to the array of casual clothing worn by the other members of staff that he and Wallen had interviewed during a long day.

Nilsson sat down opposite them and smoothed his trouser legs. His movements were precise. This was a pernickety man. Maybe that was a prerequisite of a company accountant. He then patted his bald pate and brushed away some non-existent hair at the back of his head and then gave a rueful smile. He was ready.

'I believe that you are in charge of the company finances?' Westermark asked wearily. He wanted to head back to the polishus.

'I am the financial director.' Nilsson's voice was rather high-pitched. Westermark found himself trying not to laugh.

'I've asked this question of all the staff. Is there anybody you would suspect would want to harm Tommy Ekman?'

'Harm him?' Nilsson sounded surprised. 'I thought it was an accident.'

'What made you think that?'

'That's what people have been saying round the office.'

Westermark had been finding it difficult to tow the official line, which was not to give too much away. Certainly not admit that Ekman had been murdered. With the bizarre nature of the killing, they didn't want word getting out and media speculation making things worse. Moberg wanted to make damned sure of their facts before the story broke.

'We're keeping an open mind. We need to explore all possibilities while we await forensic reports.'

Nilsson raised his eyebrows; almost the only hair visible on his head. 'Tommy was an ambitious man. He wanted this company to be the best in Sweden. That may have upset a few people along the way. He was charming, but he could be brusque.'

'Did he upset anyone in particular?'

He removed a speck of cotton from his trousers.

'No one that I could put a name to. Just generally. Things might flare up then be swiftly forgotten. I'm sure nothing went as far as anybody wanting to cause Tommy any actual injury.'

'If you don't mind me saying, you seem a little old to be involved in this business.' Westermark gestured round the room at the work on the walls. 'Advertising.'

A thin smile was returned. 'My colleagues may be younger, but Tommy wanted a mature hand on the financial tiller. The young people bring a fantastic energy to the company. That doesn't mean that they're good with money. One of my roles is to make sure budgets are kept within certain parameters.

The creative mind can conjure up ideas that are expensive to execute, particularly when it comes to TV commercials. For example, if the creatives spend too much on filming a commercial, then we can make less on the project. I know it annoys Daniel Jonsson, but, at the end of the day, we are here to make a healthy profit.'

'So how did you end up working here?'

'I worked for one of Tommy's father-in-law's companies for many years. I believe it was Dag Wollstad who recommended me to Tommy.'

Westermark had had enough. 'OK. That's all.'

'Is the company doing well financially?'

Westermark sighed heavily at Wallen. Couldn't she just keep her mouth shut?

'Yes, fine. Why do you ask?' Nilsson sounded offended by the question.

'It was just to establish whether Ekman had any financial worries.'

'I don't know about his personal finances, but he had nothing to worry about here, I can assure you.'

The room was totally devoid of character. One table. Three chairs. A barred window. It smelt of stale hopelessness. It wasn't designed to uplift spirits. It was a place for hard truths. Anita felt nervous. This was ridiculous. Why was she putting herself through this? She opened her snus tin, distractedly took out the little packet of tobacco, shoved it inelegantly under her top lip and felt it safely nestle next to her gum. It made her feel a bit better.

All the way up Lundavägen she had been on the point of turning round. It was still warm, yet she was forcing herself to go into the cold, impersonal world of Malmö Kirseberg prison. Some of the inmates were in there because of her efforts, though not the man who would be coming through that door any moment. He had put *himself* in there because of her. How would he react to seeing her? The door opened. She was about to find out.

She was shocked at his appearance. Ewan Strachan looked thin. In just a few months, he had lost the chubbiness that he had had on his arrival in Malmö in February. The slightly greying red hair had been shaved off, which only accentuated his pallid features. Even the blue eyes that had so caught her attention had lost their mischievous sparkle, partly because his right one was marred by a heavy bruise. He shuffled in and blinked at her as though he had just come out of a dark place. His surprise was replaced by the hint of a smile. Anita nodded at the prison officer who was accompanying Strachan. He hesitated.

'It's all right. Official police business.'

He accepted her lie and left the room. The door clanged and silence sat between them. She noticed the grazes on his knuckles. He had been in a fight. But he was an obvious target. He caught her gaze. Her heart gave a little leap. This was what she had been dreading. The whole point of this meeting was so that she could move on. Bury their past. Not that their "past" had amounted to much. Not even a kiss. Apart from their official dealings, there had only been four social meetings, and the last one was ruined when she realised that he was Malin Lovgren's killer and he had confessed to the murder. Two murders, actually. And therein lay another moral dilemma that was deeply rooted in her mind and impossible to dig out. Why, at his official charging, hadn't she mentioned the death of the Durham University student? Debbie Usher had been the love of Ewan's life before she had been stolen away from him by his best friend, Mick Roslyn. After Roslyn had casually cast Debbie aside, she had committed suicide – the official verdict – by throwing herself off the top of Durham Cathedral. Over their one romantic dinner, Ewan had confessed that he had pushed the girl. So, why hadn't she added this crime to the charges against Ewan Strachan? She had told herself it was nothing to do with Skåne County Police. The Lovgren murder was what they had been investigating. The one question she had never attempted to answer – was it to keep him in Sweden?

'Hello.'

She didn't know what to say.

'I hoped I would see you at my trial.'

She stared at the table. She didn't look at him when she answered.

'They didn't want me anywhere near the courtroom. I was the one who got it wrong.'

Ewan smiled at the memory. 'I noticed that your fat chief inspector took all the credit.'

'How's...?'

'Not a bowl of cherries. As you can imagine, I'm not very popular in here. Half my fellow inmates have photos of Malin Lovgren stuck to their walls.' There was no bitterness in his voice. Just the usual self-mockery that she had enjoyed.

So she didn't have to engage him in eye contact, Anita started to root around in her bag. She produced a packet of cigarettes and pushed them across the table. Now she looked at him. This time Ewan laughed.

'I've given up.' But he still took the packet and pocketed it. 'They might be useful.'

Anita stood up. 'I shouldn't have come. This was a mistake.'

'I'm glad you came.'

She stood awkwardly, not sure whether to go to the door and walk away forever. His eyes were pleading with her to stay.

'How's Lasse?'

This took her off guard. Lasse had never met Ewan, but she had been interested enough in their developing relationship to imagine introducing him to her son. Lasse had been her life, particularly after her divorce from Björn ten years before. They had done everything together. They were a mutual support system. Now he had left home to go to university and had a girlfriend, Rebecka. For the first time the awful truth had dawned on Anita that she needed Lasse far more than he needed her. Rebecka had created a hint of daylight between them. The distance wasn't wide as yet, but Anita could see the signs that would stretch the divide. Rebecka was young and self-absorbed and demanded Lasse's full attention. She hadn't lifted a finger to help all week on her first and, so far, only visit to Anita's apartment. Anita had tried to tread carefully and hide her annoyance. And when that had proved too difficult and she had said anything even slightly critical, Lasse was immediately on the defensive. The week had become tense. She was already having to cope with the fallout from the Lovgren case. Her career was in a mess. The one thing she thought she could cling to was Lasse, and he was no longer there for her. Having counted the minutes before their arrival, she had been relieved when they left. Though it hadn't stopped her from crying for hours after the front door had shut behind them. Had she been weeping for the loss of the one secure relationship in her life?

'He's in love.'

'Ah.' As though he was reading her mind, he said, 'The girlfriend?'

Anita nodded. This was a chance to tell someone. Get it off her chest. Not let it fester. She knew that Ewan would listen sympathetically. The thing that had attracted her to him in the first place had been the ease that she had felt in his company. It certainly hadn't been his looks. Yet how could she even think about confiding in a killer?

'I've got to go.'

'Will you come and see me again?'

Anita shrugged non-committally. She took the few paces to the door and knocked on it to be let out.

'By the way, I never got the chance to tell you, Anita.' She looked at him as she heard the door being opened behind her. 'I love you.'

CHAPTER 11

He had noticed the bus stop before when he had been getting to know Malmö. Part of his reconnaissance. It was on Ystadvägen, the main road out of town to Sweden's most southern point. Even at this time of night, the road was quite busy, but life on the street was quiet. He had also clocked an empty restaurant below the block of apartments. Ethnic, of course. How could people eat such muck? No wonder it closed. Maybe the owners had gone home. More likely they were still here scrounging off the state system.

Where he stood, on the other side of the street, was neatly grassed. There was a large, white building to his right. It was some sort of school and totally deserted at this time of night. There were enough trees to give him cover, and he had already worked out a simple escape route. It was just a case of waiting for the right type of victim to come along getting on or off a late-night bus. The lights from the buildings would enable him to pick the right target. As he waited, he could feel the same thrill of anticipation that he got from what he loved doing most. He had always been good with guns. He had been brought up with them. They were second nature. You started with animals. Then it was only natural to move on. Anyway, what he was shooting at were no better than animals. Terrorising. That was the only way they were going to listen. That was what his voice had told him and he was happy to obey.

A young couple wandered up to the bus stop. They held hands. The man was tall and blond. His partner was darker, but he was sure that they were Swedish. Suddenly he tensed. A bus was approaching from the Ystad direction. A yellow regional Skånetrafiken bus. It stopped. He couldn't see if anyone was getting off. The couple disappeared inside. The bus pulled out into the road and left behind it a man. The man's back was to him. His clothes suggested that he was an immigrant, but you couldn't tell these days. Even Swedes didn't dress distinctively any more. The man turned. He was middle-aged. He had a cigarette in his mouth and a box of matches in his hand. He struck the match, and in that instant he could see that the man was a foreigner. No doubt about it. He aimed. A car went past between him and his target and the man began to move. He smiled to himself. A moving target was more fun, more of a challenge. He gently squeezed the trigger.

Moberg was seething. He slammed his office door so hard that it nearly came off its hinges. Everybody in the vicinity knew whose door it was, even without seeing the chief inspector. Knowing looks were exchanged. It was a common occurrence, though this was louder and more violent than usual.

Henrik Nordlund was the first to venture in for the meeting that had been arranged to review the progress of the Ekman investigation. It was in Moberg's office, which was a bigger version of all the other featureless offices on the corridor. It had one desk with a computer on it. As a technophobe, Moberg hated the computer and tried to use it as little as possible. In one corner of the room was a separate plastic-topped table with half a dozen chairs round it, used for meetings. There was a large whiteboard on the wall for attaching information to or for writing names on during investigations. There was also a holiday wallchart on which there was a thick, black felt-tipped line running through the months that Anita Sundström had been absent. Moberg was sitting behind his desk eating a chocolate bar. Judging by the crushed wrappers which had missed his wastepaper basket, it wasn't his first of the morning. Before Nordlund could speak, Moberg swore. Then he swore again and took a bite out of the bar.

'I take it that your meeting with the commissioner didn't go well.'

'Not just him. That bitch Blom was there too.' Moberg was referring to the public prosecutor, Sonja Blom. 'That bastard Wollstad had been straight onto the commissioner. Upset by our suggestion that his daughter may have been involved. Wollstad hadn't liked my attitude or my "insinuations". Jesus, I can't believe how weak-kneed Dahlbeck is being. Wollstad barks and lapdog Dahlbeck jumps to attention. But I did get one dig in. I asked our wonderful commissioner how Wollstad knew details of the investigation that hadn't been made public or even revealed to his daughter. That had the wanker spluttering into his cappuccino.'

There was a knock on the door and Westermark and Wallen came in. Wallen appeared particularly nervous. Like many in the polishus, she was frightened of Moberg. She wished Anita was here for moral support.

'OK,' Moberg grunted. 'Before we start, just to let you know that Kristina Ekman and Dag Wollstad are officially off limits. For the moment. If we go down that route we have to tread very carefully. The evidence has to be so strong that even Blom will have to get off her snotty little arse and do some prosecuting.'

'But we have to consider that Kristina Ekman was a possible victim.'

Moberg nodded in agreement with Nordlund. 'Yes, we can look into that, whatever Wollstad says. My money is on Wollstad having something to do with this business. He certainly had commercial connections with Ekman. Gave him a foot up. Ekman's agency does the advertising for some of his companies.

61

It probably enabled him to keep an eye on him.'

'That's interesting,' said Westermark. 'Ekman & Jonsson's financial director was brought in from one of Wollstad's other companies. Bo Nilsson. Older guy who doesn't seem to fit into the trendy advertising scene.'

'Probably put in there by Wollstad to protect his investment,' Nordlund suggested.

'And keep an eye on young Tommy,' Westermark smirked. 'If he was being a naughty boy, then Wollstad would find out pretty quickly.'

'You can't escape Wollstad,' sighed Moberg. 'But we've got to look at other alternatives. Anyone in the frame at the agency?'

'We spoke to Elin Marklund. She didn't seem too distraught by her boss's death. Very composed. She wasn't letting on if she was the one who Ekman had sex with. But she's got a husband, so she's not likely to have been.'

'Has she got an alibi?'

Westermark glanced at Wallen. She gulped before she spoke, her voice hoarse. 'Marklund left the office after their drinks party at 9.57. She took a taxi home. She lives down in Skanör.'

'How can you be so sure when she left?' Moberg asked.

'I checked with the taxi firm.'

'So, either Ekman had sex with her in the office or he found someone else on the way to his apartment. Or even someone in the apartment. We need to establish his last movements. Did he go anywhere on the way home?'

'We know that Ekman must have been the last to leave the office. Could he have met someone there after Marklund left?' They took a moment to absorb Nordlund's suggestion.

'Westermark, what about anybody else at the agency who might have a motive?'

'Marklund may have shagged Ekman, but she doesn't have an obvious motive. Unless he was a crap lover.' Only Moberg smiled. 'As for opportunity; hard to tell, because we don't know when the poisonous crystals were put in the shower. Jonsson might have a motive. In theory, he has the most to gain. He ends up with the company. But that might not mean much if Wollstad has the biggest financial stake in the agency.'

'Check that out with the company's money man... what's his name?'

'Nilsson. On the face of it, no one seems to have an axe to grind. They all seem to like him. Or so they say.'

Wallen gave a little cough. It attracted Moberg's attention. 'Well?'

'I was wondering if someone at the agency could have taken Ekman's keys. Then let themselves into the apartment before replacing the keys later the same day.'

'Why didn't you think of that Westermark?' As Westermark was about to speak, Moberg waved away his unheard objection. 'Right, Klara, talk to Ekman's PA or whoever, and find out if that is a remote possibility.'

Moberg pushed himself away from his desk. Not a simple task. 'Well, we need to work out how and when the crystals were planted. And then figure out who could possibly have access without breaking in. Klara might provide a possible answer to that one. At least we've got a bit of breathing space. The commissioner's getting agitated by last night's shooting. If he's not careful, that'll become a political hot potato.'

'Is the immigrant dead?' asked Westermark.

'No; he'll live. Either this gunman is a lousy shot or he's just trying to scare people. But that's Larsson's problem. We've got our own headaches.'

CHAPTER 12

It was good to get out of Malmö. The day was bright again, and the hour-and-a-half-long drive to Simrishamn along Sweden's southern coast would be pleasant. A night with Sandra usually cheered her up. This was a last minute decision because Lasse had emailed to say that he and Rebecka couldn't come down for the weekend. Rebecka wasn't feeling well. Anita assumed it was a diplomatic illness. She didn't want to see Anita. Anita was disappointed, though not surprised. If only she could spend some quality time with Lasse alone. But there was little chance of that happening these days.

Another reason to escape Malmö was because she felt useless and unwanted. Moberg and the team were heavily involved in the Ekman murder, and the rest of her colleagues seemed to be running around trying to catch a gunman with a grudge against immigrants. All she was doing was trying to find some art thief who had a thing about Pelle Munk paintings. Not a very satisfying state of affairs.

The dual carriageway out of Malmö towards the coast wasn't too busy on a Saturday morning. The countryside of Skåne always looked at its best at this time of year. The trees were out, the earth responding to the early-summer sun and the bright yellow of the oil seed rape giving a rich and colourful texture to the landscape that was so missed during the winter months. It was the openness that Anita enjoyed. As a youngster, during the family's two years in Durham in the 1970s, she had always felt constrained by the hedges and walls that divided the fields in the British countryside. She hadn't seen them as defining boundaries, more as barriers. The Scanian landscape was all about freedom – it's only obstruction was the sea. And that was where the tamed and untamed met. To Anita, it was a glorious union. The only thing she would have imported from England was the Lake District fells. They would add the grandeur that her beloved Skåne lacked.

And the final reason to slip away from Malmö? Ewan Strachan. In hindsight, the visit to the prison had been a mistake. She had thought that by seeing him she would be able to start afresh. That her feelings for him were nothing more than a passing fancy. That she had merely been flattered by his attention. That she had temporarily fallen for someone who hadn't been after "one thing". Someone who had made her laugh when life hadn't seemed very funny. The experience had also rekindled memories of the happiest time in her childhood when her family had been a family. If they had stayed in Durham, her parents might not have divorced. Maybe that was fanciful. She had been too young, or too busy making new friends, to notice the cracks that must have been there. Yet it was in Durham that Ewan and Mick Roslyn had become friends, where enmities had started that would lead to three deaths – and to her meeting the man she was now trying to convince herself she never really loved. Far from being able to dismiss him from her mind, she found herself worrying about him. She had found out that he had been placed in solitary confinement for his own protection. She could see the evidence of the fight he had been in. Next to being a paedophile, killing a national icon – and a sexy one at that – was guaranteed to make him the target for every macho maniac in the prison. And she knew that he suffered from claustrophobia. Solitary would be playing havoc with his mind. She couldn't begin to imagine the mental torture he was going through. But he was a killer. And that fact was killing her too – inside.

As she neared Ystad, she wrenched her mind back to the weekend. But it wasn't going to be all play and no work. She would call into the gallery in Ystad to check out their Munk theft. In fact, she had decided that she would have a word with Pelle Munk himself. It was a long shot, but he might have an angle on the robberies.

Moberg was glad that he had brought Wallen along. She was the only one who could figure out how to operate the Ekmans' coffee maker. She also had worked out in which cupboard the coffee was stored. The kitchen was straight out of a style magazine. Spacious, gleaming, ultra-modern, with every appliance and gadget known to woman. Not Moberg's sort of thing. But just the kind of fitted kitchen that all three of his wives had nagged him about getting installed. All had been disappointed. He couldn't justify the money to himself. As long as there was enough room to prepare his meals, then that was all that counted.

He had brought together the nucleus of the investigating team to Ekman's apartment. He wanted Nordlund, Westermark and Wallen to get a feel for the place – to understand the environment in which their victim lived. To maybe discover a little more about Tommy Ekman himself. The truth was that they were going nowhere. Official pressure was starting to build. The news was in the papers this morning that Tommy Ekman had died in "suspicious" circumstances. They weren't revealing any more at this stage. The ease with which the murder had been carried out was not the sort of information that they wanted the general public to absorb. There were enough nutters out there who might want to have a go themselves if details were released. Fortunately, *Sydsvenskan* was more interested in speculating about the identity of the gunman behind the latest immigrant shooting to make a big splash about the death of some advertising executive. All three victims had survived, but ballistics had confirmed that the same gun had been used in both attacks.

All four officers sat round the large kitchen table with their coffees. Westermark had even found some Gille cinnamon biscuits, which Moberg was already ploughing his way through. Kristina Ekman could afford to replace them.

'Right, have we anything new?' Moberg's question was more in hope than expectation.

'I managed to get hold of Ekman's PA.'

'Well?' Moberg had tried not to bark, but Wallen had been startled by his tone.

'Viktoria Carlsson. That's her name.' Difficult cases, especially ones that didn't have a proper focus, didn't improve Moberg's mood. Yet he managed to restrict himself to a heavy sigh and not a 'fucking get on with it', which was on the tip of his tongue.

'Right... em... she said that Tommy Ekman kept a spare set of apartment keys in his office.'

'Oh, bloody fantastic,' groaned Westermark.

'Apparently, Ekman had lost his keys once when his wife was away and couldn't get into the apartment. So, from then on, he kept a spare set at the office. If he couldn't get in, he could pop back to the office and get the other keys. A precaution.'

'And who knew about these keys?' Moberg asked.

'Viktoria didn't know, but she assumed it was reasonably common knowledge. It was a joke around the office about the occasion he was locked out. He didn't like to appear foolish, so he wasn't happy when the story came out.'

'Where were the keys kept?' Moberg asked.

'In his desk drawer.'

'Locked?'

'Usually, but sometimes not. He didn't always remember to lock it.'

'And the day of the presentation?'

'Viktoria wasn't sure. But they were there the night before because she saw Ekman put them back in the drawer just as she was leaving work. She assumes he didn't lock it, as it was unlocked the next morning.'

Moberg blew out his ample cheeks. 'So, anybody at the agency could have walked into his apartment if they'd got into Ekman's office on the day of the presentation. We'll have to check everybody's movements that day. From Stortorget to here and back? It would take about half an hour if they were quick. Christ, what a ballache.'

They had already been back upstairs to the en suite bathroom and thought about how the murder had been committed. There hadn't been any great insights, as the crime still looked as horribly simple as it had when they had first come across the slumped, naked body of Tommy Ekman.

'Still no sightings of Ekman between the office and here?'

Nordlund shook his head. 'But we do know that he phoned his wife at Illstorp at ten to eleven. He rang from here. That's been confirmed. So, if Elin Marklund left around ten, there's only about fifty minutes unaccounted for – and he would need fifteen of those to walk back to the apartment.'

'Probably not long enough for a tryst in the office, but it doesn't mean he couldn't have shagged someone when he got home. After the call.'

'Unlikely.' Nordlund held his cup midway between the table and his mouth. 'Eva Thulin and her people have been over all the bedrooms with a fine toothcomb. She says there's no evidence of another woman – only his wife. He certainly didn't make love in a bed.'

'Down here then?'

'Thulin didn't find any telltale signs.'

'My bet,' said Westermark, 'is that the randy bugger had it away in the office. That means Elin Marklund. I'll speak to her again.'

Moberg took another biscuit. It was so thin that it disappeared in his paw before vanishing into his mouth. The biscuit didn't stop him speaking.

'That may prove who he was screwing that night, but it doesn't get us any further with anybody at the agency.'

'No,' said Nordlund. 'However, it does give Kristina Ekman a motive. It could have been going on for some time. She finds out.'

'Or Wollstad. We're back to the bloody family again.' Moberg began to drum his thick fingers on the table top. 'Are we sure that no one else came in after Kristina left with the kids the morning before?'

Westermark answered. 'According to the cleaner, there were no deliveries expected or workmen due. The post was delivered and the usual newspaper through the door. The cleaner was still around when the post arrived. She left at ten to go on to another house.'

'Did she clean in the en suite that morning?'

'No. She did the downstairs. The bedroom and en suite were to be done the next day. That's how she found the body.'

'I suppose what we really need to ask...' They all turned to Nordlund. 'Who would have access to the crystals? It's not something you can just pick up at your neighbourhood Netto.'

'You're right there, Henrik. In theory, that probably rules out the agency crowd. Unless it's something that you can get over the internet. Of course, our friend Dag Wollstad has pharmaceutical companies. I'm sure they could rustle up something to do the job. Which brings us back to father and daughter.'

'It doesn't necessarily rule out the advertising agency people.' Moberg was quite shocked that Wallen was advancing an opinion. 'They do the advertising for some of Wollstad's companies. One of them might be a pharmaceutical firm. At least that's easy to check.'

CHAPTER 13

Anita woke up with a hangover. It didn't happen very often these days and the older she got, the harder it was to take. She lay totally motionless in the comfortable bed in Sandra's spare room. If she moved, she would set her head off again. But the headache was worth it. She had had a good night with Sandra. They had wandered down Storgatan, which was pedestrianised during the summer months, had sat in the warm evening air and had consumed more beers than she should have done. A couple of friends had joined them before they had strolled along the harbour front. She had always loved it down by the water, with the gaily coloured fishermen's cottages, the smell of the seaweed and the cries of the gulls. Fishing these days was handled by industrial-sized vessels. A couple were in. They might be more effective and economical, but they had taken the romance out of the trade. During the summer, there were always interesting private boats around, too. It was a popular place for summer seafarers to pop into. There was one very sleek, sophisticated craft, which had come from Monaco. The wealthy owners were lounging on deck and enjoying being the centre of the locals' curiosity. And, of course, there was the Sarpen, gently undulating in the water. It was a beautiful, two-masted, rigged sailing ship, which was used by naval cadets. Two summers previously, Anita and Lasse had been out on her for an afternoon cruise with a number of friends. Lasse had loved it.

Anita had returned with Sandra to her apartment opposite the park and had had a perfect summer meal of cold herring and salads, followed by the local Scanian speciality cake, *spettekaka*, served with ice cream, and all washed down with a couple of bottles of Chardonnay. Though the booze had triggered a whole host of reminiscences and personal confessions, Anita hadn't brought up the subject of Ewan, or even her problems with Lasse's girlfriend. There was no more obvious a person to unburden her problems to than Sandra, yet something wouldn't allow her to venture into either area. Sandra could be forthright and might have given her a hard time about Ewan. But she would surely have been sympathetic about the Lasse situation. As she felt blindly for her glasses on the bedside table, she stopped the self-analysing. It was hurting her brain.

She had never needed a coffee more than this morning. Skånerost. It was her favourite. It took no prisoners, especially when Sandra brewed it. And that would be just the ticket. She wanted to be reasonably alert when she saw Pelle Munk. She had phoned the day before to make sure he was around. She thought he had understood the conversation, though she had had to repeat herself several times and shout down the phone. He was probably drunk. She would call in that afternoon before she headed back to Malmö. She gratefully accepted the mug of coffee shoved in front of her on the kitchen table. Like her, Sandra wasn't neat. The apartment was reassuringly chaotic, though Sandra's appearance was not. Her cropped, fair hair and trim figure gave off an air of control. And her senior nursing job in the town's hospital would be carried out with the utmost efficiency. It was only behind closed doors that she allowed her natural untidiness free rein.

It was some minutes before Anita had the energy to talk.

'Whatever happened to Karin Munk?'

'She's back in Simrishamn.'

'You're kidding!'

71

Anita was surprised to hear that their old school friend was back in town. She had been the most ambitious of the group and had been keen to follow an artistic career. Simrishamn was too small for Karin. It had to be Stockholm. She had been brought up there and had resented her father decamping to uncivilised Skåne when his artist's eye had fallen in love with the light. When she first came to the school, she had taken a long time to settle, but Anita and Sandra had taken her under their wing, her initial aloofness had melted away and she had been fun when in the right mood. Yet, at other times she had also been cold and uncommunicative, which they had put down to her artistic temperament. She had been by far the best artist in the school and great things had been expected of her. The last time that Anita had seen Karin was when Anita was studying at Stockholm's police academy. They had met up for drinks, but the evening had been awkward. Karin was being incredibly bohemian, and she found it difficult to reconcile her obligatory anti-establishment views with the fact that Anita was learning how to uphold the law. Anita had joined the ranks of "the oppressors". Anita couldn't really work that one out. When some of Karin's equally gauche friends had arrived, Anita had slipped away quietly and hadn't been in contact since.

'No. I think she came back to keep an eye on her dad. Her mum died about five years ago.'

'Funny. She couldn't wait to get out of here when she was younger. What's she doing now?'

'Something in the arty line. Not quite sure what. She was a bit vague. I ran into her a few weeks ago in the hospital. She brought Pelle in for some sort of check-up. He's not looking in the best of health. Either too much booze or sniffing too much paint.'

'Well, he can't be at death's door because he's putting together a new exhibition, so I'm told. That's why we think his paintings have been pinched, because he's going to be back in fashion again. If the exhibition is a success, our thief is going to cash in. That's our theory. It's the only one we've got anyway,' she mumbled into her coffee.

The drive out to Pelle Munk's home from Sandra's apartment only took about ten minutes. She passed the beach at Tobisborg, which was already busy with families enjoying the continuing sunny spell. Out on the serene Baltic, a large container ship shimmered in the distance. The main road was straight and fast, and Anita had to slow down to make sure of coming off at the right turning. Munk's place was on the opposite side of the road to an apple orchard. The road itself was higher than the house, which was in a dip, so that the rooms at the back looked directly at the bank. Anita pulled the car up next to a battered green Citroën parked under a large, sprawling chestnut tree on a patch of ragged grass. The house was a classic, single-storey, stone Scanian farmstead. It was built round a quadrangle. Three blocks were whitewashed. Here were the living quarters and garage. The roof was corrugated metal, painted a glossy rust red. The fourth side was what had been the wooden barn of the original farmhouse and, from memory, was where Pelle Munk had his studio.

All was quiet. Though the car was here, Munk might be out on a walk or down at the beach at Lilla Vik. What Anita remembered was that Munk constantly played loud classical music while he was painting. Karin Munk said that it had driven her mad as a teenager, but it was what helped her father concentrate. It inspired him. Anita walked across the cobbled courtyard and approached the kitchen door in the right hand corner of the complex. The official front entrance looked as though it hadn't been used for years. She called out 'herr Munk'. There was no reply. She tried the door, which wasn't locked. She popped her head inside and called again. She came back out and headed towards the barn-studio. Her knock on the huge wooden door produced no response, so she went in.

The studio was a massive space. On the far side, Munk had had an impressive floor length window installed so that the light could stream in. Around the room, easels were strewn – only two of which held half-finished pieces. Canvases and sheets of shiny metal were stacked against the walls. The furniture consisted of a couple of ancient wooden cupboards smeared with years of paint, and an equally mucky table on which sat an old ghetto blaster, an opened packet of cigarettes and a full ashtray. That, too, was streaked with old colour. There were two battered chairs near the table. One had a number of books haphazardly piled on it. There were paint-stained rags lying all over the floor. Anita smiled. If her mother thought she was messy, she should see this! But Anita felt empathy for someone who could live and work in such a cluttered mess. It reminded her of her unfinished bathroom, which, on a whim, she had stupidly decided to retile and repaint some months ago.

Anita wandered over to one of the half-finished paintings. This was a traditional canvas. The top half was a blur of colour; mainly yellows, oranges and dashes of purple. Could be the beginnings of an abstract sunset, she thought. Then again, it could be anything. Anita liked art, but she belonged to the "I-want-to-understand-what-I'm-looking-at" school. Her ex-husband, Björn, had always gently mocked her lack of understanding of the more obscure art forms.

'Who are you?' boomed a voice behind her. She swung round to see a tall man with tufts of straggly, grey hair sprouting above a pinched red face that didn't quite fit in with his body. In his heyday, when he had been constantly in the press, he had dominated any photographs because of his imposing physique. Now the man standing before her, though he still had the height and broad shoulders, had lost weight. His clothes hung badly on him. Anita got quite a shock. Sandra was right – he didn't look well.

'You may not remember me, but I was a friend of Karin's.'

He stared at her. 'What did you say?'

Anita noticed that he had hearing aid.

'I am Anita Sundström.' She spoke slowly and loudly. Her voice echoed round the large space. 'I used to know your daughter, Karin. We were at school together. I used to be called Ullman. Anita Ullman.'

'Ah, yes.' Again he stared at her. She found the examination disconcerting. 'I remember you. Very pretty girl.'

Anita wasn't sure if this meant that she was no longer pretty.

'I now work for the police. In Malmö.'

'And you've come to see Karin? She's not here.'

'No. I have come to see you, actually.'

Munk squinted in puzzlement. He hadn't heard her correctly.

'It's about your paintings.'

Munk shuffled over to a table and picked up a packet of cigarettes. As he took one and hunted around for some matches, he waved at her to sit. Anita sat down gingerly on the unoccupied wooden chair, but the splatters of paint appeared dry. Munk gave up his search for a match and tossed the unsmoked cigarette back onto the table. Instead he picked up a scalpel in his left hand and idly tapped it up and down on the table top.

He turned to Anita. He gestured to the unfinished paintings. 'I am afraid I'm not selling at the moment. I have an exhibition coming up. Maybe you can buy then.'

'Herr Munk, I'm not here to buy. I'm investigating the theft of your paintings. Particularly the one from the home of Jörgen Lindegren. *Dawn Mood*. Another was stolen from a gallery in Ystad.'

Munk was now standing close to Anita, still clutching the scalpel. His proximity made her feel uncomfortable, but it was probably easier for him to understand what she was saying. Suddenly his face creased into a smile. Then morphed into a throaty laugh.

'I must be coming back into fashion. I'm flattered that someone thinks they're worth stealing.'

'Your paintings are still worth quite a lot of money.' She nodded at the nearest easel. 'And with a new exhibition coming up, the value of your old works is likely to escalate. So Lindegren told me.'

He flapped his hand in front of his face as though swatting away a fly. 'The man's an idiot. The only value art has to someone like that is monetary. He doesn't feel anything. He doesn't see anything. He's not moved by art.'

'But you went to his house when he unveiled the painting for his friends.'

'Karin's idea. Thought it would be a good way to publicise the exhibition. I hated it.'

Anita could see that she wasn't going to get anywhere with him. It had been a long shot anyway. She stood up.

'It was nice to see you again.'

'And you.' Munk grinned. 'You're still a pretty girl.'

Anita found herself blushing. To cover her confusion she pointed around the studio. 'I'd make sure that these are locked up securely. The thief may come after your new works.'

Anita was glad to escape the paint fumes and get into the fresh air. The smell wasn't helping her hangover. As she feared, the visit had been a complete waste of time. If Munk wasn't careful, he would have his latest paintings stolen too. She was about to get into her car when a blue Volvo turned off the main road and came to rest beside her vehicle. Out stepped a tall woman with long, blonde hair and a short, floral summer dress. She may have been twenty years older than when Anita had last seen her in a bar in Stockholm, but there was no mistaking Karin Munk. Not that the recognition was reciprocated.

'Who are you?' She had her father's brusqueness.

'Karin. It's me. Anita.'

Karin tilted her head back as though she were appraising a

painting. Then her mouth spread into a broad smile.

'Anita! I don't believe it! You still look...'

'You've worn well, too.' They both laughed and hugged each other.

'So, what are doing here?' asked Karin as she disengaged herself. 'This is extraordinary.'

'Unfortunately, it's on police business.'

Karin suddenly looked worried. 'Is Dad–?'

'No, no, he's fine. It's just that we're investigating the thefts of two of his paintings.'

Relief flooded across Karin's face. 'I know one went from Ystad. Has another gone?'

'Yes. In Limhamn. Just the other day.'

'Which one?'

'*Dawn Mood*.'

Karin clicked her tongue in disappointment. 'That's one of Dad's favourites. I hadn't heard anything in the press about it.'

'The owner didn't want it publicised. It's best to keep these things quiet until we've had time to ask around.'

'Getting anywhere?'

Anita shook her head.

'Were you all right with Dad? He's quite deaf these days.'

Anita smiled: 'I made myself understood.'

'Got a virus a few years back. Virtually knocked out his hearing altogether. Can't listen to his beloved classical music any more. It was always his inspiration. Something to do with the frequency. It now sounds like a high-pitched whine. Sad.'

'But he's still putting together a new exhibition.'

'Oh, yes. It's his comeback.'

'We think the thefts might be connected to that.'

Karin gazed at Anita. She shook her head. 'You haven't changed. Well, not much.'

'Married, divorced and have a son at university.'

Karin laughed. 'You have been busy. But I'm surprised you're looking into missing paintings.' She paused. 'Is it because of that other business with the... in the papers?'

Anita shrugged. 'Probably.'

An awkward silence followed, which was eventually broken by Anita. 'Must be off.'

'Nice to see you, Anita.' Karin fished in her bag and took out a business card. 'Look, next time you're this way, give me a ring and we'll meet up for a drink. I'm only over at Hammenhög.'

Anita glanced at the card. *Karin Munk, Art Restorer.*

'I'd like that.'

Moberg and Nordlund sat in Rörsjöparken on the opposite side of the road from the polishus. They licked ice creams. Being a sunny Sunday, the area was full of shouting kids, attentive dads, madcap dogs, teenagers trying to look cool and a lot of tanning flesh – not all of it ideal for public display. But Swedes don't need much encouragement to expose themselves to the sun god. Moberg had used the case as an excuse to get out of the house. His wife had invited her brother's family round for a barbecue, so he was more than happy to manufacture a reason not to play host to in-laws he couldn't stand. Nordlund was glad of the company. Weekends were lonely times. Westermark and Wallen hadn't been so keen to come in to work. After keeping them hanging around for a couple of hours, Moberg had let them go and they had dashed out of the polishus like a couple of naughty school kids released by the teacher after detention.

The meeting had been frustrating. Westermark had been through Ekman's office computer. Most of the files and emails were to do with the business. A few personal emails, but nothing to make Westermark think that Ekman was having affairs all over the place. One or two to female members of staff, including Elin Marklund, were flirty in tone. But nothing overtly sexual. The only folder that didn't seem to fit in was one entitled *Sjätte November.*

'I assume November 6th is referring to Gustav Adolf's Day. But there were no files in the folder. Totally empty.' Westermark had nothing insightful to add, other than maybe Ekman had been planning a party for the staff to mark the anniversary of the death of Sweden's greatest monarch at the Battle of Lützen in 1632. 'Perhaps he was treating the little darlings to Gustav Adolf cakes,' he added facetiously.

Wallen had been through Ekman's iPhone, office and home phone records. Again, the sort of calls you would expect him to make. A lot of business contacts. Personal calls to his wife and to Dag Wollstad. Nothing untoward there. But they were still checking out all the names on the lists.

'Are we sure he didn't have another mobile?' Moberg had asked Wallen. 'Men who play around have been known to have a spare phone. Pay as you go, so it can't be traced.'

'We haven't found anything. According to his wife and his secretary, he only had the one.'

Moberg finished his ice cream first and licked his lips. 'So, where are we, Henrik?'

Nordlund was watching a young couple snoozing on the grass near a large weeping willow tree.

'If we can't find connections to other women, then Kristina Ekman's motive disappears. Or the jealousy motive, anyhow. We certainly need to establish who he actually made love to that night. If it was Elin Marklund, it may only be a recent thing. According to Westermark, she hasn't been with the company long.'

'I agree. We need to know the movements of every person in the advertising agency that day. There are over forty staff, so that'll keep Westermark and Wallen busy tomorrow. My gut feeling is that it's someone in the office. But it takes a huge amount of hate to actually commit murder as cold-bloodedly as our killer did. We have to find a person with that big a grudge.'

Now Nordlund had finished his ice cream. 'It's funny that

empty folder. November 6th. Wonder if it had something to do with Wollstad? He had Gustav Adolf's portrait hanging on his wall.'

'Maybe the old man's got a thing about ancient royals and his son-in-law was pandering to him. Anyway, I think Gustav Adolf's a bit old to be brought into this case.'

CHAPTER 14

Anita was at work early on the Monday morning. It wasn't the urgency of the case that had made her leave her apartment at seven, but the need to have people around. Her visit to Sandra's had done her good. She had done too much moping during her enforced absence from the polishus. Getting together with friends had been a boost. She would even look up Karin Munk soon and take her up on that drink. And at work she was surrounded by colleagues who, whatever she thought of some of them, took her away from the quiet apartment that no longer seemed the same without Lasse.

She took out of her drawer the typed list of visitors to Lindegren's soirée. She sighed as she thought of all the potential interviews they were going to have to get through. All they would probably end up doing was antagonising several important people, who wouldn't be able to shed light on the theft anyway. Munk himself hadn't given her any ideas. In fact, he seemed flattered and amazed that anyone would want to steal his paintings. She suspected that Munk had never been particularly bothered by the financial rewards of his work. He was still living in the same shambolic house that he had bought thirty years or so before. She would also have a word with the art fraud and theft boys up in Stockholm to see if they had any ideas. They might have the names of fences or disreputable dealers who would be able to shift Munk paintings, no questions asked.

Unless the paintings had been stolen to order for some collector. Then there would be little chance of retrieving them.

Hakim was surprised to see Anita in so early. It was now eight.

'Good weekend?'

'Yes.' He smiled at some memory. 'Very good. And you?'

'Yeah. By the way, I called in to see Pelle Munk yesterday.'

Hakim looked at her expectantly.

'Nothing of any use.'

Hakim took a magazine out of his bag. 'I'm afraid this is going to complicate things.' He handed it over to Anita. 'Pages 38, 39 and 40.'

Anita opened it. 'Not the sort of thing I would have expected you to read.'

'It's my mother's.'

Anita found the relevant feature – a big, glossy spread about Jörgen Lindegren's unveiling of *Dawn Mood*. There were several photos of grinning people with champagne flutes and canapés. Among them, Jörgen and Michaela Lindegren, Commissioner Dahlbeck, the cream of Malmö society and a far-from-excited Pelle Munk, whose strained smile spoke volumes. He'd rather be a hundred miles away. And there, prominently, was the painting. Any potential thief would only have to see the magazine, and the house, the room and the position of the painting were all displayed in glorious colour. All that was missing was a big finger pointing the way.

Anita managed a strangled cry as she slapped the magazine down on her desk. 'Well, that'll save doing a lot of pointless interviews.'

'It still doesn't explain how the thief waltzed off with the picture without having to break in.'

'I know,' Anita said reflectively. 'Makes one think it's an inside job. Insurance number?' She waved a hand in the direction of the magazine. 'He certainly went to a lot of trouble to make sure the world knew he had the painting.'

'If he needed the money, wouldn't he make sure the most expensive painting in his collection got taken? He had a Corot in there.'

'You *do* know your art.'

'If the Corot had been taken, the insurance would be more.'

'Nevertheless, we need to check out Lindegren's financial situation. Is he in trouble? And have a word with his insurance people. How much it was insured for, and if Lindegren has all his works of art covered. If it was only the Munk, then we might be onto something.'

'I think I know how it was done.'

Moberg raised an eyebrow. He needed all the help he could get with the case, and he was hoping that anything Eva Thulin could supply might point him in a more helpful direction. That's why he had made the effort to turn up at Thulin's office.

'I'm still not completely sure of the substance that was used to create the actual gas... the hydrogen cyanide. Problem is that there's no physical evidence left. However, what was nagging me was that the pellets or crystals used would have been dangerous to the person handling them. More importantly, if they were just placed in the drain, then they would probably have started working straight away. They turn into a lethal gas once exposed to the air. I'm pretty convinced that Ekman's death wasn't caused by the water in the shower reacting directly with the crystals.'

'So how on earth could the killer set off the crystals at precisely the right time?'

'That's the clever bit. We've searched the drains and the sewer outside and, believe it or not, we found the answer. We found a minute trace of jelly.'

'Jelly?' Moberg snorted incredulously.

'Yeah. Ordinary jelly. Those cubes of concentrated jelly you can buy in any supermarket.'

'This is ludicrous.'

'Not as daft as it sounds. Brilliantly simple, in fact. Our killer needed the crystals to activate when Ekman was *in* the shower. I think that the perpetrator pushed the crystals or pellets into the jelly. Then he placed the jelly under the drain cover. Along comes Ekman, gets in the shower and turns it on. The hot water from the shower then melts the jelly. That, in turn, releases the crystals into the air. Ekman probably started to feel the effects and must have turned off the shower. The water wasn't running when he was found. Tragically, turning off the water will have only made the situation worse. The fan in the shower would have speeded up the process of spreading the now lethal gas around the room. It wouldn't take much of the substance to kill him. And the beauty of the scheme is that the killing agent evaporates in the air. The evidence literally disappears. And the method of activation is flushed down the drain by the shower. We just struck lucky with our trace of jelly.'

Moberg could hear the pride in her voice. He never understood the forensic technicians. He found them a strange bunch with a warped sense of humour. Probably due to too many hours poking around dead bodies, sniffing out weird substances and obsessing over blood stains. But they had their uses.

'That's the last time I'm going to let my wife make me jelly. But what about the crystals? We need to know where to look.'

'Sorry. I can't be much help there. The effects on Ekman's system are similar to the ones suffered by the Jews in the gas chambers. The Germans tended to use Zyklon B. It was originally manufactured as an insecticide for delousing clothes. Then they discovered it worked on people. Apparently, it took ten grams to kill an insect but only nought point three grams to kill a human being.'

'Could it be Zyklon B?'

'I doubt it after all these years. The Second World War was a long time ago. Could be a modern equivalent. Your best bet is to have a look at pharmaceutical companies. That's all I can think of.'

'That doesn't make me feel any better.'

Westermark and Wallen were ploughing their way through the members of the Ekman & Jonsson staff and checking everyone's movements for the entire day before Tommy Ekman's death. They took separate rooms so that they could get through them as quickly as possible. Wallen noticed that Westermark had taken most of the women, with one obvious exception. Elin Marklund. Moberg had given them strict instructions that Wallen was to talk to her. It was time that they confirmed their suspicions that Marklund was the woman that Ekman had made love to before his death. If it wasn't her, the team would have to look somewhere else. It would also help fill in his movements that night. If they had made love in the office, then he was unlikely to have gone anywhere else afterwards. He would have gone straight home to his apartment and then called his wife. Despite Westermark's objections, Moberg insisted that Klara Wallen tackle Marklund. He reasoned that Marklund was more likely to confess to a woman than an abrasive male officer. He knew what Westermark was like and he didn't want to run the risk of Marklund clamming up because Westermark was pushing her too hard.

Wallen greeted Marklund with a smile. She always admired confident women and she put Marklund in that category. She envied their self-assurance. Her own rise through the ranks had been steady rather than spectacular. She was the first to admit that it should have been quicker because, unlike other female colleagues like Anita Sundström, she hadn't been encumbered by bringing up a family. She had had a husband. Now she had a partner. But no kids. It wasn't a biological disappointment. She just didn't want any. Now, at the age of forty, nephews and nieces filled the void that might have been there. Children were fine as long as you didn't have to live with them. As Marklund took her seat opposite the desk in Ekman's office, where Wallen was holding her interviews, she wondered if this elegant woman was a mother.

'We're talking to everyone in order to establish their movements on the day before Tommy Ekman died.'

'Why?' Marklund asked.

Wallen was taken off-guard for a moment, as Marklund was the first person to challenge the statement.

'We need to know how each member of staff spent their day. Who could have had access to this office. And who left the building during the day. We believe someone took Ekman's apartment keys from his desk and went round there some time that day – and then returned them that evening.'

'I spent quite a lot of time in here on that day. We were in early because we were running through the final pitch. Around eight. Tommy was doing the introduction, selling the agency, etcetera. As the account manager on the prospective business, I did the marketing strategy. Daniel Jonsson then did the creative work and Sven Lundin, our head of media buying, discussed where we were going to place their advertising spend. Then we all went down to the conference room for a full rehearsal to make sure the equipment we were taking with us worked OK. Got to Geistrand Petfoods' head office at Fosieby Industriområde at about twenty past eleven. We were presenting at half past eleven, though they were running late, so we didn't get in until about twenty minutes to twelve. Three agencies were in for the account and we were the last on. Tommy was brilliant.'

Marklund stopped. For a second she had lost her train of thought. Did Wallen detect a sign of moisture in the corner of Marklund's eye? Then she was businesslike again.

'We were meant to have three-quarters of an hour, but it

overran to about an hour because they asked a lot of questions, which is usually a good sign. Got back to the office at about one and, after sorting ourselves out, met up in the conference room for something to eat and a debrief.'

'You all came back at the same time?'

'Yes.' She was about to go on. 'No, actually. Daniel wasn't there. He borrowed my car. Said he had to go somewhere. We'd driven over in two cars. Mine and Tommy's. So Bo and I went back in Tommy's car.'

'So how long was Jonsson out of the office?' Wallen was sensing that there might be something significant here.

'Probably about forty minutes. Then he joined us for a sandwich in the conference room.'

'What about the rest of the day?'

'I never left the office. Then Tommy phoned through to say that we had won the pitch. It's great to get a quick answer as you can sometimes be hanging round for days before they let you know. Because it was such a big slice of business, Tommy wanted to celebrate, so all the people who worked on the pitch went up to his office for champagne.'

'How many?'

'Ten, eleven maybe.'

'And you were the last to leave?'

Marklund nodded. 'As I've said before.'

Wallen smiled an acknowledgement. 'That's fine. Oh, one last thing. Does your husband know that you made love to Tommy Ekman that night?'

'Of course he doesn't...' It was out before she could stop herself. Marklund stared at Wallen in horror. The professional mask had slipped and the guilt was plain to see.

'It was you, wasn't it?' Wallen said quietly.

Marklund's head dropped. 'Please, please, don't tell my husband.'

'Is he away?'

87

Without looking up, Marklund nodded.

'I doubt it has any bearing on the case.'

Marklund clenched her fists in anguish. 'I love my husband. It was stupid what I did. Moment of weakness. He's away so much.' Then she glanced at Wallen. 'That's no excuse, is it? I never want to hurt him. I don't want to lose him.'

Wallen was disconcerted by the change in this apparently ultra-cool businesswoman.

'Please.'

Wallen recognised the vulnerability. They had one less suspect.

CHAPTER 15

Martin Olofsson had left his journey as late as possible. By working in the cottage that day instead of in the office, he had managed to stretch the weekend to three days. He had left his wife, Carolina, at their holiday home on the coast at Vik and was heading back to their house on the edge of Limhamn. During the summer months, Carolina liked to be away from the city so she could indulge her love of walking and cycling along the beautiful southern coastline of Skåne. He was often tempted to stay with her, but the needs of the bank wouldn't allow him to be away for too long. Another couple of years and they would sell up in Malmö and move to Vik permanently when he retired. The children had left home years before and now they had three young grandchildren. He wanted more time with the little ones. And more time for golf and his other interests, particularly his latest passion, which had dominated his thoughts in recent months. Not even Carolina knew about that.

Of course, they might buy a small apartment so that they had a city crash-pad. It would be useful for Carolina's shopping trips, visits to the theatre or taking in a concert. And he would still have the occasional meeting or social function to attend. He wasn't going to give up work entirely. A consultancy role would serve him nicely.

He manoeuvred the Mercedes off the motorway and into the sprawl of the urban outskirts of Malmö. It was getting dark, though the sky was clear. Another pleasant evening. He had eaten before he left, though he would pour himself a whisky when he got home and settle down to a spot of television before going through those papers he needed to discuss at the 9.30 meeting he had arranged with Kurt. He hoped the outcome wouldn't lead to a trip up to Stockholm later in the week. He wanted to avoid that; he was tired of travelling and staying at hotels.

He had now reached Vikingagatan and its reassuring avenue of verdant trees, with branches gently swaying above the pavements – a plump green canopy in summer, a mass of bony fingers in winter. The street was deserted except for what looked like a late-night jogger. He slowed down as the car came abreast of the familiar white wall that fronted onto the street. The large house loomed in the gathering darkness. He had reluctantly had to admit to Carolina that it was getting far too big for them. They rattled around inside it. Yet he was proud that he had risen in the world and been able to afford such a property with its grand, colonnaded, semi-circular balcony overlooking Vikingagatan. He enjoyed the envious and admiring glances of the passers-by when sitting out there. He turned the car left into the side street where the black wrought-iron gates guarded the entrance to his home. They opened automatically and he pulled the car up in front of the double garage. He had had that built five years earlier – this, too, opened at the press of a button, and the Mercedes slid inside. He switched off the lights and for a moment he was in darkness. He felt for the briefcase on the passenger seat next to him with his right hand while, at the same time, he began to open the car door with his left. He was startled by the sound of the back passenger door opening up behind him. He half turned to see who was there, but it was too dim. Then something heavy hit his head and he swiftly descended into total blackness.

***

Anita held two cups of coffee. She glanced at Moberg's closed door and wished that she was inside. She knew that Moberg was having a morning meeting to discuss the latest developments in the Ekman murder. She should be in there. The case sounded intriguing, from what she had managed to wheedle out of Nordlund. She knew that he was keen for her to be part of the investigation, yet there was no moving Moberg. What annoyed her even more was Klara Wallen's involvement. Wallen was a useful cop, but she'd be eaten alive by Moberg and Westermark. Anita was convinced that she wouldn't fight her corner.

She headed along the corridor and pushed her way into her office. Hakim was on the telephone as she entered. She put the coffee down on his desk as he was finishing his call.

'Thank you. That's been most helpful.'

Anita sat down and looked across expectantly.

'That was the insurance people. Yes, the Munk was well insured. But so are his other works of art, so it's unlikely to be an insurance scam. He would make more selling it on the open market.'

'What about his financial situation?'

'I'm going round to his bank later today.'

'Of course, he could do both.'

'Both?'

'Steal the painting himself. Claim the insurance *and* sell the painting privately.'

Hakim gave a sceptical shrug.

'OK, it's a long shot. I would still love it to be him.' She sighed. 'Anyway, while you're at the bank, I'm seeing someone Stockholm have put me onto. An art dealer over on Fersens Väg. Apparently, he can fill me in on the legitimate art scene – and the not-so-legitimate.'

'She's frightened to death her husband will find out. She broke down. Full of remorse.' Wallen was reporting her conversation with Elin Marklund to Moberg, Westermark and Nordlund.

'Well, if you will shag the boss. Silly cow.' This seemed rich coming from Westermark.

'So, you don't think she's in the frame?' Moberg asked.

'I think the only thing she's guilty of is adultery. It's unlikely that you make love to someone and then kill them the same night.' Wallen glanced at Westermark. 'If you're a woman, that is,' she added.

'I agree,' said Moberg. 'What about those who had access to Ekman's office on at least two separate occasions that day?'

Westermark flicked through his notes. 'According to his PA, Viktoria Carlsson, no one went in other than those who attended the early meeting before their presentation, and then, when the team came back from Geistrand Petfoods, Ekman was in the office by himself most of the time during the afternoon. Carlsson didn't go out for her lunch until Ekman returned and then another secretary covered while Ekman was having sandwiches with the presentation team in the conference room. This other girl swore that no one entered Ekman's office – and then Carlsson took over again. Carlsson did say that Bo Nilsson, the financial guy, popped in briefly during the morning to drop off some spreadsheets when Ekman was at the presentation. So he was in there alone. When challenged, he just came out with the same story.'

'Did Nilsson leave the building afterwards?'

'Went for lunch and a wander round in the sunshine,' Westermark confirmed.

'So, he had the opportunity. Check him out. He's connected to Wollstad, so that's worth looking into. Anyone else?'

Wallen coughed nervously. 'Daniel Jonsson didn't come back from the Geistrand Petfoods presentation with the others. He borrowed Elin Marklund's car. She didn't know where he was going or what he was up to.'

'How long was he out for?'

'She reckoned about forty minutes. Then they had a debriefing meeting in the conference room.'

'He didn't mention that to me,' said Westermark. 'He implied that he came back with the others.'

'Right, find out what he got up to in that missing time. Were both Jonsson and Nilsson at the celebratory drinks in Ekman's office that evening?'

'Yes.'

'So, both could have returned the keys. Basically, anybody who was having drinks in Ekman's office could have put the keys back if they'd already been in there during the day. That might narrow the field down a bit.'

'In theory.'

'That'll do for starters.' Moberg turned his attention to the thin file on his desk. 'You've all read Eva Thulin's latest forensic findings?'

'Unbelievable.' Westermark shook his head from side to side to confirm his disbelief. 'Jelly!' Another shake of the head.

'Could it actually be Zyklon B?' Moberg mused.

Nordlund held up a sheet of paper. 'I printed this off the internet. This is what the tin looked like. Could be cat food if the contents weren't so deadly. These little greyish-white pellets did the damage when mixed with air. There may be a few tins kicking around. Probably with demented collectors.'

'That's a bit bloody morbid.'

'Nazi memorabilia comes in all weird shapes and sizes,' Nordlund answered. 'For many, it's an obsession.'

'But the chances of it being the real thing are unlikely.' Moberg frowned. 'My bet is we're dealing with a modern equivalent. And that means pharmaceutical companies. We need to establish who would have connections with these sorts of companies at the advertising agency. We know Wollstad does.

But let's eliminate the Ekman advertising people first before we return to him. Right, let's get moving.'

As the three detectives filed out, the office phone sprang into life. Moberg leant over and the receiver disappeared into his giant fist. He held it to his ear. 'Yes!' he barked.

He listened for a few moments. 'Suicide. Don't you think we've got enough on our plate at the moment?' He listened some more. 'All right, I'll put someone onto it.'

CHAPTER 16

Anita had walked down to the Gabrielsson Gallery from the polishus. It was another pleasant morning as she strolled along the canal side. On the opposite bank, the sun bathed the apartment blocks on Södra Promenarden in a gentle light before it promised to become too warm for comfort later in the day. A noisy mother duck marshalled her young on the still waters of the canal. Anita's initial annoyance at being excluded from Moberg's team had abated. She had decided that instead of feeling sorry for herself, she would do her best to solve the Munk case as quickly as possible so that Moberg would have to involve her in the Ekman murder or, at least, give her a more interesting case.

She turned into Fersens Väg. The wide, tree-lined street stretched all the way down to the glass-fronted Malmö Opera. The Gabrielsson Gallery was in an old, grey building on the right-hand side. On the pavement immediately in front of the doorway was a round advertising display stand with a conical roof. The building was several storeys high, and the main entrance was up three steps, under an elegant arch and through a large wooden door with glass panels. The gallery was on the ground floor. Once Anita had shut the door and stepped inside, the noise of the street dulled and she entered a hushed world of artworks. The building was traditional, but the display was modern. Expanses of bald, white space between the paintings. It was where potential buyers could contemplate the creations on show without distraction, where they could reflect on influence, implication, inspiration or even beauty. To Anita, however, the most creative things on show were the prices.

'Can I help you?'

An immaculately dressed young woman gave Anita a snooty look. She could tell by the way Anita was dressed, in blue jeans, red T-shirt and a creased beige jacket, that she wasn't a potential purchaser. The jacket had been the only thing Anita could find when she had rushed out of the apartment a couple of hours before.

'I'm here to see Stig Gabrielsson. He's expecting me.'

'Really?' The woman stretched the word out as far as it was possible to go, which gave her time to inject a huge dose of incredulity.

'Police. Tell him Inspector Sundström is here.'

The woman turned on her high heels and disappeared into a back office. She reappeared with Gabrielsson. He was more casually dressed than his assistant. His light-coloured, crushed-linen trousers and jacket, crowned with swept-back, dark hair and goatee beard, fitted the artistic image. His movements were mannered and slightly effeminate as he limply shook Anita's hand and waved long fingers towards two chairs in the corner of the gallery. The assistant retreated behind her desk and glared. Anita was obviously lowering the tone.

'How can I help?'

'I'm looking into the theft of a Pelle Munk painting. Two, in fact.'

'*Dawn Mood* and *Shadows*.'

'You are very well informed, herr Gabrielsson.'

He held up a hand. 'Stig, please. And word gets round quickly in the art world. I'm surprised a senior detective is chasing after Lindegren's painting.'

Anita smiled. 'He has connections.'

'Of course he has.' He, too, was grinning.

'Is he one of your clients? I notice that you weren't at his Munk unveiling.'

'That's not surprising. We don't like each other. He fancies himself as a collector. Really, he is a peasant. He thinks that people will see him in a sophisticated light. He bought a painting off me once. Never again. Tried to knock me down on the price. When that didn't work, he approached the artist directly for another piece, assuming that he wouldn't have to pay my commission. Fortunately, the artist in question told him where to shove a paint brush and he came back to me and bought the original painting at the gallery price. The point is that he wanted to own a painting by a well-known artist and not possess it because he thought it was good or actually liked it.'

'Hence the Munk.'

'Absolutely. He initially approached me about buying a Munk. I didn't have one, but I did put him onto a gallery in Stockholm. That's where he picked up *Dawn Mood*. Wish I hadn't bothered now.'

'Why do you think the Munk paintings have been stolen, and where do you think they may have ended up?'

Gabrielsson stroked his beard for a moment then glanced around the gallery before he spoke. 'The timing is interesting. You know Pelle has a new exhibition coming up soon?'

'I had heard.'

'It'll be quite an event in the Swedish art world. We haven't seen an original Munk for nearly ten years. If these new paintings are as good as his previous work, they will sell for huge amounts of money. If that's the case, then the value of the old ones will increase enormously. Not that they're cheap now. Still worth millions of kronor. A Munk is still eagerly sought after. So, either they've been stolen with the new exhibition in mind or they've been stolen to order with a collector in mind.'

'In Sweden?'

'Not necessarily. He's very popular in Germany. And a number of galleries in America have his work. If they've been stolen to order, then they may well be out of the country by now.'

'If they've been stolen to resell here, who would the thieves approach?'

Gabrielsson offered her a bashful grin. 'Sometimes gallery owners. People with contacts. No questions asked.'

'Like yourself?'

'Ah, it has been known. I see myself as a facilitator.'

'Yes, Stockholm told me that you occasionally "facilitated" art in the direction of very private collections.'

With a hint of self-mockery: 'In my defence, I only do so if I think the collector really appreciates his art. I have no time for the Lindegrens of this world. Anyway, I supply Stockholm with enough information to keep everybody happy.'

'And no one has approached you to "facilitate" the Munk paintings?'

'Not a whisper. Which is why I think they may have departed these shores. However, it might be worth your while speaking to Ingvar Serneholt.'

'Serneholt? Like the singer?'

'No relation. He's a big Munk collector. Has at least half a dozen that I'm aware of. Never know, he might have gone direct.'

Anita's mobile suddenly went off. As she tried to retrieve it from her black hole of a bag: 'Can you give me an address?'

'Certainly.' Gabrielsson stood up and wandered over to his assistant, who had been trying hard to overhear their conversation.

'Anita Sundström.'

She listened to the voice at the other end.

'A suicide? Where?' She listened. 'OK, I'll get down there now.' She snapped her phone shut as Gabrielsson came back with a piece of gallery headed notepaper.

'Serneholt's address.'

Anita took it and stuffed it into her bag. The chances of her remembering where exactly she'd put it when she got round to looking for it weren't high. Usually the entire contents of her bag would have to be disgorged.

'Thank you. Must go.'

The glint in Gabrielsson's eye was back. 'Suicide? Hope it's not one of my clients. Worse still, it might be one of my artists. They do such things. Look at van Gogh.'

'I'll see if he has an ear missing.'

There was already a number of cars parked in the street when Anita arrived. She recognised Eva Thulin's. That was good. She liked working with Eva. Not that a suicide was an exciting new case. She knew that she was being sent along because Moberg couldn't be bothered to get involved, which was fair enough given the difficult investigation he and the rest of the team were working on. But she didn't want to spend the next few years sweeping up all the stuff that he didn't want to know about. And she didn't like suicides. The emotional hurt and rejection of those left behind was often difficult to deal with. Sometimes Anita found it hard not to get involved. Suicides were also unsatisfactory because you weren't looking for a guilty party. It was a criminal cul-de-sac.

The house was impressive. Whoever lived here had money. As Anita walked through the open wrought-iron gates, all the activity was surrounding the double garage block to the side of the house. Eva Thulin emerged from the right-hand garage in her usual plastic bodysuit, and smiled in recognition when she saw Anita.

'Haven't seen you for a long time. Good to have someone sensible for a change.'

Anita grinned and then nodded towards the garage.

'Yes,' said Thulin. 'Interesting.'

'Do we know who he is?'

'A Martin Olofsson.'

Anita entered the garage and saw the telltale pipe leading from the exhaust through the window of the expensive, midnight-blue Mercedes. The garage was spacious, despite the big car sitting in the middle. The figure of a well-built man was slumped in the driving seat. All colour had drained from his face, which contrasted markedly with his dyed hair. Despite his efforts to appear younger, Anita immediately put him in his sixties. She turned to Thulin.

'I didn't think this type of suicide was very common these days. Isn't it difficult with modern cars having catalytic converters? I'm sure I read somewhere that the converters take out nearly all the carbon monoxide in the fumes produced by the exhaust.'

'You are a clever girl.' Thulin leant on the open car door. 'It was made to look like a suicide. Rather badly, as it happens. Anyhow, it certainly wasn't carbon monoxide that killed Martin Olofsson. It's the trauma to the back of his head. He was severely bashed more than once. Something solid. Metal implement? Not sure what was used just yet. He was dead before this mock suicide charade took place. I have no idea why the killer would want to make it look like suicide when it's obvious that we would easily spot the real cause of death.'

'Any idea of the time of death?'

'Probably before midnight. I might have a better idea when we get the body back to the medical examiner.'

They walked back into the sunlight. Thulin wiped her forehead. It was hot in her bodysuit.

'There's a wall all round the property, except for the gates, so no one is likely to have seen anything. Do you know who alerted us?'

'A neighbour. Heard the car running continuously this

morning. Came round to check and saw the garage door closed. Rang in.'

'Thanks, Eva. I'll let you get on. Presumably, your team are going to blitz everything in the area?'

Thulin spread her arms expressively. 'That's what we're here for.'

Anita scanned the surroundings. Either the killer had scaled the wall, or slipped in before the automatic gates closed. She saw an officer coming round the side of the house. It was Carl Svanberg.

'We must stop meeting like this,' Anita joked.

Svanberg didn't return the smile. 'No sign of a break-in.'

'Well, that means that Olofsson was targeted deliberately. Do we know anything about him?'

'According to the neighbour who found him, he was a banker.'

'That probably doesn't put him very high in the popularity stakes.' Still no reaction from Svanberg. 'Family?'

'Wife over at their weekend place at Vik. My partner, Lennart, has tried to contact her, so far without success. But he's been on to Simrishamn and they're sending someone round to the house.'

'Good. Right, now we know it was murder, this is a crime scene. We need it sealed off.' She could feel a rush of adrenaline. 'Then I'd better break the news to Chief Inspector Moberg.'

CHAPTER 17

Moberg hadn't been happy with her call. The last thing he wanted was another murder on his hands. The one he was dealing with was complicated enough. He told Anita to stay put and he would come down and see for himself. His attitude had immediately raised Anita's hackles. Moberg had spoken to her as though it was her fault that it was a murder and not a suicide. It was almost as if he didn't believe her and was coming to check up that she wasn't lying.

Anita went and told Thulin that she couldn't remove the body as Moberg wanted to see the scene. Thulin's raised eyebrows said it all. She offered Anita a briefcase, which was now in a see-through plastic bag.

'Found it on the passenger seat. It's OK, you can touch it. I've dusted it for prints.'

It was in neat black leather with a combination. Anita took it out of the plastic and tried a few numbers, but it was a waste of time. She replaced it and walked round to her car in Vikingagatan and put the briefcase in the boot. She would get someone back at the office to open it. This gave her an opportunity to check out the house and the location more carefully. The concrete wall surrounding the property was a little over a couple of metres high. The house was almost cross-shaped. The main body of the building, with its sharply pitched roof, faced the street. It had two sections jutting out – one with a fancy first-storey balcony overlooking Vikingagatan. The other was at the rear, with its own pitched roofing. The end of the house, behind the double garage, also had a semi-circular balcony. This was simpler, with a white metal balustrade. There were trees in the garden and all along Vikingagatan, and also the side road onto which the gates opened. At this time of year, they offered ample cover. The likelihood of finding any witnesses was remote, but they would have to do a house-to-house enquiry all the same. She would start with the neighbour.

By the time Anita returned to Olofsson's house, Moberg had appeared. Her heart sank when she saw that he had brought Westermark with him. His loathsome grin, half-mocking and half-lecherous, immediately put her on the defensive.

'Where have you been?' Moberg demanded.

'Talking to the neighbour who alerted us. He's retired. He wasn't sure what time Olofsson returned last night as no lights went on in the house. It was only when he was walking his dog this morning that he heard the car running inside the closed garage. Thought it was odd, so he came back ten minutes later and there was still no change, so he phoned the station. Of course, we'll have to talk to everyone in the area to see if they spotted anyone suspicious.'

'Do we know much about him?' This was Westermark.

Anita answered his question by addressing Moberg. 'He's a banker.'

Moberg snorted. 'That's one less to bugger up the world.' He arched his back wearily. 'So, why make it appear to be a suicide when it obviously isn't?'

'The killer's incompetent,' suggested Westermark.

Anita gave him a withering look. 'I think the killer knew exactly what he was doing.'

'And what's that?' Westermark sneered.

'I don't know yet. Why bother otherwise? The killer might as well have just smashed Olofsson's head in and left it at that.

Maybe he's trying to tell us something. Or tell someone something.'

'Another of your great theories. Look what happened last time.'

'That's enough,' Moberg ordered before Anita could respond. 'Do we know what bank he works for?'

'The neighbour says it's the Sydöstra Bank.'

'Never heard of it.'

'It's a private bank. Only deals with wealthy clients and companies. Specialist stuff. The neighbour used to deal with them.'

'Probably means that Olofsson's a pal of the commissioner.' Moberg turned round as Olofsson, in a body bag, was wheeled out of the garage. 'Right, Westermark, I want you to get down to the bank and start asking questions. First thing is to find out where it is.'

'Shouldn't I be doing that?' Anita asked with more than a hint of annoyance.

'You can talk to the wife. There might be a domestic angle to this one. I can't really see bankers bonking each other on the head. Give you a chance to nose around this lovely house. Isn't that what women like to do?'

Westermark's laugh was as condescending as the comment. Anita was furious as her two colleagues turned to go. As they reached the gate, Moberg swung round.

'Oh, if you come up with anything, report it to Westermark in the first instance. I want him to keep an eye on this investigation.'

Westermark's supercilious grin completed Anita's humiliation.

'You're joking!'

'No, Inspector, I'm not joking.'

Westermark had disappeared round the corner. Anita couldn't let this lie. With great difficultly, she managed to keep her temper in check. 'Chief Inspector, you sent me down here to handle this case. Surely, it should be mine. And reporting to you directly.'

'Then I thought it was a straightforward suicide. This is likely to be another bloody high-profile case. I can't afford to be seen letting you loose on it. If it were some dead Arab or junkie, that would be fine. But you're on probation as far as the commissioner is concerned. Get anything wrong on this one and you're out on your arse. Probably quickly followed by me. I can't afford to lose my job. What I suggest is that you be seen to do some good spadework on this investigation, sort out the thing with the fucking paintings and then I might... just might... be able to give you more leeway in the future. Understand?'

Anita pounded through the avenue of trees towards the huge circular expanse of green in the centre of Pildammsparken known as "the plate". She was pushing herself harder than usual and her breathing was becoming erratic. As she stretched her legs, they began to ache. She would do three circuits. She only attempted it three times when she was really fit or really furious. Today it was the latter. She couldn't believe that she was having to work under that creep Westermark, who would exploit the situation to further his career at her expense – and probably try it on into the bargain. Anita began to run even faster and started to pass more sedate joggers, who were startled at the speed she was building up. Of course, it couldn't last, and she came to a shuddering halt next to a bench and sank gratefully onto it. It took her a couple of minutes to get her breathing back under control.

A promising start to the day had ended in frustration and emotional trauma as she had taken a deeply shocked Carolina Olofsson to identify her husband's body. She was too upset to get much information out of her other than that Martin had stayed an extra day down at Vik and had set off about eight to head back to Malmö. And, no, she didn't know anybody who would want to harm her beloved husband of nearly forty years. Anita had driven her back to Vikingagatan. As it was only the garage that was a crime scene, Carolina was allowed to stay in the house. A daughter was on the way down from Gothenburg to be with her, and Anita had waited until she arrived. What had really irked Anita was that Moberg's jibe had some substance as she had been fascinated wandering round Olofsson's house and had made instant judgements as to the couple's taste and decor. Conservative had been her conclusion. During her time on "sick leave", she had become addicted to property programmes, most of which seemed to be British. That only added to their appeal. If it hadn't been for Lasse, she might have been tempted to return to Britain. And now Ewan was here. Was that another reason to stay?

As she cooled down, she became aware of a hint of a chill in the air. She stood up. She would walk back to the apartment. One thing she had had the presence of mind to do was take Martin Olofsson's briefcase into his home and ask Carolina if she knew the combination. She had: 061 132. Anita had opened it up in Carolina's presence. It seemed mainly to consist of bank paperwork. There was also a golf magazine. One of his passions, Carolina had said. He was a member of the Österlen Golf Club and played at the Lilla Vik course when he had the time. Anita knew it well, but only from driving past it on the road. The only other items in the case were a couple of DVDs. Anita explained that she had to take the briefcase back to the polishus as it had been found at the crime scene. She had neglected to inform Westermark that she had it – or even of its existence. That would give him another stick to beat her with, but she wanted to keep part of the investigation to herself for the moment. She would go and see Carolina Olofsson again tomorrow and take Hakim with her. Now the thefts of the Munk paintings hardly seemed important, and she put them to the back of her mind.

After showering, she poured herself a glass of red wine and picked up the phone. She wanted to phone Lasse because he was good at lifting her spirits. She would even force herself to ask after Rebecka, though she hoped deep down that that relationship would hit the rocks soon. He would get over it quickly. Men did. The curse for women was that they didn't. Anyhow, Rebecka wasn't right for her Lasse; he deserved better. Anita had no problem persuading herself that jealousy wasn't the reason why she didn't want Lasse staying with Rebecka.

'Sorry, Mamma, can't speak for long. We're going out in a minute.'

'You and Rebecka?'

'Of course, who else?' he chided. 'One of her friends has discovered this fantastic bar, which we're going to try out. And then we're clubbing afterwards.'

'So, she's in better spirits. Didn't seem to have much energy when she was down here.' Anita could hear the bitterness in her own voice.

'She was just a bit tired, that's all,' he said defensively.

'And are you bringing her down for midsummer?' Anita perked up at the thought. They might go down to Simrishamn. Or join the big celebrations in Pildammsparken. 'What do you want to do this year?'

There was a momentary silence at the end of the phone. 'About that, Mamma. Rebecka's folks have got a place on Gotland. They've invited me over there for midsummer. If the weather's good, we might spend the rest of the summer there.'

Anita's stomach gave a lurch. She was crushed. In the background, she could hear Rebecka calling to Lasse to hurry up.

'Look, Mamma, must be going. I'll ring you next week. Promise.'

For the next few minutes, Anita sat perfectly still, the phone still clutched in her hand. She couldn't remember the last time she felt so miserable.

***

This time it was for real. His guiding voice was clear about that. No messing about. No toying with "them". That's why he had ventured into the centre of Malmö. He had wandered through a busy Gustav Adolfs Torg. There were lots of young people milling around, happy to be alive. As he walked, unnoticed, through the square, he checked out potential targets; those whose deaths would make him happy. The scum who were flooding into Sweden and destroying the country's way of life, distorting traditional values and bringing crime and danger into safe communities. Anyone with a swarthy complexion or the run-down appearance of the typical immigrant. For him, they were easy to spot.

He wandered past the line of bus stops at the edge of the square and crossed the four lanes of road that divided the square from the gardens and cemetery beyond. He melted into the trees. From his vantage point, he could watch little groups forming round each bus stop on both sides of the road. Though a target on this side of the road would be easier to hit, it would be a more satisfying challenge to take out someone on the square side. It would also cause more confusion as bystanders would initially jump to the conclusion that the shot had come from nearby. That would give him extra seconds to disappear, with the minimum of fuss. He had plenty of cover and the dark would ensure his route out was untroubled.

He didn't want to wait long in case he was spotted and aroused suspicion. He slipped out his gun. He had already lined up his target. Three lads approached a bus stop from the square. They were smoking, and joking among themselves. There was no mistaking. Even with the occasional bus passing, he could hear their loud voices carrying across the still night. Whatever language they were speaking, it certainly wasn't Swedish. He was only going to kill one. But which one? The tallest of the three was definitely the loudest. The leader of the group. What made his final decision for him was the way the young man glanced at a couple of giggling blonde girls as they sauntered past him. Stick to your own, you bastard. A moment later the young man lurched back as the bullet hit him in the middle of his forehead.

CHAPTER 18

Hakim was reading a copy of *Sydsvenskan* while Anita drove in the direction of Limhamn. The paper was full of last night's killing of a young Libyan man in Gustav Adolfs Torg. The murder of Martin Olofsson had disappeared into the inside pages, for which Anita was grateful. The "Malmö Marksman", as the press had now dubbed him, was causing panic. It hadn't mattered so much when he was picking off immigrants in out-of-the-way suburbs, but to kill someone in one of the busiest locations in the city was a different matter. While the motive was again obviously racial, it was little comfort for the citizens of Malmö that there was a trigger-happy gunman on the loose. It was certainly winding up Hakim, who was cursing under his breath.

'It's a disgrace. This gunman is targeting the immigrant population. My parents are afraid to go out of the apartment. You know the second shooting was a few yards away from our home?'

'I didn't realise.'

'And how many Swedes will secretly be thinking he's doing a good job?'

'Look, Hakim, we've got to be professional about this, whatever we feel. Inspector Larsson will be given the manpower to catch this guy. We've got our own murder on our hands – and the Munk business to sort out. They're our priorities.'

Hakim grunted and returned to his newspaper. Anita couldn't help smiling to herself. She was sounding like a mother talking to a son, not colleague to colleague. She appreciated being with Hakim all the more after a quick meeting with the loathsome Westermark in his office first thing. She had reported back to him what she had found out from Carolina Olofsson. She had explained that she had wanted to reinterview fru Olofsson when she'd got over her initial shock. Westermark had been to Olofsson's place of work, Sydöstra Banken on Torggatan, which was only just along from the scene of the shooting in Gustav Adolfs Torg. The senior staff were horrified to hear of the murder. He was well respected and very good at his job. They couldn't think of anything that he was working on that might lead someone to kill him. Like Anita, Westermark was going to return to the bank to ask more questions, though he felt, like Moberg, that the motive was probably more likely to be personal than professional.

Not much luck either with Lindegren's bank – a local Handelsbanken. Lindegren's finances seemed to be in a "robust shape" according to the manager that Hakim had spoken to. So that route was a dead end. Anita had asked Hakim to set up a meeting with the Munk collector Gabrielsson had mentioned, Ingvar Serneholt. Again, it might be a waste of time, but, as they hadn't got a single lead to go on, they had to give it a go.

They reached Vikingagatan at exactly half past ten.

The clock in the interview room read 10.31. Daniel Jonsson didn't look relaxed at all. The intimidating presence of Chief Inspector Moberg on the other side of the table didn't help calm his unease. Even Moberg's reassurance that it was merely a routine chat didn't help.

'Daniel,' Moberg said pleasantly. 'I can call you Daniel?'

Jonsson nodded dubiously.

'Just because we want a few words with you here is nothing

to worry about. I thought it might be easier to talk about things away from the office. Get a sense of perspective. We appreciate that it must be difficult for you at the moment trying to run the company without its founder.'

'Co-founder,' Jonsson couldn't help himself correcting, almost as a verbal reflex action.

'Whatever. We're concentrating our investigation on the day before Tommy Ekman died. We think his spare keys were taken from his office by the murderer and then returned later that day. We've accounted for nearly everybody who had access – or was known to enter Ekman's office during that time. You obviously come into that category.' Moberg's raised eyebrow indicated that he expected Jonsson to say something.

'Well, yes. I was in Tommy's office that morning to go through the Geistrand Petfoods presentation. And again, I was in there for the celebratory drink.'

Moberg glanced down at a piece of paper. 'It's all here in your statement. But there's something missing.'

Jonsson shifted in his seat, though he managed to return a quizzical stare.

'You returned from Geistrand's in Elin Marklund's car.'

'Yes,' Jonsson answered slowly.

'Why was that? And where did you go *before* you returned to the office?' There was nothing pleasant in Moberg's tone now.

'I went home.'

'And that's Salongsgatan up by the Torso. Why go home?'

Moberg could feel the vibration from Jonsson's feet as they tapped the floor under the table. He could smell the nervous tension.

'I went to collect a computer stick. With all the presentation business, I'd forgotten it. I had work on it that I needed for the studio that afternoon. Stuff I'd done at home.'

'Did anybody see you?'

'I don't know. Middle of the day; not many people are about.'

'Neighbours?'

'No. I live alone and don't go out much. It's the work I love.'

Moberg spread his mighty hands palm down on the table. 'So, in theory, you could have gone to Ekman's apartment, placed the crystals and–'

'What crystals?'

'The poisonous gas crystals that the murderer put in Ekman's shower. The crystals that ensured he had a horrible death.'

Jonsson appeared appalled. 'Shit! Is that how Tommy died?'

'Oh, yes. And you've no alibi, have you Daniel?'

Jonsson adjusted his designer spectacles. 'Why? Why would I want to do such a thing?'

'I don't know. You tell me.'

'It's ridiculous.'

Moberg inspected his fingers for a moment. 'What percentage of the company do you own?'

'Twenty-five percent.'

'So, Tommy had seventy-five percent.'

'No, Dag Wollstad had a share too. Tommy brought him on board as a silent partner.'

'But now?'

'I'll get...' He stopped.

'Controlling interest?'

Jonsson screwed up his eyes. 'Partly. But I would still have to consult with Wollstad, or possibly Kristina Ekman, about important issues. I couldn't sell the company without his say-so, for example.'

'But your financial return is going to be far higher.'

'Yes, but we still have to bring in the clients. And Tommy was one of the main reasons we were successful in the first place.'

Moberg opened a folder and pulled out a glossy brochure. He idly flicked through it. 'I see in your company brochure that one of your clients is Buckley Mellor Chemicals.'

'They're British. Their headquarters are in Warrington in England. But they have a plant over here. We don't do any advertising as such for them, but we designed a new website for the Swedish end of the operation a couple of months ago.'

'And what do they specialise in?'

'Pesticides are their main business over here. Agricultural use mainly, some domestic. Slug pellets. That sort of thing.'

'Poisonous things?'

Jonsson contemplated the question for a moment. 'I suppose so.'

Moberg snapped the brochure shut. 'Fine. You can go, Daniel.'

Jonsson couldn't hide his relief as he almost jumped up from his seat.

Moberg pointed towards the door. 'Can you find your own way out?'

'Yes. No problem.' Jonsson reached the door and opened it. Then he checked himself. 'If you're interested in Buckley Mellor Chemicals, have a word with our financial director, Bo Nilsson. He worked there before he came to us.'

Moberg got up almost as quickly as Jonsson had done. 'Didn't Bo Nilsson work for one of Dag Wollstad's companies?'

'Yeah. Buckley Mellor is part of Wollstad Industries.'

Anita and Hakim came away from the front door of the Olofsson house and exchanged glances of resignation. Carolina Olofsson was still deeply upset, and there was nothing that she said in answer to Anita's questions that shed any light on a possible personal motive for murder – or murderer. The bank was something else. Carolina knew very little about her husband's responsibilities. She was one of those wives who had never had to work. Anita found it difficult to sympathise with such women.

They were near the gates when a voice called: 'Excuse me, Inspector.'

Olofsson's daughter, Sofie, had come round from the back of the house. Throughout the interview, she had sat on the sofa next to her mother, holding her hand. She hadn't said much at the time other than to confirm what her mother was saying.

'I wanted a word without my mother hearing.'

Anita nodded to her and they walked into the side street beyond the gate, out of sight of the house. Sofie took after her father in build, though she had the pretty face that her mother must have had in her prime. Anita knew from their introductions that Sofie was a doctor.

'There's something my mother didn't tell you.'

'And what is that?'

'It's difficult. In the last few months, Dad seemed more preoccupied. He went out a lot, especially when they were over in Vik.'

'He liked golf,' said Anita.

'I know. But Mamma said this was different. He was evasive. The occasional secretive phone call that he'd say was just business.'

'May well have been.'

'What Mamma couldn't fathom was a suppressed excitement. A bounce in his step. She started to think that maybe...'

'Another woman?' Anita ventured.

'Yes. She didn't mention it to you because it was only a suspicion. And she finds the whole thing embarrassing. Especially in front of strangers. I think I'm the only person she's mentioned it to. Not even to my brothers.'

'So, if there is a mystery woman, she's more likely to be over in Österlen than here in Malmö?'

'That's what Mamma thought. Though it would have been easier for him to have an affair over here because Mamma spends a lot of time in the cottage by herself when he's in town, particularly in the summer.'

'I know this is hard for you, but did your father have other affairs in the past that you are aware of?'

'No. Never. I'm sure of that.'

Anita regarded the girl who was having to come to terms with the shocking death of her father and also having to face up to the possibility that he had been unfaithful to a mother she so clearly adored.

'Thank you. That might be very helpful.'

'Inspector... you will catch the person who did this terrible thing?'

Anita reached out a hand and touched Sofie's arm. It was a gesture of reassurance. It wasn't an answer.

Westermark's enigmatic grin worried Anita. What was he up to? He had called the meeting in his office on her return from the Olofsson household to discuss "my murder case". That in itself was enough to raise Anita's hackles. What made it worse was that he had asked Moberg to attend so that the chief inspector was fully up to speed. Westermark opened the meeting as though he were chairman of some highfalutin company board. He graciously gave Anita the floor to explain what she had come up with. Her diminished role within the team was plain to see.

'I didn't get anything of much value from the wife, but then the daughter, Sofie, wanted to speak to me without her mother around. Apparently, in the last few months, Carolina Olofsson believed that her husband might be having an affair. It's not something she wanted to discuss with me, particularly as he is now on a cold slab in Lund. Dirty linen in public and–'

'Anything concrete?' Westermark interrupted.

Hakim saw that Anita was finding it hard to disguise her irritation before she answered. 'No.'

'It's an angle that we must investigate,' he added absently

and without any enthusiasm. It was obviously a lead he wasn't interested in.

'It might provide a motive. Spurned lover. Lover's husband. It was you and the chief inspector who were sure that the motive was personal.'

'That's fine. I said look into it.' Westermark couldn't get the impatience out of his voice. Anita couldn't work out why he failed to see that this was a valid route. She soon discovered why.

Westermark languidly leant back in his seat and rested the crown of his head in his intertwined fingers. 'I've had a very profitable meeting at Sydöstra Banken this morning.' He brought his hands down slowly and placed them on his desk. His pleased-as-Punch smile was directed at Moberg. 'There are significant connections between Martin Olofsson and Tommy Ekman.'

Moberg broke his silence. 'Well?'

'Sydöstra Banken recently had a review of their advertising. Guess who won the business? Ekman & Jonsson! Martin Olofsson wasn't anything to do with the marketing department, but it was he who recommended that they speak to the agency.'

'It's a bit tenuous,' said Moberg.

'That's not the only connection. One of Sydöstra Banken's principal clients is Dag Wollstad. And who was Wollstad's main point of contact at the bank? None other than Martin Olofsson.'

Moberg sighed. 'Everywhere we turn we can't escape Wollstad. Both murders have a direct connection to him. Of course, that may be coincidental. On the other hand, the financial director at the agency is another Wollstad man. And one that used to work for a chemical company owned by Wollstad Industries. I need to speak to him soon.'

'It makes you wonder whether Wollstad wanted Ekman and Olofsson out of the way for some reason.'

'The only thing that nags at me,' said Moberg, 'is that the deaths are so dissimilar. If you hire a hitman, then you would expect the murders to be carried out in the same way; not an obscure poisoning and then hitting someone over the head before making a feeble attempt to pass it off as suicide.'

'Unless it was deliberately done, so we wouldn't connect the two.'

Anita felt like a bystander, which is what she assumed Westermark wanted.

'Right.' Moberg turned to Westermark. 'If there's the possibility of a link, I want you to look into it further. I'll continue with Henrik and Klara Wallen on the Ekman case. We may find connections at our end. Anita, you and...' he said waving at Hakim.

'Hakim', answered Hakim.

'You two look into the mystery woman. Anything you find, report back to Westermark and he'll come to me. By the way, how are you getting on with the painting business? Despite all the mayhem going on, the commissioner was still wittering on about it yesterday.'

'We haven't got any real leads yet,' Anita admitted.

'Well, bloody well find some!'

Anita got the impression that Westermark had been waiting for her to appear in the car park. It was just too convenient that they bumped into each other. There was no escape, as he was between her and her car. He flicked away his cigarette, and there was that supercilious smirk again. He had one of those faces that women either wanted to smother in love or slap in hatred.

'So, what are your plans for *my* Olofsson investigation?'

Anita put her hand into her bag and fished around for her car keys. She kept him waiting for an answer until she had eventually managed to locate them in a side pocket.

'I'll go over to Vik tomorrow and make enquiries. That's if you think that's a good idea,' she added sarcastically.

'Fine by me. As long as you keep me informed.' He stroked

his clean-shaven chin. 'We should work closely together on this case, Anita.'

'Not as closely as you would like.'

'Wrong end of the stick as usual. I'm only trying to help you. You need to work well on this one to restore your reputation. If you help me get a result, then it'll look good for you.' He waved up at the huge expanse of the police headquarters building behind them. 'People round here might start to forgive you.'

'Karl, you're just so full of shit.'

The smile disappeared instantly. 'Just don't get snotty with me.' He then allowed the smile to re-emerge, but there was no humour or warmth in it. 'We could be good for each other. Just think about it.' The implication was clear. It made Anita feel ill. Westermark was turning into a caricature. It would have been funny if Anita didn't feel she was in such a weak position. Her standing in the team had been undermined by her own actions and Westermark had exploited it. He now had the power to make or break her.

She walked past Westermark to her car and unlocked the driver's door.

'Maybe we should have a drink sometime?'

Anita opened the door. 'Probably not a good idea.'

'Then we could discuss why you still have Martin Olofsson's briefcase.'

This stopped Anita in her tracks. She had meant to bring it in but had forgotten. It was still in her living room.

'There are papers in there that the bank wants back. When I checked, Thulin said she gave the briefcase to you. Doesn't look good stashing away possible evidence. You're not playing a very good game so far, are you? I want it on my desk first thing in the morning.'

CHAPTER 19

Anita's brush with Westermark was still preying on her mind when they turned into Ingvar Serneholt's short drive. It was fifteen minutes out of Malmö between Staffanstorp and Dalby. The sprawling house was set by itself and surrounded by sweeping lawns. A number of pitched roofs indicated that this 1920s home had had plenty of additions over the intervening years. You wouldn't get a place like this for under seven million kronor these days. Hakim hadn't been able to find out much about Serneholt. He was in his early fifties and unmarried. He presumably had a private income as he didn't appear to have a job. The family had been involved in the safety match business at some stage, which is where the money must have come from.

After ringing the doorbell a number of times, the man who answered certainly wasn't like the effete collector she had imagined. He had a towel thrown over his shoulder. His hair was still wet. He wore a white T-shirt and a pair of colourful Bermuda shorts. His hair and stubbly beard were starting to grey and there had been no attempt to conceal the aging process with unattractive dye. He was more faded Californian beach boy than art connoisseur.

'Hope you haven't been waiting around. I was in the pool.'

Serneholt showed them into a massive living room. Through wide windows at the back, they could see a large outdoor swimming pool. Like Lindegren's home, the walls proclaimed the fact that art was important. Yet the surroundings were less formal, and Anita suspected that Serneholt actually collected paintings for their own sake.

'Drink?'

'No thanks. We need to ask you about Pelle Munk.'

He rubbed his hair vigorously with the towel and then threw it over a nearby sofa.

'That man is a genius.'

'I don't see any of his paintings here.'

With a pleasant smile, he pointed upwards. Anita could now see that there was an area overhanging the far end of the room. Though the building was single storey, the large roof space allowed for a mezzanine floor.

'Follow me.'

They ascended a spiral staircase and came into a light, airy gallery with white walls and pine timbers. There were about a dozen works displayed. All were abstract, though Anita had now seen enough of Munk's work to pick out his paintings.

Sernholt went over to a small console by the wall, touched a button and music began to play. It was a vaguely familiar classical piece, though Anita couldn't name it. There were two black leather sofas, back to back, in the middle of the space – each one facing a display wall.

'I come up here when I'm pissed off, put on some music and just let the art flow over me. It restores my faith in the universe. Munk's art is like that. Life-affirming. Wouldn't you agree?'

'I'm afraid it's lost on me. I think Hakim has more appreciation.'

Serneholt raised a disbelieving eyebrow as he watched Hakim examining one of Munk's paintings.

'That's *Reflex*.'

To Anita it was a series of squiggly lines.

'Acrylic on aluminium. All these are from his most creative period.' Sernholt pointed at a painting, which was on a canvas.

It seemed to be split in the middle. The top half was green with a red surround, while the bottom half was purple with a blue surround. '*Saturday & Sunday*. I think it's stunning.'

To Anita it was more like a bad weekend.

'I've studied Munk and his work. Met him a few times, of course. His work is spontaneous. Not planned at all.' Serneholt's excited enthusiasm for the subject was at odds with his laid-back persona. 'So, a painting can change in form or feel at any stage. It allows him to explore colour, light and texture. And his main inspiration? Classical music. Depending on what he's listening to shapes the painting he's working on. I found out what he was listening to while creating all these. That's why I'm playing Mahler's *Fifth* now because he painted *Outcome* over there while listening to it. If I listen to the same piece, it allows me to connect with the painting and the artist at the same time.'

Anita had had enough of the lecture.

'I believe that you're the biggest private collector of Munk's work.'

'Sadly, I only have nine. I've tried to get more but without success.'

'So, you'll be interested in his new exhibition?'

His eyes lit up. 'Of course! It'll be a great event and I'll have my chequebook out. It's such an exciting prospect. The Swedish art world is holding its breath.'

Hakim had moved on to the next painting. Anita sceptically wondered if the young man had any idea what he was gazing at. The Impressionists were the outer limit of her artistic appreciation.

'We're trying to track the theft of a couple of Munk's paintings.'

'Ah, yes. *Shadows* from over in Ystad. One of his earlier pieces. Not his best, in my opinion.'

'And *Dawn Mood* from a house in Limhamn. That's the one we're really investigating.'

'Now, that's really worth stealing. I would have bought that myself, but I was in Bali at the time.' In response to Anita's quizzical glance. 'Extended holiday. It's tiring doing nothing, so I needed a break in the sun. No, by the time I heard that *Dawn Mood* had appeared in a Stockholm gallery, it had been snapped up by some businessman down here.'

'And you haven't been approached by anyone wanting to sell it to you?'

Serneholt laughed. 'No such luck. Not that it doesn't happen. I've been tipped the wink before. But that's not my style. That's not how I collect.'

'But works like *Dawn Mood* can be stolen to order?'

'Yes. It happens all over the world. Even in our law-abiding Sweden,' he gently mocked.

'With your knowledge of Munk and that particular art scene, what would your money be on?'

He rubbed his ear as though trying to get water out of it. 'Sorry. Organised crime goes in for this sort of thing. But I don't know whether there's any down in these parts. That's more your department than mine. I would talk to Stig Gabrielsson in Malmö.'

'He put us on to you.'

Sternholt puffed out his lips in amusement. 'Did he? Well, there's a man who knows where everything is – or can be found. Anything he tells you can be taken with a large pinch of salt. Did he imply that I might have *Dawn Mood*?'

'Not exactly,' Anita answered guardedly. 'He reckoned that the painting might be out of the country by now. Germany, possibly.'

Serneholt folded his arms and casually leant against the end of one of the sofas. 'That sounds like he's saying it's not worth investigating. Don't be put off, Inspector. Gabrielsson is unscrupulous. I've dealt with him on a few occasions in the past. Then he popped up the other week trying to sell me an unknown

Munk that had turned up. It was very good. To the inexpert eye, one could easily have been fooled. The colours were right and the composition was typical of the great man, but there was something about the brushwork that wasn't quite as it should have been. I've spent so long looking at these paintings that you begin to understand the flow of his style. Gabrielsson protested his innocence, of course, but I still sent him away with a flea in his ear. He must have known it wasn't an original. If not, he's in the wrong business. Probably has a team of tame artists somewhere churning out fakes which he sells to gullible businessmen who don't know any better. If *Dawn Mood* was stolen to order, I would put my money on Stig Gabrielsson being involved in some way – if not in the theft, then in the disposal.'

A run round Pildammsparken didn't help her sense of restlessness. There were two cases that didn't seem to be getting off the ground, though they would have to take a closer look at Stig Gabrielsson's activities. It was all the personal problems that seemed to be mounting. She was upset by the Lasse situation and his distancing himself from her. It was difficult not to take it personally, even though the truth was that he was infatuated with the wretched Rebecka. Maybe a summer stuck with her on Gotland would make him see sense. The nagging doubt that Anita couldn't remove was that his infatuation might turn into love. And love was also on her mind. She couldn't get Ewan out of her head, however hard she tried. It was so stupid. So pointless. She got herself a drink.

As she poured a glass of red wine, she also had a more immediate concern. Westermark. She hated the fact that she had to report to him. And he was delighting in her discomfort. The bloody briefcase. It was daft not handing it straight in. Now she had given him more ammunition. She was also dreading the inevitable move he would make. The more she said "no", the more he would contrive to make her life as difficult as possible.

But if she didn't stand up to him, he would take it as encouragement. Swedish laws on sexual harassment were complicated enough, but if it reached a stage where she had to make a formal complaint, she might as well just quit. She might win her case, but her career would be down the drain. She would be earmarked as a troublemaker. The men would assume she had led him on in the first place. Once the atmosphere in a team is soured, it never recovers. She would be seen as the bad apple.

As she came back into the living room, she spotted the offending article. She put down her drink and lifted the slim, leather case onto the coffee table. She took out her notebook and looked up the combination again. She scrolled the numbers round on the first set of dials – 061 – and then repeated the process on the other – 132. Then she flicked the catches and the lid sprang open. She rummaged through the bank papers yet again. None seemed to be remotely relevant. The golf magazine she quickly discarded. She searched all the compartments of the case. Nothing there either. No secret love letter. No clue to any untoward behaviour at all. No hint of another woman. Then there were the two DVDs. One was *Casino Royale*. She couldn't stand Bond films. Björn had loved them and had dragged her off to the cinema whenever the latest one came out. She put it down to it being a boys' thing. The other DVD was a *Kurt Wallander* story – *Before the Frost*. She could see where Olofsson's tastes lay – adventure and crime. She rather enjoyed the Henning Mankell books because they were set in Ystad, a place she knew well. She liked the local references. Nostalgia set in and, for lack of anything better to do, she decided to put the *Wallander* DVD in her recording machine. She had watched one or two episodes of the popular TV crime drama before, and Krister Henriksson, the actor who played the titular hero, was always good value.

Anita sat back, clicked the remote control and settled back with her glass of wine for an hour or so of undemanding entertainment. Except what came on the screen was totally different. The man sitting in the old-fashioned, upright chair was somehow familiar. He spoke in English.

'This is an important time for Sweden, and the work you have put in so far is vital in the battle against the enemies of Christ. You have so many in your midst. Your streets are full of the heathen, the tainted, the coloured, the depraved, and, of course, the malevolent Jews. Yet feeble governments have welcomed them into your country over many years, and what has Sweden got in return? Attacks on your womenfolk, the spread of drugs amongst your youth, and the theft of jobs from the native people of your beautiful land.'

It was the clerical dress and the northeast English accent that brought it back to her. He had been on TV the day before she went back to work. And here he was spouting out his anti-Semitic, anti-Muslim, anti-everything sentiments. Anita watched with a mixture of appalled fascination and rising indignation as the cleric regurgitated his Holocaust denials, his railing against the tide of immigration and the Muslim threat from within Sweden's borders. In short, he was attributing all Sweden's ills to the minorities within the country's society.

'I know that it is important to you all that Sweden is restored to the proud, God-fearing country that you so love. But before that can become a reality, you must be at the forefront of a battle to cleanse your society of the alien races that infest your streets. Your hero, Gustavus Adolphus, said: "War is not a river or a lake, but an ocean of all that is evil." Your war is here and now. Take courage, for the one true God is with you in your work.'

The screen went black and the words "Bishop Clive Green" appeared in white lettering.

Anita sat in shocked silence. Her emotions were seething. She had no religious beliefs herself, but she couldn't credit a supposed man of God coming out with such grotesque views. To her, he was distorting the facts, playing with dangerous ideas and appealing to the baser instincts. What distressed Anita most was that Bishop Clive Green's gospel of hatred would strike a chord with many disaffected Swedes, of which there were a growing number. Immigrants were blamed for everything. It was poisonous opinions peddled by such people as Green that were presumably influencing the likes of the "Malmö Marksman". It was only a matter of time before those with far right-wing views would turn words into action. She knew that even the foreign press had picked up on the corrosive campaign carried out by both Neo-Nazis and Muslim youth on Malmö's dwindling Jewish community. Attacks had increased in recent years and there had been little sign of official action or sympathy, even after the chapel at a Jewish burial site was firebombed. Also, there had been harassment from various quarters of the large Muslim community, and there was continuing unrest in areas of the city, like Rosengård, which had seen rioting the year before.

Anita gazed at her untouched wine. More to the point, what was this DVD doing in Martin Olofsson's briefcase? And who had made the recording? It wasn't of the interview that Bishop Green had given on the television. The message was so specific to Sweden that there was probably a reasonable chance that it was made in the country. Most worrying of all, who was it aimed at? Bishop Green was very sure of his audience. Preaching to the converted? By his tone of voice, most definitely. And that disturbing call to action at the end! It was nothing less than incitement to violence. Yet all this bile was delivered in measured tones. That's what made it so chilling.

CHAPTER 20

'Yes, I was at Buckley Mellor Chemicals for five years.' Bo Nilsson's thin face was impassive. The contrast between Nilsson and Moberg was comical. Nilsson's height didn't exceed by much the large computer screen on his desk. Moberg loomed, Brobdingnagian, on the other side. Nordlund was next to him.

'And before that?' Moberg growled. For some reason he had taken an instant dislike to Nilsson.

'At a finance company in Lund.'

'It wouldn't happen to be owned by Dag Wollstad?'

Nilsson feigned surprise at the question. 'Yes. He bought it over in 1992. Is that significant?'

'Not necessarily. So, you've been a Wollstad man for nearly twenty years.'

'I don't think he has any complaints about my work. In fact, he holds me in quite high regard,' he added pompously.

'Know him well?'

'Not well, no. I have been at business meetings at which he has been present, and the occasional company social event. Like the Trotting Derby out at Jägersro a few years back.'

'Did you win anything?'

Nilsson was momentarily taken aback by the question. 'A little. I don't believe in gambling as a rule.' This was accompanied by a polite laugh. 'It's not good practice for an accountant. It was merely a harmless flutter.'

Nordlund wrote something in his notebook.

'Let's get back to the chemical company,' said Moberg. 'Presumably, through your job, you became familiar with the production processes involved. The chemicals, poisonous substances, that sort of thing.'

Nilsson rearranged the position of a calculator on his desk. Everything neatly in its place.

'I assume you are trying to tie me in with the substance that caused Tommy's death.' Before Moberg could interrupt, Nilsson held up a restraining hand. 'I heard it from Daniel Jonsson. The answer to your question, Chief Inspector, is that I did not need to know what went into Buckley Mellor products. I am still ignorant of the processes. I merely helped to keep a tight control of the budgets and ensure that each year the company achieved its profit forecasts. At that time, I was not the finance director, but the number two.'

Moberg was becoming irritated by this pedantic number cruncher. 'But you knew people who produced the pharmaceuticals. People with know-how.'

'They were colleagues. Nothing more. I hope you're not suggesting that I could possibly have had anything to do with Tommy's death.' Despite his size, Nilsson wasn't afraid to eyeball the chief inspector. 'I hardly think it is in my interests to kill my employer.'

'But who was your employer? Ekman or Wollstad?'

'Tommy Ekman, of course.'

'But weren't you put into this company to safeguard Wollstad's investment? To be his eyes and ears?'

Nilsson stared hard at Moberg before answering. 'I don't know where you got that idea from. Wollstad recommended me because he felt I could do a good job for his son-in-law. Which I did. Still am doing, despite the appalling events which have engulfed us.'

'Are you trying to tell me that a man like Dag Wollstad didn't ring you up from time to time to check that everything was running smoothly here?'

'No, he didn't. If he wanted to know how the company was doing, he would talk to Tommy.'

Now Moberg was convinced that Nilsson was lying.

Anita made sure she arrived at the polishus before Westermark had dragged himself out of his bed, or someone else's. She placed Martin Olofsson's briefcase on his desk and hurried out again. She popped into her own office and slipped the Bishop's DVD into her desk drawer. *Casino Royale* remained in the briefcase. It really had been *Casino Royale*. She wanted time to think through how best to reveal the Bishop's "message" to the team – and she wanted to do an internet search on Bishop Green first. She switched on her computer. The one that she and Lasse had shared at home had disappeared with him off to university. Not that she was a great emailer or interested in surfing the net. But just occasionally it would have been useful to have a computer in the apartment. Like last night. The sudden urge to look something up had to be done through the traditional route of reference books. If that proved fruitless, she would have to look up whatever it was at work the next day.

There were a lot of entries for Bishop Clive Green. The sixty-eight-year-old cleric had been born of humble origins near Newcastle. He had studied theology at a Roman Catholic seminary outside Durham. His early life was uneventful and included spells in Africa and South America. In the 1970s he became involved in a society that was set up to oppose the liberalism of the second Vatican council. Then his increasingly hardline views started to cause the Vatican unease. Some believe that he was made a bishop in Argentina in the hopes of keeping him quiet. It seems to have had the opposite effect, and his opinions became more strident, particularly his Holocaust denial stance. Eventually, the Vatican acted and he was excommunicated.

Since then, he had moved around to wherever his views found a home. Had Lutheran Sweden played host to the rogue Roman Catholic? If it had, there was no way of knowing when he was recorded or where he was now. The interview that Anita had briefly caught on television had taken place in Switzerland, though Sweden was the only country to air it. It was now on YouTube and had received an alarming number of hits.

Before driving cross-country to Vik, Anita briefed Hakim on what she wanted to dig up on Gabrielsson. Basically, anything he could find, from known associates to whether the gallery was viable. She knew that she should take Hakim with her, but she wanted to work alone on this. It would give her time to think. And it would also give her the chance to prove that she was working on a positive lead, even if it had been dismissed by Westermark and Moberg. She was turning it into a challenge.

The weather had broken, and the rain followed her most of the way across to Simrishamn. Despite the dismal light, the auriferous oil seed rape fields and the fresh green of the trees lifted her spirits. This was her Sweden. Ten minutes after leaving Simrishamn, she was driving down the narrow lanes – they could hardly be described as streets – of the lower part of Vik. It was an old fishing village that had attracted weekenders, including a number of dreaded Stockholmers. The single-storey cottages were quaint and picturesque. Some had moss-covered roofs, pleasingly contrasting with the ones constructed of the more traditional red corrugated iron. Most of the homes were whitewashed and nearly all were well cared for with neat garden areas. Anita parked her car close to the small harbour, where a couple of pretty little brightly painted boats bobbed on the ebbing tide, and walked along to Olofsson's weekend home. She knew nobody would be there as Carolina Olofsson had gone to stay with her daughter in Gothenburg. It was the neighbours that Anita wanted to talk to. See if she could discover more about Martin Olofsson and his habits. If he were having an affair, then it was over here in the east and not in Malmö.

The Olofsson's weekend cottage was neat, even by Vik standards. The bottom half of the building was made of stones cemented together with traditional mortar outlined in white paint. The top half was whitewashed. In the window was a model of a ship. That appeared to be compulsory round these parts. The rain gave the garden a sparkling, heavy lushness after the recent dry spell, and dabs of colour were splashed about at random. Anita wasn't sure what the flowers were called, but she appreciated their beauty.

When Anita knocked, there was no reply from the immediate neighbour. If most of the properties were owned by weekenders, then she wasn't going to have much luck. But the house on the opposite side proved more successful. She found Matilda Blomquist relaxing with a coffee. Blomquist invited Anita in while simultaneously expressing the village's horror at Martin's death. 'Terrible business,' she repeated three times as she poured Anita a coffee from her thermos jug. Blomquist also insisted on bringing out some cinnamon biscuits. She was a middle-aged woman who had time on her hands, but she was a full-time resident and therefore a potential source of useful information.

Anita trod carefully at first. She established that Blomquist knew the Olofssons well, particularly Carolina. 'Such a nice woman. Devoted to Martin.'

'What did Martin get up to when he was down here?'

Blomquist helped herself to another biscuit. 'Not much. Liked to relax after a busy week in Malmö. Loved his golf, of course. Nearly every weekend I would see him taking his golf clubs to his car. I'd get a cheery wave. I think it was his way of unwinding. He'd be away for the day. Carolina would go out walking.'

'Right up until recently?'

'Oh, yes. He was golfing last weekend. It would be the Saturday.'

'These biscuits are very nice.'

It was the right thing to say. 'I make them myself.'

Anita took a bite and gave an appreciative nod. 'Did you ever discuss politics?'

'That's a funny question. Not really, though I do know that Carolina is a strong Social Democrat because she campaigned for them at one election.'

'And Martin?'

'Don't think he was interested. Just let Carolina get on with it.'

'Did they ever discuss religion?'

'No.'

'Or the influx of immigrants?'

Blomquist sniffed loudly and raised her eyebrows.

'That's the only cross words we ever had in all the years they've been coming here. I happened to mention the number of immigrants I'd seen on a visit to Malmö. It was a shopping trip. I like to go when the summer fashions are coming in. Luckily, we don't have them round here. Immigrants, I mean. But my comments upset her. She said that Sweden had always welcomed them. They need a safe haven. That's what she said. She got quite heated.' Blomquist bristled at the memory. 'Haven't dared mention the subject again.'

'One last thing then I'll leave you in peace. Was Martin a lady's man?'

'Not in a flirty way. But he was a gentleman.'

'Do you think it's possible that he had another woman?'

Matilda Blomquist was so shocked at the suggestion that she couldn't answer immediately. When it came out it was an indignant: 'Martin? Never!'

Anita turned the car off the main road, drove past the verge-side apple trees and into the half-full car park of the golf and conference complex. It was made up of neat, red-roofed, low-slung buildings and exuded affluence. Anita couldn't get her head round golf but could understand the attraction of wandering around the Österlen course, which took full advantage of its coastal location. The big expanse of the Baltic was more interesting than small white balls. At the well-appointed clubhouse, she managed to track down the club secretary and then talk to one of the members, who seemed more interested in propping up the bar than probing the greens. Both confirmed that Martin Olofsson had played regularly at the club, mostly weekends. When she asked the florid-faced member in the bar if Olofsson had mentioned another woman – all guys together enjoying a few drinks – the reaction was virtually the same as Matilda Blomquist's. The suggestion was greeted with disbelieving laughter. Martin didn't seem the type. Pleasant but boring was the verdict. After all, he was a banker.

Anita wasn't getting anywhere and was about to take her leave.

'Had Martin been ill, before you know what...?' enquired the member.

'I don't think so,' Anita answered. 'Why do you ask?'

'Just that he hasn't played here for about a month. Maybe he was away.'

That didn't fit in with Blomquist's description of Olofsson going off with his golf clubs.

'No, he was here.'

The member returned to his whisky. 'Probably rushing off to Dag Wollstad's place.'

'Wollstad's place?'

'Yes. Saw him once turning into the entrance to Wollstad's estate when I was driving past. When I mentioned it the next time I saw him here, he was a bit evasive. Maybe it was business. And none of mine.'

'When was this?'

'Couple of months ago.'

CHAPTER 21

Anita had taken advantage of her trip to meet up with Karin Munk for lunch at Röken, a fish restaurant on the seafront at Simrishamn. She had rung up Karin on the spur of the moment outside the golf club, and Karin had said she was free and would meet her in half an hour.

Röken was a basic but pleasant spot for a seafood lunch. A modern building near the yacht club, its wide windows overlooked the seemingly endless sea, which disappeared into a sunlit horizon. To the right was a curved wall of huge boulders that provided shelter for the closely packed yachts, whose masts were swaying gently in the warm breeze. It was the kind of scene that Anita would have liked to paint if she had been remotely artistic. How would Pelle Munk have interpreted the view? she wondered.

The first fifteen minutes in the restaurant, as the two of them helped themselves to the free entrée salad and glass of beer, had been awkward. By the time their set meal of plaice and prawns in a lobster sauce arrived, they had moved on from the meandering small talk that is inevitable when an old friendship is rekindled, and had found a topic that sparked off the reminiscences. Old boyfriends. Nils Kjellberg to be exact. Anita had dated him first.

'After you dumped him, he came after me!' smiled Karin at the recollection. 'I usually ended up with your rejects.'

'Rubbish,' Anita protested. 'Tall, blonde, attractive, artistic and sophisticated. The boys thought that anyone from Stockholm must be exciting. You were quite a catch.'

'I liked Nils. He was my first, you know. I lost my virginity in Dad's studio,' Karin said, her eyes flickering happily at the guilty remembrance. 'I lured poor Nils in there on the pretext of showing him Dad's pictures. Not that he was remotely interested in art. But it gave him a kick to make love to the daughter of a famous painter. That was fine by me.' She sipped her beer. 'That made him memorable. Trouble was, he couldn't stop talking about you, so I dumped him too.' They both laughed.

'Oh, he was a handsome boy.' Anita had her own memories. 'Remember that lovely head of hair he had?' Karin nodded. 'Virtually bald now. Ran into him in Malmö a couple of years ago. Shopping in Indiska. Buying something for his wife or girlfriend. Run to fat, too. Actually, he was embarrassed when he saw me. Couldn't get out fast enough.'

'How awful! Awful that he's lost his looks.'

The conversation moved effortlessly on to Anita's marriage, Björn, Lasse, divorce and the life of a working single mother. As someone who spent her professional existence asking questions, it was a strange experience being interrogated by her old classmate. Karin seemed genuinely interested in what had happened to her since their last meeting in that Stockholm bar.

'What about you, Karin? What have you been up to in the intervening years?'

Karin swirled the last dregs of beer in her glass. 'Not much. Never married. So never divorced.'

'But you had great plans to be an artist. You were so talented at school.'

Karin sighed. 'There's talented and there's *talented*. It's not easy to carve your niche in the art world; create a style that's really yours. I wasn't distinctive enough, and I couldn't escape Dad's shadow. His paintings are different. His work demands attention whether you love it or loathe it. My work was well painted. Technically good. But there was something missing. That indefinable quality that sets you apart. I could have gone and lived in some artistic community and churned out pictures for the tourists, but that's not enough.'

'But you're still involved.'

A rueful grimace. 'Art restorer. Oh, I'm good at that. Because I understand and appreciate art, I can relate to the paintings I restore. I enjoy it. I help bring good paintings back to life. It's not quite the same, though.'

They had been talking for so long that they were the last people in the restaurant. The owner wanted to close up. Anita wandered out with Karin to where their cars were parked. The conversation had suddenly flagged and Anita's mind was drifting back to work.

'I saw a number of your father's paintings at Ingvar Serneholt's place.'

'Who's he?' Karin asked.

'A rich collector. Family made money in matches. Loves Pelle's work.'

'What's he got?'

Anita gave an embarrassed shrug. 'Can't remember the names. They all look...'

'The same?'

'No.' Anita tried to backtrack. 'Not at all. Just the titles aren't always obvious from the painting. Or vice versa. Oh, I know! Something to do with the weekend.'

'*Saturday & Sunday*?'

'That's right.'

They reached the cars and they gave each other a hug.

'Must do this again,' said Anita.

'Sure.'

Anita unlocked the car door. Then she stopped as a thought struck her. 'Karin, do you know a Stig Gabrielsson? Runs a gallery in Malmö.'

'Yes. I've had a couple of restoration jobs through him. Why?'

'He's on our radar. Do you think he could be behind the thefts of your father's paintings?'

'I'd be surprised.'

Anita shrugged. 'Just a thought.'

Westermark strode across Gustav Adolfs Torg, ignoring the busy flow of shoppers, office workers and tourists criss-crossing the cobbles. His mind was so focused that he didn't even indulge in his usual passion of eyeing up the beautiful women of the city. Malmö had more than its fair share, many tall and blonde, but Westermark's taste was eclectic. He was excited. He should have phoned in as soon as he knew, but he wanted to savour the delicious moment when he could break the news to Moberg. He knew the chief inspector would be pleased. A chance to score points over Anita Sundström. Not that he thought of her as being a serious threat to his career advancement any more.

Westermark quickened his pace. He never got over the thrill of a case coming together. From the moment he was involved in an investigation when nothing appeared to make sense, to the gradual discovering of evidence; the joining up of those seemingly unconnected dots, and finally things starting to slot into place. And if he was an integral part of the process, the final successful outcome was nothing short of exhilarating. Maybe sleeping with an attractive woman was the only comparable thrill. For a moment, he was distracted by the thought of Anita Sundström. She was the unsettling presence in his life. Women had never been important, other than as a means of sexual recreation. Even as a child, his philandering father had, perversely, turned him against his mother. Why hadn't she stood up to him? Why hadn't she walked out? It hadn't occurred to him that she had stayed to try and keep a fractured family together. Instead of his gratitude, she had earned his disdain for her weakness. The low esteem in which he had held his mother, before she withered away in a cancerous haze, was his starting point in judging women. Yet Anita Sundström challenged all his deep-rooted views. Beautiful as she was – and he had had a number of good-looking women – it was not just the physical attraction that set her apart. To him, she was strong, independent, and had the courage to stand up to people like Moberg. And she loathed him. He knew that. She made it plain. But what really drove his contradictory desires of hatred and lust was that he knew that she was a bloody good cop. And as long as she rejected his advances or challenged his growing status in the force through her own successes, he would put her down at every opportunity. He would use any mistake, any lowering of her guard and any means at his disposal to break her. Both in work and, eventually, in bed.

By the time he reached the polishus, he had pushed Anita from his mind. He took the stairs two at a time and rushed into Moberg's office, where the chief inspector was discussing the case with Nordlund. Moberg was about to ball out Westermark for barging into the room but held back when he saw the triumphant expression on his colleague's face.

'Well?'

'We've got the connection!'

'Bo Nilsson or Daniel Jonsson?'

'Nilsson.' Westermark paced the office in his excitement. 'My contact at Sydöstra Banken, Lars Allbäck, told me that not only did they handle the Ekman & Jonsson business but also Bo Nilsson's personal account.'

'I didn't think it was that type of bank,' Nordlund ventured.

'No, it isn't normally. But for special customers, they do oversee various accounts. And with Nilsson being connected to Wollstad, the bank was obviously happy to oblige.'

'So, he's connected. Doesn't make him a murderer, though

139

the little bastard is hiding something,' mumbled Moberg.

'It does!' Westermark sat down as he couldn't keep his legs still. 'A couple of weeks before he died, Ekman came round to the bank to have a meeting with Martin Olofsson. Apparently, Ekman wanted the bank to scrutinise the agency accounts because he felt that there was something going on. He thought money was missing. He wanted the bank, discreetly, to look into Ekman & Jonsson's financial structure and Bo Nilsson's role in particular. Basically, Ekman suspected Nilsson of fiddling the books.'

Moberg ran his hand across his mouth. 'If Nilsson had his hand in the till, that would give him a motive to get rid of Ekman. Afraid of being found out.'

'And to kill Olofsson,' Westermark carried on, 'as he was the one who was going to do some digging on the quiet. Lars Allbäck only found this out yesterday when he was going through Olofsson's files.'

'I think we had better find out if Nilsson had a gambling habit,' said Nordlund. 'He looked uncomfortable when you mentioned flutters at Jägersro.'

'That might fit,' said Westermark. 'According to Allbäck, Nilsson's account has fluctuated quite considerably over the past few months.'

'Money going out on bets, money coming in from embezzling.'

Moberg smiled at Nordlund's observation. 'Makes perfect sense. My God, we could have our man!'

'Exactly!' Westermark exclaimed animatedly. 'We know he was in Ekman's office by himself in the morning. The PA said he was dropping off spreadsheets. He went out to lunch and wandered around in the sunshine, according to his statement. He could quite easily have gone to Ekman's apartment. Then he was back in Ekman's office for the drinks celebration. He had the opportunity to take and return the keys. And, of course, he has the pharmaceutical connection with Buckley Mellor Chemicals for the poison.'

'Right,' said Moberg decisively. 'We've a lot to do. Need to really go into Nilsson's habits to see if there is a gambling problem. Full check on his finances. He may have other bank accounts outside Sydöstra. We also need to discover if Olofsson had actually found any financial impropriety at the agency. See if Jonsson knew anything about the missing money. And we have to find out where Nilsson got to that lunchtime – and then check if he has an alibi for when Olofsson was killed. I want to know everything there is to know about this little bugger.'

Why she was parked outside the gates of Dag Wollstad's estate, Anita wasn't entirely sure. What had seemed a good idea when she got into her car outside Röken didn't seem so clever now that she had driven deep into the Österlen countryside. She was having second thoughts. She knew that Wollstad was off limits. Yet Martin Olofsson had made at least one trip here which, it seems, he didn't want others to know about. That in itself was odd, as Olofsson was Wollstad's banker. What was more normal? So why be secretive? Yet the timing was strange. A weekend? Maybe someone like Wollstad was always on the go and expected everyone to fit in with his timetable, however inconvenient it was for everybody else. You didn't say "no" to Dag Wollstad. The fact was that Olofsson was regularly going somewhere, presumably to meet someone. He set off, ostensibly to go golfing, but he hadn't been to the club for over a month. His wife was suspicious of his behaviour, yet no one else, apart from her, seemed to think that a romance was a likely scenario. At least by talking to Wollstad or someone in his entourage, she could verify the golf club member's story. If she found nothing here, she would have to investigate some other avenue.

She let the handbrake off, gently touched the accelerator and began to navigate the long drive.

Anita was shown into the room with the portrait of Gustav Adolf by a plump and unfriendly woman who was probably the housekeeper. She had informed Anita that Wollstad was out of the country at the moment. Anita then asked if she could talk to Wollstad's PA, only to be curtly informed that she was away on the same trip. When Anita had insisted on seeing someone who might have access to Wollstad's appointment book, the housekeeper reluctantly left her in the room that Moberg had met the business magnate. Anita was surprised when Kristina Ekman appeared. She was as cold and as beautiful as Nordlund had described. She lit a cigarette before she spoke.

'Found my husband's murderer yet?'

Ekman eased herself elegantly into an expensively embroidered chair of 18th-century style. Anita wasn't offered one, so she was left hovering awkwardly.

'Not yet. But we are making progress.'

'That's not what my father's contacts say.'

'So why ask the question?' It was out before Anita could stop herself.

Ekman bristled. She wasn't used to being questioned. The glare was hostile.

'I am not working on your husband's case. I'm looking into the murder of Martin Olofsson.'

At least this elicited a reaction of sorts. Half a raised eyebrow. 'My father's banker. Or one of them. I hardly think I'm in a position to tell you anything about him.'

'We're simply trying to establish if Martin Olofsson visited your father here in the past couple of months. I was wondering if it was possible for someone to check your father's business diary to see if Olofsson had appointments with him.'

Ekman stubbed out her cigarette and stood up. She left the room without a word. Anita was left to contemplate Gustav Adolf. The famous king had been her grandfather's hero, though she hadn't been old enough to appreciate most of his stories at the time. She supposed her fascination with the past had been inherited from him. Though, ironically, she had learned more about history in general during her two years at school in Britain than all her time in the Swedish educational system. With a global empire, Britain had more of it.

Ten minutes later, Ekman returned.

'I have looked at my father's appointments over the last three months. He had meetings with Olofsson on three occasions.'

This information raised Anita's hopes. 'They were here?'

'No. In Malmö. Two at the bank and the other at a company office.'

'Could Olofsson have made social calls here in that time?'

Ekman gave a mirthless laugh. 'You don't know my father. His life is business. He wouldn't welcome social calls unless they were from his family. You can be sure that Olofsson has not been here. I assume that's all?'

Anita's dismissal couldn't have been curter.

CHAPTER 22

Moberg wasn't sure whether he was pleased or angry. His morning meeting with Prosecutor Sonja Blom and Commissioner Dahlbeck had gone really well at first. He had been able to report that the investigation was starting to take shape. He outlined all the evidence they had against Bo Nilsson in the Tommy Ekman case – possible motive, opportunity and access to the crystals. And now they had a motive for his murdering Olofsson too. What had been discovered since his meeting with Nordlund and Westermark was encouraging. It seemed that Nilsson was more than keen on an occasional flutter. He was a regular gambler at the trotting races but was also known to the staff at Malmö's opulent casino in Kungsparken. It was not the sort of place that a company's financial director should frequent. His bank accounts confirmed the erratic nature of his finances. There were two large deposits made in the past two months, though it had to be conceded that they might be big wins.

They had discovered that Nilsson lived on his own, though he had an ex-wife in Falkenberg. Wallen had been sent to speak to her, and the woman knew nothing of his gambling. He had frowned on such practices during their marriage. In fact, one of the reasons she had left him was his meanness. So the habit had taken hold in the last couple of years. Certainly the ex-wife believed that Dag Wollstad would never have entrusted Bo with any senior position of financial responsibility if he thought he was cavalier with his personal finances. Wollstad always checked his people out. The team had yet to discover what had caused this sudden change in Nilsson's behaviour.

As for the murder of Martin Olofsson, they needed to talk to Nilsson before they could establish whether he had an alibi for that Monday night. Westermark was going to bring Nilsson in for questioning later in the morning. What they had established at the bank was that Olofsson's notes indicated that he thought something was definitely amiss at the agency, though there were no specifics. His investigation was at an early stage. Both Blom and Dahlbeck were pleased at this turn of events mainly because it meant that Wollstad wasn't implicated. Dahlbeck had said all along that Wollstad couldn't have been connected directly with the case, and he had been right to make him off limits. Potentially embarrassing for the force to have involved him. And the sooner these murders were cleared up, the sooner everybody could concentrate on the "Malmö Marksman".

Blom had left the meeting and Dahlbeck had asked Moberg to stay behind for a moment. Then he had torn into the chief inspector. Why the bloody hell had Anita Sundström gone to Wollstad's country home and questioned his daughter Kristina? She had no right to be there and Moberg had been warned not to let anyone go near the family. Moberg had no answer, which made him even more furious. He could think of no reason on earth why she should have gone. She wasn't even working on the Ekman case. So Moberg wasn't able to stand his ground with the commissioner and had to take the censure. The commissioner said that if Moberg didn't sort her out, then she would be out of the force. And good riddance.

Moberg had stormed off to Anita's office to give her a bollocking she would never forget. But she wasn't there. Hakim said that she had a hospital appointment. Moberg was even more enraged. He didn't want to have time to simmer down. She deserved his full wrath.

***

Doctor Axelsson's continuous tapping of his pencil against his lips was beginning to seriously bug Anita. Why wasn't he in the park playing with the other kids instead of sitting in this stuffy room prying into her private thoughts? She was also finding it hard to concentrate because she knew she should have told Westermark or Moberg about her investigations yesterday. They hadn't thrown up anything dramatic other than that it was unlikely Martin Olofsson had a lover; he didn't play golf when he said he did and he may have visited Wollstad one weekend. The golf club member might have been wrong about that one. Anita was jolted back by Axelsson's next question.

'Do you know why you fell in love with Ewan?'

Anita sighed heavily. 'Is this relevant?'

'I think so. It might help explain your actions.'

Anita shifted uneasily in her seat. She wasn't very good at this sort of thing. She took after her father, who had never been forthcoming when it came to expressing his feelings. She admired some of her friends, like Sandra, who could quite openly discuss any subject in the frankest of terms. Björn had often teased her about her reticence over talking about intimate matters, especially in public. Privately, she was sensual, sexual, physically and emotionally expressive. She knew that the one thing Björn missed was their lovemaking, and that gave her some satisfaction. But exposing herself to other people was anathema to her. Which was daft really, as in her work she expected other people to expose their private lives in minute detail.

'He was different.'

'How?'

'Well, he wasn't Swedish for starters.'

'Is that important?'

'After my abysmal record with Swedish men, yes.'

'Go on,' Axelsson prodded.

Anita took out and started to fiddle with her snus tin. It was a prop. 'Ewan made me laugh. He didn't make demands on me. Didn't seem to expect anything. We never even got round to...'

Axelsson waited. Then he filled in the gap, 'Having sex?'

Anita laughed out loud. 'No. We never even got round to kissing.'

She was amused to see that Axelsson was astonished.

The moment seemed to open the flood gates. She had fallen for Ewan gradually as the case had progressed. They got on so well. She felt relaxed in his company. She described the awful moment when she was sent to arrest him at the train station when he was first suspected of Lovgren's murder. It was at that moment that she realised that she had feelings for him. And now that he was in gaol, she kept thinking about him. Worrying about how he was being treated. His beating by his fellow prisoners had upset her badly. And then she confessed. She'd retraced the steps Ewan had taken during his brief time of freedom in Malmö. She had visited the places they had been together – the Moosehead bar in Lilla Torg, the cafe in the Malmö art gallery. And the places she knew he had been to – The Pickwick pub and Café Simrishamn 3. At The Pickwick, she had recognised Alex and David from Ewan's descriptions. They were the two expatriate Brits who had befriended Ewan on his arrival in Malmö. She didn't think it was a good idea to make herself known to them. She assumed that they didn't want to acknowledge their connection with him now. Yet she could picture Ewan in the pub. It was his natural habitat.

Above all, there was the guilt she felt for loving a man whom she knew she mustn't. She couldn't reconcile the contradictions.

'I think that's all for today, Anita.'

'You mean you can offer me no insight? No advice?'

'Do I need to?'

Anita shook her head slowly.

'I'm here to listen. You've expressed thoughts that you've buried deeply. I've helped you to unearth them. Now I think it's time you moved on. Whether Ewan is part of that process is up to you.'

Her timing couldn't have been worse. Anita had decided, against her better judgement, to report back directly to Westermark on her trip to Österlen. She didn't want to give Moberg or Westermark any more reasons to reprimand her, and thought it best to go through the correct chain of command on the case. As she walked into Westermark's office, Moberg was just coming out. The moment she saw the chief inspector she knew something was up. She was ushered into the room and Moberg slammed the door behind him. It was like being trapped in a cave with a big bear blocking her escape route.

'What the fuck were you thinking of?'

Anita was taken aback.

'What?'

'Visiting Wollstad's home.' This came out as a strangled yell.

'I was following up on the Olofsson case. The mystery woman, who I don't think exists by the way.'

'And you didn't happen to think this mystery woman was Kristina Ekman?'

'Of course not.'

'So why bother her? Now I'm getting loads of shit from the commissioner. Didn't I say the family were off limits, or was I just talking to myself? Or does Inspector Sundström think she knows better than the rest of us?'

Anita could take the aggressive sarcasm. It was Westermark's obvious delight that aggravated her.

'I was following up a lead. I didn't even know Kristina Ekman would be there. I just wanted to check something out.'

'Without checking it out with me first?'

'It was on the spur of the moment.'

'There are too many spurs of the moment with you. The commissioner wants you off the force. And you're playing right into his hands you silly b...' Moberg just managed to rein himself in before he blurted the word out.

Anita lost her temper. 'I followed up a valid lead. Olofsson made mystery trips when he was supposed to be playing golf. I got a tip-off that he went to Wollstad's country place. I was doing what any competent police officer would have done.' Her eyes were blazing by the time she had finished.

Moberg shrugged. 'It doesn't matter now.' This took the wind out of her sails. 'The Wollstads aren't involved. The killer is Ekman's financial director, Bo Nilsson. We just have to prove it now. So, Anita...' and this time he added a condescending smile, 'you can get back to your paintings and we'll wrap this up.'

When she left the office, it wasn't Moberg's expression that she couldn't get out of her mind; it was Westermark's. There was a cat that had swallowed the cream.

Anita had taken Hakim down to the ice-cream parlour on Drottningtorget. She needed to get out of the office to escape the smug arrogance and excess testosterone. She was off the Olofsson case and stuck with this wretched art theft investigation. Her one chance to get her teeth into some proper policing, and she had given Moberg the perfect excuse to shove her ignominiously off the case. Maybe her findings were insignificant. That didn't stop her wondering what Olofsson had got up to on his supposed golf days and, if the golf club member had been correct about him driving into Wollstad's estate, why Kristina Ekman had lied to her.

She might be feeling pissed off and unwanted, but it cheered her up to see Hakim's childlike glee at licking his ice cream. The Italian stuff served here was particularly good.

'So, while I was getting myself into trouble yesterday, did

you find out anything useful about Gabrielsson?'

Hakim couldn't answer immediately as he had swallowed a mouthful of ice cream.

'Stig Gabrielsson has been running his business for about twenty years. Like many gallery owners, he's a failed artist. He sold insurance before that. Started to cash in when the Öresund Bridge opened up the market. Even tried to set up another gallery in Copenhagen. It failed. Most of his income seems to be from legitimate sales, though according to your art theft contact up in the Stockholm police, he's known to them.'

'That's what they told me.'

'Apparently, they first came across him in Stockholm when he tried to sell some fakes. Small stuff, but the police made a deal with him. They said they wouldn't prosecute if he would feed them information on stolen artworks. His tip-offs have led to a couple of high-profile arrests over the years. They turn a blind eye as long as he's useful.'

'So he's still allowed to try and sell Serneholt a fake Pelle Munk?'

'Exactly.'

'We'll need some pretty hard evidence against him if we decide he's behind these thefts. Great!'

Anita returned to her ice cream. It didn't taste as nice as it had before. This was hopeless. She looked across the square. At the top of the tall building opposite was Tommy Ekman's apartment. That's where the real action was taking place. That's the investigation she wanted to be on.

She finished off her cone. 'Well, let's go and rattle Gabrielsson's cage. At least we can have a go at him for trying to sell the fake to Serneholt.'

CHAPTER 23

Nilsson furrowed his brow. He was trying to recall where he was on the night that Martin Olofsson was murdered. He was also trying to ignore the intimidating atmosphere in the interview room. 'Monday night, you say.'

'It's not that difficult,' Westermark said with a hint of annoyance. 'It was the beginning of this week, for God's sake.'

'I must have been at home. In my apartment in Limhamn. A quiet night in.' Nilsson fussily brushed the sleeve of his jacket with his hand. 'By the way, should I have my lawyer here?'

'Only if you think you need one,' said Moberg.

Nilsson flashed a confident smile. 'No. But I don't know why you're asking me about Monday night.'

'Because that's when Martin Olofsson was killed in his car. Not far from you, as it happens.' This was Westermark again. It had been decided beforehand that, initially, Westermark would lead the interview and Moberg observe.

'The banker. Yes, I heard. Very distressing.'

'It was. He had strong connections with Ekman & Jonsson.'

'Did he?'

'Oh yes. It was he who recommended that your company got Sydöstra Banken's advertising.'

'I know there's a connection with the bank and Dag Wollstad, so I suppose it was only natural. The agency now has its account there. My contact is Lena Lowén. And I actually bank there too,

151

though I didn't know Olofsson.'

'But he knew you.'

'Really?' Nilsson appeared genuinely surprised.

Westermark suddenly leaned across the table so that the startled Nilsson instinctively jerked backwards. 'He was investigating *you*.'

'I don't understand.' Moberg noted the panic in Nilsson's eyes.

'Your boss, the late lamented Tommy Ekman, thought that you were taking money out of the company. So, he called on his banking friend, the late lamented Martin Olofsson, to pry into your accounting practices.'

'This is absurd,' Nilsson protested.

'Is it? Why would Ekman instigate an investigation if there was nothing untoward?'

'I was recommended by Dag Wollstad himself. I was put in a position of trust. How could I–?'

'Quite easily. Advertising agencies are notorious for their extravagance. Making expensive commercials, client wining and dining... it must be simple to salt a little off here and there. Then a bit more. And so it grows.'

'But why would I? I have a perfectly decent salary.' Nilsson was starting to regain his composure.

Westermark pushed himself away from the table. 'We've been looking into your bank account.'

'You've no right–'

'We've every right when we're investigating a double murder. We've discovered that your account has gone up and down like a fucking yo-yo in recent months.'

'Well, I've had things to spend it on...' Nilsson blustered.

'We know you have. At the trotting track. At the casino. You seem to be a bit of a gambler.'

Nilsson hurriedly glanced around the bare room in search of invisible help. 'It's the odd flutter.'

'It's more than that, isn't it? Why else were you embezzling Ekman & Jonsson?'

Nilsson shook his head vigorously, though his eyes were now fixed on the table.

'You see, this gives you a motive to kill both Tommy Ekman and Martin Olofsson. With both of them out of the way, you're in the clear. No one knows about your financial thieving.'

'You can't possibly be accusing me of...' Nilsson sat with his mouth open in horror. From the body language of his inquisitors, that is exactly what the two policemen were thinking.

Nilsson pulled a handkerchief from his suit jacket pocket and dabbed his forehead. Then he nervously twisted the material in his hands as his accusers sat impassively. Every movement seemed to rubberstamp his guilt.

Nilsson then neatly folded the crumpled handkerchief and replaced it carefully in his pocket. He was back to his neat movements. A man once again in control of his thoughts and feelings. He rallied.

'I had no idea that Tommy was investigating me. Or that the bank was either. How could I have killed anyone if I didn't know what they were up to? I had no motive.'

It was Moberg's turn to lean forward. 'But we know you were stealing from the company.' They didn't know for sure. Or, more to the point, they had no proof.

Nilsson was about to object again before deciding against it. 'Yes. All right. I did. But it was only a temporary measure. I had a personal liquidity problem. I was going to pay it back. Every öre. That's the truth.' This confession didn't seem to be doing the trick. Nilsson became panicky again. 'Please, please, believe me! I had nothing to do with the deaths of Tommy or the banker.'

There were no customers in the gallery when Anita and Hakim arrived. And there was no sign of Stig Gabrielsson.

The supercilious assistant sat at her desk cutting up pieces of art board with a shiny new scalpel. She informed them, without bothering to look up, that Gabrielsson was in Germany, then Denmark, on business. Anita and Hakim exchanged glances. Delivering stolen Munks? was the unspoken question. When was he due back? The next day. Or the day after. She never knew with Stig. Not that she seemed bothered one way or the other.

'Tell him to contact me as soon as he returns,' demanded Anita to a still-bowed head.

Before they left, Anita let Hakim have a brief wander round. When they emerged into the sunshine, he said. 'Some good things and some real rubbish.' Anita didn't bother to ask for an explanation of which was which. She wouldn't know the difference.

They stood in the shade of a plane tree and watched the traffic stream past.

'So, is Gabrielsson over in Germany flogging the stolen paintings?' Anita asked.

'Possibly.'

'I'm not sure if he stole the paintings, but I'm sure he knows something about it. Maybe after the event.'

They began to walk up the street in the direction of the library and Slottsparken.

'Is it worth finding out who actually painted the fake Munk?' Hakim suggested. 'Sometimes, when a well-known artwork is stolen and doesn't reappear again, copies can be sold to collectors who think it's the missing original. Gabrielsson might be up for such a scam. He could make more money selling two or three fakes than he could getting rid of the original.'

'That's a thought. Maybe Gabrielsson was testing out his con on Serneholt. Serneholt is an acknowledged expert. If he fell for it, then anyone would. But he wasn't taken in.'

They came to a halt opposite the library. The old part, visible from the road, resembled a German schloss. It was built of red brick and looked solid and reassuring. The 1997 annex, designed by the Danish architect, Henning Larsen, reminded Anita of a couple of biscuit tins, and was tucked away behind. Some people liked its innovative style, but Anita's taste in architecture was similar to her taste in art – she remained unimpressed.

'One thing still nags me, Hakim. Whoever stole the Lindegrens' painting somehow managed it without breaking in. It could still be that Lindegren's wife left the house unlocked. But, if so, the thief was bloody lucky to stumble across the property that particular night. No, someone got in and out without disturbing Michaela Lindegren. And that disturbs me.'

They crossed the road and wandered into the park.

'It seems strange,' observed Hakim, 'that Gabrielsson implied that Serneholt might have the paintings, and that Serneholt virtually accused Gabrielsson.'

'And neither of them have time for Lindegren. I'm sure Serneholt wasn't happy to have missed out on *Dawn Mood*.'

Hakim stopped abruptly. 'Serneholt said that he had nine Munk paintings. Yet there were only seven on display on that upper floor.'

'You are observant. They might be in another part of the house. Or in another property. He's rich enough. But the other two might be our missing paintings. He certainly can't show them off publicly. I think we'll pay our playboy another visit tomorrow.'

'Blom says we've got enough to hold Nilsson for now. He's admitted to the embezzlement, which gives him the motive to kill both Ekman and Olofsson. He had opportunity in both cases as he doesn't have any alibis – and he could have had access to the crystals that killed Ekman. What Blom wants is positive proof. At the moment, it's all circumstantial.'

Moberg was convinced that they had their man. He was sitting with Westermark and Nordlund in the sports bar on

Östergatan. At that time in the late afternoon, it was almost deserted. Old football matches were being replayed on the TV screens. Moberg needed a cold beer after his confrontation with Blom. Every meeting he had with that woman either wound him up or drove him to drink. High-flying prosecutors from Stockholm were a natural irritant. At least she had allowed them to keep Nilsson in custody for another forty-eight hours.

'Any chance of a confession?' enquired Nordlund. 'That would save some time and trouble.'

'He still denies it, despite the evidence stacking up against him.' answered Westermark as he toyed with his beer bottle.

'Do we know why Nilsson started gambling?' Nordlund asked.

'Do we need a reason?' asked Moberg.

'It just seems strange that such a methodical man, who his wife described as being mean, should suddenly get hooked on gambling. There must be a root cause. Find that out and we might get a better idea of the man and how he operates. It takes a lot to push someone from embezzlement to meticulously planning the murder of two people.'

Moberg drained his glass. 'You may have a point, Henrik. Anyhow, we need to get weaving. I want Nilsson's apartment taken apart, I want someone down at the pharmaceutical company to find out if he got any dodgy stuff from there, and I'm going to grill the little bastard again. He did it. And we're going to bloody well prove it!'

CHAPTER 24

Anita was woken by the thud of *Dagens Nyheter* hitting the floor of her hallway. Five o'clock. The free newspaper was always delivered at 5 o'clock. Normally she wouldn't hear it, but she had been awake for some time. So many things flitted through her mind as she vainly tried to get back to sleep. The thought that Lasse was slipping away from her into the clutches of a girl she didn't like plagued her. The fact that she had poured out her heart about Ewan to some bloody adolescent with a psychology degree and a scrawny goatee hadn't helped. What irked her was that her feelings for Ewan seemed stronger now than before. How the hell was she meant to "move on"? Axelsson was an idiot. The revelations hadn't made her feel better. They had made her feel stupid. Finally, all the permutations at work were confusing. She no longer knew where she stood. Was Moberg conspiring to get rid of her? Was he deliberately undermining her confidence? She was on a case, then off again. She was being sidelined when the department was being stretched to the limit by the murders of two of the city's leading businessmen, not to mention the immigrant shootings, which had got both the ethnic communities and local politicians putting the pressure on. And, as she tossed and turned, there was the spectre of Karl Westermark. Their loathing was mutual yet, deep down, was she flattered that he so obviously wanted her? All these conflicting emotions raged as the early-morning sunlight winked through the chinks in the Venetian blinds. She realised how easy it would be to succumb to Westermark's animal desires – and her own. It was almost a year since she had last had a man. It was much longer since she had actually enjoyed sex. She imagined Westermark would be a good, but selfish, lover. The horror at the direction in which her thoughts were travelling made her get up and head for the kitchen. A strong coffee would dispel the demons of the night.

Skånerost did give her a boost, and the time sat at the kitchen table enabled her to order her thoughts. In the cold light of day, they weren't quite as bad as they had appeared at two in the morning. But only just. *Dagens Nyheter* was full of speculation about the "Malmö Marksman". Mad immigrant hater, hired gun, spurned lover, inter-gang rivalry and even a maverick Mossad agent. Take your pick. The newspapers, as usual, were doing their best to exploit everyone's anxieties. There was also a small piece on the progress the police were making into the death of banker, Martin Olofsson. A spokeswoman had said that they had a significant lead on the case. She knew that this was only the commissioner's attempt to give the press some positive news to deflect the fact that the investigation into the rogue gunman terrorising the city was going nowhere. Whether it really was a "significant lead", she was unsure. Moberg and Westermark seemed to think it was. The trouble was that she didn't know enough about the case to make a real judgement. That in itself was infuriating. She must crack this Munk business quickly and then they would have to involve her in the big investigations: if not Moberg's, then with Larsson on the Marksman case.

She pushed the newspaper away and poured herself a second coffee. The trouble was that she had hit a blank wall. She was pretty sure Gabrielsson was involved, but he was out of the country. Maybe their visit to Serneholt would reveal something. But without a search warrant, she couldn't root around to see if he had the two stolen paintings stashed away somewhere. All the other avenues she and Hakim had looked down had proved to be dead ends. The two thieves with a penchant for stealing works of art in the Skåne County Police records both had alibis. One was in hospital on the night of the Lindegren theft, after falling out of a third-storey apartment building in Halmstad while trying to escape the owner who had returned home to find his house being burgled. The other was dead; he had lost his fight against liver cancer. Unless there was a new kid on the block that they hadn't heard about, then she didn't know where to turn.

An hour and half later she picked up Hakim from the polishus and they made their way out of town to Serneholt's home. Anita couldn't help noticing that Hakim appeared preoccupied, even nervous.

'What's the matter?'

'Nothing,' came the defensive reply.

'Look, I've got a son not much younger than you. I can tell you've something on your mind.'

Hakim ran his hand across his mouth before replying. 'It's daft really. Embarrassing.'

'When it comes to embarrassing, you're talking to the department's queen. Whatever it is, just spit it out.'

'It's my parents.'

Anita stopped the car at a set of traffic lights. She glanced sideways at the young man. 'Your parents? What about them. Are they giving you a hard time over the job?'

'Oh, no. It's just that...' Another awkward pause. The light turned green and Anita's foot gently squeezed the accelerator. 'They want to meet you.'

'Meet me?' she spluttered.

'Yes.'

'Why?' She was gently amused. 'To see that I'm not leading their son astray?'

'Please don't mock me.'

'Sorry. I'm not mocking you, Hakim. I'm just surprised.'

'I think they want to know that I'm doing a good job. That I'm showing you respect and not letting my family down. Living up to their standards.'

Anita grinned at the road ahead. 'Old-fashioned parents. I like that. Of course I'll meet them. When?'

The relief on Hakim's face was obvious. Anita suspected that he had also had a sleepless night worrying about Anita's possible reaction to his rather unusual request.

'After work today. Only if it's convenient,' he added quickly. 'Just for a cup of tea or coffee. You don't have to stay long.'

Anita smiled.

'I'd be delighted to meet your parents.'

'Shit!' Anita wasn't happy when there was no answer after ringing Serneholt's doorbell. She sent Hakim off to ask at the neighbouring house if they knew where Serneholt was. He came back to say that Serneholt had left early that morning to catch a flight to Stockholm. He was due back sometime this evening. The neighbour only knew about it because Serneholt was expecting a delivery and she was going to take it in for him until he returned.

'A pity he didn't give the neighbour his keys. Wouldn't mind an hour by ourselves in there.'

She caught Hakim's disapproving scowl.

'Don't worry. I was only musing. OK. Let's go back to town. I'll ring him tonight and we'll come back tomorrow morning.'

On the way back into the centre of Malmö, Anita pulled the car into a self-service garage area off busy Lundavägen and parked.

'You can drive the car back to the polishus. I've got something to do.'

Hakim looked puzzled. 'What?'

'You have to learn not to question a senior officer's instructions.'

'Sorry.'

Anita got out of the car and Hakim moved over to the driver's side.

'I'll see you when I get back. In the meantime, see if we have anything on Serneholt on file. Handling stolen goods would be a nice start.' She slammed the door shut and watched Hakim manoeuvre back onto the main highway. Then she crossed the road and headed towards the prison.

Nilsson's apartment was modest and neat. It was in an unassuming red-brick block just behind Linnégatan. It was a Limhamn address and that was what probably mattered to Nilsson, concluded Westermark. The block was one of four forming a square that hemmed in a large area of garden. The garden didn't consist of much more than lawn and a hedge running round its perimeter, but it was a place where residents could sit and relax in the sun. There were one or two flowering cherries and a small border on one side full of berberis and hypericum. As Westermark, with Wallen's assistance, poked around the one-bedroomed apartment, he found it difficult to imagine why someone on Nilsson's salary would want to live here. Maybe this was downsizing caused by his financial recklessness.

Westermark glanced through Nilsson's CD collection in the living room. Lots of ABBA and easy listening. He sighed heavily. He had Nilsson down as a seat-at-the-opera type, but there wasn't even a Mozart or a Sibelius. His DVDs were mainly history documentaries, with a few romcoms thrown in. Westermark wandered into the small kitchen and glanced down into the garden below. An old man was sitting on a bench reading a newspaper. A mother was playing with a child of about three. She wasn't attractive enough to keep his attention for more than a moment. He was more interested in calculating how long it would take Nilsson to walk to Martin Olofsson's house in Vikingagatan. He reckoned it wouldn't be more than about ten minutes. Easy to get there, hang around for Olofsson to turn up (though they hadn't found any witnesses yet), kill him, set up the car to make it look like suicide, and then pop back to the apartment. His thought process was disturbed by a call from Wallen in the bedroom next door. 'Karl.'

Wallen was holding up a photograph of a young woman. She was pretty. It wasn't a family shot. The skirt was too short, the pose too provocative and the smile too inviting.

'Found it in his bedside table. Inside a bible.' She turned the photo over. 'Signed. *To Bo. Love Milena.*'

'Any other signs of her in here?'

'No. Nothing in the wardrobe or drawers.'

'Take the photo round to the neighbours. Find out if she visited Nilsson.'

Wallen gazed at the photo. 'Do you think she's the reason that Nilsson took up gambling?'

'We won't find out if you don't go and do as I tell you. Now!' Westermark added sharply. Wallen reddened and scuttled out of the room.

'Police business?'

Anita shook her head. Ewan was mocking her in an affectionate way. The black eye had healed, though he was still as gaunt as the last time she'd seen him.

'I'm glad you came, whatever the reason.'

She wanted to say that she had come to reassure herself that everything was over between them. That the strange love link they had formed no longer existed. She wanted emotional closure so she could get on with her life. Yet, as she sat opposite him in the same room they had talked in before, she knew it was hopeless. She wanted to lean over and kiss him; to hold him close and feel his arms around her.

'I've got a friend.'

'A friend?'

'Yes. Jovan. He's Serbian. He's taken a shine to me and defends me when the other inmates get threatening.' Ewan smirked. 'And he doesn't even want sex for his services. I just think he hates Swedes for putting him in here; and I'm a foreigner, so I must be all right. And he also likes Newcastle United, so we have a bond. Every time he sees me, he puts his thumb up and says "Alan Shearer". I mentioned that I interviewed him once years ago when I covered sport. He believes Shearer must be my mate.'

'I'm pleased someone's looking after you.'

'Oh, I gave him your cigarettes. He says "thank you".'

Anita smiled.

'How are things? Is your career getting back on track after I fucked it up?'

'I didn't know...'

'Word gets round, even in here.'

'It could be better.' She felt herself relaxing. She was half-tempted to have a bitch about Moberg and company but thought better of it. However awful it seemed to her, she knew Ewan would see the funny side of it. Maybe that was the root of his attraction.

'Lasse?'

She spread her hands out in a gesture of despair. 'Lasse. Never have kids! He's not even coming back for midsummer. And then he's spending the summer in Gotland with the dreaded Rebecka.' She found herself confiding her thoughts and frustrations about Lasse and how they were causing her more heartache than her job. She didn't care that it was Ewan who was the recipient of her angst. He was so easy to talk to. He listened patiently.

'He's young,' said Ewan when she had finished. 'We all do things without thinking about other people at that age. He'll come back to you, maybe in a different way from before. But he'll come back.'

'Do you think so?'

Ewan leant across the table and squeezed her hand reassuringly. She let him, and found herself disappointed when he withdrew it again.

'Either he'll realise that Rebecka is a selfish madam and find someone else, or they'll both grow up. I'm sure, deep down, he still appreciates his mum. It's just uncool to acknowledge the fact at the moment.'

Anita felt better.

'So, why did you come?'

She glanced away. 'I must be going.' She stood up.

'Anita. I'm sorry. Sorry for all the problems I've caused you.'

Anita knocked on the door. She felt in her bag and pulled out her snus tin. She threw it across to Ewan, who caught it.

'A present for Jovan.'

Ewan's face lit up with delight.

'I hope you'll come back again.'

'I don't know.' As the door was unlocked she knew she wouldn't be able to keep away.

Moberg now felt he had the information that he needed to pin the murder charges on Bo Nilsson. That's why he was enjoying Nilsson's discomfort on the other side of the table in the interview room. Nilsson had his solicitor at his side, though he didn't seem to have gained much reassurance from his legal representative's presence. Moberg had Nordlund for company. He realised that a combination of Westermark and himself would be unwise. One of them, inevitably, would overstep the mark.

He had a file on the table in front of him. Inside were notes from a meeting he had had half an hour before with Westermark and Wallen. They had come back with some very incriminating information, though Nordlund's visit to Buckley Mellor

Chemicals had been less productive. There was no obvious connection, and it would be difficult to find someone to admit to supplying Nilsson with poisonous substances. He would have to skirt round that suspicion at this stage. Moberg began quietly.

'You've admitted that you took money from Ekman & Jonsson–'

'Only temporarily,' Nilsson interrupted.

Moberg smiled sweetly. 'Only temporarily. However, you must have taken a lot of money over a period of time to warrant Ekman calling in the bank to investigate.'

Moberg waited for a response which never came.

'We know you frequented the casino and the trotting track. Why the sudden gambling? We have it from your former wife that you were a stingy sod. That's why she left you.'

'That's ridiculous. We were just incompatible.'

'It was my good friend here, Inspector Nordlund, who suggested that there must be a reason why a man like you changes the habits of a lifetime.' Moberg flicked open the file in front of him and took out a photograph, which he slowly pushed across the table towards Nilsson. The widening of the eyes and the sweat on the upper lip reassured Moberg that he was closing in on their man. 'Recognise her?'

Nilsson was about to protest when Moberg flipped over the photograph so that both he and his solicitor could see the inscription on the back.

'I take it that you do. Who is Milena?'

'Milena is a friend.'

'I can see that,' Moberg said scornfully.

'I have nothing more to say about her. You had no business going to my apartment.'

'Oh, I think we did. Milena wasn't the only thing we discovered. You said in your statement that you were at home on the night that Martin Olofsson was murdered.'

'I was,' Nilsson said vehemently.

165

'Not according to your neighbour.' Moberg made great play of reading his file notes. 'Göran Brante. He says he ran into you leaving the apartment at half past seven.'

'I was going–'

'And another witness saw you returning just before eleven. She spotted you from her kitchen window as she was making her late-night cocoa. So where were you between half past seven and eleven o'clock?'

Nilsson glanced in panic at his solicitor, who leant over and whispered something in his ear.

'Basically, you lied to us, and now you have no alibi for the second murder. Neither do you have one for when the murder of Tommy Ekman was set up. And we've established you have motives for killing both men.' Moberg looked at Nordlund before playing his ace. He was certain this would get the reaction he was after. 'I think we might have enough evidence to charge you with the murder of Martin Olofsson.'

The solicitor was about to intervene when Nilsson blurted out, 'No, no, I didn't. I couldn't have! I was with Milena on Monday night.'

'And where was this?'

'A small apartment in Segevång. I bought it for her. That's where we...'

'So that's when your money troubles started. Milena what?'

'Milena Tadić.' Nordlund wrote the name down.

'I assume she's a prostitute.'

'No, she's not!' Nilsson answered angrily, before adding in a quieter tone, 'Well, not now.'

'We'd better have Milena in and see what she has to say, however unreliable.'

Nilsson's head sank into his hands.

'She's not here at the moment.'

'Where is she?'

'Montenegro. That's where she's from. Left yesterday. She's

visiting her mother outside Podgorica. I paid...'

'Of course you did. How long is she away for?'

Nilsson was almost weeping. 'A month.'

'How convenient that your alibi is out of the country. You're a betting man, Bo. What are the odds on your story being a load of crap? You were out waiting for Martin Olofsson that night. Inspector Nordlund, I think we have enough to keep herr Nilsson here a bit longer while we find the witness we're after to make his stay permanent.'

CHAPTER 25

It was six o'clock when Anita reached Hakim's parents' apartment. She had decided to walk as she thought the exercise would do her good. It had taken twenty minutes to cross the park and walk past the sprawling hospital and along the first stretch of Ystadvägen. She had hoped that the stroll would enable her to forget about her visit to the prison. It hadn't.

She knew this area reasonably well. It was her side of the railway line from Rosengård, where much of the immigrant population lived, but it was still a very ethnic part of town. It was where she did most of her clothes shopping. There were two big second-hand stores that she enjoyed mooching around. *Myrorna* was on the other side of the street from where she was walking and further along was her favourite, *Emmaus*, which was housed in an old industrial complex. The older she got, the more she found herself buying clothes she liked in the second-hand chain stores rather than in the big retail shops in town. And also she saved money.

The dull apartment block she was heading for was at right angles to the busy main road. It badly needed a lick of paint, there was rubbish clinging to the half-dead bushes on either side of the entrance and graffiti daubed across the walls of the bike shed. She remembered that one of the so-called Malmö Marksman's shootings had taken place round here. Not very comforting for Hakim's parents.

Anita rang the buzzer and waited. A couple of minutes later, a nervous Hakim appeared. As a mother, she could tell that the poor young man was going through agonies. She could imagine Lasse being mortified if she had asked him to bring home his employer to be vetted. Not that that was likely for some time, as she suspected her darling son would find all sorts of imaginative and convenient barriers to taking up paid, full-time employment.

Hakim led her up two flights of stairs, along a corridor and then onto an open-air walkway. A number of apartment blocks surrounded a central garden area. The grass was bare in places. A few ornamental trees, still in blossom, broke up the monotony of the buildings. Loud samba music was belting out of an open window on the other side of the garden. She liked the rhythm of the music but found herself immediately irritated by the volume – she was showing her age. Though the apartments weren't exactly run down, they had a tired feel about them. The residents wouldn't have much in the way of disposable income.

As soon as Anita entered the neat apartment, she was greeted by the unmistakeable figure of Hakim's father. Tall and angular like his son, the only points of difference being the thinning hairline and the thick moustache. This would be Hakim in thirty years' time. He wore a shirt and tie, despite the warm day. He wasn't going to receive guests without showing them the courtesy of dressing smartly. Anita wished she had made more of an effort. Beside him was the bubbly figure of his wife. Her traditional clothes were vibrantly colourful and, despite her chubbiness, she had once been a handsome woman. Anita was surprised that she didn't wear any kind of head scarf.

Hakim's father smiled. It was full of warmth.

'Inspector Sundström, welcome to our home.' He spoke in English. Hakim had warned her that English would be the language of choice rather than Swedish. His mother had found it difficult to learn the tongue of her adopted country despite the many years they had lived there.

'Please, call me Anita.'

'Very well, I am Uday and this is my wife, Amira.'

They shook hands, which made the handing over of Anita's gift of a box of chocolates from the supermarket a rather awkward manoeuvre. Once the preliminaries were concluded, Anita was ushered into the living room. It wasn't very big and had a rather suffocating atmosphere, partly due to an embroidered curtain of deep reds and golds which separated it from the kitchen. Amira noiselessly passed through a gap in the curtain and almost immediately reappeared, accompanied by Hakim's sister, Jazmin, with plates of sweet cakes and small cups of strong Turkish coffee. Jazmin was very western-looking, with her black hair severely shaved either side of her head, helping to accentuate the uncut mop on top. It didn't detract from a pleasant face, which was dominated by fierce, brown eyes. She wore a T-shirt and jeans. Anita could sense her parents' disapproval. All four of the Mirza family sat down rigidly and looked at Anita, who had been given the most comfortable chair. She couldn't work out if she was being scrutinised as a suitable boss for Hakim or if these earnest people felt the need to prove Hakim's worthiness to her. Then Anita realised that she must make the first move and take a cake. Once she did so and remarked how delicious it was, the family relaxed, except for Hakim who was obviously going through purgatory.

'And is Hakim working diligently?' Uday asked. Hakim's eyes rocketed towards the ceiling.

Anita couldn't help herself smiling. 'He hasn't been with us long, but he shows a lot of promise. One day he may make a good detective.' Amira beamed with pleasure.

'Of course, we would not have chosen the police as a profession for our son. However, the young will go their own way these days. In Iraq you quickly learned not to trust the police.'

'I understand.'

'We had hoped that Hakim would become a painter. He has the talent. A wonderful eye. An understanding eye. That's rare.'

Uday pointed at one of a number of paintings on the wall. It was a sparse desert scene with a single white house. The colours evinced the heat and the light. The sky was azure and unbroken. It was very striking. 'I once ran one of the best galleries in Baghdad.'

Uday went on to tell Anita about how good life had been in the Iraqi capital. It had been a great cultural centre, where east and west mixed easily. They had had a large house with a swimming pool. Uday jetted around the world meeting artists, attending exhibitions and selling works. He produced a folder with copies of paintings that he had sold from his gallery. Anita dutifully thumbed through it as Uday continued his story. Then Saddam Hussain had begun first to squeeze then terrorise the intellectual classes, and Uday had taken the decision that it would be better for his family to get out altogether before he disappeared one night, as so many of his friends had done, and was never seen again. It broke their hearts, but neither their resolve nor their faith ever wavered. They left Iraq with virtually nothing. Firstly, they had lived in Rosengård, and now in this apartment, thanks to the money Hakim brought in. Yet the family appeared grateful that Sweden had taken them in, even though they were conscious that many locals now were not so keen on them being here.

'My children are Swedish now, like many others who have sought sanctuary here. Yet a madman wanders the streets attacking us.'

'Yes, Dad, that's enough,' put in Hakim.

'A neighbour of ours was shot at the bus stop round the corner.'

'We're doing our best to capture this man.' Anita wanted to sound reassuring. She knew from gossip at the polishus that the investigation was going nowhere, despite extra personnel being drafted in from other forces around the country.

'The police will never find this person,' pronounced Jazmin. 'They don't want to. They hate us.'

'That's enough, Jazmin,' admonished Amira. 'I am most sorry for Jazmin's rudeness, Anita. Please have another cake.'

'I'm sorry about my sister,' Hakim apologised when he let Anita out of the main door of the apartment block.

'No. It was fine. You have a very nice family.' Hakim looked relieved.

'Jazmin is hot-headed. She's embarrassed that I'm a cop. Her friends rib her about me.' He added with a self-mocking smile, 'I'm not cool.'

'She should talk to Lasse. I'm not cool any longer, either.'

Nordlund could see that Moberg wasn't as happy as he should be after detaining Bo Nilsson. The financial director had almost been in tears as he was taken away. All the way down the corridor he had protested his innocence.

'What's the problem?' the older detective asked.

Moberg pulled a face. 'I misjudged him. I thought when I talked about charging him he would collapse and confess. He did break down but came up with an alibi of sorts; though he'll find difficulty proving it as his whore is away in some eastern-European fleapit. I'm sure Nilsson murdered both men – he had motive, means and opportunity – but we may never be able to prove that he killed Ekman. That was such a clever murder. The use of the gas and the delayed timing makes it all the more difficult for us. If we can't find the evidence that he did it, then it'll become the perfect crime. That'll bug the hell out of me until my dying day.'

'The trouble is,' said Nordlund, 'is that no one at Buckley Mellor Chemicals is going to admit to providing Nilsson with whatever he used, now they know what he wanted it for. They would become an accessory. Anyhow, according to their records, nothing has gone missing.'

Moberg idly picked up his cup of coffee. 'Could Nilsson have got hold of an old container of Zyklon B? Let's check it out.'

'What are we going to do about Milena Tadić?' asked Nordlund.

'We've no extradition treaty with Montenegro. And once she's heard that her sugar daddy has been locked up, I expect she'll never grace our shores again. Anyhow, she'd be regarded as an unreliable witness from the prosecution's point of view. Too much incentive to lie on Nilsson's behalf. And the defence will probably have a job getting her back. But that's their problem.'

'One difficulty we have is placing him in the vicinity of Olofsson's house. And we still haven't got the murder weapon. Sonja Blom won't get the case to court until we tie him in with one or the other.'

Moberg drained the last of his coffee in one gulp and then put the cup down on his desk. 'It's bought us some time. But not much. Can't keep the little shit locked up for very long without formally charging him. Blom will tell us to let him go if we don't find some concrete evidence quickly. The commissioner is now putting pressure on me to tie up these murders because he wants all hands on the "Marksman" case. He's getting serious grief from the mayor's office now that the story's gone international. And the bastards in Stockholm are getting twitchy because it's painting Sweden in a poor light. Politicians make me sick.'

They drew up outside Ingvar Serneholt's house at about quarter past nine. It had rained overnight, freshening up the air, though it hadn't made much impact on the faded green lawns of Serneholt's impressive spread. The sky was a gun-metal grey, promising rain. Serneholt should be expecting them as Anita had managed to get hold of him at about half past nine the night before. He explained that he had been in Stockholm viewing some paintings that he was considering buying. Yet there was no answer when Hakim rang the door bell. Maybe he'd slept in, Hakim suggested. He would hardly be having a swim in this weather.

Anita sent Hakim round to the back of the house. He returned to say that there was no one around but that there were lights on inside. This made Anita angry. She was damned if she was going to waste another journey out here. She tried the door. It was unlocked.

'I'll go in and call out,' announced Anita in response to Hakim's worried frown. 'If lights are on, he must be here somewhere.'

Hakim reluctantly followed her in.

'Hello!' There was no reply.

They walked into the huge living room. Anita called again. Her voice echoed round the space. It was strange that so many lights were on in the morning, despite the grey day. Spotlights glared from the ceiling, and table lamps illuminated the darker corners. Hakim hopped from foot to foot nervously. He was uncomfortable at being party to his boss's illegal entry.

'He must be somewhere,' Anita said, scanning the room. 'He'd be stupid to leave his door unlocked with all this expensive art around.'

She went to the windows and glanced out at the swimming pool. The water wasn't as inviting as it had been on the day they first came. She turned round. 'I'll look about. You pop up the stairs and check that none of his precious Munks are missing.'

Anita went through an open door in the far wall. She found herself in a large dining area with a baronial suite of heavy oak, which sat fourteen. There was no sign of Serneholt. Suddenly she heard Hakim cry out, 'Oh, my God!'

She rushed back into the living room. Hakim was leaning over the gallery balustrade shaking violently. The electric light accentuated his ashen face.

'He's... he's...'

The next moment he was violently sick.

CHAPTER 26

By the time Eva Thulin arrived with the forensics team, Anita had managed to gather her thoughts. Her first reaction on seeing a horror-struck Hakim had been to get him away from the dead body of Ingvar Serneholt. She took him out into the garden and sat him down on the grass. A cop's first death was always a jolting experience at the best of times. But to find a man with his throat cut and his blood spattered everywhere was a real shock. Hakim would eventually get used to it, but at the moment he wasn't going to be much use. Anita had immediately rung the polishus. She re-entered the house and gingerly ascended the spiral steps. Serneholt was slumped on one of the sofas, his head arched back, his mouth gaping as though yelling into the wind. The pose laid bare in gory vermillion the neatly cut throat. The macabre thought struck Anita that the pattern of the blood that striated the black leather sofa resembled one of Pelle Munk's more flamboyant works of art. The blood had dried and was gleaming in the spotlights. Both blood and lights pointed to the conclusion that the murder must have taken place during the night. Certainly after nine thirty, when she had rung Serneholt to arrange this morning's meeting. He was dressed in a casual shirt and trousers, though he had no shoes or socks on. His bulging eyes were gazing at the wall where Munk's painting *Saturday & Sunday* had been. Anita could see that it had been cut out of the frame. Did Serneholt disturb their Munk thief? That might explain the lack of footwear, though he might well be the type to pad about the house in bare feet. Yet he was sitting in a relaxed position. Had he let someone in and then been taken by surprise from behind by his visitor? That might explain the unlocked front door.

Anita didn't touch anything. Eva Thulin would go mad if she did. So she stood and observed. That's what Henrik Nordlund had taught her. If you're first on the scene of a crime, use that precious time to take in as much detail as possible before the circus of forensics and crime-squad detectives wade in and distract you. There was no sign of a drink anywhere. If Serneholt had been expecting a guest, he would probably have offered something. She stared at the blank space where the painting had been. She assumed that as Serneholt had described *Saturday & Sunday* as "stunning", then it must have been one of the main pictures in his Munk collection. So it was worth stealing. Maybe the thief was also the murderer. There may be similarities with the Lindegren break-in. She needed to check. It was interesting that the painting chosen was on traditional canvas and not one of the works on a metal sheet. Easier to transport and hide. Simple enough to put two and two together and come up with the probability that the likely murder weapon was the same instrument that was used to cut the canvas. A scalpel? Eva Thulin could confirm that and also tell her whether the painting was cut out before or after Serneholt's murder. "Before", there would be no traces of blood on the inside edge of the frame. "After", there would be. Even if the perpetrator had wiped the scalpel after the killing, Thulin's technicians and their fancy equipment would still be able to discover some traces. "Before" would point to a burglary and then the thief being disturbed by Serneholt. "After" would probably indicate that Serneholt had let the murderer in. One other thought occurred to her as her eyes flicked from one painting to the next – it wasn't likely that Serneholt had anything to do with the original Munk thefts. When she heard vehicles drawing up outside the house, she made her way down the spiral staircase back into the living room. A counter-thought popped into her head. Was this bloody scene the physical evidence of the falling out of thieves?

While Eva Thulin's team of technicians went about their business, Anita was relieved to see Nordlund come through the door.

'The chief inspector and Karl are busy with Nilsson,' Nordlund explained. Thank God for that! Anita wanted to shout. She quickly explained the situation and left Nordlund to inspect the scene while she went to find the neighbour Hakim had spoken to the day before. Valerie Wigarth was already at the end of Serneholt's drive talking to Hakim, who had regained some semblance of his old self. Wigarth had come out to see what all the fuss was about. Hakim nodded to show Anita that he was all right.

'I know it's awful,' Anita agreed with Wigarth after the latter had expressed her horror that such a thing could happen in such a pleasant and law-abiding neighbourhood. 'However, you can help us by answering a few questions.'

'Of course, of course,' she said, wringing her hands. Anita put Valerie Wigarth down as the sort of woman who would delight in telling her friends what an appalling experience it all was, while enjoying their envy that she was playing such a vital role in the investigation.

'Do you know what time Serneholt returned last night?'

'Exactly. Two minutes past nine. He came round to collect the parcel that was left for him. The one he asked me to look out for. I know the time because I have a clock in the hall.'

Anita glanced over to Wigarth's house, which was a short distance away. It wasn't as big as Serneholt's, though it still oozed prosperity beyond Anita's sphere.

'I know your house isn't that close, but were you aware of any visitors that Serneholt may have had last night?'

'I think he did. I am sure I heard a car pull up.'

'Time?'

'After ten. I'd gone to the kitchen to make a warm milk drink. It helps me sleep, you know. It was definitely after ten. Probably about ten thirty. That's when I usually make my drink.'

'You didn't see the car?'

She shook her head apologetically.

'Did you hear it go?'

She thought for a moment. 'I'm pretty sure I did. Yes, I'm positive. I was in the bathroom at the time. I was getting ready for bed. I didn't think much about it because Ingvar tended to have late visitors. He often has parties, and there are cars everywhere. He had one the other night. More of a night person than a morning one, if you know what I mean.'

'But what time was that?' Anita said, trying to keep the exasperation out of her voice.

'Oh, well, that would have been about quarter past eleven.'

On returning to the murder scene, she caught up with Nordlund and Thulin. Thulin confirmed that the murder could have been committed by a scalpel blade – and that there was evidence of traces of blood on the inside of the frame. 'Whoever had done this was pretty nifty with their weapon of choice,' was Thulin's verdict.

'By the way, the neighbour heard a car arrive about half ten and leave forty-five minutes later. How does that fit in with the time of death?'

'At the moment, I'd put the death between ten and twelve. But we'll need the medical examiner to give us a more precise time.' Thulin looked down at the body and the blood spatters everywhere. 'And I was just opening a tin of ravioli when the call came in.'

Anita came down the staircase with Nordlund. They walked over to the picture windows and looked over the serene water of the swimming pool, achromatised by the heavy cloud cover.

'The chief inspector wants me to front this case.' Anita's features sank into a frown of disappointment. 'Publicly, that's how it has to be. But, as far as I'm concerned, it's your case, Anita.' Anita could have hugged him. She was back in business.

Eva Thulin organised the removal of the body as Nordlund looked on. He then went in search of Anita, who had been checking all the windows and entrances with Hakim. They met in the dining room.

'No signs of a break-in,' reported Anita. 'Just like at Lindegren's home. My guess is that Serneholt let the killer in.'

'Is it your art thief?'

'Looks that way. The likelihood is that they were discussing Serneholt's art collection. That's why they were up in the gallery. Otherwise, if it had been a normal social call, I suspect he would have entertained in the living room.'

'What's your first course of action? I have to tell the chief inspector something when I go back,' Nordlund added with a wry smile.

'After a further look round here, we'll do a house-to-house to see if we can establish if anyone saw the car that came last night. It might not be our murderer. He might have come later. But we do need to identify the visitor. Then I need to discover exactly where Stig Gabrielsson was last night.'

'He's your main suspect?'

'Unfortunately, he's our only one at the moment.'

'All right, I won't get in your way any longer. I'll head back.'

As Nordlund turned to leave, he stopped for a moment. 'Serneholt is another Gustav Adolf fan.'

'What?'

'The painting,' Nordlund said, pointing to a portrait of the whiskered king at the opposite end of the surprisingly formal dining room, which contrasted sharply with the rest of the house. 'Dag Wollstad had one in his home.'

'That's right. I've seen it.'

'Anyway, good luck. And don't forget to report to me first.'

'Don't worry, Henrik. You know me.'

'Exactly!'

There were still a couple of technicians at work when Anita went back up to the scene of the crime. She wanted one last look while Hakim went off to fetch Serneholt's laptop to take back to the polishus. There might be something on it that would give them a clue as to the events which had led to the death of this rich art collector. The motive for the murder seemed plain enough. The missing painting. But why had their thief gone so far? Stealing paintings didn't naturally sit in the same criminal bracket as murdering people. There must have been more at stake – it can't have been a simple burglary that went wrong. The body was now gone, but the blood spatters remained. She gazed at the back-to-back sofas. Serneholt had been sitting relaxed, possibly at ease with his guest. Was he discussing his love of *Saturday & Sunday* when he was attacked? The killer must have leant over from the sofa behind to be at Serneholt's back. Why wasn't he sitting next to him? It seemed more natural if they were discussing the work. Otherwise, the murderer would initially be facing the painting on the opposite wall. Anita looked at the picture's squiggly silver lines, which she could now see were created by the metal showing through the blue paint. It did have an almost hypnotic quality that she hadn't appreciated on first viewing. She had been put off by the pretentious title. *Restore*? *Revolt*? Oh yes, *Reflex*. There was something about the painting that seemed faintly familiar. Of course it was. She had been here before, she chided herself. Yet something was still niggling her as she descended the staircase. Try as she might, she couldn't put her finger on it.

CHAPTER 27

Moberg was feeling increasingly frustrated. Nordlund had reported back about the Serneholt murder. It was another complication. He had told Nordlund that he was to keep on top of the case. He felt nervous letting Anita Sundström anywhere near it. He knew he couldn't remove her from this one as it appeared to be tied up with her ongoing Munk investigation. It just added to the crap flying around an ever-more-paranoid polishus as the murders multiplied. To make things worse, despite the numbers assigned to tracking down the "Malmö Marksman", Larsson's team weren't getting anywhere. The gunman didn't seem to exist. The only grain of satisfaction Moberg could gain from the situation was that at least at his end he had made progress. He was convinced that they had their man. Yet, annoyingly, they couldn't actually place Nilsson at the scene of either crime. They were concentrating mainly on the Olofsson murder as that was going to be, in theory, easier to prove. The only sighting of anyone out of the ordinary around Olofsson's home was a jogger, who had been noticed a couple of times late at night before the murder – and hadn't been spotted since. The jogger wore a hood, so no one could actually say whether the figure was male or female. The only identifying feature was a small, black backpack. And there was no confirmation that he or she had been around on the night of the murder. That's the trouble with working on a case which relies on wealthy people in their

181

fancy houses barricaded behind high walls and hedges. Nobody sees anything. Besides, whoever the jogger was, it can't have been Nilsson. The description was of someone taller.

As for the Ekman murder, Moberg was equally sure that Nilsson had somehow got hold of an old can of Zyklon B. Further discussions with Buckley Mellor Chemicals only reiterated what they had said before, that nothing was missing. Nordlund had talked to the main scientist on site, who claimed that none of the products that they produced at the plant could have been responsible for the manner of death that was described to him. Information from a rather disreputable dealer in Nazi memorabilia in Gothenburg had established that it was still possible to get hold of Zyklon B if you had the money and contacts. According to their police colleagues in Gothenburg, the dealer claimed he had never actually seen a can in real life and certainly had never supplied one to any customer. They were more likely to find the item in Germany or Poland. Westermark and Wallen had spent the day virtually ransacking Nilsson's office, his apartment and that of his "girlfriend", and had found nothing resembling a can of Zyklon B. Forensics had been over each location thoroughly, and couldn't find a trace either.

Moberg sighed and wondered what delights his wife would have waiting on the table for him tonight. He might pick up an Indian carry-out on the way home, just in case she served up those disgusting meatballs she was so proud of. They were always mushy and underdone. At least his other two wives had been able to cook. If she produced something edible, he could eat both. The culinary distraction couldn't quite dislodge the irksome thought that Nilsson wasn't exactly the kind of person who would ferret around Europe finding obscure Nazi poisons. He suspected that it would take time to locate and obtain a can of Zyklon B. And there hadn't been that long between Tommy Ekman instigating the financial investigation into Nilsson's activities and his murder. That murder had needed planning. It didn't sit comfortably. Still, Nilsson had to be their man, and if the only way to get a conviction was to frighten a confession out of him, so be it.

Anita was having a problem trying to find anybody who had seen the car that Valerie Wigarth had heard the night before. Not that witnesses tended to be particularly forthcoming at the best of times. In general, Swedes don't like being disturbed in their own homes, and often have little or no contact with their neighbours. Fortunately, Wigarth had been an exception. Without her, they would have had nothing.

Anita had dropped Hakim at the polishus with Serneholt's computer and told him to head off home. He had had a traumatic day. She only hoped that his mum didn't serve up a tomato-based dish tonight. She had given him instructions to be at work early the following morning to go through police records to see if Serneholt had had any previous brushes with the law. But now her immediate priority was to talk to Stig Gabrielsson. He was in his gallery when she walked in late that afternoon. He didn't look surprised to see her.

'Lost another Munk?' he asked jovially.

'Yes.'

Gabrielsson was taken aback by her answer. 'Really? Which one? Where from?'

'I was hoping you'd be able to tell me.'

'Come on, Inspector, I've been away. And you know that because you called in before. Inga told me.'

'When did you get back?'

'Arrived by train this morning. Haven't had time to steal anything.'

'Where were you last night?'

'Copenhagen.'

'That's only half an hour away. I'm no mathematician, but

by my reckoning you could easily have nipped across to Malmö last night.'

Gabrielsson suddenly lost his good humour. 'Look, what the hell am I meant to have stolen?'

'*Saturday & Sunday.*'

Gabrielsson gave an involuntary whistle.

'That's an important work. Or is Serneholt just pretending it's gone to get you off his back. That would be typical of the creep.'

Anita looked straight at him. 'He's not pretending anything. He's not even pretending to be dead. The thief slit his throat last night.'

Anita found herself sitting inside The Pickwick pub. She was in a corner, nursing a pint of Bombardier. Ewan had said it was good. The bar wasn't full, as many of the early evening customers were in the street, gathered round the wooden tables that hugged the outside wall. The hanging baskets full of petunias and lobelia swayed in the slight breeze. Despite the warm summer evening, Anita was happy to be inside. She was enjoying listening to the banter, both in Swedish and English, from the diverse, multinational clientele which frequented the popular hostelry. She had also ordered some food. It would save her having to worry about making something when she got home. This wasn't really a matter of soaking up the atmosphere of Ewan's world; more an excuse not to go back to what was becoming an increasingly lonely apartment. After her last conversation with Lasse, the apartment had suddenly seemed less like his home. She knew she was being stupid and maudlin to think like that. It was still full of his things. They were solid reminders of his physical presence, but somehow she felt that he'd moved out, both mentally and emotionally. Anita was fighting the voices in her head which were telling her that her son was gone. She had been deserted.

'Your fish and chips,' a pleasant young man said in English, and put down a plate in front of her. 'Anything else I can get you?'

'No thanks.'

The interruption allowed her to refocus her thoughts on more immediate matters. After her chat with Gabrielsson, she had returned to the polishus and gone over with Nordlund what they knew of events surrounding Serneholt's murder. At least they had the late-night visitor. The odds were on the murderer being the Munk art thief. And she had Gabrielsson, too. His alibi sounded flimsy. He was only half an hour away from Malmö by train. He could then have driven out to Serneholt's, killed him, stolen the painting and returned to Copenhagen. He claimed that he had had a meeting in the early evening, then went down to the bars in Nyhavn and ended up having a meal by himself. Spent the night in a friend's apartment – the friend was away. Basically, he couldn't prove any of it, though he reckoned that the attractive waiter who served him would remember him. He had left a hefty tip – his trip to Germany had been lucrative. Anita was going to head over to Copenhagen first thing in the morning to check Gabrielsson's story and, on her return, Nordlund suggested that they run through all the evidence. By then they should have the forensics and initial medical examiner's report.

She took another sip of beer. It wasn't bad. She had developed a taste for British beer during her year in London with the Met. Then she heard a raucous laugh. She recognised the wild-haired Scotsman whom Ewan had befriended. Alex was greeting a couple of men sitting on stools at the bar. As she watched him shake hands and joke, she suddenly wished Ewan was with her.

The voice had sounded angry. It still reverberated around his head. He was happy to obey, and he had known where he would strike next. He had planned it in advance because he knew that a lot of foreigners shopped in the area. He slipped through the wire-mesh gate. This side of the complex was surrounded by a huge fence. There were a number of cars parked near the gate. Beyond was what may once have been a large industrial site. He didn't know what it had been before because he didn't know Malmö that well. The huge metal building immediately in front of him was the rear section of the supermarket. Even at this time of the evening, there was a lorry unloading produce. Everyone involved in the operation had a swarthy skin. This was definitely the right place to be. They were all a possible target, but this time he was determined to create more of an impact. It was the shoppers he was after.

Adjoining the back of the supermarket and the building next to it was a low-slung metal roof, supported by tall posts painted in a garish yellow. Under its shelter were more parked cars. Beyond was a second-hand clothes shop and an Allsorts outlet. As he waited, he could hear the traffic on busy Ystadvägen coming from the other side of Allsorts. In front of him there was another main road. Lantmannagatan met Ystadvägen at a major junction at the extremity of this group of buildings. He would hardly call it a retail complex. Too shabby for that. He had thought that he would be able to escape over Lantmannagatan and disappear into the mass of apartment blocks on the other side of Ystadvägen. But he had dismissed this idea as the road was too wide and he would have to cross an open area beyond, between a school and the apartments, before reaching cover. He would return the way he had come. He'd melt into the side streets once he was across the car park.

His first plan had been an audacious swoop into the supermarket itself and to take out a number of the shoppers. That would make the front pages around the world. But he decided it was too risky. His work must continue. The second-hand clothes shop was closed, so no one would come in behind him. *The roof cast a long shadow at this time of day, so he could hide behind one of the parked cars and pick off a couple of people coming out of the supermarket. He took out his gun, held it by his side and waited for possible targets.*

It could have been anyone. There was hardly what he would have called a native Swede in sight. It was a young couple who took his fancy. He was tall and wore a dark T-shirt and jeans. She had long black hair and a green top with the supermarket logo. She must be one of the girls who worked on the tills, going home after her shift. They each carried bulging plastic bags. Kill them now and they wouldn't be able to produce more of their kind. He balanced his hands on the top of the car roof and took aim. The couple seemed lost in their own thoughts as they ambled towards him, oblivious to their fate. This would soothe the fevered voice.

CHAPTER 28

It didn't take Anita long to walk to the new Triangeln underground. It was one of the two new stations built underneath the city to take the line from Copenhagen through to Malmö Central. It had caused disruption for years, and only cut a few minutes off the old journey time. Many thought it a waste of public money. Anita rather liked it. Triangeln had two entrances, and she approached the one nearest Möllevången. Even at that time in the morning, there was a forest of bicycles near the station entrance. Many were parked haphazardly, some had wheels or pedals missing – a security precaution. They were tightly packed and, not being a cyclist herself, Anita wondered how some of the bikes could be disentangled. The entrance itself, she mused, had an appropriate shape. It looked like an enormous, aerodynamic cycling helmet. Inside, the engineers had dug deep, and it took three separate escalators to reach the cavernous platform. It was an extraordinary space – like a vast cathedral nave with a gigantic curved roof. In the centre, instead of an aisle, was a long platform, with sturdy concrete pillars, which seemed to stretch into infinity. Lights, softer than neon, mesmeric in their different hues, blinked, sometimes rhythmically, sometimes randomly, in parallel lines along the grey expanse of the wall on the other side of the track. Free art for the commuters interested enough to work out its significance. It was like no other underground station she had ever been to. She had got used to the old-fashioned stuffiness and claustrophobic environs of the London tube during her time at the Met. Triangeln was the antithesis; a cold, awesome, subterranean temple to transport, and Anita loved it. Down here she could escape the Malmö landmark that defined her life. The Turning Torso taunted her from every part of the city. Its fifty-four storeys of white Rubik's cube dominated the townscape and oversaw every aspect of city living – and was a constant reminder of what she had done. In the depths of Triangeln station, she could pretend it didn't exist.

The Copenhagen-bound train slipped in three minutes late. The new route hadn't improved the service's timekeeping. Commuters and holidaymakers headed for the airport converged on the open doors and pushed their way on board. Anita managed to find a seat. The carriage was full. Many in Malmö worked in Copenhagen. A lot were Danes who found housing cheaper on the Swedish side but still earned their living in the Danish capital. Anita picked up a free *Metro* newspaper. The killing of a young couple last night had taken place early enough to make the front pages of all the local papers. It was a mindless, cold-blooded attack. She read on. It sounded as though it was outside the second-hand clothes shop she frequented. She knew the supermarket well, too, as it had a wonderful selection of fruit and vegetables. She always bought dates, figs and other exotic indulgences from there whenever she was in the area. It was also uncomfortably close to where Hakim and his family lived. She hoped the Mirzas hadn't been shopping there at the time. It was their nearest supermarket and catered for those from the Middle East. She was glad not to be in the polishus this morning because she knew there would be pandemonium. The commissioner would be panicking, and the politicians would be shouting for immediate action in the face of the press coverage that was elevating the "Malmö Marksman" to mythical status.

The train sped over the Öresund Bridge before diving down into a tunnel below sea level and coming to a halt beneath Kastrup Airport. All the heavy luggage disappeared as the holidaymakers disgorged onto the platform. Danes returning from foreign climes took their place and the carriage filled up again. After her investigation was over, she would treat herself to a holiday in the sun. Greece or Italy. Maybe she could persuade Lasse to come without Rebecka. Some hope! Of course, now she had a murder on her hands, it might go on for ages. At least Moberg would take more interest in the case now instead of bawling her out all the time because she couldn't find the art thief. So much hinged on this trip to Copenhagen. She had taken a photo of Gabrielsson on her mobile phone to show to the staff at the restaurant he claimed he ate at. He certainly wasn't acting like a man who had committed a particularly gruesome murder. And if he did have an alibi, then she didn't know where to turn next.

Nyhavn was already quite busy with morning coffee-drinkers. Overlooking the water, this had once been a rough quayside area with bars bursting with sailors, prostitutes and those looking for a wild time and a fight to finish off the evening. Now it was all smart restaurants and cafés. The old clientele had long been banished, and now the prosperous locals mingled with the tourists at the waterfront tables. Anita found the restaurant where Gabrielsson had supposedly dined. Outside were a couple of tourists drinking in the sights and sounds of a new Copenhagen day. At another table, a young businessman was engrossed in his financial paper. Anita sat down and waited to be served. She might as well have a relaxing coffee while she worked.

A girl came out to take her order. When she returned, Anita asked in Danish, 'Were you working two nights ago?'

She smiled and shook her head. 'No. I only do mornings. But Franco was.' She glanced at her watch. 'He's due in about half an hour.'

Anita was on her second coffee when Franco turned up in a leather jacket over his waiter's shirt and waistcoat. Her heart sank. He had Mediterranean good looks accentuated with sexy stubble. If he was the one who had taken Gabrielsson's eye, then she had no suspects left. The girl sent Franco out to see Anita as soon as he had taken his jacket off. He greeted her with a perfect set of white teeth. He would be wasted on Gabrielsson, Anita thought as she forced herself to concentrate on the reason for her visit.

'Can I help you, madam?' he said in poor Danish.

'I believe you were working here two nights ago,' she replied in English. He grinned gratefully.

'Yes.'

Anita took out her phone and brought up Stig Gabrielsson's photo. 'Was this man in that night?'

Franco screwed up his eyes. Then he nodded slowly. 'Si. Yes.'

'Are you sure?'

'He gave me a big tip! He seemed to like me.' She could see why.

'Do you know what time he left?'

Franco raised his hands dramatically. 'It must be, oh, about eleven. Maybe after.' Then he suddenly slapped the top of his forehead with the palm of his hand. 'He paid by card. We will have a record of the time on his bill.'

'That was a waste of time. But the coffees were nice.' Anita was describing her trip to Copenhagen to Nordlund, Hakim, Wallen and Eva Thulin. They were in one of the conference rooms. Nordlund was letting Anita chair the meeting. 'The waiter identified Gabrielsson, and the copy of the bill I have here,' she said, waving a small piece of paper, 'confirms that he paid for his meal at 23.17. What time do you estimate the murder took place, Eva?'

'Now we reckon between ten thirty and midnight at the latest.'

'Given that it would have taken him fifteen minutes to walk to the station then catch a train over the bridge, there's no way he'd get to Serneholt's before midnight. So that rules him out, though I still think he may have a connection with the first two thefts. But I doubt he'd touch *Saturday & Sunday* with a bargepole, given how it's been acquired.'

'Any sightings of the car that went to Serneholt's?'

'Nothing,' said Wallen, who had been drafted in to help while Moberg and Westermark were trying unsuccessfully to bully a confession out of Nilsson. His lawyer had advised him not to answer any more of their questions and the interview had been terminated when Moberg lost his temper and had become threatening.

'What can you tell us about the murder, Eva?'

'Neatly done. The assailant got behind Serneholt. Probably kneeling on the other sofa. His throat was sliced right to left, which makes me think that the killer is left-handed. The blood traces on the inside of the frame indicate that the painting must have been cut out after the murder.'

'Would the murderer be covered in blood?' asked Wallen.

'Not too much. Probably the left arm, but the assailant was behind his victim, so most of the blood went forwards and sideways.'

'I was just thinking that there might be some in the murderer's car, if he'd come in one.'

'We'd better go over Gabrielsson's car, just in case,' said Anita. 'OK, Hakim, any luck with Ingvar Serneholt's background?'

Hakim got out a notebook and scrutinised his scribblings. 'His family money came from his father, who was high up in the Swedish Match empire. They made a fortune in the days when people lit fires and smoked cigarettes.'

'You mean when Henrik was young!' laughed Anita. 'Sorry, carry on.'

Hakim returned to his notes. 'Serneholt's father left his money to Ingvar. As an only child, he got the lot. He did work briefly as an accountant when his father was alive, but as soon as he died he left. He worked in an art auction house in Stockholm for about a year, then seems not to have worked since. Moved down to Malmö fifteen years ago. He's appeared in the papers from time to time, usually in the gossip columns. A lot of lady friends. Went out with the actress Maria Broman for a couple of years. As for breaking the law, he has a couple of speeding fines and he was done for possession of cannabis in 1999. And he was once attacked in a club here in Malmö by a cuckolded husband. Serneholt had to go to hospital but didn't press charges.'

'Well done, Hakim. Does the husband have a name?'

'Ingelin. Victor Ingelin.'

'When was it?'

'Two years ago.'

'Let's check him out. We need to talk to Serneholt's set. It might throw up some art-world connections. Anything else?'

There was silence around the table. Then Nordlund spoke. 'I suppose the key thing to ask is whether the murderer was after the painting and killed Serneholt because he was there, or whether the murderer was after Serneholt and wants us to think that he was killed for the painting.'

After the others left, Anita and Nordlund had a brief chat. She wanted his approval of her approach. The senior detective thought she was handling the situation well so far, but she would find it more testing the longer the investigation went on. And, as there were no immediate suspects, they could be in for a long haul.

'Do you think the Ekman and Olofsson case will be wound up soon?' asked Anita, partly out of curiosity and partly because she wanted Westermark out of the way for as long as possible.

'The chief inspector seems convinced that Nilsson is the perpetrator.'

'But what do *you* think?'

'All the evidence that we have points in his direction.'

Anita picked up the reticence in his voice. 'But?'

Nordlund composed his thoughts before he spoke. 'It's the way that the two men were killed that intrigues me. The first was very clever and well thought out. Where he got the idea from I haven't a clue. But the Olofsson murder – why bash him over the head and then make it look like suicide when the killer must have known that it would take us five minutes to realise it wasn't? Very different MOs.'

'Except they both involved gassing of some sort.'

'Exactly. Very German. The chief inspector even thinks that Zyklon B may have been used. To me, the killer is being very deliberate, giving us a message. Or sending someone else a message.'

'That echoes my thoughts when I first came across Olofsson's body.'

'If it's not Nilsson, have we got a mad neo-Nazi running around?' Nordlund wondered.

'With the "Malmö Marksman" picking off immigrants, that's the last thing we need.'

Nordlund pulled a face in agreement. 'Anyhow, must get on. Oh, just one other thing. You've been in Martin Olofsson's house?'

'Yes. Spoke to his wife.'

'There weren't any paintings or images of Gustav Adolf anywhere?'

'Not that I remember. Why?'

Nordlund shook his head. 'It's nothing.'

It was lunchtime, and Anita was alone in her office checking through Serneholt's police record to see if anything jumped out at her. She scooped the last of her Turkish yogurt from the pot as she stared at the screen. There wasn't anything. The door opened and she assumed it was Hakim coming back with something to eat. But it was Karl Westermark standing in front of her.

'You've got your own little murder now, Anita. Well, Nordlund has.'

Anita ignored him. She dropped the yogurt pot in the bin.

'Getting anywhere?'

She had to look at him to answer. 'Ask Henrik Nordlund. As you say, he's in charge.'

'No need to be like that. I'm just being friendly.'

'I'd have thought you'd be too busy cracking your case to bother coming in here.'

'Anita, I came in here to ask you out for a drink after work.'

'Karl, it's a waste of time. I don't want to have a drink with you.'

Instead of taking the hint, Westermark sat down on the chair in front of her desk.

'I thought it would be a good chance to put any previous misunderstandings behind us. There's so much for us to talk about.'

'I can't think of a single thing.'

He gave a thoughtful frown. 'I can think of something. How about your visits to Ewan Strachan in prison?'

This gave Anita a jolt. How had Westermark found out?

'Of course, I could have a drink with the chief inspector instead and discuss it with him.'

Anita felt a surge of panic. A bead of sweat trickled down her back. Ewan was private. He was a hidden part of her life. Questions would be asked as to why she had gone there. The prison authorities would report that it had been on "police business". What police business? Her standing in the department was already at rock bottom. Stories circulating that she was seeing Strachan, the convicted murderer, would call into question her motives behind the shooting of Mick Roslyn at the top of the Turning Torso. They would wonder whether she had been trying to protect her lover all along. Given the spin someone like Westermark would put on the story, her career as a detective would be finished. And the bastard knew it.

'How about that place on Eric Dahlbecksgatan? Where the department went for a drink last Christmas. About seven?'

Westermark smiled as he left.

CHAPTER 29

Anita cradled a glass of white wine as she waited nervously. She was at one of the tables that spilled onto the pavement whenever the weather justified it. It was just warm enough to be able to sit outside, though in an hour it might be too cold. Hopefully, she would be back in her apartment by then. She had made sure that she got to the bar first so that she could choose her ground. It was darker inside, and she didn't want Westermark to get any ideas.

The afternoon had been wasted wondering how she was going to deal with a randy Westermark who had discovered her guilty secret. Somehow, she was going to have to provide an explanation for her prison visits, or Westermark would make the most of the situation. He would give her a simple choice – lose her career or sleep with him. She had been distracted when Hakim reported that Victor Ingelin, the man who attacked Ingvar Serneholt in a fit of understandable jealousy, was up north visiting family. He had been away from Malmö since before the murder, so that was a dead end.

'You're looking sexy tonight.'

Anita squinted, the evening sun glinting on her glasses. Westermark had made an effort and was wearing a new shirt and trousers. He stank of some aftershave that made Anita wince. She was glad that she had just come in the clothes she had put on that morning. Her jeans needed washing, but they weren't putting Westermark off. His leer made her self-conscious about the close-fitting, blue, v-necked T-shirt she was wearing. Too much cleavage? She wished she'd put on a burka.

'Are you sure you want to sit out here?'

'It's safer.'

He laughed and pointed to her drink. 'Another?' Anita shook her head.

By the time Westermark sat down opposite her with his bottle of beer, she had decided what to say about Ewan. He took her off guard when he mentioned his case.

'We're struggling with Nilsson. Little prick won't crack. Circumstantial evidence isn't good enough for that bitch Blom. It's driving Moberg demented.'

'And you?'

'Not totally convinced. I made the connection between Ekman and Olofsson, and then tied in Nilsson, but something's not right.'

Anita was surprised that Westermark was admitting to having misgivings. He was an arrogant man with few self-doubts. There was no denying that he was more than a competent detective. After all, it was he who had reckoned that Ewan was guilty of Malin Lovgren's murder right from the beginning. His problem was that he too often thought with his balls.

'Maybe the two murders are connected but you've got the wrong link.' Anita hadn't given it much thought since being pushed off the case, but Nordlund had filled her in on some of the Ekman details that had been denied to her. There were still unanswered questions from her own dealings with the Olofsson killing. Maybe his "golfing" trips and Kristina Ekman's lie about Olofsson's visit to Wollstad's estate were more significant than Moberg had thought.

'Talking of the wrong link, how's the boyfriend? The unpleasant sneer had returned.

'How did you know?'

'I asked your Arab sidekick where you were the other day. He said he'd dropped you off on Lundavägen. You don't have to be a detective to work out where you were heading, but it helps. I checked things out and I discovered it was your second recent visit and that you requested to see a prisoner called Ewan Strachan.' He was very pleased with himself.

'There is a reason for it.'

'I'm not interested. I just want to make sure that news of your secret assignations doesn't go any further. Come back to my place tonight and it won't. You know you want to, really.' Anita just stared at him. 'We'd make great love.'

'Do you have to blackmail women to get them into the sack?'

Westermark was totally unabashed. 'Not usually. But you've been a harder nut to crack. You can't resist forever. And afterwards, I'm sure it would improve our working relationship.'

'Well, I'm afraid you're going to have to remain disappointed... and frustrated. There's a good reason for visiting Strachan.'

Westermark raised a sceptical eyebrow. She took an inward gulp of air before diving into her story.

'If you remember, Strachan and Roslyn fell out over a girl at Durham University. She supposedly committed suicide, but Gazzard, the British inspector, thought that one of them had actually pushed her off the cathedral tower. I was trying find out the truth so that I could put Gazzard out of his misery.'

She could see the flicker of uncertainty in his eyes. Was he falling for her lie? Despite the need to get Westermark off her back, she couldn't help feeling guilty about betraying Ewan. But she could never ever admit to anyone, outside the psychologist's consulting room, her love for him.

'And did he tell you? He seems to make a habit of confessing to you,' he added nastily. Anita knew then that she had won.

'No. Maybe it was suicide all along.'

Westermark simply grunted.

'Sorry, Karl, but I'll have to turn down your kind offer.' She drained her glass in an unladylike manner and stood up. 'We mustn't do this again sometime.' She left him scowling.

The dream was so weird that it woke Anita up. Even though she couldn't remember the content, it had left her unsettled. She glanced at the digital bedside clock. The fluorescent red 4:03 looked at her accusingly, as though she had no right to be awake at such an hour. She knew that going back to sleep was impossible. Of all the things that were flashing through her mind as she got up and went to the kitchen, it was Henrik Nordlund's question about Gustav Adolf that came to the forefront. She hadn't noticed any representations of the famous Swedish king in Olofsson's house, but there had been something. Now what was it? She put a small pan of water on the hob. It was too early for coffee. Tea was more soothing at this hour. She popped an Earl Grey teabag into a mug. Then the dream came back to her. She had been on the verge of making love, and she had had an awful feeling that it was with Westermark. She shuddered and desperately pushed the image out of her mind. Fortunately, it was quickly replaced by the realisation that there had been a Gustav Adolf connection with Martin Olofsson. The DVD. The barbarous British bishop. As she poured the boiling water into the mug, she tried to dredge up the reference. She had been so disgusted by Bishop Green's general message of hatred that she hadn't taken in specific references. But there was definitely something about Gustav Adolf, or the name he was known by in Britain, Gustavus Adolfus.

Anita drank her tea quickly, got dressed and was in her car by twenty-five past four. The streets on the way to the polishus were empty, the only traffic being a couple of clanking dustcarts. She parked in the police car park and made her way into headquarters. Two weary cops passed her with barely a glance.

She didn't recognise them and assumed they were part of the extra police brought in from other forces to find the "Malmö Marksman". She knew that everybody was on high alert, as it was now suspected that the killer was a professional. The young couple who had been murdered outside the supermarket had both been shot cleanly in the forehead. The gunman had to be good to hit two people so quickly and so accurately.

Anita reached her office and switched her computer on. While it was galvanising itself into action, she slipped along the corridor to the coffee machine and got a cup. On her return, she took the *Before the Frost* DVD out of her desk drawer and slipped it into the machine. Bishop Green came on the screen and started speaking. She tried to remember where the Gustav Adolf reference came. It wasn't at the beginning. She started to flick through. Then she remembered. It was at the end. She flicked on and then stopped and watched. This was the bit:

'But before that can become a reality, you are at the forefront of a battle to cleanse Swedish society of the alien races that infest your streets. Your hero, Gustavus Adolphus, said: "War is not a river, or a lake, but an ocean of all that is evil." Your war is here and now. Take courage, for the one true God is with you in your work.'

Well, there it was. But what was the significance? What was it that troubled Henrik Nordlund? Serneholt had a painting of the king. So did Dag Wollstad. Half Sweden probably had some reference to Gustav Adolf in their homes. Olofsson had this message in his briefcase. And Nordlund had mentioned to her the empty file on Ekman's computer entitled *Sjätte November*, which was the date of Gustav Adolf's Day. So what?

Anita drank her coffee pensively. She should have stayed at home and gone back to bed. Now she was wide awake in the office at five in the morning. She idly flicked through the disc again and then replayed the Gustav Adolf reference. Nothing. She was about to unload the disc when she suddenly sat bolt upright. Slowly she put down her coffee cup. She stared at the screen. She flicked the image back then freeze-framed it. There is was – the thing that she hadn't been able to put her finger on.

'Oh, my God,' she whispered under her breath. 'This is going to turn everything upside down.'

CHAPTER 30

Anita was nervous. She had downloaded the Bishop's speech onto her computer so that she could show it on the big smartboard in the meeting room. After making her discovery, she had gone for a long walk around the streets of the city centre so she could get things straight in her mind. She passed the early risers, the office cleaners and the daybreak commuters, before calling into a small café when it opened at six. She sat down and called Nordlund. Fortunately, she hadn't woken him, and she briefly explained what had happened. She could hear the excitement in his reaction to her news. He would be in the polishus by seven and they could discuss what to do next. Moberg wasn't going to be pleased, so Nordlund suggested that they prepare thoroughly before breaking the news. As Anita fiddled with her pile of notes, she knew Moberg's biggest problem would be why she hadn't reported the Bishop's disc before, or handed it in to Westermark with the other contents of Olofsson's briefcase. God knows what Westermark's reaction would be, particularly after his unsuccessful attempt to blackmail her into slipping in between his sheets.

When the meeting started, Moberg, Nordlund, Westermark, Wallen and Hakim were all seated round the table. Westermark's stare was hostile. Nordlund, who as far as Moberg was concerned was handling the Serneholt case, opened the proceedings.

'In the course of our investigation into the murder of Ingvar

Serneholt, we've discovered a link with Martin Olofsson which might be hugely significant. I think the best way to start is for Anita to show you a DVD of a speech by a British bishop called Green.'

'Where's this DVD come from?' Moberg asked.

Anita held up the *Before the Frost* DVD cover. 'It was in this.'

'But where did that come from?' Westermark was immediately suspicious as he thought there had only been one DVD in Olofsson's briefcase – a James Bond movie.

Anita paused. 'It was in Olofsson's briefcase.'

'What the hell are you doing with it?' Westermark exploded.

'I thought it was an ordinary programme. I hadn't seen it before. It was only when I played it, I realised that it was something different.' There was a kernel of truth in her explanation.

'This is fucking outrageous–'

'That's enough, Karl! I'll sort it out afterwards,' said Moberg ominously. 'Let's just bloody well get on with this.'

Anita played the speech to the assembled detectives. They watched in amazement as the clergyman poured forth his epistle of hatred. When it stopped, the room was in silence. This was broken by Westermark.

'He has a point.'

Before Anita had a chance to angrily jump in – she had seen Hakim's discomfort as the film was being screened – Moberg turned to Westermark.

'Don't ever say anything like that in my hearing again. It's people like that clerical twat that make our job even harder.' He looked across to Anita. 'Carry on.'

'We'll go into what he said later. Henrik's got some views on that. But I want you to look closely at this.' She flicked back the film and then freeze-framed the image. The Bishop was sitting on a chair.

'And?' said Moberg.

'I want you to look carefully at the top left-hand corner. Above his head. Can you see? It's the bottom of a painting.'

'It just looks like squiggles to me,' said Wallen.

'Exactly. Squiggly silver lines against a blue background.' Anita enlarged the corner of the painting on the smartboard screen. 'The painting is called *Reflex* and it's by Pelle Munk. This hangs in the gallery section of Ingvar Serneholt's house. This film must have been shot there. So why has Martin Olofsson got a copy of a film of Bishop Green? This is a call to arms to people with extreme right-wing views. Is there anything in your investigations that point to Olofsson's political leanings?'

'No,' answered Moberg. 'This could all be coincidence.'

'But it could mean that Serneholt's murder wasn't anything to do with stealing a Munk painting. By pinching the artwork, maybe the murderer is deliberately steering us in the wrong direction. Whatever, we have a link between Olofsson and Serneholt.'

Moberg turned his large frame so that he was facing Nordlund. 'What do you think, Henrik?'

'The views expressed by Bishop Green suddenly throw a political angle into our investigations. I mentioned at the beginning that I thought that the manner in which Ekman and Olofsson were killed was significant.'

'You mean the gassings?'

'Yes. Ekman was gassed in a shower. Olofsson was found dead in a car full of fumes. We know that he was actually killed by a blow to the head. The gas was a statement. Zyklon B and carbon monoxide were both used by the Nazis in the concentration camps to obliterate the Jews. Serneholt had his throat cut. The Nazis were happy to kill that way too. OK, that's pretty tenuous, but what if all these men are connected by political views and that the murderer is someone of diametrically opposed opinions who's reeking revenge on people he sees as racist, fascists; what you will?'

'But we have no proof that Ekman was like that,' responded Moberg.

'No. But there's another strange connection with the three of them. Gustav Adolf.'

'Oh, come on, Henrik. What's some ancient monarch got to do with things? We need evidence, not theory. I can see where you're going with this, though. If you're right, and Serneholt's murder is somehow connected to the other two, then Nilsson's in the clear because we were looking after him downstairs when the crime was committed. I'm still not convinced there's a connection to Ekman but I'm prepared to keep an open mind. Do we know where this bishop is?'

'We're trying to find out,' answered Anita. 'But it's highly unlikely that he's still in Sweden.'

'We need to look into the backgrounds of all three victims and see if there's a right-wing slant to all this. And Nilsson too. Well, one thing's for sure: it's certainly not the work of the "Malmo Marksman", because his victims are all on the other side.'

'At least we've made a start with the chief inspector.'

Anita had to agree with Nordlund, though she wasn't sure that they would get Moberg totally on board. He certainly wasn't going to lump the cases into one investigation. The others had left; except Hakim, who was helping sort out the computer. He was the one who had set it up for her before the meeting. Youth had its uses.

'Inspector Nordlund, you mentioned Gustav Adolf,' said Hakim as he clicked the laptop lid shut. 'So did that horrible priest, though he called him Gustavus Adolphus. I don't know much about him except for his name day and the square in the centre of town.'

'Don't schools teach any Swedish history anymore?' Anita sighed.

'Actually the square in town is named after a different Gustav Adolf. Gustav the Fourth. That's because he ruled the country from Malmö briefly, before he was deposed. No, our Gustav Adolf – Gustav the Second – was Sweden's most famous monarch, coming to the throne in 1611 at the age of seventeen. After his death, he became known as Gustav Adolf the Great. The rest of Europe knows him by the Latinised name, Gustavus Adolphus. He was a masterful soldier and led Sweden to military supremacy during what was known as the Thirty Years' War.' Anita was amused to see Nordlund become so animated. This was a side of his character she hadn't seen before. 'He had many military successes, like the Battle of Breitenfeld, which saw a victory for a protestant alliance over the German Roman Catholics. Through that he changed the political, as well as the religious, balance of power in Europe. He was poised to become a truly great European leader when he was killed on November 6th at the Battle of Lützen in 1632.'

'That's why we have "Sjätte November", Gustav Adolf's Day,' put in Anita. 'Commemorates his death.'

'He created a Swedish empire and heralded a golden age. One that Dag Wollstad looks back on fondly.'

'I saw the portrait at his place,' said Anita.

'Gustav Adolf's cropped up everywhere. Serneholt has a painting of him, too, and the Bishop made a pointed reference to him in his speech, which we believe now, thanks to you, was filmed at Serneholt's.'

'I've just thought,' interrupted Anita. 'There's another Gustav Adolf reference. It was staring me in the face all along. Olofsson's briefcase. The combination was 061132. It didn't occur to me before, but, as you say, that's the date that Gustav Adolf died in battle.'

'And we found an empty folder on Tommy Ekman's computer entitled *Sjätte November*.'

'There's something I must get. Something I found on Ingvar

Serneholt's computer.' Hakim hurried out of the room.

'He's keen,' Nordlund remarked.

'I wish I could tap into his enthusiasm. Mine's run out.'

'This case will reignite it.' Nordlund gave her paternal pat on the shoulder.

When Hakim came back into the room five minutes later, he had a piece of paper in his hand.

'I only came across this before the meeting. Didn't mean anything until you mentioned "Sjätte November". It might be nothing, but it was in a file just sitting on his desktop.'

'It has the same name as Ekman's file,' noted Nordlund.

Hakim laid the sheet of paper on the table, and Anita and Nordlund leant over to look at it more carefully.

Sjätte November Gruppen – April 16th

> *DW*
> *AG*
> *IS*
> *MO*
> *LP*
> *TE*

'Is this all?' Anita asked.

'Yeah. I clicked on "details" and it was last opened the day before, on April 15th this year. It wasn't hidden or anything.'

Nordlund pointed to the *IS*. 'As it's on his computer, I assume that that stands for Ingvar Serneholt himself.'

'There's *MO*. Martin Olofsson?' Anita felt that there was something hugely significant in front of them.

'*TE* at the bottom,' said Hakim. 'Tommy Ekman?'

'That could be all three of our victims.' Now Anita's old enthusiasm was starting to stir. The feeling was almost physical. Her eyes were shining.

'*AG*? *LP*? Mean anything?' Nordlund asked.

'No. But *DW* might.'

Nordlund was already there. His mirthless smile at Anita

said it all. 'If that's Dag Wollstad, the chief inspector isn't going to like it. What's more, Dag Wollstad might well be the next intended victim if our killer is working off a similar list.'

'But what on earth is "Sjätte November Gruppen"?' Anita wondered aloud. 'And why would someone want to kill the people in it?'

CHAPTER 31

It was midafternoon, and Anita was beginning to feel tired as she headed along the side of the canal. She had been awake since the early hours and so much had happened since. She had decided, with Nordlund's approval, that they would try and do some more background checks before they presented their information to Moberg. They had to be pretty sure of their ground because he was unlikely to be receptive to anything that involved Dag Wollstad. But now there was the possibility that the industrialist might be a possible target. And who were the other two people on the list? Maybe they were targets too. Her first port of call was going to be Stig Gabrielsson. He was a short cut to finding out more about Serneholt. Gabrielsson certainly knew Serneholt, and he might have information about the playboy art collector that wasn't generally known. They disliked each other enough for Gabrielsson to have some dirt on his rival. And she also wanted to ask Gabrielsson a question that she had forgotten to put to him before – where had he got the fake Pelle Munk painting from?

When she arrived at Gabrielsson's gallery, the assistant was locking up. This seemed odd, as it was only around three on a Friday afternoon.

'You're finishing early,' Anita remarked.

The assistant almost jumped when she heard Anita's voice. The glacial poise had melted away.

'Stig's instructions.'

'And where is the delightful Stig?'

'I don't know.' The woman was flustered.

'You don't know. So how do you know what his instructions are?'

The assistant dropped the gallery keys on the ground. She hurriedly retrieved them and stuffed them into her bag.

'He told me before he left.'

'Left for where?'

'I've said I don't know. That's the truth. He said I was to close up early on Friday and keep the gallery closed until he returned.'

'And when will that be?'

'He didn't say.'

'So when did he tell you about closing the gallery?'

'Two days ago. Right after your visit here. Whatever you said to him, he was really shaken. He was all over the place for a while. Then he suddenly announced he had to make another trip abroad. I asked him where, but he said he'd be out of contact for a few days. Then he left his instructions and off he went. He didn't want to hang around.'

This was a surprise. Anita couldn't understand Gabrielsson doing a runner. Why? He wasn't a suspect, thanks to his alibi. Yet his behaviour made him appear guilty.

'What's your name?'

'Inga.'

'Inga, get your keys out and unlock the door. I want a look around.'

'I'll ask you again. What did you vote in the last election?'

Nilsson turned to his lawyer.

'My client has already said that he voted for the Moderate Party.'

'I think Fredrik Reinfeldt is doing a good job and deserved a second term,' added Nilsson to justify the reason for his choice. 'And Anders Borg seems to have a firm grip on the country's financial situation, despite these difficult times for Europe.'

Trust a bloody accountant to bring up the Finance Minister. How could you take a senior politician with a ponytail seriously? Westermark thought that this line of questioning was an utter waste of time. But Moberg had told him in no uncertain terms that this is what he must do. It was all because that crazy bitch Sundström and old man Nordlund had come up with some cockeyed idea that there was possibly a political angle to the killings. He hated politics at the best of times and had never bothered to vote. Anyone standing for the "Rise in Salary for Public Servants" party may have conquered his apathy. Money played a big part in Westermark's raison d'être. His lifestyle wasn't easy to finance on his existing wages and he always had an eye on the next rung on the ladder, even if it meant pushing someone else off in order to reach it. Yet pissing around asking tomfool questions wasn't going to lead to greater things. He had been the one to connect Ekman and Olofsson. Though he was convinced their murders were linked, he had been having doubts about Nilsson's involvement. What he didn't want was Anita Sundström charging in with a totally new connection between the crimes – and bringing in the Serneholt affair, too. There was no way that he would let her steal his thunder. And if the cow hadn't kept the Bishop's DVD from him, he could have scuttled this stupid right-wing idea before it was even floated. Now Moberg had to pay lip service to it to cover his back, though he agreed with the boss that they were clutching at straws. Also, like the chief inspector, he thought that the Serneholt murder was a totally separate business and was plainly to do with those god-awful paintings.

'So you swing to the right?' he asked wearily.

'I would say more a liberal conservative.' Nilsson sounded more like his old confident self. He was on safer ground.

'But you sympathise with the Sweden Democrats?'

'I do not, Inspector. They're so far to the right that they wouldn't have let Milena Tadić into the country.'

'Right. So what about Tommy Ekman? What were his views on immigrants or Jews or whatever?'

Nilsson ran a hand through his non-existent hair. 'I don't think we ever really discussed politics or immigration issues. He once made a very off-colour joke about a Norwegian.'

'We all do that.'

This was hopeless. The interview was only making him hate Anita Sundström even more. He had felt humiliated when she had walked away from the bar the night before. He had been so sure that he had ensnared her, only to see her wriggle free. Did he believe her story? He did remember the discussion about Strachan and Roslyn and a girl falling off some tower in England during the Lovgren investigation. Yet he was sure that she still loved the bastard. Maybe he would look into the tower story. Could Strachan be guilty of a second murder? The thought cheered him up.

'Interview terminated at 16.37.'

Anita returned to the office, somewhat perplexed. The search of Gabrielsson's gallery hadn't yielded any new information, other than that he had a lot of scalpels. There was no sign of the fake Pelle Munk painting, and Inga said that she knew nothing about it. According to her, they hadn't had a Munk painting in the gallery for a couple of years. Yet Gabrielsson had disappeared within hours of her informing him of Serneholt's murder. She had to admit that he had appeared shaken by the news when she delivered it. What did he know that made him so frightened?

Nordlund and Hakim had been busy on the phones but had little to report. Nordlund had spoken to an old journalistic contact on *Sydsvenskan* who knew nothing of anything called *The November 6th Group*. He had also spoken to Stockholm, and they had no such group on their radar either. The trouble was that they needed someone who was on the list that was still alive. Moberg wouldn't countenance them approaching Dag Wollsad without a cast-iron reason. Maybe they were barking up the wrong tree. The initials, other than Ingvar Serneholt's, might belong to other people entirely. The only nugget of information they had dug up that afternoon was the whereabouts of Bishop Green. He was safely back in Argentina.

There seemed nothing more to be achieved, and they decided that they would come in on Saturday morning and have a recap session; and tackle Moberg on Monday.

Klara Wallen got back into her car. She was looking forward to tonight. She was going on a night out with some of the other girls from the polishus. "Girls" was a misnomer – more "women of a certain age". A meal, a couple of bars and maybe a club – if she didn't have to come in first thing in the morning. She had mentioned it to Anita, but she never came out with them these days. Anita could be fun when she let her hair down. They had shared some good nights out in the past. But Anita had changed. Wallen knew that she was having counselling because of the Roslyn shooting, and understood her reticence to mix socially with the other women at headquarters. Wallen admired Anita. Especially the way she seemed able to hold her own in the presence of Moberg and Westermark. Anita had an inner strength that she didn't possess. It was always Anita she turned to when the strain got too much. Anita had comforted her a number of times when she had retreated into the toilets in tears. Strangely, she wasn't sure whether she really liked her. But as a colleague, she was supportive. Wallen dreaded having to work too closely with Moberg or Westermark. She had been relieved when she had been assigned to the task of trying to find witnesses on the night of the Serneholt murder. The team's first house-to-house – more like mansion-to-mansion – had been unsuccessful. She had had to repeat the process because there had been a couple of houses where there had been no reply when they called the first time. She was glad she had come back. Persistence often paid off.

Wallen flicked through her mobile's address list and found Anita's number. She called.

'Hi, Anita. Klara here. I've just spoken to someone who says he saw a jogger here a couple of times. The last time was on the night of the murder, about eleven. The light wasn't good and the jogger had his hood up, so he couldn't describe him. But the witness said the jogger definitely had a small backpack. Black, he thought. Given the height and build, and the backpack, he could be the same one that was reported around Olofsson's. Oh, and one odd thing. The jogger wore gloves. My witness thought it strange on a warm evening.'

CHAPTER 32

The Saturday morning meeting involving Anita, Nordlund, Hakim and a hung-over Wallen, was a rehearsal for putting the case across to Moberg on Monday. They felt there were definite connections between all three murders, and they had to be convincing. Firstly, there were the Gustav Adolf associations. Their main piece of evidence was now Serneholt's list with the initials. Moberg hadn't seen this, so it was important that he wasn't given the opportunity to dismiss it. It was the only concrete thing they had that appeared to link Ekman, Olofsson and Serneholt – and possibly Dag Wollstad. The nagging doubt was that the initials may not belong to the people they had in mind. They needed corroboration. Wollstad couldn't be approached at the moment, so who were the other two – *AG* and *LP*? And, of course, the list may be no big deal – it could just be some rich man's club and nothing suspicious at all. But if they were right, then three of them were dead, and that's got to be more than coincidence.

'What we need to try and establish is what the four men we think we know are on the list were doing on the day of the meeting, April 16th,' suggested Anita. 'What day in the week was that?'

'Saturday,' said Hakim.

'That'll be harder because their movements are unlikely to be in their business diaries. At least we can check and confirm whether they could have been together or not on that day.'

Then there was Nordlund's theory that the murders could have been politically motivated – the methods used fitted in with Nazi concentration camp killings. Certainly the first two – Serneholt's was far more tenuous. The problem with this angle was whether the three murdered men followed far right-wing ideologies. The Bishop Green DVD was filmed at Serneholt's and turned up in Olofsson's briefcase. That would indicate that both men shared the Bishop's views. Yet Anita's talk with Olofsson's neighbour at Vik made plain that Carolina Olofsson was an ardent Social Democrat and that Martin wasn't really into politics. Westermark had reported back that Nilsson had no idea about Ekman's political views. The information was gleaned before Nilsson was released; Prosecutor Blom reckoned they hadn't enough to hold him any longer for the murders, though it seemed likely that charges would eventually be brought for embezzlement. Moberg had not been a happy man.

'What do we know about Serneholt's views?'

'I've done some digging into the family history, and there's a strong German wartime link,' said Hakim.

'Fire away.'

Hakim produced some pages he had run off the internet, and other notes that he had assembled into a neat file. He was certainly thorough.

'The money he inherited came mainly from his mother. Ingvar Serneholt's father worked for Swedish Match and ended high up in the company by the time he retired.' Hakim glanced up from his notes. 'You probably know all about Ivar Kreuger's matchmaking empire?'

Though Anita did, she wanted to allow Hakim the chance of explaining his findings without interruption.

'Fill us in.'

'To cut a long story short, by 1924 his companies were producing seventy per cent of the world's matches. There were factories in thirty-four countries. Kreuger became so rich that he was giving loans to prop up entire national economies. In gratitude, countries would grant him match monopolies in return. Eventually, it turned out that he was cooking the books and was found out by the Wall Street Crash. After a last failed throw of the dice, he shot himself in a Paris hotel in 1932. Though his empire collapsed, Swedish Match still had factories and monopolies all over the world, but especially in places like Eastern Europe.'

Hakim shuffled his papers before continuing.

'The company was taken over by the Wallenberg family. Then the Second World War came along and the Germans marched through Europe. Thanks to Kreuger's monopoly contracts, Swedish Match had exclusive rights to produce and sell matches in Germany, Poland, Romania, Hungary, Yugoslavia and the three Baltic States. Suddenly, they were all under German occupation, or were on Germany's side. Swedish Match stood to lose a fortune if the Germans decided to confiscate their holdings or alter the terms of the monopoly agreements. In the early 1940s, the agreement with Poland was worth twenty-nine million dollars alone. Fortunately for Swedish Match, the Germans allowed the agreements to remain intact. That is until the arrest of the "Warsaw Swedes".'

'I've heard of them,' said Nordlund, who was engrossed in Hakim's research.

'Well, I haven't,' announced Anita. 'Please enlighten us.' She gave Hakim an encouraging nod.

'Obviously there were a number of Swedes working in the occupied territories. A group of seven Swedish businessmen in Warsaw joined the Polish underground and became the vital link with the Polish government in exile in London. Some of the seven were Swedish Match employees. They were betrayed, and arrested by the Gestapo in 1942. The businessmen's activities put Swedish Match's European commercial interests in serious jeopardy. The seven appeared before the German High Court in 1943 and four were sentenced to death. A fifth was given life imprisonment, while the other two were acquitted but remained in custody.'

'It's fascinating, Hakim,' Anita interrupted, 'but what's the relevance to Ingvar Serneholt?'

Hakim raised his hand in annoyance. 'I was just coming to that. The Germans didn't carry out the sentences but used the "Warsaw Swedes" as bargaining chips. The SS negotiated directly with Swedish Match. Serneholt's father was part of that team because he was a director of operations in Nazi Germany at the time. He dealt with Walter Schellenberg, Himmler's Chief of Intelligence, and was the go-between with the Nazis and the Wallenberg family. After the war, he ended up marrying a wealthy woman with a Wallenberg connection. Anyhow, it's believed that these negotiations led to various Swedish concessions, such as the export of ball bearings, which helped the German war effort. Used in tanks and other weapons and machinery. Later, as the war went against the Nazis, Himmler used the neutral Swedish connection to try and broker a peace deal with the Allies. These allegations are unproven, but the men in Gestapo custody were released over a couple of years.' Hakim paused. 'That's it.'

'An interesting story,' said Nordlund after a short silence. 'However, it doesn't make Ingvar Serneholt a Nazi sympathiser. Or his father, for that matter.'

'No. But his father lived and worked in Nazi Germany. He'd be exposed to the Nazi regime. He could have ended up having Nazi sympathies. I understand a lot of Swedes did at that time.'

'Not our most glorious period,' opined Nordlund.

'Serneholt senior – he was called Ingvar too – mixed with some dubious characters. He may have passed on his ideas to his son. After all, his son obviously allowed a Holocaust denier to air his views on film in his house.'

'Well done, Hakim.' Anita was taken by the young man's confidence in putting across his information and expressing his views. 'It certainly is suggestive. And it's these ideas that could have resulted in his murder. Our problem is to link it with the other two. And even if the men are connected ideologically, we have no idea who would have an obvious motive for killing them.'

'More to the point, if they are in this *November 6th Group*, what is it they're doing that makes someone want to kill them?' Nordlund was right as usual, thought Anita.

Hakim pointed to the Bishop Green DVD that Anita had brought into the meeting. 'The priest was inciting a war against incomers to Sweden, including the Jews. Should we be looking at the activity against ethnic groups in Malmö?'

'That makes sense,' answered Anita. 'We've already got the "Malmö Marksman" gunning down immigrants. Remember, there have also been numerous well-publicised attacks against the Jewish community. They've even made the foreign press, and I read that the Simon Wiesenthal centre in America has asked Jews to exercise extreme caution when travelling in southern Sweden. The attacks have been blamed on Muslims, but they've been attacked themselves. And don't forget the Bosnians and Serbs, who've been having their own turf wars. It's turning into quite a melting pot. Worth looking at, because potential suspects could emerge from any of these groups. If that's the case, the question is, how could they have found out about this obscure group if none of our contacts have ever heard of it?'

'We've got the jogger with the black backpack,' piped up Wallen, who had been drinking from a large bottle of water throughout the meeting. 'I know we haven't got a sighting on the actual night of Olofsson's murder, but he was definitely about at the time of Serneholt's killing. And wearing gloves on a warm evening.'

'Yes. That's interesting. We're pretty sure a car was at Serneholt's until quarter past eleven. Maybe the driver wasn't the killer and the jogger went in afterwards. As with the DVD, the jogger could link Olofsson's murder with Serneholt's. And we know Olofsson had various business links to Ekman, but there's nothing to connect Ekman to Serneholt, unless it's the list. As for Gabrielsson's disappearance, I don't know where that fits in. OK,' concluded Anita decisively, 'we'll present all our evidence and theories to the chief inspector on Monday morning and see what he has to say. Enjoy what's left of your weekend.'

The drive over to Vik on Sunday morning was wet. It was the heaviest rain that there had been for weeks. The windscreen wipers on Anita's car found it difficult to cope with the deluge and the constant spray from the vehicles going in the other direction. The weather matched her mood. She was sure that they were on the right track, though she was unsure of what Moberg would make of it. He was still convinced that Nilsson was their man. If he was right, then the Serneholt murder wasn't connected. Maybe the Bishop's DVD was a red herring and that Nordlund's gassing theory was just that – a theory. The more she thought about things, the more she began to doubt herself. And she knew that Westermark would do everything he could to torpedo her ideas. She wasn't looking forward to Monday morning.

The rain had eased by the time she arrived in Vik. She parked her car and walked to Olofsson's weekend cottage. She knew Carolina would be there because she had phoned ahead. Anita had hoped that she would be back in Malmö and that it would save her a journey. But Carolina hadn't gone back to their Vikingagatan home since Anita had interviewed her with her daughter. Anita could understand why.

Carolina let her in and had some coffee ready in a thermos. Anita could see that she was still traumatised by the loss of her husband. She was distant, and lapsed into periods of deep thought before politely answering Anita's questions. Yes, Martin had gone off on April 16th to play golf as usual. No, he wasn't into politics and let her get on with her Social Democratic canvassing.

'Did he ever express any right-wing political opinions? Or have, say, any thoughts on the number of immigrants in Sweden?'

The question had brought Carolina out of her trance. 'Not that I can remember. If he had, he would have had an argument on his hands.' She glanced down to her wedding ring. 'I think that's why we got on so well. I had my causes, and he was relaxed about them. His life revolved around his work, his golf and his family.'

Anita finished off her coffee and set it down on the table. The room had a number of family photographs, including some of Martin by himself. She wondered if these had been put on show since his death.

'Have you heard of Bishop Green?'

Carolina didn't seem to have heard her, so Anita repeated the question.

'That abhorrent man! Yes, I saw him on the television not that long ago. How could they allow someone like that to voice his rabid racism on our television screens? What has Sweden come to?' Carolina was suddenly animated. 'I don't believe in censorship, but letting someone peddle such lies! It would almost be laughable if it weren't for the realisation that some people will believe what he has to say.'

People like her husband, thought Anita. She hadn't the heart to say where she had come across the Bishop, and was evasive when Carolina asked her why she had asked the question.

A brief visit to the Österlen Golf Club confirmed that Martin Olofsson hadn't played a round that day. Anita had expected that; so Olofsson could have attended that meeting on April 16th. As he was over in Vik and pretending to go golfing, then the most likely location for *The November 6th Group* meeting was Österlen. And Wollstad's was the most obvious venue. It fitted in with Olofsson's furtive manner in recent months. If he was part of a right-wing group, then he was hardly going to admit it to a strongly opinionated wife like Carolina Olofsson.

As she had to drive past Pelle Munk's house on her return journey, she decided to call in. It wasn't because she felt that there was any need to update him on the theft of the paintings as he wasn't the one who had lost them, but more to show that the police cared about finding his works of art. And, as it was Sunday, Karin might be around. She had enjoyed their lunch together. She had sensed that they could rekindle the genuine friendship that had lapsed over twenty years ago. Karin's blue Volvo was parked next to Munk's green Citroën. Both vehicles had seen better days.

As Anita came into the courtyard, the sun was making a tentative appearance through rapidly brightening stratocumulus clouds. The earlier rain hadn't deterred Munk, who was sitting on a bench with a glass of wine.

'Hello, herr Munk,' Anita said loudly.

Munk raised his glass to her. 'Welcome. I remember you. You're the pretty one.'

'I don't feel it at the moment.'

'Believe me, you are. An artist knows these things. Come and join us. Karin!' he shouted. Karin appeared at the kitchen door. 'We have a guest.'

Within minutes, Anita had a glass in her hand and was invited to stay for a late lunch. While Karin was in the kitchen getting the meal ready, Munk fixed Anita with his piercing blue eyes. 'Now, pretty policewoman, have you come here on official business?'

'No. But I do have news that another of your paintings has been stolen.'

'I haven't heard anything,' he said, draining his glass and filling it up again from the bottle on the table in front of them. He wouldn't have, thought Anita. That was a detail of the Serneholt murder that hadn't been released to the press. 'Which one?'

'*Saturday & Sunday.*'

Munk's eyes narrowed. 'Ingvar Serneholt?'

'Yes,' Anita said in surprise. 'The painting was cut out of its frame.' Then she remembered she had mentioned Serneholt and that particular painting to Karin when they had met up for lunch.

'I hope they didn't damage it.'

'We don't know as yet. But they certainly damaged Serneholt.'

'What do you mean?'

'Haven't you heard? He was killed when the painting was stolen.'

Munk looked stunned.

'Did you know Serneholt?'

'I met him once. Bit of an art groupie. He invited me over to his pad... near Malmö somewhere.'

'When was this?' Anita couldn't help slipping into police mode even when she was making a conscious effort not to.

Munk shrugged his broad shoulders. 'Can't remember. Some years ago.' Munk raised his left hand and painted a stroke with an imaginary paintbrush. 'I didn't realise owning my paintings could be so dangerous,' he joked. 'Do you know who did it?'

'Not yet.' Anita didn't want to go into the details, so she changed the subject. 'Are you all ready for the exhibition?'

Munk didn't respond. Anita thought he hadn't heard what she said. 'The exhibition?' She spoke as clearly as she could. 'Is it all ready?'

He just grunted, waved a hand dismissively and took another

drink. Anita didn't pursue it any further.

After lunch, Anita and Karin walked down to the beach at Lilla Vik. It was only a five-minute walk; across the main road, through an apple orchard, past a spankingly painted, traditional timber house with a fabulous view over the sea, and down a short, steep slope to the shore. Anita had walked here so many times over the years and had never got over the sense of release it always gave her. It was a place she loved and carried around in her heart wherever she went. Now that the sun had returned, families had come down to enjoy the rest of their Sunday. Some were walking their dogs, others were playing Frisbee with their kids. No one was actually swimming, but a few were splashing along the water's edge, where the waves gave up being boisterous and fizzled into the sand. Anita liked it best in the winter when the place was deserted and she could pretend no one else in the world existed.

'Your father didn't seem very keen to talk about the exhibition.'

'It's just nerves,' Karin sighed. 'It's a big thing for him. His comeback. He doesn't know how the world will receive his new paintings. Will it be as good as the original work that made him famous? I've been mounting some of them this weekend. But I know it'll be great.' Karin stopped and gazed out to sea. 'It'll revitalise him. It'll bring the old Pelle back to life.'

'It's a pity about Ingvar Serneholt's murder.'

'Is that the guy you told me about? The one who owned *Saturday & Sunday*?' Karin looked shocked.

'Yes.'

'Oh, you're joking!'

'He was looking forward to the exhibition. I think he was keen to buy some more of Pelle's work.'

Karin turned and began to walk away. 'That's bad timing.'

CHAPTER 33

'If anybody but Henrik had come up with this stuff, I'd have told them to find another job.' Moberg was looking at Anita when he spoke. The meaning was clear. 'But I respect your opinion and judgment, Henrik,' he said turning to Nordlund. 'And, as we have had to let Nilsson go because of a lack of evidence, we've got to pursue this.'

'Except for this list that *he* found,' objected Westermark dismissively, referring to Hakim, 'there really isn't anything to tie all three murders together.' He had sat through Nordlund, Anita, Hakim and Wallen explaining their findings in a meeting room which was plastered with photos of the victims (before and after death), scene-of-crime shots, maps of murder locations and a very small gallery of possible suspects. He could see his pivotal role in linking the Ekman and Olofsson murders being hijacked by Anita.

'I know. But we have to take this list seriously until we can find an explanation for it. We have to discover what *The November 6th Group* is.' He turned to Nordlund. 'Is it a political group, as you and Sundström believe, or is it a commercial think tank? Or merely a social club? They might all be bloody golfers for all we know. Depending on what it is, the motive will become clearer. Does the group pose a threat to the killer? Or is it someone with a grudge against rich people?' Moberg shook his head. 'If someone else has got a copy of this and is using it as a hit list, for whatever reason, we have no choice... we have to speak to Dag Wollstad. He might be the next target.'

'At least we can confirm whether Wollstad was on his estate on April 16th,' said Anita. 'We can assume Ingvar Serneholt was at the meeting, as he had the list. Martin Olofsson wasn't where he said he was, so he could have made the meeting too. We don't know about Ekman, but his wife could confirm his movements on that Saturday.'

'The commissioner's not going to like this, but if he thinks we're concerned about Wollstad's safety...' Moberg didn't bother finishing the sentence. 'I'll see him and sort it out. Then I want Westermark and Sundström to go Wollstad's.' Moberg had no desire to meet Wollstad again.

'Why her?'

'Because, Westermark, I want you to talk to Wollstad and I want Sundström to tackle Kristina Ekman. She seems to be living out there at the moment. It will have to be very low key, so I don't want either of you two startling the horses.'

Westermark glared at Anita. She smiled sweetly back.

'In the meantime, we all need to start digging deeper into the background of our three murder victims. We need more concrete connections. See if we can find out anything about Bishop Green's movements while he was in Sweden. He must have been in Malmö. Who else, other than Serneholt, did he meet?' Moberg eyes swivelled round the room. 'We've got three murders on our hands and not one proper fucking suspect!'

It wasn't until the next day, Tuesday, that a meeting with Wollstad was arranged. The nervous commissioner had wanted it all done officially so that there would be no recriminations. After the last time, Dalhbeck was relieved that Moberg wasn't going. On the other hand, Anita was not looking forward to her trip to Illstorp one iota. Stuck in a car with a randy and resentful Westermark wasn't her idea of a nice day out. She had managed to avoid him since the Monday morning meeting. As she was preparing to leave the office, the phone rang. It was Moberg.

'Change of plan. Turns out Kristina Ekman is back in town. She's at her apartment. Go over there now with Hasim.'

'Hakim.'

'Whatever. Westermark will have to go to Illstorp alone. Nordlund and Wallen are out.'

'What about you?'

'I've upset Dag Wollstad enough already. Westermark's got a high enough opinion of himself to cope with Wollstad. If Westermark establishes that Wollstad's part of this November group, then we're to offer him protection, though I'm sure he can afford his own. If he thinks we're talking out of our arses, then at least we've been seen to do our duty.'

Kristina Ekman's face only dropped for a fraction of a second when she answered the door and saw Anita and Hakim. She was back to glacial politeness when she showed them into her large living room. Hakim was silent. Anita could sense his amazement at such sumptuous trappings of wealth. Kristina didn't offer them coffee, and Anita could tell that she wanted them out as quickly as possible.

Kristina, sitting like a ramrod, with the attitude of an elegant actress in a 1930s Hollywood movie, arched an eyebrow.

'Is this about that banker again?'

'No. It's about your husband's murder.'

'They've put you on the case?' The mock surprise was derisive. Anita ignored it. 'We need to establish where your husband was on April 16th this year.'

'Why?'

'Because of this.' Anita took out a photocopy of Serneholt's *Sjätte November Gruppen* list.

Kristina took the piece of paper in her finely manicured fingers and perused it. 'What's this?'

'That's what we're trying to discover. Hakim found it on Ingvar Serneholt's computer. He's the man who was murdered last week.'

Kristina turned her gaze on Hakim. 'Never met him, but I do know of him. Comes from a wealthy family. But I've certainly never heard of *The November 6th Group*.'

'We believe *IS* stands for Ingvar Serneholt. The *MO*, Martin Olofsson. That's your father's banker I asked you about before. Our interest in this may tie in with an empty folder we found on your husband's office computer, which was entitled "November 6th". And there is a *TE* on the list, as you can see.'

'It's unlikely to be Tommy, as I don't think he knew Ingvar Serneholt any more than I did.'

'Had he met him?'

'I don't think so.'

'There's also a *DW*. We thought that might be your father.'

'That sounds pretty ludicrous. And where was this meeting meant to be taking place?'

'We thought you might be able to help us with that.'

'Hardly. As I said, I've never heard of this... group.'

'We think it has something to do with Gustav Adolf.'

'There might well be a clue in the date, I suppose,' Kristina said sarcastically.

With great difficulty, Anita didn't rise to the bait. She hadn't taken to Kristina Ekman on their first meeting. Now that unfavourable impression was replaced by unadulterated dislike. Just then the phone rang. 'Excuse me.' Kristina got up and went over to the instrument, which sat on an intricately carved wooden table in the corner of the room. It looked Indian and expensive.

'Titti speaking.' She listened carefully to a voice on the other end of the line. 'I'll have to call you back. I have the police with me at the moment, but they'll be gone very soon.' Another pause. 'Speak to you in a minute.'

Kristina returned to her seat. She reached over to a small, black lacquered Chinese box on the coffee table and took out a cigarette, which she twirled in her fingers. She didn't attempt to light it.

Anita was about to resume when Hakim jumped in.

'What were your husband's political beliefs? Views on immigration?'

Kristina studied Hakim before answering. She made no effort to hide her contempt. 'He was a man who believed in Sweden.'

'That could mean anything.' Hakim carried on, ignoring Anita's warning glance. 'What did he vote, for example?'

'That was between Tommy and the ballot box. But if you want to know what his political persuasions were: he supported governments that he felt were in tune with the needs of entrepreneurial businesses like his own. As for immigration, Tommy thought that if ethnics were prepared to work and not scrounge off the system, then they had a part to play in Swedish society.'

'And did he employ any "ethnics"?' There was real anger in Hakim's voice.

'That's enough, Hakim,' Anita snapped. 'Fru Ekman, I apologise for my colleague's overeagerness. But we do need to establish where your husband was on Saturday, April 16th.'

Kristina stood up again. This time she wandered over to a small chest of drawers. Even in jeans and a casual, cream summer top, she retained a sophisticated elegance. She pulled open the top drawer. Anita thought she was about to produce a diary or filofax, but instead it was a silver lighter. She lit her cigarette, returned the lighter to the drawer and pushed it shut.

'That's simple enough. I was over at Illstorp with my father that weekend.'

Anita hopes were raised. This could be the confirmation they needed, that the murder victims were all together at Wollstad's.

'As for Tommy, he was in Hong Kong.'

'Hong Kong?' This was a blow.

'Yes. Hong Kong. He was out there on business. The Chinese market is becoming more important.' Kristina Ekman puffed on her cigarette and then let a delicate stream of smoke escape from her lips. 'So, that can't be Tommy on your list – or my father. I was with him all that day. I can assure you that neither Ingvar Serneholt nor that banker came anywhere near the family home. I suggest that you spend less time worrying about silly little lists and make more of an effort to find my husband's murderer.'

They had reached the man-made lake. The light breeze caused a slight ripple on the surface of the clear water. No invasive duckweed to be seen. The grass round the lake was neatly cut, though the vegetation on the banks themselves had been allowed to grow just enough to give the waterside verges a semblance of wildness. On the far side, a family of ducks was swimming serenely towards the cover of some tall reeds. In the middle, two swans circled slowly.

'Magnificent creatures. I love swans. Strong. Independent.'

Westermark assumed that Dag Wollstad was equating the birds with himself. And why not? The house and grounds were a testament to Wollstad's hard work and ultimate success. Westermark had contrasting emotions when meeting wealthy people, which he only did through his job. There was always a mixture of envy and admiration. Envy he reserved for those with money who hadn't accrued it through graft, or had used other people to help them up the greasy pole. Like Serneholt and Ekman. Wollstad was different. Such was the scale of his tangible achievement that all Westermark could do was award him total respect. Westermark had never been within sniffing distance of such staggering affluence before. The industrialist had already given him a tour of some of the rooms of the house. Now, one of Sweden's richest men was taking him down the wide gravel drive and through an estate that only money could have created. The style was formal, but without the flair of the French or the Italian landscapers. White, rectangular tubs containing dwarf conifers were placed at regular intervals along the drive, on either side of which well-cut lawns melded into birch and pine woodland. It made Westermark feel good. Wollstad was talking to him as an equal, and not as some annoying policeman who had disturbed his busy schedule.

They had already discussed the November 6th list. Wollstad had to call his PA to confirm that he was at home all that weekend and that Titti (his affectionate diminutive for Kristina) and the grandchildren had been there also, as Tommy had been away in Hong Kong on business. And he certainly wasn't the *DW* on the list. Ingvar Serneholt and Martin Olofsson might be in the group, but that was their business. 'Sounds to me more like a social circle.' Of course, he knew Olofsson through Sydöstra Banken. He had held him in very high regard as an efficient and sound banker. He also knew that Olofsson had been friendly with Tommy as they had sometimes played at the Österlen Golf Club at weekends. To his knowledge, Olofsson had never been out to Illstorp. As for Serneholt, he had met him a couple of times on social occasions. The last time? Probably about three years ago. When he was younger, he had come across Serneholt's father while still working at Swedish Match. From what he remembered, Serneholt senior had died some years ago.

Wollstad had dismissed the police offer of protection as he was sure that he was not an intended target. 'Anyhow, I can handle my own security.' Westermark could believe it. However, Wollstad was seriously concerned that there seemed to be little progress in finding the killer of his son-in-law and of such a respected banker as Martin Olofsson. Quick action was needed on these murders to restore the commercial sector's confidence in the police. It didn't look good for the Scanian business community. As he felt he was now in Wollstad's confidence,

Westermark had gone beyond what he should say about the investigation, discussing how *he* had cleverly connected Nilsson to Ekman and Olofsson. And now that Wollstad and Ekman had nothing to do with the list, then Sundström's only thread connecting the three murders was snapped. He would enjoy telling her.

They came to a halt at the water's edge.

'I hear positive things about you, Karl. It is Karl?'

'Yes, sir.' Westermark felt a swell of pride.

'I'm assured that you're destined for great things. And I'm sure finding my son-in-law's killer, and that of Martin Olofsson, would further your career.'

'I am desperate... we are desperate to conclude this case. However, the Serneholt killing has caused complications. Muddying the waters, as it were.'

'I understand. And is anyone in particular muddying said waters?'

Westermark saw his chance and slyly tiptoed as he stuck the knife in. 'Inspector Anita Sundström and her sidekick, enthusiastic though they undoubtedly are, tend to clutch at rather tenuous straws. Hakim,' he said slowly to emphasise the name, and accompanied doing so by raising his eyebrows, 'is a trainee, and perhaps can be forgiven. He found that list I showed you, and Sundström seems convinced there's a link between the three murders. She also found a DVD in Olofsson's briefcase with a British cleric spouting some pretty out-there views about immigrants and Jews and suchlike. Not all that daft, some of them, in my opinion, but that's by the by.'

'Does he have a name? The cleric?'

'Bishop Green.'

Wollstad shook his head. The name obviously meant nothing.

'Anyway, the DVD was filmed in Serneholt's house. Hence the link.'

'But you obviously don't consider there is one.'

'No. I think the Ingvar Serneholt and Martin Olofsson connection is coincidental. But Sundström has come up with a theory that there's some right-wing conspiracy – this *November 6th Group* – that the killer cottoned on to, and is using the list for his targets. Waste of time, if you ask me.'

Wollstad turned away from the lake and began to wander back through the grounds towards the house.

'Like me, you don't appreciate time wasters. Karl, I wonder if I can ask a favour of you?'

'Don't ever do that again!' Anita was furious with Hakim. They were in the lift on the way down to the ground floor of Kristina Ekman's building. 'In situations like that, I ask the questions and you keep your mouth shut. I'm the senior officer. Your job is to listen and learn.'

Hakim shuffled awkwardly before her glare. He looked like a recalcitrant child, and that immediately softened Anita's anger.

'I don't like her either, but that's no excuse to be aggressive in your questioning. You have to remember that she's lost her husband. Also, she happens to be a Wollstad, so that means that we have to treat her with kid gloves. If this gets back to Moberg, we'll both be in trouble.'

The lift came to a halt and the doors slid open. They made their way through the foyer and onto the street. The traffic noise hit them. Up in the apartment the sounds had been muffled. Good triple glazing.

'Pity about Tommy Ekman being in Hong Kong. Rather ruins the theory that they were all in something together.'

Anita was annoyed with herself as much as with Hakim. The list had appeared a real breakthrough. Now they still couldn't connect Tommy Ekman to Ingvar Serneholt. They were back to square one. No motives, no suspects.

By now they were in Drottningtorget. Her favourite ice-cream parlour was across the square.

'Do you want an ice cream?'

Hakim mumbled a sheepish 'Yes.'

'Not that you bloody deserve it.' Neither of them did.

CHAPTER 34

The whole team discussed the evidence so far. Thulin was brought in to go over the forensics again. No traces of the murderer at Ekman's apartment. There was no way of verifying the substance used to cause the gas that had killed him, other than that it was encased in jelly. It could be Zyklon B if the perpetrator had been able to get hold of an old wartime supply.

They had found female hair in Olofsson's car, but that had turned out to be his wife's. No fingerprints anywhere and no murder weapon, though Thulin was now ninety-per-cent sure that it was a heavy spanner, judging by the trauma marks. A couple of strong whacks by someone who must have been in the back seat at the time of the assault. That meant the killer was already in the car, or had slipped in while Olofsson was parking the vehicle in the garage. The killer must have taken the spanner away with him, as a thorough search of the surrounding area had yielded nothing.

With Serneholt, they knew the murder weapon of course – a scalpel. As for evidence of visitors to the house, that was nigh on impossible. Serneholt had held a party there a few nights before, so it was difficult to isolate any individual.

There was no trace of the mystery jogger, who hadn't been seen again in either murder location since. Medium height; dark-blue, hooded top, and black backpack was the best description they had. And on the night of Serneholt's murder, definitely wearing gloves, which, if he was the perpetrator, would explain the lack of fingerprints on the picture frame at Serneholt's – and possibly the same explanation would cover Olofsson's car. They had already talked through Westermark's visit to Dag Wollstad and Anita's to Kristina Ekman. Westermark had taken particular delight in pointing out that Tommy Ekman was on the other side of the world on April 16th. 'And Dag Wollstad said he wasn't at any meeting with Serneholt or Olofsson. He had only met Serneholt at a couple of social gatherings, and the last was around three years ago. So, there's no link there.'

'Do you believe him?' asked Moberg, more out of hope than expectation.

'I think he's a very honourable man.'

Moberg could see that their impressions of the industrialist were totally different. Just because he personally couldn't stand Wollstad, it didn't follow that Westermark wasn't right. He must learn to have more respect for Westermark's judgement. After all, he had been right all along about Ewan Strachan being Malin Lovgren's killer.

It was time for Moberg to summarise the cases so far and decide on some action.

'Tommy Ekman is gassed in his shower. Martin Olofsson is killed in his car. Both are linked through business and now we know socially, through playing golf over in Österlen. There are similarities in the way they were killed; well, gas was involved in both crime scenes. Nilsson is our best bet so far, as he had motives to get rid of them both. Trouble is, we can't place him at the scene of either killing.'

Moberg stood up and pointed to the photograph of Serneholt sitting on his sofa, gorily covered in blood. 'Then we have Ingvar Serneholt. Art collector-cum-playboy who has a painting stolen – one of three thefts involving works by Pelle Munk. This may be exactly what it seems – an art theft gone wrong.' He waved a hand in the direction of Stig Gabrielsson's photograph. 'And Gabrielsson seems to have done a bunk. So, he may well be up to his neck in the Serneholt business.

'On the other hand, Serneholt is linked to Olofsson because of the Bishop Green film. That implies that they both hold very radical right-wing views. On top of that, we have *The November 6th Group* list, which appears to link them again. But the list also dismisses any connection with Tommy Ekman, as we know he was thousands of miles away on April16th. And possibly Dag Wollstad can be discounted too; according to what he told Westermark, he isn't the *DW*. And Kristina Ekman denies that she or her husband ever met Serneholt. Basically, there's absolutely nothing that joins Ekman to Serneholt; therefore, I don't believe that the three murders are connected. My gut feeling is that two of them are, but the problem we have is whether the combination is Ekman and Olofsson or Olofsson and Serneholt. Our mystery jogger was seen around the homes of the latter. Is that another connection or a coincidence? Are there two joggers wearing similar gear, given that the locations are about fifteen kilometres apart? At the moment, we have to assume that there are two murderers out there. Thoughts?' Moberg's exasperation with the situation was evident in his voice, though he was trying hard to be systematic in his approach.

There was a reflective silence in the room. Then Nordlund spoke.

'Given that we have no reason to believe that Ekman has any right-wing views – and that Dag Wollstad has been known to give money to the Social Democrats in the past – then my right-wing theory is probably off the mark. I've been too influenced by that invidious recording of the Bishop's. It's probably an irrelevance in terms of the killings. And the Gustav Adolf link is tenuous at best, so may I suggest we go back to the beginning?'

'In what way?' Moberg asked.

'Tommy Ekman's murder. That's where it all began. We're

pretty sure that only someone at the advertising agency could have had the opportunity to plant the poisonous crystals. Unless it's some grand scheme where Wollstad is getting rid of business rivals or a misbehaving son-in-law, I suggest that we go over all the evidence again to see if we've missed something. Maybe if Anita got involved. A fresh eye. Maybe she could reinterview those who we know were in Ekman's office the day before the murder.'

'Why? What's she going to find that we didn't?' After his moment of triumph over the Hong Kong revelation, Westermark wasn't keen to see Anita reinstated in the heart of the investigation. 'It could still be Nilsson.'

'I still think it is,' agreed Moberg. 'In that case we're looking at the Ekman and Olofsson killings being linked; Nilsson couldn't have murdered Serneholt, as he was in custody. Besides, he has no motive to get rid of Serneholt. Westermark, I want you to carry on looking for the evidence we need to nail Nilsson for the Olofsson murder. I want you to interview everybody who lives in that vicinity again. We need a sighting. And we need to find that bloody jogger, or joggers. But, as we can't rely on that, I think Henrik is right. We must take another look at the agency. Sundström, you can talk to all the people again and double-check their stories.'

This was more like it, Anita thought. 'As you believe there's a link between the Ekman and Olofsson murders, presumably we need to try and establish if the principal agency-people have alibis for the second killing.'

'Yeah.'

'And can I talk to Nilsson?' Anita asked.

Westermark shook his head vigorously. Moberg ignored his silent protest.

'Yes. But don't balls it up.'

Anita worked late at her desk that evening going through all the statements and evidence gathered so far on the Ekman murder.

She had talked to Nordlund beforehand and he'd put her in the picture with his impressions of the case. He had suggested that she also discuss it with Westermark, as he had carried out the questioning at the advertising agency. She ignored that particular piece of advice. She noticed that Klara Wallen had been at most of the initial interviews, so she would have a word with her in the morning.

Those who had been in the office during the day, and again that night for the celebration, were: the financial director, Bo Nilsson; Daniel Jonsson, Ekman's business partner and creative director; Elin Marklund, the account manager; and Sven Lundin, the head of media. The latter three had been at the early-morning meeting prior to the new business pitch. They were all at the evening drinks; Nilsson had popped in during the day to drop off some spreadsheets, according to Ekman's PA, Viktoria Carlsson. Carlsson was there all day, except during her lunch hour when her place was taken by another secretary, Ida Kanfors, as Ekman always insisted there was someone on hand if a call came through to his office. Kanfors reported that no one had entered Ekman's office during that time.

The team had established that Nilsson and Jonsson had had opportunities during the day to go to Ekman's apartment. Sven Lundin could account for his movements all day, and both the secretaries were with other members of staff when they went out for lunch. Kanfors wasn't at the celebration that evening, so she was ruled out. Elin Marklund was the most interesting in that she had made love to Ekman, so was hardly likely to kill him, unless there was something darker about the relationship. Her movements appeared to be accounted for, and she was more concerned about her husband finding out that she had been unfaithful.

Anita had also sifted through the other forty-odd statements from the remaining staff. The only one that had caught her eye was from the senior copywriter, Jesper Poulsen. He was Jonsson's creative partner and had worked on the pitch for Geistrand Petfoods. As the other most senior creative, Anita wondered why he hadn't been at the early-morning meeting. She would definitely have a word with him.

It was after nine by the time she left the polishus, and she decided to pop into The Pickwick for a drink. There was a strange atmosphere around Malmö at the moment. People were trying to carry on as normal and the pub was full of the regular clientele chatting loudly. Yet the dark shadow of the "Malmö Marksman" seemed to be hanging over the town. Even though it wasn't an ethnic pub, some of the regulars lived in parts of the city where the attacks had taken place. And ever since the killing in Gustav Adolfs Torg, it was apparent that no area was safe. She knew that the police were doing their utmost to try and catch the man. This was, after all, perhaps the most high-profile investigation in the history of Malmö crime. But it was the lack of progress on the case that was causing public disquiet. She knew Larsson's team was convinced that the perpetrator was local, because he could disappear so easily. Larsson had made an appeal on television for people to come forward with information. Someone must know this man. Someone was shielding him. The biggest problem was that they didn't have a proper description of him. They had trawled through all the usual suspects, all the anti-Islamist groups, right-wing fanatics and general nutters. Nothing. And "nothing" meant widespread nervousness and a paranoid police commissioner.

Anita ended the evening talking briefly with a couple at the same table – a South African and his Swedish girlfriend. Like so many men who frequented the Pickwick, this expat had been lured by a Swedish siren. Anita had nearly done the same to Ewan. He was never far from her thoughts. She desperately wanted to see him again, though she knew it was a hopeless situation. Now visits were out of the question, thanks to Westermark's interference. She had got away with her excuse of trying to get Ewan to tell her about the death of the Durham student. That would no longer wash. Westermark would be keeping an eye on any future contact.

By the time Anita got back to the apartment, it was after eleven. As she put her mobile on the kitchen table, she realised that she had missed a call from Lasse. She immediately rang him up, but only got his voice mail. He would be out with the awful Rebecka. At first, she was cross with herself for missing the call – the noise in the pub had been loud most of the time she had been there. Then she was deflated. She always loved talking to Lasse, and she had wasted an opportunity. By the time she was getting ready for bed, panic had set in. If he had rung, then maybe something was wrong. He needed help? An accident? Worrying about Lasse was almost a default setting in her make-up. In a state of agitation, she rang his mobile again. This time, in an anxious tone of voice, she left a message asking if he was all right. Of course, she now couldn't sleep properly and only dozed fitfully.

She was woken by her mobile buzzing beside her bed. It was two o'clock. It was an SMS from Lasse telling her that there was nothing to worry about, and he had only called to ask if he could borrow some money. After the initial relief, Anita started to fret that he was squandering his meagre funds on Rebecka – or, more to the point, she was encouraging him to spend too much. By the time the morning came, she was tired, annoyed and confused.

It had taken a long shower and three strong coffees to get her mind back on the job that Moberg had set her. Anita had already decided that Bo Nilsson would be the first person she would speak to. He was Moberg and Westermark's chief suspect, so it was important for her to form her own opinion about the financial director before she talked to the other agency staff. Nilsson opened the door of his apartment and reluctantly let Anita and Hakim enter.

'Should I have my lawyer here?' were his first words.

'No. Just a few questions.'

Nilsson looked like a man whose world had imploded. He had been told to keep away from the agency while the financial irregularities were investigated. He had thrown everything away for a young prostitute who would probably never return to Sweden. And if she did, it was unlikely that she would come and console him. He had the haunted look of the hunted. He was in Moberg's sights, which was not a comfortable place to be.

As Anita went over old ground, she gradually formed the impression that this was a man who had got out of his depth, but he didn't strike her as a natural killer. If she forced herself, she could, at a pinch, see him plan Ekman's death. But as for Olofsson's murder, she doubted he had the strength or stealth to administer the blows that had killed the banker.

'Have you heard anything about *The November 6th Group*?'

He shook his head. 'Is it something to do with Gustav Adolf's Day?'

'Possibly. I have a list here with various initials.' She handed over the photocopy of Serneholt's list. 'We think that they may stand for Dag Wollstad, Martin Olofsson, and a man who was murdered the other day called Ingvar Serneholt.' Nilsson scrutinised the piece of paper. 'We thought that *TE* was Tommy Ekman, but he wasn't in the country on that date.'

'No. He was in Hong Kong. I remember sorting out his expenses when he got back,' he said with a rueful smile.

'Do *LP* or *AG* mean anything? Or an alternative *TE*?'

'I don't think so. Then again,' he glanced quizzically towards the window. 'I have no idea about the others, but *AG* could be Ander Genmar.'

'Ander Genmar? Who's he?'

'Genmar is the CEO of Genmar Financial Services. I worked for him when he had a successful company in Lund. Genmar sold out to Wollstad in 1992. That's how I first came to work for Wollstad. Since then, Genmar has gone on to build a very successful financial organisation. Mainly insurance.'

'Where does he live?'

'He used to live in Lund. May still be there.'

Anita nodded to Hakim and they stood up and prepared to leave. At least they had gleaned one useful piece of information.

'By the way, I know you've been asked about your political views, and those of Tommy Ekman, but is there anybody at the agency who you would regard as left-wing? Anti-fascist? Or ideologically opposed to Ekman?'

Nilsson considered this question carefully, as he did all that he was asked. 'Jesper Poulsen.' The answer was said with certainty.

'The copywriter?'

'Bit of a leftie. But copywriters tend to be. They all want to write the great social novel. Poulsen is no different.'

'His name suggests he's Danish.'

'Yes. Daniel Jonsson head-hunted him from a big Copenhagen agency. Poulsen often expressed strong opinions on the Danish attitudes to immigrants, which he felt were not a credit to his nation. Not that he expressed it like that. I don't think he was Tommy's cup of tea.'

'Because of his attitudes to immigrants?'

'No. He just seemed to get under Tommy's skin. He wasn't afraid to argue a point in meetings. Everybody else tended to go along with what Tommy wanted; he didn't appreciate being contradicted.'

'Why didn't he get rid of him?'

'Poulsen is a brilliant copywriter and works well with Jonsson. They're regarded as one of the top creative teams in Sweden. They've won many awards both here and internationally. We won a lot of business through Poulsen's efforts.' Nilsson was hit by a thought. 'Strangely enough, Poulsen has a right-wing connection. Nazi, you could say.'

'What?'

'His mother was a Lebensborn child.'

***

They were back at the falafel stand on Linnégatan again. It was Hakim's turn to pay this time. The weather wasn't as warm as their last visit and there was rain in the air.

'What's Lebensborn?' asked Hakim, his mouth half full of falafel.

'It was some sort of Nazi breeding programme during the Second World War. I think it was the brainchild of Heinrich Himmler. It was all about racial purity. Biologically fit, blue-eyed, blond-haired Aryans. It was their ideal.'

'So they wouldn't have been very happy with the likes of me.'

'Afraid not. They set up these Lebensborn homes in Germany, then across the occupied countries. Like Norway. And obviously Denmark, if Poulsen's mother is a product of the scheme. They often kidnapped young blond children from other countries, or encouraged their soldiers to mate with women from these places. Many of the women who ended up pregnant after having relationships with German troops had few alternatives other than turning to a Lebensborn home for help.'

Hakim ruminated over this information as he ate his remaining piece of falafel. After swallowing it, he wiped his mouth. 'It must have been difficult for these women after the war finished.'

'Not only for the women. The kids, too. In Norway, many of the children were put in lunatic asylums because they were regarded as a national embarrassment. Many were abused and mistreated.'

'It wasn't their fault,' said Hakim indignantly.

'No. They suffered for the sins of their parents. You know that girl from ABBA – Anni-Frid? She was a Lebensborn child. Saw a documentary on her. Her Norwegian mother fell in love with a German soldier. But Anni-Frid was brought to Sweden after the war, so escaped the ill-treatment.'

They began to wander back to where Anita had parked her car.

'If Poulsen's grandmother is one of these women who fraternised with the Germans, wouldn't that make him more likely to support the right wing? Alternatively, could he have gone the other way, as Nilsson suggests?'

Both thoughts had occurred to Anita. 'We'd better go and ask him.'

The gun lay on his bed. He stared at it. To him it was a thing of beauty. It wasn't an innate object. It was an extension of him. He couldn't imagine life without firearms. They gave him pleasure. They gave him power. They gave him a purpose. He took out a cigarette and lit it. He expelled the smoke from his mouth and watched it dissipate. It reminded him of the smoke that had coiled from the old hunting rifle the first time his father had let him fire it. He had loved the feel of it in his hands. The excitement it gave him on those early hunting trips. It was the rifle that his father had been using when he had been shot dead. They all said that it had been an accident. Even his mother. But he knew better. It had been the Finn. The outsider. He had waited until he was old enough to avenge his father's death. He had enjoyed using the old man's weapon to shoot the Finn. The authorities put that down to a hunting accident too. All those trees. It was bound to happen from time to time. It had been his first killing, and it had never been quite as satisfying since.

He leant over the bed, picked up the gun, caressed it for a moment and dropped it into the leather bag on the chair next to the door. The smooth hard metal nestled against the soft cotton T-shirt. The voice was insistent. The instruction was clear. He zipped up the bag. He finished his cigarette before flicking it out of the open window. He pulled the window shut and, with the bag in his hand, he left the room. This time it was going to be different. He had a specific target in mind.

CHAPTER 35

Anita and Hakim crossed Stortorget. It was busy in the early afternoon. The heavy drizzle wasn't deterring the shoppers as they streamed in and out of Södergatan. Anita liked the elegant buildings in the square, but it was the wide open space that she enjoyed wandering through. In August during Malmöfestivalen, a giant stage was erected at one end, as part of the week-long, free arts festival. Then the town really came alive with every conceivable type of music and performing arts – from jam sessions to juggling, there was something for everyone; in tents, in squares and in parks. At the corner of the square, Ekman & Jonsson was located.

Anita had already popped back to the polishus to tell Moberg and Nordlund about Ander Genmar. Moberg was going to delegate that task to Nordlund and Westermark. She hadn't mentioned Jesper Poulsen, as he wasn't on their list of suspects and might turn out to be just another time-wasting diversion. She wanted to speak to Poulsen first, so that she could eliminate him from their enquiries and not give Moberg yet another reason to criticise her. While they were back in headquarters, she had phoned Gabrielsson's gallery. She had caught Inga, who had called in to check the post. The gallery was still officially closed and she hadn't heard from Stig Gabrielsson since he had rushed off abroad. She was getting worried about him as he hadn't gone away for so long before without being in touch.

Anita's dad would have called the advertising agency "swish". The interiors were very modern and weren't entirely in keeping with an old building. She had already asked to speak to Viktoria Carlsson, Ekman's PA; Daniel Jonsson; Elin Marklund; and the secretary who had covered for Carlsson during her lunch break. She also had Sven Lundin, head of media, down on her list, mainly because he had been at both the morning meetings and the presentation, though he hadn't been at the celebratory drink for long. As the meeting had only been fixed up the day before, she hadn't had time to add Jesper Poulsen to the list but had assumed he would be in the agency on a Friday afternoon anyway. However, on her arrival, Anita was informed that Jesper Poulsen had flown up to Stockholm for the day to record some voice-overs and wasn't due back in the office until Monday. She got hold of his home address and decided to see him on Saturday morning.

They had already spoken to the two secretaries before they were shown into Jonsson's large, glass-fronted office. There were two rectangular, veneered desks with shiny, tubular-metal supports. Both had computers. Jonsson's had two large Apple macs on his desk, together with piles of papers, a large sketch pad, two thick advertising annuals, a coffee cup and a half-drunk bottle of water. Hanging on the two end walls were mounted advertisements, stills from TV commercials and various framed awards. Through the glass partition, there was an open-plan room where a motley group of art directors and copywriters were working at their computers. It wasn't how Anita had imagined an advertising creative department. She had expected it to be noisier and more chaotic. Everyone was working quietly at their screens.

'Do you mind if I carry on while we talk? I've got this urgent job that needs to be out by tonight,' said Jonsson, peering through his designer glasses as he manoeuvred some unseen element of a layout around his screen. Anita thought her spectacles had been a rip-off, so heaven knows what Jonsson had paid for his.

'Fine,' said Anita. 'I presume this is where you work with Jesper Poulsen?'

'Yeah. Jesper's up in Stockholm today. Voice-over session.'

'So, we know your movements on the day of the Geistrand Petfoods presentation,' said Anita as she scanned the notes that had already been taken in previous discussions, 'including the time after the presentation when you borrowed Elin Marklund's car and briefly disappeared.'

'As I've said before, it was to collect some work that I'd done at home.'

'So you say.' Anita wanted to make Jonsson uneasy. The accusation was left unspoken. It certainly had the effect of making him shuffle about in his chair. Jonsson was still on their list of potential suspects. He had the opportunity and some sort of motive. It was his company now, even if Dag Wollstad – or possibly Kristina Ekman – was calling the financial shots.

'So, did you and Jesper Poulsen work together on the Geistrand Petfoods pitch? You do call it a "pitch"?'

'Yes, we worked on the pitch.' Jonsson pointed a finger at the staff through the glass. 'We had other creative teams involved because it was potentially a big piece of business. But Jesper and I came up with the main campaign that we presented to the client.'

'I was wondering why Poulsen wasn't involved in the actual pitch?'

Jonsson smiled. 'We didn't want to go in mob-handed like other agencies. Tommy always believed that too many people just intimidate the client. We just went in with the core people that the client would be dealing with most often if we won the business.'

Anita scribbled a note on her pad. 'Why wasn't Poulsen at the meeting when you ran through the presentation before you left the office?'

Again a smile swept across Jonsson's face. 'Despite the unruffled image we like to portray to the clients, ask any ad agency about a pitch and they'll tell you that it's often a frenzied process. People working late, the creatives desperately trying to get everything together at the last minute. There are always changes right up to the moment we rush out of the door with the work under our arms. Seat-of-the-pants stuff. Normally, Jesper would have been at that meeting, but he was rewriting some radio commercials. The night before the pitch, we were working until after midnight. And then Tommy was unhappy with some of the radio scripts, and Jesper came in early the next morning to rewrite them.'

'What time?'

'I think he said around six.'

'So he was the first in that morning?'

'I was in just after seven and he was the only one about. Tommy arrived about the same time as me.'

Anita could sense Hakim sitting alertly at her side. He was thinking the same as she was – Jesper Poulsen had been all alone in the building. He was also at the celebratory drink in the evening. How had that escaped notice?

'I hear that Poulsen and Ekman didn't see eye to eye.'

'Who told you that?'

'Office gossip.'

'Well, there was some truth in it. Jesper believes in the work we do and isn't afraid to fight for it. To me, that's healthy. Sometimes Tommy found that difficult because Jesper can be very opinionated about creative work. Occasionally, Tommy could be quite savage in his criticism of our ideas. That would wind Jesper up. It's only because both of them wanted the agency to be the best. They set high standards.'

Jonsson pressed a key on his keyboard, and a moment later the printer next to his desk sprang into action.

'Did you come across Martin Olofsson?'

'Yes. A couple of times. Meetings with Tommy.'

'Did you know he was investigating Bo Nilsson?'

'Not then,' he replied. 'I do now! That's why Nilsson's suspended. He's the last person I would have suspected of nicking from the company.'

'Where were you on the evening of Monday, May 23rd?'

'The Olofsson murder?' He was peering at the screen.

'Yes.'

He looked up and fidgeted in his seat again. He was either nervous or the ergonomic design wasn't working.

'I was here.'

'Alone?'

'Yes. As you can imagine, it's been almost twenty-four/seven since Tommy... you know.'

Anita stood up and Hakim followed suit. Jonsson leant over the printer and retrieved the copy he had made.

'By the way, do you jog?'

Jonsson pulled a face. 'You're kidding. Walking is bad enough. I leave daft things like that to Jesper.'

Just then Anita noticed a black backpack shoved down by Poulsen's desk.

'He's a keen jogger?'

'Fanatical. He often jogs into work in the morning from Ön. And home again at night.'

Ön was a short jog from Olofsson's house. Anita really did need to speak to Jesper Poulsen now.

After reading Wallen's notes, Anita was intrigued to meet Elin Marklund. They waited for her in the conference room. Hakim was fascinated by the spooling TV commercials, and squealed with delight when a humorous one came on for a well-known brand of yogurt. 'I love that one.'

Elin Marklund appeared, dressed in a short skirt and neat top. Anita was amused at Hakim's embarrassment at the amount of leg on show. Even in these days of equality, Marklund knew what pleased male clients – and, presumably, her boss, until his untimely demise. Klara Wallen had told her that Marklund had seemed very self-confident until she'd broken down after being confronted with her infidelity. But at that moment, there was no air of fallibility as she sat on the other side of the table and awaited Anita's questions. Anita got her to go through the events of that day. Marklund explained about the meetings at the office, the pitch itself, coming back in Ekman's car because Jonsson had borrowed hers, and then how she had stayed in the building until the drinks in Ekman's office that evening. Her story totally tallied with Wallen's notes.

'And then you know what happened.'

As Marklund told her version of events, Anita sensed that this woman liked to be in control. Her manner, her poise, her clear, precise way of talking all added to the impression. So why did she let herself be seduced by her boss? Maybe it was Tommy Ekman's charisma. Or was she just lonely? She had been full of contrition when confronted by Wallen. Had it been genuine remorse, or fear of her husband if he found out? Neither scenario seemed to fit with the confident woman on the other side of the table.

'Your husband. What does he do?'

'Pontus works in the oil industry. Goes all over. Middle East, America. He's based in Canada at the moment. He's on the security side of things.'

'Is that why you're not with him?'

'Partly. He's never in the same place for more than a year or so. And I have my own career. The arrangement works.' Then she flashed a rueful smile. 'Most of the time.'

'And where were you before you joined Ekman & Jonsson?'

'At an agency in Copenhagen. The same one as Jesper Poulsen. He recommended me for the job here. Before that, I was in a small design company here in Malmö. It doesn't exist any longer.'

'Where were you on the evening of Monday, May 23rd?'

She looked puzzled. 'Why?'

'Just tell us.'

'That's easy, actually. I took a day's holiday because Pontus was here on a flying visit. He had been over in Norway on business and managed to squeeze in a couple of days at home.'

'And how did you spend that evening?'

Marklund raised an eyebrow. 'Do you really want to know? It was his *last* night.'

Hakim couldn't hide his blush.

The last person they saw was Sven Lundin. He was a chubby man in his forties, with a shock of brown hair. He smelt of stale cigarettes and his teeth were slightly stained with nicotine. He greeted them with a pained smile and apologised for keeping them waiting. He had been on the phone to a TV company negotiating a better rate for some client's next campaign. Anita guessed that he had then rushed out of the building for a quick drag before facing them.

'My colleagues have already talked to you. We know that you were in Tommy Ekman's office for the early meeting at around eight.'

'That's correct,' he said, flicking a speck of ash off his jacket sleeve. 'Tommy, Elin and Daniel.'

'And then you came down here to the conference room to run through the pitch. Did you go back into Ekman's office again that day?'

He nodded his head. 'Yes. Very briefly. I was there for literally a few minutes as I had to dash off home reasonably early that day. My eldest daughter was in a school concert. You can't miss those sorts of things.'

Anita felt a pang of guilt. She had failed to make some of Lasse's school events because of work. The memories still plagued her.

'Just one more thing. How long would you say that Daniel Jonsson was away from the office after you'd finished the presentation at Geistrand Petfoods?'

Lundin coughed. A smoker's cough. An unpleasant, rasping sound. 'Elin and I came back in Tommy's car,' he said in a flat, matter-of-fact voice, 'and then we met here for a sandwich and to talk about our impressions of how the pitch went. It was certainly less than an hour. Forty minutes or so.'

'Why did you go in two cars?' Hakim asked. 'Such a short journey.'

'Well, Daniel and I went in Tommy's car because Elin had to go somewhere first on the way to the pitch.'

'Wait a minute,' Anita exclaimed. 'Are you saying that Elin Marklund set off first by herself?'

'Yes,' Lundin answered warily.

'How much earlier?'

'I don't know. Half an hour.'

'Did she say where she was going?'

'Not that I can remember. You'd better ask her yourself.'

Anita turned to Hakim. 'Go and find her and say we want another word.'

Hakim got up and hurried out of the room.

'Is that all?' Lundin asked.

'Yes. Yes, that's all, thank you,' Anita said distractedly. Her mind was whirring.

As Lundin walked out of the door, Hakim re-entered. 'She's finished work for the day. Left ten minutes ago.'

CHAPTER 36

The trees gave him good cover. He could see her wandering around the living room of the ground-floor apartment, with a cup of coffee in her hand. He had been here on the edge of Pildammsparken for half an hour. At nine on a Saturday morning there were usually joggers and dog walkers about. Today, the sky looked unpredictable and there was a sharp southwesterly wind. The clouds scudded across the sun and spots of rain tapped among the leaves of the beech trees.

He wasn't sure when and where he would strike. This was purely a reconnaissance mission. Stake out her home. He knew that he needed to get the pair together. It would then fit the pattern he had set. He'd already been to the young Arab's apartment block. He'd had to be careful, as he had carried out two of his attacks in the vicinity, including the killing of the couple outside the ethnic supermarket. The whole area was on high alert. Anyhow, it would be better to kill them in another part of the city. It would spread the fear and snuff out a potential problem at the same time. That's what the voice had told him.

Now he could see that she was organising herself to go out. She was gathering her things, and then she disappeared from sight. A couple of minutes later, she came out of the side entrance of the apartment block and walked straight towards him. He didn't flinch. She was quite attractive for a police inspector.

The short, blonde hair he liked. Under her old leather jacket, the jeans and T-shirt showed off her figure, which was still good for her age. But the clothes were slovenly, he thought. Why couldn't professional people dress better these days? And the glasses were off-putting. He never fancied women in spectacles. She got into her battered Volkswagen and he watched her drive off. He stepped through the trees and zapped his car lock. He jumped in, started the car and pulled out into the street. He could see her car some way ahead. He wasn't sure where she was heading. With luck she would pick up the Arab.

Anita drove along the coastal road of Limhamnsvägen. To her left were a series of impressive apartment blocks with magnificent sea views, while on her right was an expansive ribbon of green belt that ran down to the shore. Much of the area doubled as part-time playing fields. She saw some white-clad men heading towards a metal container at the edge of one of the fields. She recognised them as members of the local cricket club. The container would house their equipment, she supposed. She remembered her father taking her to a cricket match in Durham when they were living there. He thought that he should try and understand the quintessentially British sport. It had totally defeated him, though she had enjoyed playing round the boundary and marvelling at the size of the mighty medieval cathedral that dominated the background. Today, Malmöhus's cricketers had the Turning Torso as their backdrop. It was strange to reflect how the two buildings had played their part in her life and were now always synonymous with Ewan Strachan. She would always be amazed at their grandeur but would forever hate them.

The road twisted away from the old cottages that were once the heart of Limhamn, and came under the shadow of the vast cement works that dominated the landscape at this end of the bay. It was a sprawl of grey, cylindrical blocks of concrete, ugly chutes, a complicated system of metal piping, and topped off with a slender apology for a chimney. It overlooked the old harbour and Ön. "The Island", beyond the cement factory, was tethered to the mainland by a man-made causeway. It was being developed into a highly desirable residential area. Easy to see why, as long as you didn't look back towards Limhamn. The panorama was breathtaking. The water of the Sound between Sweden and Denmark was blue and inviting. It shimmered and twinkled under the Öresund Bridge elegantly curving to the left, while in the other direction, the Turning Torso loomed like a benevolent ghost; straight ahead Copenhagen was framed on the skyline. Ön was now covered in cleverly designed houses and smart apartments, all making the most of the vista. This was a place on the up, literally. More and more developments were commandeering the limited air space and jostling with one another for the best outlook. But you had to pay for the privilege. Jesper Poulsen could afford it.

Anita parked her car and approached the first in a series of pristine white blocks. Each of the apartments had circular balconies – with sea aspects of course – and large Art-Deco-style bay windows, behind which Anita assumed were the living rooms. Dividing the blocks were stretches of neatly mown grass, which extended to the waterline beyond. Anita glanced towards the bridge. For a moment, she thought of Jörgen Lindegren and his missing painting. She could almost see his house from here. That investigation was on hold. She had more important matters on her mind.

Jesper Poulsen wasn't in.

Anita came out of the apartment block and decided she would make her way down to see Elin Marklund. She lived in Skanör, on the peninsula about half an hour's drive south of Malmö. As she headed for her car, she noticed someone jogging along the northern shore of the small island. This part was still bereft of buildings, though Anita supposed it would disappear under expensive concrete before long. The jogger wore a dark-blue, hooded top. Anita watched him reach the grassed area and begin to head along the path on which she was standing.

When the jogger reached Anita, she blocked his way.

'Do you mind?' he snapped.

'Jesper Pouslen?'

He pulled up. He wasn't breathing very heavily, though sweat covered his face.

Anita took out her warrant card. 'Inspector Anita Sundström.'

He pushed the hood from the top of his head. Poulsen was a wiry man. She knew he was thirty-eight. His very blond hair was cut so short that it resembled facial stubble. The deep blue eyes were glacial. A legacy from his German grandfather?

'I need to talk to you.'

'I already made a statement to the police a couple days after Ekman died.'

'Can we sit over there?' Anita moved towards the water's edge and sat down on a bench. After watching her for a few moments, Poulsen reluctantly followed. Instead of sitting down next to her, he started to do stretching exercises, using the end of the bench like a piece of gym equipment.

'Keen jogger?'

Poulsen didn't bother to answer her.

'The morning of the Geistrand Petfoods pitch, you were in really early.'

'So? I had work to finish.'

'And you were the only one in the office at that time?'

'No one else would be that daft.'

'It meant that you could have gained access to Tommy Ekman's office.'

'And stolen his keys? Of course I could have. But I didn't.'

'Did you go out of the office during the day?'

'Damn right I did. We'd put so much work into the pitch that I treated myself to a couple of pints round the corner in Lilla Torg.'

'By yourself?'

'Yeah. Outside the Moosehead.'

'For how long?'

'About an hour. I wanted to get back and find out how the pitch had gone.'

'Time?'

'I left on the dot of twelve. Back about one.'

Anita gazed out to sea. The wind was whipping up the water.

'I get the impression that you weren't very keen on Ekman.'

He stopped his exercising and stood with his hands on his hips. 'I thought he was an utter arsehole. I didn't fall for all that false charm that the girls in the office loved. But he was a brilliant businessman. A ruthless bastard. He made things happen. E&J was on an exciting journey, as the cliché goes. I was happy to go along for the ride even if we had arguments along the way.'

Anita took her snus tin out of her bag and took off the lid.

'You shouldn't be using that filthy stuff,' Poulsen said in disgust. 'No wonder it's banned in the rest of the EU.'

Anita defiantly popped a sachet under her top lip. Poulsen pulled a disapproving face.

'Why did you come to Malmö?'

He made a sweeping gesture which spanned the bridge to the Turning Torso. 'What's not to like?'

'There must be more to it than that.'

'When I came over from Copenhagen, property was a lot cheaper. It was a good opportunity workwise, too. E&J were just starting to go places. I could help make that happen. Get in on the ground floor. Besides, I was pissed off with the Copenhagen scene.'

Anita nodded. She could understand. But she could sense that there was something more to Poulsen's move across the Öresund.

'Someone described you as a "leftie".'

He grimaced. 'It doesn't take much to be considered a leftie in an advertising agency. If you're slightly to the left of Mussolini, you're considered subversive.'

'So, why advertising?'

'That's the first interesting question you've asked so far, Inspector Sundström. I can't really justify it. Others in the business would say we help create jobs, lubricate economies, keep the commercial world ticking over. Most of that is crap. The reality is that we make people discontented because what they once thought of as luxuries, we have persuaded them are essentials. We appeal to their worst instincts – all dressed up in that horrible word "aspiration". The reason I'm in advertising? I just love the creative process. When we get it right, it gives me a buzz like nothing else. It's a purely selfish emotion. But it doesn't sit happily with my conscience. Maybe that's why I do all this running. Work out my frustrations, clean out my brain.'

'Maybe you should put this in your book.'

'I have thought...' Poulsen stopped himself when he saw Anita's wry smile.

'Apparently all copywriters want to produce the "great novel".'

He had the grace to grin. 'It'll get written one day. I'll make you buy a copy.'

Anita was now benefiting from the snus. It kept her calm.

'Will your novel include your Lebensborn mother?'

'What the fuck?' He took a menacing step towards Anita.

'It's obviously a touchy subject.'

'It's none of your business. I think we've said enough.' He turned away towards his apartment block.

'It could be why you killed Tommy Ekman. And Martin Olofsson.'

Poulsen stopped. Slowly he turned around. 'That's madness.'

'I suspect one of the reasons you moved over from Denmark was because of your mother. Or, more to the point, your grandparents.'

Poulsen came back to the bench and sat down next to Anita.

His temple throbbed, though he was trying to keep his anger in check.

'Have you any idea what my grandmother and mother went through?'

'I should imagine it was tough.'

He snorted in derision. 'My grandmother fell in love with a German SS officer. By the time she gave birth, he had been killed on the Russian front. Or that's what they told her. The bastard was probably already married and survived the war. Himmler encouraged that sort of thing. My grandmother's parents disowned her and she was taken in by the Lebensborn home. It means the "fountain of life". What a sick joke when you think of the lives that were devastated by it. You know that the nurses were ordered not to respond when the children cried, whether it was for food or a simple hug. Emotions were expunged. They were programming the future generation of world rulers from the cradle.

'After the war, my grandmother had nowhere to turn – no Danish family, no German family. Then my mother was taken from her and put in a home. God knows what abuse she suffered there. The Danish authorities wanted these children out of sight – they didn't want reminders that there had been fraternisation with the occupying forces. Literally sleeping with the enemy. They had their hands full. There were well over five thousand "German babies".'

As he twisted his hands, Anita realised that Poulsen was not a man who could forget, or forgive.

'My grandmother was so distraught that she walked into the sea over there somewhere,' said Poulsen pointing in the direction of Denmark, 'and was never seen again. One less national embarrassment.'

'What happened to your mother?'

'When she was ten, she was taken in by an uncle. He tried to be kind, but word got out, and her school life consisted of other children telling her that her father was a Nazi war criminal and her mother a prostitute. She never got over the shame, even when she found fellow sufferers after *Danske Krigsbørns Forening* was formed.'

'I've heard of *Children of War Denmark*. They share their experiences, don't they, and get counselling?'

'My mum didn't join until it was too late. She was very ill by then, but it gave her some comfort knowing that other people had gone through the hell that she had. She didn't have much time to share her experiences, but one thing she did have in common with the others was guilt.'

'Why? It wasn't their fault.'

'They were atoning for the sins of the parents. It makes no sense, but it's true nonetheless.'

'What about your father?'

'I don't know who he is. I'm the result of a one-night stand. She could never trust anybody to form a long-term relationship. She brought me up as best she could and then I took over caring for her when she became ill.'

'And you escaped to Malmö when she died?'

He nodded. 'Escape is the right word. I learned at an early age how ugly intolerance is. We're too quick to judge. Look at all the problems we have now. Anyway, two months after Mum died, the E&J job came up.'

The wind was getting stronger. The fleeting clouds were looking more threatening.

'Of course, I soon began to realise that there are just as many bigoted people over here. The far right seems to be coming out of the woodwork all over Scandinavia. I leave behind the Danish People's Party and find the Sweden Democrats instead. They're all scum. Despite that, I'd prefer to live in Malmö than Copenhagen any day. You're not even legally allowed to live with a non-EU spouse over there these days. No wonder they're all coming over to Sweden.'

He stood up to stretch his legs. 'So, who told you about the Lebensborn connection?'

'Bo Nilsson.'

He raised his almost-bleached eyebrows. 'That'll have come from Ekman.'

'How did Ekman know?'

'I'm not sure. Maybe he did some checking up on me before he gave me the job. It only came up once. He seemed interested. Fascinated, actually. After he saw that it wasn't a subject I wanted to talk about, he never mentioned it again.'

'We think that Ekman and Olofsson, and a man called Ingvar Serneholt, who was murdered the other day, might have been part of a far-right group.' She knew she was fishing. 'Maybe that's why Ekman was so interested in your German connection.'

'Is that why you think I killed him?'

'Not only him. A jogger, wearing a blue, hooded top, was seen in the vicinity of both the Olofsson and Serneholt murders.'

'Half the joggers in Malmö dress like me.'

'Where were you on the evenings of Monday, May 23rd and Monday, May 30th?'

'I have no idea. I think you've wasted enough of my time, Inspector.' With that Poulsen turned and jogged off.

He watched the man jog away from her as she remained seated on the bench. It appeared that she was working on her own. He wouldn't bother to follow her any more today. He would wait until Monday, when he could pick her up again at the police headquarters. It was safer following her movements than the Arab's. Then he could work out his strategy. He would have to think on his feet and grab his opportunity to strike where there was a safe escape route. And they had to be together. The voice was adamant. At least he had now seen both his targets.

He felt the inside of his jacket. The gun reassuringly nuzzled against his chest. It would be strange killing a white Swedish woman. He had never done that before.

CHAPTER 37

Moberg's wife hadn't been pleased when he had left for the polishus after breakfast that morning. She had wanted him to go to IKEA with her to choose the new bed that she had been pestering him to buy for the last year. He had lost his temper and shouted that he had three fucking murders to solve and that a new bed wasn't high up on his list of priorities just now. After slamming the door, he was quite relieved that he wouldn't have to go back home until tonight. He wondered how long she would put up with his unreasonable behaviour. He must start making an effort – he couldn't afford a third divorce on his salary.

Nordlund and Westermark were waiting for him.

'Ander Genmar is on holiday,' said Nordlund. 'Interestingly, it was a very sudden decision, according to a couple of people at the group's head office.'

'I think this list shit is getting us nowhere.' Westermark resented having to spend valuable time in Lund looking for Genmar and then wasting more time talking to office employees. 'People take spur-of-the-moment holidays. Maybe he saw a good deal.'

'Where is he?' Moberg asked.

'Spain,' answered Nordlund. 'He has a villa near Marbella. They usually go for the whole of September. He and his wife left two days after Serneholt was killed. It's suggestive.'

'I know Henrik is still backing Sundström up on this right-wing conspiracy thing, but we only have evidence to connect two of these people; through the Bishop Green film. The Wollstad association is pure fantasy. And we know Ekman couldn't have been at this supposed meeting.'

'Henrik?'

'Karl may well be right. The trouble is we can't ask anybody about the meeting as we either don't know who they are, or the ones that we do know are dead. Except for Genmar.'

'Have we contact details for Genmar in Spain?'

'Yes,' said Nordlund. 'I rang last night. However, there was no answer. Nor this morning when I tried.'

Westermark was restless. 'Look, Chief, I think we should be concentrating on Nilsson. The big question we've got to ask ourselves is how he got the poison. Crack that and we've got him – and solved two murders. The Serneholt slaying has something to do with the art world, and nothing to do with the advertising agency. End of story.'

'Coffee?'

'Thank you.'

Elin Marklund went through to the kitchen. Marklund had seemed totally unfazed when Anita had turned up on her doorstep a few minutes earlier. The rain had come during the drive down the E6. She had branched off to Höllviken, the community that straddled the route to the peninsula. She drove on to Skanör and parked near a small, whitewashed church with crow-stepped gables at each end, which commanded a view of the distant Öresund Bridge. Skanör was a beautiful spot with protected wildlife wetlands spreading to the south. Anita could see a couple of avocets using their long, curved beaks to plunder the muddy marsh. Beyond was the beach and a colourful line of beach huts. It was a place in which she would like to linger, but a combination of the rain and the need to talk to Elin Marklund overrode any such thoughts.

Anita had walked to Marklund's house. It was situated not far from the church along an unmetalled road. The residents parked their cars on the grass verges around their homes. A smart red Saab sat next to Marklund's quaint, white-fronted cottage. By the standards of this prosperous area, it was a modest home. Somehow it didn't fit with Anita's image of an advertising executive with a husband in the oil industry. As Anita waited after ringing the doorbell, she glanced at the yellow blanket of cowslips on the rough grass that surrounded the building. It was a wild flower that she loved. The lilac trees beyond were now in full bloom and their scent wafted on the breeze. Marklund had answered the door in old slacks, sloppy T-shirt and espadrilles, very much the off-duty look. Anita thought she was prettier out of her business uniform. There certainly wasn't an ounce of fat on her. No kids, Anita thought with a tinge of envy.

The room was more traditional than expected. Anita had assumed a high-flyer to surround herself with trendy furnishings and arty knick-knacks from trips to exotic locations. This was more like a traditional Swedish house. An older person's home. There was a model of a small sailing boat in the window. There were even a couple of brightly painted Dala horses. Among the photos, there were a couple of a girlish Elin with a grey-haired couple. Grandparents probably. On the mantelpiece was an old black and white photograph of a handsome young woman. Her thick, raven hair waved to just above her shoulders – a typical late 1940s style. She had a pretty smile.

'That's my grandmother,' said Marklund as she came in with a tray bearing two mugs of coffee and two cinnamon buns.

'Very striking.'

Marklund laid the tray down on the old wooden coffee table.

'Granny was from Denmark.'

Anita took hold of her mug. 'Thanks.' She took a sip.

It wasn't as strong as she liked, but it was much needed. 'I've just spoken to Jesper Poulsen. I had an interesting chat. He was talking about his grandmother, too.'

Marklund took a bite out of her bun.

'I can't imagine that had anything to do with the case.'

'It might do.'

Marklund didn't disguise her surprise.

'What do you make of Poulsen? I sense a lot of anger there.'

'I like Jesper. A lot people don't know what to make of him. He's not the most diplomatic person, which doesn't make him very popular in the office. Rubbed a few of his colleagues up the wrong way.'

'Tommy Ekman?'

'Particularly Tommy. He wasn't used to staff standing up to him.'

Anita nibbled at her cinnamon bun. It tasted delicious. She hadn't had one since Lasse was last at home. She decided to buy some on the way back.

'The real reason for my call is that you weren't entirely truthful about the day of the presentation.'

'Wasn't I?'

'You left the office early – in your car. There were two cars – Ekman, Jonsson and Lundin went to the presentation in the other. Where did you go?'

Markland appeared amazed. 'I thought I'd covered everything. Yes, I did take my car because I needed to go to the pharmacist.'

'The pharmacist?'

'Tampax. My period came early. Caught me unawares. Would have been embarrassing at the presentation...'

'Where was the pharmacy?'

'The one outside *Entré*.'

'Bit out of the way if you were going to Fosieby.'

'My car was parked near the central station, so it was easier to go that way. And I know where the toilets are in *Entré.*'

Anita was thankful that Hakim wasn't with her. Too much information.

'What time would that be?'

'I was at Geistrand Petfoods at twenty past eleven, so I must have left the office about half an hour earlier.'

'If you went to *Entré*, then you must have passed Tommy Ekman's apartment.'

'I suppose I must have.'

'Anyway, that explains it. We have to follow up everything. You understand.'

'That's your job.'

After Anita had finished her bun, she got to her feet. 'One last thing. Who does Pontus work for?'

'Fraser Oil International.'

'Thanks for the bun.'

The rain had eased a little as Anita headed down a tree-lined path that ran along the back of Marklund's house and retraced her steps to the church; Marklund said it was a short cut. She reached her car and got in. For a few minutes she sat and watched trickles of rain run down the outside of the windscreen. She was concentrating hard. What had been wrong about the house? There was something.

Anita caught Moberg in mid-sandwich. In fact, it was more mid-meal, judging by the amount of empty plastic wrapping strewn around his desk.

'Wasn't sure if you'd be in today.'

Moberg grunted, as he was still demolishing his last mouthful.

'I've been to see Jesper Poulsen, the copywriter; and Elin Marklund.'

'Anything interesting?'

'Yes.' Anita sat down. 'Marklund hadn't told us that she set off early to the presentation in her own car. She says she went to *Entré* shopping centre to get some Tampax. That time of the month.'

Moberg put down the rest of his sandwich. 'Please. Not while I'm eating.'

'She would have passed Ekman's apartment, so she would have had opportunity. She's no motive though.'

'And this Poulsen guy?'

'He's more interesting. He was the first in the office on the day of the presentation. Finishing off some radio scripts. That gave him about an hour alone in the building. Plenty of time to get the keys.'

'How come this wasn't clocked before?' Moberg was annoyed. He hated sloppiness in his subordinates. 'Anything else?'

'Poulsen and Ekman didn't get on. Fights over work. And Poulsen has strong political opinions. His mother was a Lebensborn child. I think it's an obsession with him. Chip on his shoulder. Obviously loathes right-wingers. If Ekman and the rest were politically involved, then that would give him a good motive. He also happens to be a fanatical jogger, with the same colour top and black backpack as reported in the sightings. I saw the backpack in his office.'

'Pick it up. The backpack. Send it to forensics and see if Thulin can match it to anything in Olofsson's car or Serneholt's house. It's a long shot, but we might as well clutch at a few straws. That's all we've got.'

'I'll go first thing Monday.'

Moberg had returned to the remnants of his sandwich. 'You know Westermark thinks that the political route is a waste of time.'

'But what do *you* think?'

'I think we need more suspects. The less we find on Nilsson, the more worried I am that he's the wrong person.'

Anita wasn't used to such admissions from the chief inspector. She could see that the lack of progress on the cases was getting to him.

'At least Poulsen gives us another.'

'This Ander Genmar has rushed off on an unexpected holiday. It might be a coincidence. Then again...' Moberg leaned back in his chair. 'Gut feeling about Poulsen?'

Anita tapped the desk top with her fingers. 'Yes. It could be him.'

'Do you want to bring him in?'

'I'll speak to him again on Monday.'

'Is he methodical enough to plan Ekman's murder?' That was a good question which Anita wasn't sure she could answer. 'And we still have no idea how the murderer got hold of the means to gas Ekman.'

Anita shrugged. That was baffling. She made a move to go.

'The Mirza kid. How's he shaping up?'

'He's keen. A good eye. Methodical. I think he'll make an excellent cop one day – if the system doesn't wear him down.'

'We need people like him.' Anita was surprised at this admission. 'Might shut the Sweden Democrats up. They were moaning on the other day that Sweden has taken in more Iraqis since the 2003 invasion than all the other major European countries combined.'

'Hakim's family came over here when he was young. He thinks of himself as Swedish.'

'Maybe the people we're dealing with disagree with that. And that definitely includes the "Malmö Marksman".'

CHAPTER 38

He followed her all the way from the apartment to Stortorget. She had got up early. He had expected her to leave for the polishus after seven. Instead, she had emerged at quarter to nine. She hadn't taken her car, so he had followed her on foot. At this time on a Monday morning, it was simple to keep out of sight among commuters heading to work. He was feeling tense this morning. Maybe it was the target that was worrying him. The others had been easy. This policewoman was different. She was upholding the laws of Sweden, even though those laws had been twisted to allow in so many foreigners. But he had no choice. The voice had been insistent. As she walked, he could tell by the slight telltale bulge that she was carrying a regulation police Sig Sauer pistol. He would have to bear that in mind when he struck. His other victims had had no means of defending themselves or fighting back.

She had walked across the bridge by the library and stopped for a few moments. The sun glinted off the canal. She had better enjoy the sight now because she was unlikely to see the day out. He wanted to make sure the killings were done today, and then he could disappear quickly. He didn't want to stay in Malmö a minute longer than he had to. The murder of two cops would result in the whole country on the lookout for him.

In the corner of the square, she hung around, checking her watch. He hovered, pretending to admire the varied architecture, while he took in ways of making a quick exit. When he glanced

271

back, the young Arab was with her. He immediately felt for his gun. There wasn't an obvious escape route, so he let them go into the building. He would bide his time.

Jesper Poulsen wasn't pleased to see Anita again. Jonsson had vacated the office to let them speak to him. This move had set off whispered chatter in the rest of the creative department on the other side of the glass.

Anita got straight down to business. 'We need to know where you were on the evenings of Monday, May 23rd and Monday, May 30th.'

Poulsen stared at Anita and then at Hakim. 'Unless I go for a run, I never do anything on Monday nights.' He sighed. 'If you must know, I always write on Monday evenings. Or try to. It's the only time I get.'

'The great novel?'

'I know it sounds pathetic. And I realise it means I haven't got an alibi, but I had nothing to do with the deaths of those men. I didn't even know who they were before their names appeared in the papers.'

Anita noticed that the black backpack was still lying next to Poulsen's desk.

'We'll take that away with us if you don't mind.'

'What for the hell for?' Poulsen snapped.

'We need it for forensics. If you're innocent, then you have nothing to worry about.' Anita nodded to Hakim, who leant over and picked the backpack up carefully. He put it in a large plastic bag, which he had fished out of his pocket.

Poulsen almost spluttered with rage. 'I don't know why you're picking on me. There's probably about a dozen people in the agency who jog. Christoffer, Fanny... Elin... em... Niclas... they all jog. So does Emma. Are you taking away their stuff?'

'Did you say "Elin"? Elin Marklund?'

'Yeah.' He had calmed down. 'I got her into running when

we were working together in Copenhagen.'

Anita took a step towards the door. 'We'll get your bag back to you as soon as possible.' Her hand was on the handle when she half turned to a still-seething Poulsen. 'What do you know about Elin Marklund's husband?'

He was surprised by the question. 'Not much. I know he's in the oil business and I know they met while she was still working in Copenhagen. I was over here by then. But she's kept her maiden name; presumably it's easier for work purposes.'

'What's his surname?'

'Pontus Stennevall. He's never come to any agency social dos as far as I know. Always away protecting oil fields. Come to think of it, I don't believe I've ever met him.'

He followed them when they came out. The Arab was now carrying a plastic bag. Instead of heading for the police headquarters, they made their way through the shopping thoroughfares and on to Triangeln. He had no idea where they were heading. He was getting frustrated. No opportunity to take out his gun and finish them off. The streets were now too busy. There was no cover. Keep composed.

They carried on past Triangeln down Södra Förstadsgatan before turning left. This was more promising. They were heading for Möllevångstorget. The square was full of market stalls with cheerful striped blue-and-white or red-and-white canopies. The stallholders were mainly ethnic, as were most of the customers. He knew the area's reputation as being home to many incomers, though it was now becoming more fashionable among Swedes. That would push the unwanted out. The cops would be more exposed here. And he had cover. He could pick them off and get away in the confusion, camouflaged by the stalls. But they went beyond the market and into Simrishamnsgatan, one of the streets leading off the square. They then disappeared through a doorway to the right. He idled past the window. It was a café. He could see the woman taking a seat near the back while the Arab went to the counter. None of the tables and chairs matched and were set out randomly. He crossed over the road and weighed up his options. There was no point in shooting them through the window as they were near the back of the café and he couldn't be certain of success. He could walk in and gun them down where they sat, but the layout and the number of people already inside would hamper his escape. He'd rather be in the open. He'd rather wait.

Anita sat down in the Café Simrishamn 3 while Hakim bought them a couple of coffees. She was paying.

Hakim came back with two mugs and a large cinnamon bun for Anita.

'What next?'

'The first thing we'll do is go to the market. I want some fruit and vegetables. I've been eating too much crap lately, now that I'm just cooking for myself.'

'My dad comes here on a Monday most weeks. So it must be good because he's very particular.'

Anita took a bite out of her bun. It was nice, but not as good as the one Elin Marklund had given her.

'Do you think Poulsen is our perpetrator?' Hakim asked.

Anita picked an unruly crumb from her bottom lip. Not very elegant, she thought.

'Poulsen has possible motive. Well, he didn't get along with Tommy Ekman. That might give him a reason to kill his boss, but not the banker. However, he'd have a strong motive if there's a political angle to the murders, which I'm now convinced more than ever there is. His views are blatantly obvious. And he had opportunity in all three cases. He was by himself on the morning we assume the keys went missing from Ekman's office, and he was out of the building for lunch on the day the poison was planted. When we leave here, you can go to the Moosehead and check out if he was there that day. He has no alibi for the other two murders.'

She looked vaguely around for the sign to the toilet. 'As for the means, Martin Olofsson is easy. Clonk him on the head with a heavy spanner. Serneholt was killed with a scalpel. Advertising agency studios probably still use them, despite the technological revolution. And we must remember that a jogger with his general description was seen near Olofsson's and Sernholt's homes. If we prove that these are politically motivated killings, then Poulsen goes straight to the top of our list of suspects.'

They finished their coffees and prepared to leave the café. The door with the "ladies" symbol seemed to be blocked by a table. She could either make a fuss or hold on.

'Two more things we need to do, Hakim. When we get back to the polishus, I'll check that Marklund's husband, Pontus Stennevall, really did pop back over from Norway at the time of the Olofsson murder. He's her alibi. And I want you to get hold of any CCTV footage from the pharmacist's outside *Entré* for the day before Ekman's murder. It's the one just along from the *Systembolag*.' It was also virtually opposite the apartment where Ewan had strangled Malin Lovgren. It's where Anita had first met him. Little did she know the effect he would have on her life. Damn him!

He was seated on a bench in the square waiting for them to come out of the café. From his vantage point, he could see along Simrishamnsgatan. He had had to share the bench with a withered old man with a long, grey beard. Another bloody Arab. The seat along from his was occupied by a whole group of them talking loudly and waving their arms. Is this how they repay the Swedes? Do nothing but scrounge off the state? Why don't they bugger off to whatever Middle Eastern hellhole they'd crawled out of? Maybe he would come back at a later date and send a few of these off to see Allah.

He stiffened when he saw the woman and the young Arab step out of the café and head straight towards him. For a moment, they disappeared from view as a couple of cyclists crossed their path. He was now totally alert. He was going to strike here. He sat still and watched them closely. They were making for the first row of stalls, and the woman began inspecting the colourful display of vegetables. They were playing into his hands. He got up slowly so as not to attract any attention, and worked his way round to the opposite side of the row. When they were in his sights, he would draw his gun and fire through the gap between the canopy and the trestle. Then he could make his escape through the throng and be shielded by the other stalls. He would cross the road – the traffic would hold up any potential pursuers and give him vital seconds. He would probably make for the new underground station at Triangeln.

Anita was still casting an eye over the array of fresh vegetables and fruit. In her head, she was trying to match the produce to recipes she could use when cooking for one. She had better not buy too much as it would go to waste. But the choice was so tempting.

'Hello, Inspector.'

Anita turned to see Hakim's father, Uday, with a bulging shopping bag. Hakim was hovering around hoping that his father wouldn't say anything embarrassing. The dreaded words "when Hakim was a boy…" sprang to mind. Anita stepped away from the stall to speak to Uday.

'I see you've been busy, herr… sorry, Uday.'

Uday beamed back. She had remembered his name.

'I come here every Monday. Not as good as Baghdad, but I mustn't grumble.'

'No, you mustn't, Father.'

Just then a young female cyclist came to an abrupt halt between them and the stall. At the same moment there was a small explosion. Then another. The female cyclist tipped over and collapsed against Anita, who had automatically ducked as she had realised what had caused the sound. Someone cried out. Everything stood still for a second. Uday slumped to his knees, clutching his arm with his hand. Blood appeared through his fingers. His vegetables rolled across the cobbles. The cyclist moaned, still straddling her bicycle on the ground. Anita could see Hakim shouting and pointing. She jumped up. Someone was running through the maze of stalls. She quickly assessed the situation. The woman on the ground was still alive. Part of the handlebar on her bike was pulverised – it had taken most of the impact. Uday wasn't critically injured. People were rushing to help. It was a communal reflex action. As the incident had happened so quickly, there was no time for panic to fully set in. Anita shouted at the stallholder to ring for an ambulance and the police. And then she drew her pistol and ran after Hakim, who had dropped the plastic bag with Poulsen's backpack in, and was now in pursuit of a burly, blond man.

He couldn't believe it. That fucking cyclist had appeared from nowhere. He wasn't sure if he had hit either of his targets. He couldn't hang around and have another go because they had now disappeared below the level of the stall and were out of sight. Then he saw the young Arab cop pop up and point at him and bellow something he couldn't catch. He quickly turned and ran, bumping into two young women. One fell to the ground and the other shrieked when she saw the gun. He dashed along a line of stalls then jinked left to avoid another. When he reached the main street that ran along the end of the square, he just ploughed on. A car screeched to a standstill as he used the bonnet to lever himself into the middle of the road. He heard screams and shouting behind him.

Now there was no hindrance in the street in front of him. He stretched his legs. He would be clear soon. Down into the underground and out the other side, and he would be invisible again. He glanced over his shoulder. The young cop was in full chase. Did he have a gun? He realised that he was gaining on him. The glass roof of the station was straight in front of him. The entrance was on the other side. Coming up on his left were ranks of parked commuter bicycles. He would dodge behind them and try to pick off the Arab. Halfway along, he leapt to his left and ducked down behind a forest of spokes. He didn't have time to take aim properly but let off two shots. The Arab seemed to stumble. He didn't wait to find out what had happened to him.

He made a dash for the entrance of the station, barging past a woman with a child's buggy. The buggy spun away from him. The woman yelled obscenities as she desperately tried to stop her baby tumbling out. He was now under the glass roof and on the first of the three down escalators. He ran down the moving steps and onto the next level. A swift glance back. The bloody Arab was still with him as he launched himself down the second escalator.

At the bottom, he ran across the large atrium and turned to the right onto the last escalator, which tumbled down to the station concourse. He leapt the last three steps onto the extensive platform. A train was just pulling out and a large number of people were walking straight towards him. When someone spotted his gun, there was a terrified warning shout. The wave of panicking passengers parted like the Red Sea as people tried to get out of the way. He quickly looked over his shoulder and saw the Arab was still with him. He shouldn't have looked. His foot caught the side of someone's trolley suitcase and he fell forwards. The gun went off, and the noise reverberated loudly around the cavernous space.

It only took a second to get to his feet. He was now clear of disembarking passengers at this end of the platform but could see a crush of people at the far end leaving by the other exit. He instinctively knew he couldn't outrun the Arab and he would be held up by the crowd ahead. He sidestepped behind one of the colossal, grey cement pillars supporting the lofty roof. He could hear the Arab slowing down. He nipped round the back of the pillar just as the Arab reached it. He grabbed the panting young man from behind and held his gun to the young policeman's head.

As Anita gave chase, she managed to get her mobile out with one hand and speed-dialled the polishus. She could see Hakim way in front of her and then two shots rang out. She saw Hakim stumble and thought for a horrible moment that he must have been hit. He regained his footing and continued running after the retreating figure of the gunman. The bloody idiot. She knew he wasn't armed. She got a voice on the phone. The gunman had vanished into the station. 'Sundström here,' she yelled. 'Get any armed officers you can to Triangeln station now! There's a gunman just gone down there.' She didn't have time to give any more information. She knew the response would be quick because the force had been on high alert since the last "Malmö Marksman" killings.

When she got to the top of the first escalator, she purposely regulated her breathing and psyched herself up for whatever may be ahead. Fortunately, her runs round Pildammsparken meant she was fairly fit. She hurried down the slow-moving staircase. By the time she reached the top of the last escalator, frightened passengers were surging towards her in the opposite direction. It only took a few bounds and she was on the platform. She was just in time to see Hakim slowing down and then being grabbed by the throat and wrenched backwards, out of view. The gunman was four pillars down. With her pistol held in both hands, Anita made her way carefully to the next pillar. Her mouth was dry, and she could feel sweat starting to trickle down her back. Her hands began to shake ever so slightly. She had never wanted to be in this position again after that dreadful day on the top of the Turning Torso. Now she was called upon to use a gun again, this time deep beneath the city, instead of high above it. She felt rising panic. She forced herself to stay focused by fixing Hakim in her head. It was him that mattered, not her. He was her responsibility. How could she face his parents if he didn't come out of this alive? She had no idea who she was dealing with. Was this the "Malmö Marksman" or some other mad gunman? All she knew was that Hakim was in grave danger. A boy not much older than her Lasse. The thought made her angry. Her anger carried her to the next pillar. By the third pillar, her fury was replaced by steely determination.

'Hakim?' she called out as she pressed against the side of the pillar.

'Don't come any nearer or I'll blow his head off.' The voice was gruff. Was that a Norrland accent? It wasn't local anyway. Larsson had got that wrong.

Then the man appeared. His arm round Hakim's neck, his gun tilted under the young man's chin. She would always remember the fear etched on Hakim's face. In contrast, the gunman was almost relaxed. And he looked so ordinary. About forty, was Anita's immediate calculation. Drab clothes, undistinguished blond hair, square-set jaw – no wonder he hadn't been noticed. He was like a million others.

Anita had already slipped her pistol down the back of her jeans – out of sight under the flap of her jacket – before stepping out to face him. She held her hands up to show that she wasn't carrying a weapon.

'I'm unarmed.'

'Where's your gun, then?' He knew she had one.

'I dropped it back there in the confusion.'

'If you let me walk out of here, I'll let him go.'

'You'll never make it. The station will be surrounded by police by now. Do the sensible thing and hand over the gun.' Anita surprised herself at how calm she was.

'No way. Any false move and I'll kill you both.' He suddenly laughed. 'That's what the voice told me to do.'

The man was ranting.

'What voice?'

'The voice. She told me.'

Anita had no idea what he was talking about. He was unhinged. Now she was playing for time. Slowly, the gunman began to edge backwards along the platform, with Hakim clamped to the front of his body like a shield.

'Look, we can help you. We have people who can deal with any problems you may have.'

'You don't understand. There's nothing wrong with me. This is a job.'

Anita didn't know what to make of this maniac. Job? What on earth was he babbling on about?

'Take me instead of him.'

The gunman pondered the offer. 'That might be an idea. No one is going to shoot me with a female cop as my captive.'

He motioned with his gun for Anita to come forward. Behind the man, there was a sudden commotion. Armed police were piling down the far escalator. The gunman was distracted for a split second. Both Hakim and Anita sensed it. Hakim broke the gunman's grip and threw himself forward onto the ground a split second before Anita whipped out her pistol from behind her back and fired. The bullet hit the man's left shoulder and he twisted round like a top. He fired his gun, but he had lost his balance. The report was drowned by the whoosh of an approaching train as he tried to regain his footing and fire once more. Anita let off a second shot, aiming for the hand that held the weapon. It missed. The gunman tried to take avoiding action and moved too near the platform edge. Too late, he lurched backwards just as the 12:14 for Copenhagen swept into the station. The driver couldn't stop in time.

CHAPTER 39

Anita didn't know whether to hug Hakim or clip him round the ear. She met up with him at the hospital in the late afternoon. Uday's arm was in a sling. The female cyclist had superficial wounds, and had already left the hospital. The mental scars would last a lot longer.

'Are you OK?' she asked Uday.

'I am, thank you. Today was like being back in Baghdad,' he added with a grin.

'Hakim, take your dad home and I'll see you tomorrow.'

'I'm sorry I rushed after him like that.' Hakim scratched his head distractedly. 'I was just so mad.'

'You were unarmed, you–'

'I know. It won't happen again.'

'I'll hold you to that,' she said sternly.

Hakim grimaced.

'Is it the "Marksman"?'

'They don't know yet.'

The underground station was closed for four hours as they cordoned off the whole area. The gunman was virtually unrecognisable when they brought the body back up off the track. His head had been retrieved separately. The train driver was in shock and had been taken away. Larsson had appeared with his team and had interviewed her. The man's gun was now with forensics. If they could match it to the bullets recovered from previous victims, then they had the "Malmö Marksman". To complicate matters, the man had no identification on him or even a mobile phone. It was going to be difficult to identify him unless they could trace where he had bought the gun.

Anita had recalled the few words that they had exchanged. She thought that there'd been a trace of a Norrland accent, though she couldn't be totally sure. She told them what the man had said about the voice. Her impression was that the gunman was deranged, but that that was hardly an informed medical opinion. Larsson had smiled. What she hadn't understood were the gunman's words "This is a job". Larsson suggested that maybe he considered killing immigrant Swedes as his life's work. They may never know, because now they couldn't ask him. Certainly the Möllevångstorg location, with its largely ethnic population and market, fitted the pattern of the previous shootings. All Larsson was really concerned about was identifying the man as the "Malmö Marksman". If it was him and they were spared the expense of a trial, then everyone was happy.

It wasn't until she had left the station and come up into the daylight that the enormity of what she had been through hit her. The incident on the top of the Torso, which had so emphatically changed her take on survival and her own mortality, suddenly crashed in on her again. Before then, it had all been virtual; now it was all too palpable. She felt nauseous. Now another man had died because she had shot him. OK, the bullets hadn't actually killed him, but they had led directly to his death. The only crumb of comfort was that she had saved the impulsive Hakim from a lunatic's clutches. She knew she had taken the right action. It didn't make her feel any better. What was her psychologist going to make of this?

Hakim nodded to his father and Uday began to walk slowly down the corridor. His son hesitated for a moment.

'Thank you.'

***

The next day was frustrating for everyone in the polishus. They were waiting excitedly for news from forensics about the gun. Anita had never known a police station in such a state of heightened anticipation. A number of staff had come in to congratulate her. She didn't miss the irony that many of those same colleagues had been avoiding her since her return to work. She and Hakim had even been graced by a very brief visit from Commissioner Dahlbeck. Significantly, Westermark was nowhere to be seen, though Moberg couldn't keep the smug grin off his face. If his small team had solved the problem of the "Malmö Marksman" – albeit totally by accident – he would never let Larsson hear the end of it. After all, his colleague had had an army of cops at his disposal and come up with zilch.

But euphoria is often a precursor to despondency. There was still so much to do, and Anita seemed to be hitting a brick wall. She was becoming exasperated. Hakim had gone to the pharmacist's and picked up their CCTV footage covering the inside of the shop: the counter and the door area. If Elin Marklund had been there, they would find out. Anita couldn't phone Canada to ask about Marklund's husband until five at the earliest because of the time difference. While Hakim was out, she had taken a photo of Jesper Poulsen, cut out of the Ekman & Jonsson company brochure, along to the Moosehead bar in Lilla Torg. That had produced nothing as the two people serving on the lunchtime in question were not due in until the evening shift. While she was out, she even checked if Gabrielsson had returned. The gallery was closed.

The first murmurs of excitement spread from Larsson's office along the corridor late in the afternoon. Then the news came that confirmed that the gun at Triangeln station matched up to the bullets from the other crime scenes where the "Malmö

Marksman" had struck. There was a sense of exhilaration as well as relief. Someone opened a book on how quickly Commissioner Dahlbeck would get himself on TV claiming the credit for finding the gunman. Anita slipped away to a side room where Hakim was going through the CCTV footage. The sense of dejection hadn't left her. It was hard being upbeat. They trawled through the film until they came to the period that Marklund should have been inside the pharmacist's. They went through the sequence three times. Elin Marklund was nowhere to be seen.

Anita sent Hakim home early. He still seemed in a state of shock after all he had been through the day before. He had nearly lost his father – and his life. He had to learn what a career in the police is all about but, despite all the training and rule-book procedure, nothing quite prepares you for a real life-or-death situation. Some officers were lucky – she had colleagues who had spent thirty years in the force and had never had to face a dilemma such as Hakim had yesterday. But she knew the world was changing – and the old, comfortable Sweden was changing with it.

She phoned Fraser Oil International at ten past six. The person she had to speak to wouldn't be around for another hour. While she waited, Wallen popped her head round the door.

'Coming for a drink? There's a big celebration going on. We're heading for some bar in the centre.'

'I've got to wait around to make a call. Might join you later.'

Wallen smiled. 'You're back in favour.'

That's why Anita had no intention of joining them.

While she waited, she picked up the small photograph of Lasse she had on her desk. She was still gazing at it when she tried to phone his mobile. She was put onto his voice mail. She didn't bother to leave a message.

Suddenly, she sat up. She stared at the photograph. That's it! That's what was missing!

At seven, she rang Canada again and spoke to someone who

could help. She didn't prevaricate. The questions were well rehearsed and to the point. By the time she put the receiver down, she was wearing a very thoughtful expression. She stared at the phone for at least a couple of minutes before picking it up again. She punched in a number and waited.

'Chief, Anita here. Sorry to disturb you at home, but there's something I think you need to know.'

CHAPTER 40

'He doesn't exist?'

Moberg shook his head in disbelief. They were sitting in his office. The call had come at a good time for him. His wife was about to serve yet another unpalatable meal. Something healthy with leaves. He would get a big carry-out on the way home.

'Fraser Oil has never heard of a Pontus Stennevall,' Anita explained. 'Or a Pontus Marklund. And none of their employees were over in Norway the weekend Elin Marklund says her husband made his flying visit. It figures. When I went to her home on Saturday, there was something that didn't seem right. Then it came to me. She had family photos everywhere but none of a husband. She had plenty of her grandparents, particularly of her grandmother. But not one of the person who in theory was most important to her – her husband. They can't have been married that long. I don't reckon they've had time to fall out.' Moberg wasn't so sure. He had two lots of wedding photos stuffed out of sight somewhere. A third would surely follow soon.

'But what about that stuff about her not wanting her husband to find out she had been screwed by Ekman?'

'That's why she wasn't looked into more closely.'

'That would make her a very cold-hearted bitch. A farewell fuck. A quickie in the office, and then send him off home to a hideous death.'

Anita realised how hungry she was and she was aware of the faint rumble in her stomach. 'Marklund no longer has an alibi for Olofsson's murder. And on the day of the presentation, she didn't call in the pharmacist's, as she claimed she did. We have CCTV footage that proves the lie. By her own admission, she went past Ekman's apartment, so she would easily have had time to plant the jelly in the drain with the poison pellets or crystals. It would only take minutes.'

'Anything else?'

'Yes. Poulsen says that he introduced her to running. She's probably our jogger. She's quite tall, so is about the right height from the descriptions we have.'

She could see Moberg weighing up the evidence in his mind.

'Do we have a motive?'

Another stomach rumble was on the way. 'I can't think of one, unless *The November 6th Group* is a political organisation and Marklund has a good reason to destroy it.'

Anita thought Moberg's grimace wasn't encouraging.

'We can't find Ander Genmar. He's gone to ground in Spain. Even the Spanish police can't locate him. His villa's empty.' Then he surprised her. 'What would you do next?'

'I think we should search her house. And her home computer, if she has one. If she's working off that list, she must have got it from somewhere. Could she have taken it off Ekman's computer? It would explain the empty *Sjätte November* folder. If she could get the keys from his office, she could also have got into his computer.'

Moberg stood up decisively.

'Right. Tomorrow morning we double-check that Marklund isn't married. Official records here and in Denmark. Marriage registration. All that stuff. Ask the ad agency people if they've ever seen the husband. Discreetly. We don't want to alert her. I'll go and see our tight-arsed prosecutor to get a search warrant. We'll hit her just as she gets home from work.'

Anita smiled. They were getting somewhere at last.

Moberg heard her stomach rumble.

'Hungry? I know just the place.'

Nordlund took the call. Wallen had rung through to say that Elin Marklund had left the office. She was making for her car. Nordlund turned to Anita. 'She's on her way. With the rush-hour traffic, it should take about forty minutes.'

Anita felt that surge of excited anticipation. A difficult case was on the verge of a major breakthrough. The more the team had dug that morning, the more obvious it was that there was no husband called Pontus Stennevall. Four Pontus Stennevalls did exist and all were checked out. None of them were married to Elin Marklund. And no one that they spoke to at Ekman & Jonsson had actually seen or spoken on the phone to Marklund's husband. Now Anita was sitting in Nordlund's car, with Hakim in the back, waiting for Marklund to show up. There were also four uniformed officers in a police car parked behind them. The search was going to be thorough.

Only Westermark had been sceptical at the lunchtime meeting. 'I interviewed the woman. She wouldn't have killed Ekman after making love to him. Women just don't do that. It can't be her.' Westermark was losing out to Anita, and he knew it. Moberg sensed something wasn't right with Westermark. He decided not to let him go down to Skanör.

While they waited for Marklund to return from Malmö, Nordlund filled Anita in on the latest news of the "Malmö Marksman". They had taken fingerprints from his left hand – his right had been too mashed up by the train. They had put the prints into the national data base and found a man called David Löfblad. He had been arrested a couple of times for gun-related incidents in some place north of Umeå. And had one conviction for grievous bodily harm. He had been out of the country for about three years in the late 1990s. One of his neighbours thought that he might have been a mercenary, because Löfblad occasionally came out with tales about Africa and hinted at armed action. Bit of a loner. Another neighbour described him as "weird". Most significantly, his disappearances from his home coincided with the dates of the shootings in Malmö.

'Why Malmö? Why come all this way? He could have found plenty of immigrant targets nearer home. He could have a field day in Stockholm.'

'It seems strange,' Nordlund admitted. 'God knows what goes on in some people's heads. You reckoned he was babbling? A voice instructing him? Some religious fanatic?'

Any further speculation was curtailed when they saw Marklund's red Saab approach. She parked it on the grass verge. Anita and Nordlund got out of their car and walked down the road towards Marklund as she was putting a key in the lock of her front door.

'Excuse me, fru Stennevall,' said Anita.

Marklund swung round. Her eyes betrayed her alarm at seeing so many police officers.

'Or should I say, "fröken Marklund"?'

'I don't know what you mean.'

'Where's your husband?'

'In Canada. You know that.' A hint of resistance entered her voice.

'Fraser Oil International has never heard of him. And you lied about visiting the pharmacist. That's why we're going to search your home.'

'What? This is intolerable. You've no right–'

'We have every right.' Anita held up the warrant. She turned to the uniformed officers. 'In you go.'

The four uniformed officers filed past Marklund, whose confidence suddenly seemed to deflate. 'After you,' Anita indicated, and Marklund stepped though the door.

Elin Marklund sat in the living room as though in a daydream while the police officers noisily went about their business.

As Nordlund organised the search on the ground floor, Anita and Hakim went upstairs. There were two bedrooms and a bathroom. The higher level replicated the lower. Old-fashioned furniture and fittings. One room – obviously used by Marklund – had a sturdy double bed. In the large wooden wardrobe hung Marklund's trendy designer clothes. The contrast between receptacle and content couldn't be more marked.

'Found it!' Hakim called from the other bedroom. 'A laptop.'

Anita went through. This room contained a single bed and a small table on which the laptop was positioned. Hakim had already turned it on. The screen lit up, the icons blipped on, one click, and there was the Google homepage.

'She hasn't even got a password on this. Crazy lady.'

Anita left him to it and went into the bathroom. There was a laundry basket on the floor next to the shower. Anita put on a pair of plastic gloves and rummaged through it. She pulled out a dark-blue, hooded top. She called to one of the uniformed officers, who could be heard in the bedroom next door. He came in.

'Bag this lot.'

Anita went back downstairs. Marklund was still sitting in silence, as though she was unaware of the activity all around her. Anita almost felt sorry for her. Her composure had been replaced by vulnerability.

'Was this your grandparents' house?'

Marklund looked up uncomprehendingly.

'This house. Was it your grandparents' home?'

Marklund nodded slowly.

Anita went over to the black and white photograph of the young woman. She pointed at it.

'Is this all about her?'

Marklund gazed at the photograph without answering. When she spoke, she was barely audible.

'What you're after. It's buried out the back.'

CHAPTER 41

'Tell me about your grandmother.'

The interview room was featureless and bland. Yet the most extraordinary stories had unfolded in these drab surroundings. Elin Marklund was back to her composed self. She was calm. Almost at peace with herself. She sat alone on one side of the table as the tape recorded her story – her confession. She had refused to have a lawyer sit in on the interview. Opposite her were Anita and Nordlund. Anita was relieved that Moberg or Westermark weren't involved. They could conduct the interrogation at their own pace. She and Nordlund had been surprised how meekly Marklund had given in. How co-operative she had been. She hadn't been interviewed straightaway because the team decided to go through her computer first. And they had sent off to forensics the worn, brown, metallic canister with the Zyklon B label and Degesch company logo slashed around the middle in red lettering against an orange background. Great care had been taken while digging it up behind Marklund's house.

It was Thursday morning. 10.27.

'Hanna. That's her name. She was Danish. And, as you gathered from her early photo, Jewish.'

Elin took a sip from the bottle of water she had asked for before the interview began.

'Like many Danish Jews, she managed to escape to Sweden after the Nazi occupation of Denmark. She was one of the lucky ones. Her parents weren't. They were rounded up. It was a brave Danish fisherman who got Hanna and a few others over here. The Öresund may not be that wide, but that crossing was very dangerous with so many German patrol boats around. Hanna was welcomed with open arms by a Swedish family. After the war, she stayed on as she had no people to go back to. Her parents died of malnutrition at Theresienstadt, Hitler's so-called show camp. Hanna married Oskar Marklund. They had a son, my father. I never knew him, as my parents died in a car crash when I was only a few months old.'

'So, your grandparents brought you up. And the house in Skanör was their home.'

Marklund twirled the water bottle around in her manicured fingers.

'Yes. Mainly my grandmother's because Oskar died when I was eight.'

'You must have been close.'

Marklund looked across at Anita. 'Very. She taught me the importance of tolerance. She loved Sweden because it was a country that sheltered the oppressed. She was proud to be taken in by such a liberal state. She cherished our values. I'm glad she didn't live to see the Sweden of today, where immigrants are treated with suspicion and distain. The Jewish community here is persecuted. And we're turning into a nation of Islamophobes. Do you know, there are at least fifteen thousand xenophobic Swedish websites? They seem to think that the Jews are world conspirators and that the Muslims are taking over through mass immigration.'

'I understand what you're saying. However, we need to know about Tommy Ekman,' prompted Anita, whom Nordlund was happy to let lead the questioning.

'Tommy Ekman. Smooth Tommy Ekman. I thought he had hired me because of my excellent track record. I soon discovered he was less interested in my mental attributes and more interested in my physical ones. I'd only been at E&J a few days when he hit on me. That's when I invented a husband. It didn't keep him at bay for long. Suggestive remarks when we were alone and endless flirty emails. Then he called me in for a late meeting one evening a couple of months ago. He'd been out with clients all afternoon on a boozy lunch. He must have topped that off with a lot more drink when he got back. He tried it on again. It was easy enough to fend him off as he was very drunk. Then he started coming out with things about some group he was in. All to do with Gustav Adolf. It didn't make much sense. He burbled on about how he and his powerful friends were going to take Sweden back for the Swedes, as it had been in the golden age of Gustav Adolf the Great. It was a side of him that no one in the company had seen. We all thought he was apolitical. But that evening the mask dropped. I don't know whether he thought I'd be impressed or if he was just showing off, but he unlocked a drawer in a cabinet he kept in his office. He produced this canister. He was so proud of the bloody thing. Said he'd bought it off a dealer on a business trip to Germany. I couldn't believe it when I twigged what it was. It was horrifying. And he just thought it was funny. It didn't occur to him that I might have Jewish blood. Mind you, it hadn't occurred to me that Tommy was a fascist, racist or whatever. It was the first time I'd heard him express any political views before.'

'And after?' asked Anita.

'Not after either. He came to me the next day in a panic and said I was to forget about what I'd seen or I'd never get a job in advertising again.'

'But you didn't.'

'No. After the initial revulsion, I became angry. I wanted to find out more. Late one evening, when the building was empty, I went to his office and got on his computer. I found the *Sjätte November* folder. I downloaded it onto a memory stick.'

'It makes interesting reading.' Anita's first reaction to what they'd found in Ekman's files, downloaded from Marklund's computer, had been one of disbelief. The information would send shock waves around Sweden. The people mentioned had been above suspicion, which is why the group hadn't registered with the national police monitoring right-wing organisations.

'Oh, yes. Such respected, wealthy men planning to change the face of Sweden. Using their money to spread fear. Paying people – including young Muslims – to hound an increasingly frightened Jewish community. As a cop, you must know more than most how difficult it is for Jews to live in Malmö at the moment. And then fermenting trouble amongst the immigrant populace, particularly Muslim. They paid agitators. Every incident is catalogued. I'm sure you've cross-checked the dates?' They had.

'Why are all the activities referred to taking place here in Malmö?'

'I assume it's because all the names on the list live here in Skåne. They have to start their revolution somewhere. And we have a large immigrant population in Malmö. Strangely, if you read the material from their meetings and correspondence, they don't seem to be archetypical neo-Nazis and racists. Or certainly they don't think of themselves as such. In their eyes, they're not fascist Swedes like Per Engdahl or Sven Olov Lindholm in the past. They see themselves as patriots – saviours of Sweden and its values. More like medieval knights on a crusade, or warriors following their hero, Gustav Adolf, and building an empire everyone would look up to. What they seem to have forgotten is that welcoming refugees to Sweden is an integral part of our contribution to civilisation. It was only Tommy who seemed to have true Nazi tendencies, though he kept that well concealed. Hence the hidden Zyklon B. Even then, it was like an exciting game to him.'

Anita got out her snus tin. She offered it to Marklund, who shook her head. Anita took a sachet and glanced at Nordlund.

'When did you decide to kill Tommy Ekman?'

Marklund paused before speaking. It was as though she wanted to get the story right so that they could understand why she had done what she had.

'At first, I wanted to do something about what I'd found out but didn't know what to do.'

'Why didn't you come to us?'

Marklund snorted in derision. 'The police! You're joking. For all I know, you're in Wollstad's pocket. Everything would have been covered up. The group have untold wealth. They can buy silence and make things or people disappear. Or at least they could. But not now. Now I can have my day in court and they – or the police – can't shut me up.'

Her calmness cracked as she squeezed the water bottle tightly. For the first time, Anita could see the vehemence, the passion, the anger and the hatred in those smouldering brown eyes. For the first time, she could really imagine this woman as a murderer.

'We're here to uphold justice,' put in Nordlund.

She gave Nordlund a scathing glare. 'Even after this, you'll never bring Dag Wollstad to account.'

'We will if we discover he's behind this. Inciting civil unrest is a serious crime,' Anita said with conviction. 'Back to Ekman, please.'

'What made up my mind was that disgusting cleric. On the film.'

They had recovered a copy at Marklund's home.

'The bile he came out with, so cold and calculating. You've seen it. Tommy even filmed that with equipment from the agency. The cleric went on about the Holocaust and how it hadn't really happened. Just clever Zionist PR. I was so consumed by bitterness and revulsion, but I felt powerless to do anything. All I could think about was my grandmother and what she had been through, and how her parents had died. And then, suddenly,

I thought I knew what I had to do. Do to them what they pretended hadn't happened to the Jews. I had a list of leading members of the group. They were only initials but I worked them out from other notes in Tommy's files. I read up about Zyklon B and worked out how I could use it. It helped that I'd studied chemistry at university before I decided advertising was more glamorous.' Her background should have been checked out more thoroughly, thought Anita.

'Then, a few days before, Tommy told me he'd be at home by himself on the night of the pitch. Wife and children away. He suggested that I should pop round for a drink. He was never very subtle. I said I'd think about it, though I had no intention of taking him up on his offer. Then I realised he was presenting me with an opportunity.'

'You knew about his spare set of house keys?'

'Nearly everybody did. I also remembered where the key was to the cabinet where he kept the Zyklon B. The canister was easy enough to pinch. I erased all the *November 6th Group* files the day after Tommy was poisoned so you wouldn't find any information before I had a chance to get to the others. I didn't dare go in the day he actually died in case I gave myself away.' She pulled a face. 'I'm not used to killing people. So I took a sick day. You know the rest.'

'I think so. But just let me get this straight. When you left the agency early, ostensibly to go to the pharmacist's on the way to Geistrand Petfoods, you picked up your car from near the station and then drove directly to Ekman's apartment.'

'Yes.'

'You let yourself in, found his bedroom and put the crystals in the en suite shower.'

'I figured it would be the one he'd use.'

'There's something that's still bugging me. Why did you make love to Ekman?'

Marklund blew out her cheeks and smiled. 'It wasn't meant

297

to happen. I had to hang around during the celebration drink so that I could put his spare house keys back. I didn't get an opportunity before. I knew that if they were missing, then you would conclude that it was someone from the agency. When we were alone, he thought he'd forgotten his house keys and was about to go into the drawer. To distract him, I seduced him. Well, it wasn't as though he needed much encouragement. So we did it on the desk. Afterwards, he went off to the bathroom to sort himself out and I put the keys back. The ironic thing is that he found his normal keys in his briefcase and didn't go into the drawer after all.

'Afterwards, I realised that you'd probably discover that we'd made love, and that you would draw the conclusion that, having done so, I was very unlikely to have killed him. Especially if I seemed horrified at the thought of my "husband" finding out.'

'It worked very well. You were discounted early on.' Anita caught Marklund's eye. 'Didn't it make you feel guilty having sex with someone whose life you were about to end?'

'No.' Her denial was flat and unemotional. 'He died the same way as his sick heroes dispatched millions. I hope he suffered as much as they did.'

Anita put away her snus tin.

'OK. Martin Olofsson?'

'I used to jog in the areas where I knew the main members of the group lived. I got to know their evening routines. Olofsson was fairly simple. I'd expected him the evening before. He obviously stayed an extra night over in Österlen. I'd have liked to have gassed him too, but modern cars aren't much use any more. So I hit him with a spanner. You won't find it. It's somewhere out there in the Öresund. Then I made it look like a gassing. The Nazis used carbon monoxide to kill many of their victims in specially designed vans.'

'But it was obvious that it wasn't a suicide.'

'It wasn't meant to fool you. I wanted to send a message to the others in the Group. Someone is coming to get you! It frightened off Ander Genmar. He disappeared somewhere.'

'Spain.'

'Ah. And I couldn't find Lennart Persson.'

'That gives us our *LP*. Who's he?'

'He owns half the warehouses in Sweden. Very rich.'

Anita shifted in her chair. She nodded to Nordlund to carry on.

'So, Ingvar Serneholt was your next victim?'

Marklund stroked her right earlobe thoughtfully. 'He should have been.'

'What do you mean "should have been"?'

'I did go out to his place a couple of times to work out how I was going to kill him. Then someone beat me to it. I don't–'

'Hang on,' interrupted Anita. 'Are you saying you weren't responsible for Ingvar Serneholt's murder?'

'No. Someone did me a favour.'

'But you were seen there that night. The jogger.'

'Oh, I was there all right. But Serneholt had a visitor.'

'Did you see who it was?'

'No. But I was surprised that he was entertaining someone with such a crappy car. I thought he only mixed with the Porsche set.'

'What was the make of the car?'

'Citroën.'

'Colour?'

'Difficult to tell in that light. Brown... green. Could even have been dark blue.'

This piece of information had Anita's mind racing. She thought she knew whose car it might be. It wasn't a happy thought.

Nordlund broke the silence.

'And what were you going to do about Dag Wollstad?'

'He was the biggest fish. To be perfectly honest, I hadn't the faintest idea how I was going to get him.' She spun the water bottle round in her hands. 'But, thanks to you, I know now. You've given me a platform.'

Nordlund looked at Anita. She nodded.

'I think that's all for now, Elin. We'll need to get this down as a full statement.'

Anita leant over and switched off the tape recorder. She and Nordlund got up out of their chairs. Nordlund went to the door and opened it. A female uniformed officer came in to keep an eye on Marklund.

Anita stopped by the door.

'One other thing. Tommy Ekman refers to some event or series of events that he was masterminding. Something to make people sit up and take notice. But there's nothing specific in the files. Just hinted at.'

'I wasn't sure myself. That was until the "Malmö Marksman" started his shooting spree.'

CHAPTER 42

The early morning sun tried its hardest to shine through the window of Anita's car. All it really did was show up how dirty it had become since she'd given the vehicle a wash. She couldn't remember when that was and promised herself to give it a thorough clean when she got home. There were so many domestic tasks she had neglected recently. Like finishing her bathroom. It was ludicrous to have such mundane thoughts when there was so much at stake. The last twenty-four hours had been hectic. Many discussions had taken place – many important decisions had been made. In the next few hours the cases should be resolved, if she had got her thinking right. She felt all the nervous tension of a sprinter on the starting blocks. Nordlund was next to her and Hakim sat fidgeting in the back. All of them were armed. She wasn't going to let Hakim be exposed if the situation flared up this time. The car in front contained Chief Inspector Moberg, Westermark and Wallen. Behind her were three police cars with uniformed officers – two from Malmö and the other from Ystad. This was their patch, and Moberg, for once adhering to protocol, didn't want to rub the local force up the wrong way by keeping them out of the loop. The five cars were parked on a quiet country lane near Illstorp. They had a search warrant and a warrant for the arrest of Dag Wollstad on charges relating to conspiracy and incitement to violence.

Anita had reported back to Moberg straight after her

interview with Elin Marklund. The whole team had gathered together and listened as the tape was played back. The confession added flesh to the bones that had been taken off Marklund's computer. One thing was unequivocal – Wollstad was heavily involved. Possibly the driving force. There was a series of emails between Ekman and Wollstad which left no doubt.

What hadn't been on the tape was Marklund's view that the "event or events" referred to by Ekman in one email to Wollstad was the work of the "Malmö Marksman". This piece of news had been greeted with a shocked silence. Larsson had then been brought on board. Though they now knew the gunman was one David Löfblad, there was no mobile on him or personal ID. However, Larsson agreed that it made sense if he had been summoned down from the north to do each "job" – the word he'd used to Anita on the station platform. That would fit in with his disappearance after each shooting. Then he'd go back home. Far from being a local man as they had believed, he came and went as he was instructed. He was pointed in the direction of immigrant targets. The last attack at Möllevångstorget was an obvious one, given the ethnic market and usual customers. There would be a safe house provided for his use. The police up north had been through Löfblad's phone records and there was nothing to tie him into Wollstad or any of the others in the *November 6th Group*. They had been cleverer than that. Lately, he had bought at least four pay-as-you-go mobile phones in Umeå. None were found. He must have dumped each one after he had received his orders. A search of Wollstad's house might produce the evidence they needed.

Last night, there had been a high level meeting with Commissioner Dahlbeck and Prosecutor Sonja Blom, with frequent calls to national headquarters in Stockholm. Both were extremely nervous about moving against such a high-profile and influential figure as Wollstad. But the evidence against him was so compelling that they had reluctantly agreed to send Moberg in with a warrant for his arrest. Moberg was delighted. He would enjoy his next meeting with the arrogant Wollstad. The whole team was excited. They were on the point of blowing wide open a dangerous organisation committed to causing civil unrest that might have operated for years without being detected. The only person who was subdued and seemed lost in a world of his own was Karl Westermark. Anita assumed that he resented her success. He had been right about the Ekman and Olofsson murders being connected – just wrong about the reason. It was she who had arrested the killer – not him. He had hardly spoken a word at the final briefing and had slipped away as soon as it had finished. That morning, as they gathered at the Polishus, he was preoccupied. No barbed comment, no lecherous leer, no gung-ho cockiness. Anita should have hated herself for it, but underneath she was rather pleased that Westermark seemed to be suffering.

At eleven o'clock, Moberg got a call – they had been given the official go-ahead from the commissioner. With a broad grin, he started up his car, and for the last couple of kilometres the rest followed in convoy and then swept up the long drive. The officers poured out of the cars and, led by the massive frame of the chief inspector, headed for the main door. He was about to open it unannounced when Kristina Ekman appeared at the entrance. She was smartly dressed in expensive casual slacks and a short-sleeved, floral top. Her blonde hair was pinned up. She was every inch the "ice maiden" that Moberg had come to regard her as.

'Fru Ekman, we have come to see your father. We have a warrant for his arrest. If you'll stand aside, we can go about our business.'

Her look was mocking.

'You're too late, Chief Inspector. My father isn't here. In fact, he's no longer in the country.'

'Where is he?' Moberg bellowed.

'I have no idea.'

Moberg furiously brushed past her and barked out an order to search the house from top to bottom.

Over the next two hours, the house was turned upside down. All the computers were impounded, files were boxed up and taken out, and every member of the household was questioned. A van arrived to take all the potential evidence back to Malmö. The staff knew nothing, except that their employer had left in the early hours of the morning. Just before one, Moberg got a call on his mobile. Wollstad had left on his private jet, which he kept at Sturup airport, just after five that morning. The destination was logged as Malaga. The plane had spent an hour on the tarmac in southern Spain. After refuelling, it took off again. Spanish air traffic control had no record of where it was heading. Moberg stamped his foot in frustration.

At quarter past one he called a halt and they began to leave the estate. Moberg gathered together Anita, Nordlund, Westermark, Wallen and Hakim in front of the house. 'The bastard has evaded us. He'll be holed out where there's no extradition treaty, you can sure of that. He has companies all over the world, so I'm sure he'll live out his days in comfort.' He was seething. 'What really pisses me off is that someone back in Malmö must have tipped him off. That bitch Kristina was expecting us. Someone's in Wollstad's pocket, and I'll kill the shit if I ever get hold of whoever it is. I'll be amazed if we find anything. They've had all night to get rid of any evidence.' He could hardly bring himself to speak. 'Come on!'

Moberg stalked off to his car, trailed by Nordlund, Wallen and Westermark. Kristina Ekman watched them from the doorway. There was triumph in her eyes. And for a split second, Anita thought she saw a hint of a glance between Kristina Ekman and Westermark. It happened so quickly that she fancied she must have imagined it.

Anita nodded to Hakim and they went over to her car

outside the main door. Kristina Ekman eyed them up.

'I'm sorry to disappoint you, Inspector Sundström.' Even beautiful mouths could look ugly when they sneer, thought Anita.

'Your father, your husband and their sick friends aren't going to come out of Elin Marklund's trial very well.'

'We'll see. I wasn't surprised to hear it was Marklund, you know. I always thought she looked a bit crazy. I expect she'll only get some paltry sentence. Our so-called justice system is pathetic. She should be shot.'

'I thought you'd be grateful that we've found your husband's murderer.'

'*You* should be grateful that you're still alive.'

The comment took Anita by surprise. It required a few seconds to process the remark. And then it was like scales falling from her eyes and restoring her sight. Of course, of course!

'It all makes sense. *You* were at that meeting on April 16th. *TE*. We assumed it was Tommy Ekman. But, of course, he was in Hong Kong. Your family call you "Titti", don't they? It was Titti Ekman who was there.'

There wasn't a shred of emotion on Kristina Ekman's face. Hakim stood there, dumbfounded.

'It was *you* who was giving the "Malmö Marksman" his orders. I didn't understand at the time, but Löfblad referred to "The voice. She told me." The attack at Möllevångstorget wasn't just one of his random shootings to create fear.' She could hardly believe it as she was saying it. 'We were the targets! Hakim and myself! Were we getting too close to discovering the truth about your deranged group? Löfblad made a reference to the voice telling him to kill us. I thought that was he just babbling insanely. Jesus! You're behind all this!'

'I have no idea what you're talking about. I think it is time you left.' She gazed at Anita and then at Hakim. It was a look of utter contempt. 'Goodbye, Inspector Sundström. Thanks to your interference, I've got a business empire to take charge of.'

Kristina Ekman turned on her elegant heels and marched back into the house.

'We've got to do something about her,' said an incredulous Hakim.

Anita stepped towards the car.

'I'm afraid we're unlikely to prove she had anything to do with it unless one of the Group testifies against her. Half of them are dead and the other half has fled the country.'

They got into Anita's car. The sun was beating down. It was a beautiful June day. But to Anita it was grey and forbidding. And she knew it was going to get a lot worse when she arrested Ingvar Serneholt's killer.

CHAPTER 43

They drove along the winding country roads from Illstorp in silence. Anita was too busy thinking to bother about conversing with young Hakim. She couldn't get it out of her mind that it was Westermark who had tipped off Wollstad. It was an irrational thought, yet it would explain his whole attitude and demeanour over the last couple of days. And what was his price? A fast car? A fancy apartment? A Swiss bank account? She loathed him, but she had always acknowledged that he was good at his job, despite being headstrong and over-confident. His personal behaviour was despicable at times, particularly in regard to her. Maybe a place in the widow's bed was the price he had asked. It would never be proved. Should she mention it to Moberg? No. She had no evidence. A guilty glance is hardly proof enough to finish a career. The more she thought about it, the more she was sure that it was Westermark, yet there was nothing she could do. She consoled herself with the thought that at least the *November 6th Group* was broken up and Wollstad was hardly likely to return to Sweden. Kristina would run his conglomerate, though her activities would now always come under close scrutiny from the security services.

There was one positive to come out of this morning's farce. Once Westermark knew that she knew, he would leave her alone. And she could visit Ewan again without fear of him stirring up trouble. She knew it would be sensible to cut her ties with the incarcerated Scotsman. Her involvement with Ewan was as foolish as it was pointless. It had no future. Yet at this moment in time, she didn't care.

They reached Brösarp and got onto the familiar main road that ran along the coast through Kivik and Vik to Simrishamn. All she had told Hakim was that they were heading for the centre of Simrishamn. She wasn't sure how she was going to handle the situation when they got to Valfisken, the gallery in the library building. Pelle and Karin would be setting up the exhibition in the gallery area. The launch was due tomorrow. Karin Munk had sent her an invitation to the private viewing. "Plus partner". Had Karin done that just to emphasise that Anita didn't have one?

Anita drove her car through the centre of the town and it rumbled over the smooth-topped cobbles of Järnvägsgatan towards the railway terminal at the end. She turned right into Stenbocksgatan and immediately right again into the Simrishamn police station car park. The local force was based on the ground floor of a modern red-brick office block. On the opposite corner, over the road, was the library.

'I'm just popping into the station to let them know we're here,' she said to Hakim as she got out of the car.

'Then what are we going to do?'

'Arrest Pelle Munk.'

Valfisken was a very modern building of glass and brick, with steeply sloping panels of red roofing. They proceeded through the atrium entrance and down past the library to the gallery beyond. The exhibition was being mounted in the large, white open display area. The high, multi-pitched, wooden ceiling created a sense of airiness that many similar artistic spaces lack. It was perfect for Pelle Munk's colourful new works, which contrasted startlingly with the stark background. To Anita, the paintings looked just as inaccessible as the old ones. Nothing new there. The usual obscure titles too. *Tumult, Immune, Manipulation, Penetration* – and a rather gaudy effort defiantly called *Strong Response*. Was it an attack on his critics? Anita suspected only they would know.

Karin Munk was busy organising a small army of helpers in the hanging of her father's works. Anita could see that Pelle was missing. She hadn't seen his car when they passed his house on the road into Simrishamn, so had assumed he would be at the gallery.

Karin noticed Anita and waved across. 'Come for a sneak preview?'

Anita felt awkward. Here was Karin organising her father's come-back exhibition and Anita was about to make sure that Pelle would never attend the event.

'Hi, Karin. It's looking great,' she lied.

'I think Dad is going to be so proud.'

'Where is he?'

'Back home. Not feeling a hundred per cent. I suspect it's pre-show nerves. It's been a long time.'

'Actually, it's Pelle I need to speak to.'

'Really?' Karin queried. 'What about?'

'Can't say until I've seen him.'

Karin gave her a quizzical look. 'You'll find him at home. Sorry, I must get on. I'm still not happy with the lighting.'

'Of course.'

Anita walked back with Hakim to the gallery door and out towards the atrium.

'This is going to be awkward. I don't want to go in mob-handed. I'll pick up Pelle Munk and bring him back to the police station over the road. They're expecting us, and I'll formally charge him there.'

'Have you any evidence?'

'Enough to bring him in. I'll tell you all when I get back.'

'Are you sure you'll be OK by yourself?' Hakim asked with

a hint of concern.

Anita was touched.

'It's going to be difficult enough as it is. I've known him since I was a kid. It's going to destroy Karin. I think that's one friendship that'll be lost forever. Just when we were getting reacquainted.'

'What shall I do?'

'You like art. Go back in and tell me if it's any good. Come across the road in about half an hour.'

Hakim wandered back into the gallery. Karin noticed him and came over.

'Do you know why Anita wants to speak to my father?'

'Sorry. No idea. She wouldn't tell me.'

It took Anita ten minutes to reach Munk's house. There was no sign of his car. She had realised that it must have been *his* car outside Ingvar Serneholt's when Elin Marklund described it. The testimonies of Marklund and neighbour, Valerie Wigarth, plus the forensic evidence, meant that only Munk had the time to kill Serneholt. And a scalpel was an artist's weapon. And she had seen for herself he was left-handed, too, which fitted Thulin's prognosis. Pelle Munk had also been at Jörgen Lindegren's unveiling of his painting. Somehow, he must have got a key to allow him to get in later to steal it. So, he could have easily done both thefts – from Lindegren's and the Ystad gallery. But there were still two questions that Anita needed answering. Why had Gabrielsson disappeared? And, more importantly, why did Munk want his paintings back? The interview would be revealing.

Anita knocked on the kitchen door. When there was no answer, she called out Pelle's name. No response. She walked through the kitchen into the living room. It was as chaotic as she remembered it as a teenager. It smelt of stale nicotine. Old furniture with not a hint of co-ordination. An ancient television sat in the corner. On the stained coffee table in front of the TV stood an empty whisky bottle and an ashtray bulging with cigarette butts. A whisky glass lay on its side in the middle of the sofa. A couple of paintings hung on the wall. Traditional scenes. She remembered that they had been painted by Pelle when he was a young man. He could paint then, thought Anita. Again she called his name and was greeted with silence.

She went back through the kitchen and out into the courtyard. The garage, with its faded, red, timber doors, was to her right. She walked over to it and pulled back the catch. There was the ancient green Citroën. Even dirtier than her own car. She tried the driver's door. It was locked. She peered through the window. A tartan rug lay across the back seat. Had it covered up Serneholt's painting? Forensics would take the car apart. There would be traces of his blood somewhere. She closed the garage door behind her and walked over to the studio.

Anita was now fully alert. It suddenly occurred to her that Pelle Munk might not want to accompany her to the station. He was a big man, albeit not in the best of health. He had already killed. For once, she was glad that she had her pistol with her. She took it out and gently pushed on the studio door. It creaked as it swung open. Slowly, she moved inside. The room still had the two unfinished paintings on their easels that she had seen on her first visit. He hadn't done anything more to them.

'The pretty one. I thought you might come.'

Anita swung round with her outstretched arms pointing the pistol at the figure. The sun streaming through the large picture windows had almost bleached out the silhouette of Pelle Munk. Anita had to squint to focus on him.

'You don't need that,' he said pointing at her gun. He was slurring his words.

Anita suddenly felt foolish and placed the pistol on the table behind her to show that she wasn't about to use it.

'I'm sorry, Pelle, but I need to take you in.'

Munk stepped forward and she could see him clearly now. He cocked an ear.

'What?'

'I need to take you in,' she said loudly.

He glanced around his studio.

'A stupid dream. Just look at them.' He waved a hand dismissively in the direction of the two easels. 'Crap.'

Anita didn't understand what he was talking about. She watched him stride over to the first easel and he kicked it viciously. It crumpled in a heap of broken wood. He surveyed the wreckage.

'You were bound to find out,' he said bitterly.

Hakim had spent the last twenty minutes watching electricians putting up atmospheric spots to help highlight the paintings. He had enjoyed seeing them close up. They were not in a style to his particular liking but, unlike his senior colleague, he could appreciate the technique. That had always been his strong point. He had been a passably decent painter himself, but what had interested him – and it was something his father had taught him – were the methods used by the great artists, from the masters to the modernists. His father had joked that he knew his maulstick from his licked finish. What fascinated him was how Munk's new paintings would compare to the ones he had seen at Serneholt's home. But as he went round the walls, a shadow of concern crossed his features. There was something wrong. By the time he had inspected his sixth painting, he was sure.

His eyes swept around the room. This wasn't good. Inspector Sundström might be in serious trouble. He rushed out of the gallery. By the time he had reached the street, he had his mobile out and was frantically ringing her number. He was almost hit by a car as he blindly rushed over the road to the police station, with the phone buzzing in his ear.

Anita jumped when she heard her mobile burst into life. She put her hand in her pocket.

'Leave it,' a voice commanded.

Anita was taken completely by surprise. With the crashing of the breaking easel and the mobile ringing she hadn't heard anyone come in. But she knew the voice straightaway before she saw Karin standing behind her. She was holding Anita's pistol. In her left hand. The mobile continued to ring.

'Karin?'

'You must be cleverer than I imagined. You wouldn't be here otherwise. I always thought you were too pretty to be bright, Anita. When you're young, it's looks that count. I was jealous of you. Maybe I still am. That's why we could never really be friends.'

'Karin, put the pistol down. It's your father we want.'

Karin's burst of laughter was shrill. 'Not so clever then. You haven't worked it out, have you?'

Anita's mobile stopped ringing.

'I know it's difficult for you to take in–'

'Shut up! Dad has nothing to do with this.'

'Please, Karin,' Pelle Munk appealed to his daughter. 'Stop this now.'

'Sit, Dad.' The painter slumped into the chair like the broken man he had become.

'Are you saying you stole the paintings and...'

'Killed Serneholt? Yes.'

Anita was shaken by the revelation. She had found it hard enough to admit to herself that Pelle was guilty. It had never occurred to her that Karin could have been involved.

'I was trying to revive Dad's career before it was too late. Give him something to live for. An alternative to the booze. But with his hearing gone, he lost his music; his inspiration. He lost the will to paint. I stole his original paintings so he could see what great work he had done. I thought it would stir his artistic spirit. I took the one from the gallery in Ystad, but that was a minor work. I needed one of the great pieces.'

'Lindegren's *Dawn Mood*.'

Karin nodded. 'I'd done some restoration work for Lindegren on a couple of his older paintings. He'd given me a door key so I could work on them when he and his wife were away. I still had it. I knew how upset Dad had been after the unveiling party. He'd always loved *Dawn Mood*. So, I let myself in and took it back. It was wasted on Lindegren.'

Anita focused on the painting lying on the floor among the busted bits of easel. "Crap", Pelle had just called it. Now she saw what had happened.

'And it still didn't work?'

From the corner of Karin's eye, a tear rolled down her cheek.

'No; his talent had deserted him.'

'So, you got someone else to paint them?'

'Yes. Me. I could never find my own style, but I could mimic his.'

'But why kill Serneholt?'

Karin was still pointing the pistol at Anita's head.

'Serneholt was an expert on Pelle Munk. His most fervent collector. I got Stig Gabrielsson to show one of my "Munk" paintings to Serneholt. Stig was up for anything that would make him money. I was using it as a test. If Serneholt needed confirmation that it was real, we could have got Dad to say that it was authentic. But it never got that far. Serneholt spotted that it was a fake and sent Gabrielsson packing. That gave us a problem. Serneholt was bound to come to the exhibition. He would have exposed to the world that Pelle Munk's new works weren't painted by him at all.'

'So you had to get rid of him.'

'There didn't seem to be any other option. Serneholt let me in. Delighted that the great Pelle's daughter had come to see him.'

'The scalpel. The tool of an art restorer's trade.'

'I stole the painting afterwards to make it look like an art theft. Once I knew you were on the case, I thought we would be all right. You wouldn't suspect us.'

'But your dad's car?'

'I thought it would be less noticeable if it were spotted. People don't tend to remember old bangers.'

Anita stared at the pistol. How was this going to play out? It certainly explained why Gabrielsson had run away. He must have known who had killed Serneholt and wondered if he would be next. He had been party to the fake and was the only other person to know about Karin's great deception.

'What now?'

'I'm sorry, Anita. But by stumbling in here, you've left me no choice.'

'Pelle,' Anita called across to the painter, 'Stop her!' He didn't move, still hunched in the chair. Either he hadn't heard or didn't want to hear.

'Come on,' Karin commanded.

'Don't do this, Karin. You'll never get away with it.'

Karin waved the pistol at Anita and motioned towards the door at the back of the studio.

There was now a tinge of hysteria in her voice. 'Maybe not, but I'll not have you, Anita Ullman, of all people, showing up my father! Ridiculed by the art world! Never! His reputation will stay intact with you dead. I'll admit to the murder, but no one will ever find out about the paintings. No one! Even your young sidekick doesn't know why you suspected my dad.'

Karin shoved Anita in the back and she stumbled forward.

'Open the door.'

Anita turned the handle, and they were out of the back door of the studio and in the garden. The pine trees around the boundary shielded them from prying eyes. They were standing on the coloured paving Anita remembered as a child. Where she had played as a youngster with a lonely big-city girl, whom she had made the effort to befriend. Now that friend was about to put a bullet in her head. This was where it was all going to end. This was to be her place of execution.

'It's not too late,' Anita pleaded.

As she turned to face her death, she saw in Karin's eyes that there was no reasoning with someone who had so much demented devotion to her father that she was prepared to kill for him. Anita suddenly yearned for one last hug from Lasse. One last chance to say how much she loved him.

Karin held the pistol and lined it up. This was no childhood game.

The shot was sudden. Karin stared at Anita without moving. Blood appeared at the side of her mouth. It trickled down her chin. In slow motion, Karin sank to her knees and then keeled over. The pistol dropped from her grasp and her blood slithered across the weathered concrete slabs and began to run into the mossy fissures between them. The image was hauntingly similar to a Pelle Munk creation.

Anita watched her in disbelief. Behind her was Hakim. Next to him was a uniformed officer.

Hakim lowered his pistol.

'The paintings. They weren't his. And she had left the gallery.' It came out in a breathless rush.

Anita felt a surge of affection for the tall young man with the swarthy complexion who stood awkwardly in front of her.

'Thank you,' she managed to mouth. Then she began to shake uncontrollably.

TITLES IN THE SERIES

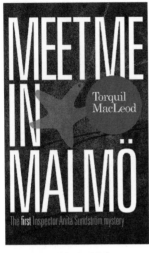

Meet Me in Malmö
ISBN 9780857161130

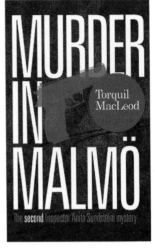

Murder in Malmö
ISBN 9780857161147

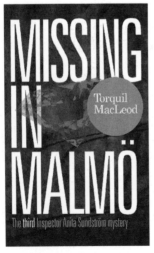

Missing in Malmö
ISBN 9780857161154

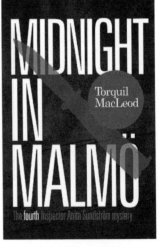

Midnight in Malmö
ISBN 9780857161307

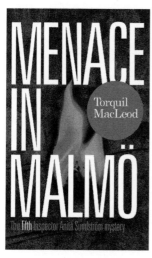

Menace in Malmö
ISBN 9780857161734

Malice in Malmö
ISBN 9780857161871

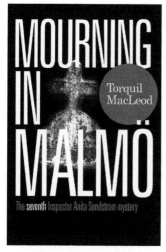

Mourning in Malmö
ISBN 9780857162076

Mammon in Malmö
ISBN 9780857162106